ST. MARTIN'S SUMMER

BY

ANNE H. M. BREWSTER.

"Our poet knows you will be just, but we
Appeal to mercy. . . . . 'T is in you
To make a little sprig of laurel grow
And spread into a grove, where you may sit
And hear soft stories, when by blasting it
You gain no honor, though our ruins lie
To tell the spoils of your offended eye."

BEAUMONT & FLETCHER, *Thierry and Theodoret.*

BOSTON:
TICKNOR AND FIELDS.
1866.

UNIVERSITY PRESS: WELCH, BIGELOW, & CO.,
CAMBRIDGE.

PREFACE.

OOR La Fontaine! Racine took him one evening during Holy Week to church. "*Le bon homme*," as his friends called him, was not at all learned, nor was religion, in the old sense of the word, one of his prominent characteristics; therefore he grew horribly weary with the length of the services.

To occupy him, Racine gave him a Bible which contained the Minor Prophets. La Fontaine opened it at the prayer of the Jews in Baruch. Struck with the sublime fulness of this grand diapason of supplication, he could not control his surprise and delight, and commenced elbowing Racine restlessly.

"O my friend," he whispered, eagerly, "what a fine genius this Baruch had! But tell me, who was he?"

And for some time after he was so full of Baruch that every friend he met in the streets of Paris was greeted with the question, "*Avez-vous lu Baruch? Ah, c'était par ma foi un beau génie.*"

Poor great La Fontaine!

I have often thought during my journey in Southern Italy of "*Avez-vous lu Baruch?*" when expressing my sincere enthusiasm. And while relating with innocent delight all this which was new to me in "*Les Petites Prophètes*" (the Minor Prophets) of the grand Bible of Art and History, I have been probably like *le bon homme* La Fontaine.

Many of my readers may have known these Minor Prophets of art their whole lifetime, may be familiar with every word of beauty they have uttered through countless ages, — words which have served as texts of inspiration for great poets from the time of that "golden world" where

> "The holy laws of homely pastoral,
> And flowers, and founts, and nymphs, and semi-gods,
> And all the Graces, found their old abodes,"

up through passionate passages of perilous human contests and gorgeous mediæval splendors, on to this nineteenth century where men are driving out

> "From clouds of steam majestical white horses,"

making true the prophetic words of Baruch, that wise "old man of noble extraction and learned in the law," — "Bringing down every high mountain, and the everlasting rocks, and filling up the valleys to make them even with the ground." But the Bible of the Beautiful is ever young and ever new, and the earnest, unaffected admiration of those to whom this Bible has been opened for the first time has its own peculiar charm; therefore, though my readers may be more learned, they must show as much good-natured patience as did the cleverer friends of the great French humorist, to my reiterated exclamation, "*Avez-vous lu Baruch? Ah, c'était par ma foi un beau génie.*"

Then there is a kinder view which can be taken of these pages, for, as Bold Fletcher said to his audience, —

> "We would fain please ye, and as fain be pleased;
> 'T is but a little liking, both are eased."

There are seasons of quiet that come in the midst of great trials, rare and short to be sure, but precious. All outside interferences seem to arrange themselves, and social tangles unweave their knots most graciously, as if to lend us a short rest and peace, — it may be to give strength for future trouble, — fresh discipline, — Mother Nature holding the soul back, as it were, with tender solicitude and pensive prevision on the edge of a moral winter.

During such a season were these pages written, and the pleasure of writing them under the influence of that sweet lull added greatly to the diversion of sad thoughts. Therefore, as they have performed such a gentle office to me, I would not have them ungently judged.

And now as I gather these journal leaves together, and think of that pleasant period, I name them, and that part of my life, after the sweet autumn season of the year which they resemble, —

"St. Martin's Summer."

CONTENTS.

ST. MARTIN'S SUMMER.

"WE."

VEVAY, Hotel des Trois Couronnes,
11th January, 185-.

E never do anything for the last time consciously without sadness, some one has said; and I am feeling a sort of tender mournfulness as I write the above heading in my new journal.

"Vevay, Hotel des Trois Couronnes," is put here for the last time,—and the first, too, in this fresh book; the last time, at all events, for many years, for to-morrow we commence our journey into Italy, and to accomplish our pleasant plan of delightful travel and leisurely study there will keep us from revisiting Suisse for a long while.

I talk of "We" as naturally as if this "we" was the same which was meant on the first pages of the large, closely-written volume I packed to-day in the box which is to be sent to America,—that book which contains the sorrowful record of five gloomy years. A *lustrum*, as those old Romans used to say,—and indeed, it has been a period of purifying and light-giving; so much light and clearness of mental vision, that I sit sometimes and grow weary over the thought that, with such light at the beginning, I might have made straight much that was hopelessly crooked and wilful. What use, however, in such a thought?

> "We can but fill the hour with its best deed,
> The knowledge which the tardy morrow brings
> Impeaches not the wisdom of the act,
> It came too late to guide."

And now back again to my starting-point of "We." First, however, let me notice that Rhone valley, and the Lake, the clear starlit sky, and the beautiful terraced garden beneath my window, which looks like some chateau pleasure grounds of the gay French days of Watteau. Yes, they are all very beautiful, and the memory of them will be delightful; but, according to the opinion of the German lad across the street, at the Pharmacie Mayor, the memory will also be sad.

"Ah, Madame," he said to me this afternoon, as I was buying some cologne of him, "you will long heart-achingly for these Alps. You may think you can leave them as you do other beautiful countries, — but you cannot, Madame. Once live among mountains and they become like kindred, — and when you go away the *Heimweh*, or home-sickness, is sure to cling to you as well as to the native-born Suisse."

How strange these Germans are! There is such a deal of dreamy sentimentality about them, which consorts drolly, like some curious marriages, with their sharp, keen eye to the main chance. This young German looked pensive and sighed most touchingly; but he did not forget to charge me outrageously for the cologne, notwithstanding he could talk so tenderly about the Alpine *Heimweh*. But the Irishman is forgiven for his wit, therefore let the German's droll romance stand him also in good stead.

Down in the garden I see Janet walking up and down the short slab of stone which forms the landing-place of the broad flight of terrace steps leading to the lake. She is enjoying the loveliness of the night, which is cold, still, and beautiful, and doubtless thinking of the approaching departure — separation to her — a little solemnly. She leans on the stone parapet, gazing clear off into the dim distance. Like Thekla, over that glorious young Max's grave, she may be murmuring,

> " There where he lies buried
> Is now the whole earth to me ! "

The eye cannot in this dark night trace around the beautiful indentations of the lake shore, nor could it from this window or that terrace see the enchanting spot where lies Janet's "whole earth."

Under the shadow of that beautiful old Montreux church is a grave containing two human beings. One, whose life had only a breath, a look, a sigh, and then back again to its native heaven. Another, who lived honorable years, loved, served his kindred nobly, received priceless love in return, lay down to die in the midst of life's best gifts, and is now mourned with a silent unending grief, "too deep for tears."

It is a lovely resting-place, that old graveyard. The picturesque church hangs suspended, as it were, from the mountain's side; its fine spire, with ogive piercings, draped with clambering ivy, points upward, and at sunset this stone finger of Hope throws down its protecting, assuring shadow directly over the earth-bed in which lie Janet's best memories.

I stood by it alone yesterday at sundown, and wished I could have Janet beside me to show her how peaceful and happy the place looked; and this afternoon, when she walked off there to make, as I knew, her last pilgrimage to that dear spot, I prayed that the same soft shadow might rest just as lovingly as it seemed to my eyes, and bring down into her heart the same quiet, soothing thoughts it had to mine.

Music fills the air. Venitia is condescending to use the hotel piano. Her own Erard full-grand has been packed up for a day or so, in order to be sent round by Marseilles and down the Mediterranean to our new home in Parthenope,—as she, with pretty poetic pedantry, calls our intended abiding-place Naples, Neapolis, — for to us it will be new.

She is capricious to-night, and is playing only broken bits and passages, nothing continuous. Like us she is feeling the breaking-up and departure, but not as we, nor for the same cause; for she has no past, has had no awakening, and is at that happy age when she feels only the inconveniences of the present, and is free from those sorrowful memories which might make her dread a future, or any change, no matter how hopeful and bright it might look.

And yet her trust in this unknown future is a blind, unconscious feeling, not that trust which arises from wisdom; for though Venitia has much knowledge, she has but little wisdom.

> " Knowledge is of things we see,"

but true wisdom is faith, — a faith more than a believing, for belief is a work of reason, faith a result of love, — a trust in that which we do not see. But, after all, it is only through many losses that this diviner wisdom comes; and it is the possession of this that makes Janet so much calmer than either of us; she has a true tranquillizing faith and trust in the unknown Future of this life.

" It soon becomes the Present," she says; "and if it be a present of sorrow and suffering, they, being human, after a season, pass away even from the memory; but if it shall be a sweet present of joy and happiness, they, being divine, remain forever. There is a lethean stream, my friend, flowing through our being, which, in time, quiets all murmurs, stills all unrest, and even throws a soft mist over the memory of past joys to prevent the disturbing effect of regret."

But now back again to " we." Who and what are "we?" For I make it a rule always, in commencing a new journal, to describe my social surroundings, if at all differing from those which were with me at the beginning of the previous one. As my memory sweeps back, endeavoring to contrast *this* present with that past, it flaps a wearied wing, so wide and broad is the gulf of difference stretching out appallingly into a *mare tenebrosum* of hopeless separation from that past!

Enough of my individual self. My journal does not need that text dwelt on at the beginning. It is a sermon which all these pages are to hold and develop. Let me talk of those social domestic surroundings which, to a woman most especially, make her real " we " — her daily, hourly associates — of Janet and Venitia; for they are mine, — my " we."

These names did not touch the pages of the other journal during all its first three gloomy years. These two human beings, who are now so much to me, — one,

Janet especially, — I did not know even the existence of; and should that other journal be lost during its long voyage "home," those who love me and who love to read these pages would be in a state of perplexity and wonder, while reading this one, who my new friends could be.

They are two sisters. A couple of years ago, when I came to this old Europe to seek, if not a grave for my body, one at least for my dead hopes, which lay in most unseemly state unburied, I met these two women under most pleasing social circumstances. Chance threw us much together; our tastes and pursuits we found to be alike. We were all three comparatively alone, not only in Europe, but in life, with only passing acquaintances which are most often to travellers like us but bits of straw hanging to the fringe of a garment, easily caught and as easily shaken off.

A severe illness of Venitia enabled me to be of service to Janet, and I grew deeply attached to her; we united with each other, made one home together, and without vow, or engagement, or troth-plight, only a loving look of need for each other's presence daily, I think we shall spend our future of this life together.

Janet is a widow, about my own age, or a little older. She is neither handsome nor homely, but has those nameless charms, those indescribable attractions, which are the only ones that can hold love after beauty of form and feature and intellect have grown familiar to us. She has also —

> "A calm unfaltering voice, and the grace
> That comes with the knowledge of life."

She is a thoroughly educated woman. I do not mean by this her skill in Latin and Greek, nor her cleverness in positive sciences and mathematics, all of which she possesses, but I mean that her soul is so fully developed, — drawn out, — that it seems to my mortal comprehension complete. She has a fine, highly cultured intellect, it is true, but, better than all, a judgment so clear that it is almost inspiration, and a pure, well-balanced character, every fibre firm and strong.

Janet is an American by birth and feeling, although the most of her life has been spent in Europe. Her father was for many years consul at some southern European port. The effect produced on Americans, particularly on some characters, by living in Europe any length of time, is very unsettling. Artificial habits are acquired, views of society and life, totally at variance with those entertained at home, are insensibly taken up, and this proved to be the case with Mr. Howard, Janet's father. After losing his consulship he never returned to America, but went into a foreign banking-house, and remained the rest of his life abroad. For some reason or other he changed his abode many times, and they seem never to have had a settled or comfortable home. Janet has only visited America once since her childhood, and that was when she first grew up, just before the death of her mother, at which time she spent a few months with her kinsfolk in the United States, but returned to Europe to take charge of her young brothers and sisters, after the news of that saddest of all sad losses, her mother's death, reached her.

She is strongly attached to, and quickly drawn towards, that which she considers American. Of course, never having lived in her birthplace, she is more governed in her opinions and feelings by the views which she has taken at a distance, of our truly interesting government and its romantic success, than by actual experience. She has known intimately distinguished Europeans who have regarded the United States as the Utopia of their dreams. In her girlhood she often made one in the charming circle which gathered at La Grange around "that hero of two worlds," Lafayette, a delightful atmosphere which developed, if not created, artists and political dreamers.

After Janet became a woman, she knew De Tocqueville, and, later, Ampère, and certainly can theorize about the American States as patriotically, poetically, and with as much enthusiasm as the best dreaming philosopher of them all.

Her early life was one of bitter sorrow. Wrong, injustice, disgrace, every biting drop that could be distilled in the alembic of grief, fell on her young heart. After she had passed her early womanhood, without ever thinking of love or its sweet comforts, this great joy of life came to her. Here, on this beautiful lake shore, while striving to eke out a slender income, educate her young sister and some orphan nieces, and nurse a dying, broken-hearted widowed sister, she met with Paul Dale, a prosperous, cultured Englishman. She has told me, by short bits from time to time, her story, for Janet is not one who talks much of that which touches her feelings most: but her short, rapid utterance is very touching, of —

"How strange it should have seemed, and yet it did not, for Paul and me to love each other. I had no faith in mortal man left, and he came to teach me, by his own truth and excellence, perfect faith."

Paul Dale must have been a man worthy of love. He gathered up the whole family and his Janet most tenderly to his heart; he took them to his beautiful English home; used his delightful wealth generously, made life pleasant to the dying widowed sister and her children;

soothed Janet, and when her heart ached with the sorrow caused by the deaths of the darlings for whom she had labored so courageously for years, he filled the goblet of life to overflowing with his own rich purple love, and pressed it tenderly to her lips. She dared not grieve, even when their only child, the boy for whose birth Paul had wished so earnestly, breathed one short breath and then died.

"O no," she has said to me, "I never uttered a murmur, for had I not Paul? And so long as death, which seemed then to be my only pursuing sorrow, did not touch him, I could not mourn."

At last, of her whole large family there were only two left, — Janet and Venitia, — the oldest and youngest! All had died just when prosperity came, and they could so well have enjoyed life together. Paul adopted Venitia, of whom he was very fond, and directed her education with as much care as taste. The girl early showed remarkable musical ability. To give her every advantage in her musical studies, he left England and resided in Germany for a while.

Then came death again; and this time it took Paul, and with it Janet's best part of life. She brought him here, and laid him down under the shadow of that old church spire, where their baby boy was sleeping his little slumber, and where she also hopes to lie some day, "God willing," she says, with a soft submission most touching in one so self-sufficing and firm.

And now a few words about Venitia, — then I must clasp my journal and go to bed, as it is past midnight. The beautiful girl has just been in to say good night and give me one of her caresses, which are so different from Janet's, though much more profuse. Janet's touch my heart, Venitia's only my body; and yet we both love each other dearly. Let me describe her as she looked, standing by my window a few moments since, gazing out on the night and the lake, and talking of Italy and our journey with all the keen fresh taste for novelty which youth gives.

Venitia, whose rather fanciful name was given her from her birthplace, Venice, is really a beautiful woman. Her figure has the majesty of an empress and the grace of a nymph, which give her that double charm of infantile innocence and womanly reserve. Her height is full, her development fine; large, well-formed limbs, statue-like in their mould. She has a well-shaped, well-poised head, with a great wealth of waving hair, a rich brown in its hue. Her fine brow expresses capability of thought as her eyes do of feeling, and these eyes are the glory of her face.

The arch of the brow is a little prominent, and gives her a stern expression; the setting and shape of the eye and whole facial outline is Greek; but the full face, owing to the firm brow, is not so flat as the Greek form, and therefore not so insipid. Her eyes are large, their expression, and that of the mouth, as imperious as those of a Juno. Indeed, she has often been likened to the Juno in the Villa Ludovisi at Rome, a profile engraving of which I have had framed, and christened it playfully "Venitia." There is the same mouth line, the same liquid reflective eyeball and resolute curve of the brow and lip, the firm, high-arched lines, indicative of strong will, contending with the soft flowing ones of loveliness.

The color of the eyes is a tender poetic gray, which deepens to an intense black in earnest moments from the enlarging of the pupil, and there is an expression in them sometimes that amounts almost to inspiration; but the fire is too redundant, too intrepid, and at times there is a sombre mysterious look in them which tells of distant thunder and far-off lightning; they need toning down, with some great emotion that shall shake her being to its very centre.

Her mouth, that feature which tells so much of one's character and culture, is faultless. Some one has well said, that all the features of the human face are made for us but our mouths; these we make for ourselves. Venitia's is full of expression; the rich hued lips are as quivering and trembling as "shadowy water with a sweet south wind breathing over it"; and the curves are those soft, delicate ones, which only culture and the early discipline of refinement can give; but there is that same imperious line triumphant, which hardens her whole face, and which must be the one that makes the striking resemblance to the Juno; for I have seen a simple fragment of a female head on a mutilated gem pronounced to be that of the haughty queen of the gods, simply from this imperious mouth line.

A pallor which the Italians call *morbidezza* is the hue of her skin, golden and transparent in its high lights like ivory. Titian knew and felt to the very tingling point of his fingers the rich loveliness of such flesh.

Does this description sound exaggerated? To me it seems tame; for words can scarcely give the effect produced on me by such beauty as Venitia's. I lie on the lounge sometimes and watch her with half-closed eyes, as I would a picture or statue, her graceful motions, every attitude an unconscious *pose* of statue-like beauty, and think of luscious fruit, delightful sounds, warm coloring, and great sculptors' creations. Why, to paint Venitia, a

Raphael and Titian should unite; for she has the pure beauty of a Madonna, combined with the rich full size and attraction of a Magdalen.

She has all the organization of an artist, too, — quick perceptions, keen enjoyments, is sympathetic, and to a certain point creative; but, with all this beauty of mind and mould, there is a mysterious, veiled, inexplicable something about her, which keeps her from developing completely; she is by some enchantment locked up from herself and from others.

Venitia's life melody is not only yet unwritten, but even unprefigured; here is the fine human instrument with its rich assemblage of strings and keys; preluding chords, too, are heard full of promising beauty, but the life-theme is not hinted at. To some women this theme never comes; the whole human existence is but a gentle soft preluding; and others even have preludes full of complicated harmonies, sounding like intricate themes, but the life pieces end as mere voluntaries, nothing more, and so it may be with our Venitia.

We are very proud of her. She gives us no cause for uneasiness or discomfort. There is none of the restlessness and caprice about her which might be pardoned in one so gifted and charming. She is pure and sparkling, too, like a first-water diamond, — yes, that is just it, — for she is almost as hard.

MIDNIGHT ON MONT CENIS.

E left Vevay last Thursday for Geneva. On board the lake steamer Rhone, we met a Milanese whose conversation amused us; she was not young, — about mid-age; not at all pretty, but had an intelligent face. Some chance accident introduced us, a courtesy, I think, such as the offer of a seat or something of the like. She talked rapidly, freely, and well; described Milan, Genoa, and Turin with graphic distinctness; drew a rapid sketch of Italian literature, and touched on Italian politics with a forked tongue.

We talked of books over Heine's "Lutèce," which I was reading, and a novel of De Balzac she held in her hands. She spoke contemptuously of French authors, was well read in English literature, — as cultivated Italians are apt to be, — and said she "adored the classic writers of England," as she called the poets and dramatists of the Elizabethan day. When we approached Geneva we all leaned over the guards of the boat together.

"Look!" she cried, "at the ugly place. It is a great phalanstery town; but that is the spirit of the day, — so no wonder. In the last age this community idea was dreamed of by philosophers; in this nineteenth century the people carry it into execution. The philosophers meant it for the improvement of the mind and condition of the poor; the people of this day use it to give to themselves the luxuries of the old *noblesse*, — the temporal sensual ones, — and ragged half-price business they make of it, with their mammoth hotels and community-cafés, their woven cotton lace, and their thin coatings of silver and gold."

Her lips curled scornfully, she drew in her sharp pointed chin and threw back her head with a haughty, resentful air, as she added, in low hissing words with half-closed lips, as Italians speak when at white-heat rage, —

"Ah, the influence of the South is over! No more beauty, no more poesy in life. The reign of the cold, rigid North is supreme, with its *chemins de fer* (railways), its *fils de fer* (telegraphs), and all other *choses de fer*" (iron things).

Then she muttered from Dante's *Inferno* this passage:

"Lo 'mperador del doloroso regno
Da mezzo 'l petto uscia fuor della ghiaccia."

"That Emperor who sways
The realm of sorrow, at mid breast from the ice." *

I have no doubt she felt full of gall and bitterness as she thought how prone to earth lay her beloved Italy under this detested rule of the Teuton.

Venitia, with graceful kindness said to her: "Beautiful Italy, seated in your loveliness on the earth, like poor uncrowned Constance!

'Here I in sorrow sit;
Here is my throne, bid kings come bow to it.'"

The Italian turned sharply, with tears actually glittering in her keen black eyes, and looked at the lovely girl as if she adored her. The boat touched the pier and

* Cary's Dante; *Inferno*, Canto XXXIV.

knocked all to bits the nice little scene, while in the hurry of landing, porters' bustle, the noise of luggage, and all the other busy attendants of going on shore, we lost sight of our chance acquaintance.

After securing the *coupé* in the diligence, and setting a commissionaire, or errand-porter, to work about the passports, we took a farewell look at the "phalanstery town," as our boat friend had called it. We went to the head of the city, to our favorite spot, *Place St. Antoine*, to give a good-by gaze to the beautiful view on which we had looked so often that it had become a possession of memory.

The Savoy Alps stretched out snowy fortifications between us and that wondrous ice-bed, above which towers the "monarch of mountains," Mont Blanc. Deut D'Oche, our old Alpine neighbor, seemed to peep familiarly over the Chablais at us, to tell us "God speed." To the northeast there was the Mole, with its solitary peak, and the Voirons, seated like matrons in the midst of their forests; while to the right, Mont Buet, with its snowy dome, and the dark rocky outworks of the Grenier, summoned us onwards.

At half-past four we returned to the hotel and dined, then went to the Diligence Bureau, received our passport, and were soon snugly packed away in the *coupé*. The journey from Geneva to Chambèry was the coldest part of the route. We left Geneva at six in the evening, and reached Chambèry at six the next morning, where we staid till midday. At one o'clock in the afternoon we were again on the road. The diligence was lifted upon the rails, and we flew along quite swiftly up to St. Jean, which we reached at nightfall; there we took horses again and commenced the mountain passage.

The passage of Mont Cenis is the least interesting in a picturesque sort of view of all the Alpine entrances into Italy; but it is a superb road, and is as safe and comfortable in mid-winter as an ordinary journey away from the Alps. It is considered a masterpiece of engineering, its ascent and descent are so gradual and secure. Fabbroni, the great engineer, gave seven years' study, thought, and labor, and France over a million of dollars, to accomplish it.

The first Charlemagne crossed Mont Cenis with his army, when it was a true feat to make the passage, for it had to be done on foot and in litters. The road remained impassable for diligence as late as 1800. Then came the second Charlemagne, who wished to go into Italy over mountains as high as his ambition, but he was not of the race of those

> "First men who led black horses by the mane";

nor was he of this third race, of which his nephew is a type, — who merits, better than his uncle, Carlyle's title "Hero of Tools," — who is now driving out over these Alps, —

> "From the cloud of steam majestical white horses."

He, the second Charlemagne, the great Napoleon, commanded this fine road, and a greater miracle it was then than the tunnel can be now. We talked of the history of this celebrated road, and the great change the tunnelling of the Alps shall make in a few years. The idea sounds more poetical than the journey then shall be, for the tunnel will alter materially this midnight pass which has its own peculiar charm.

The peal of a bell across the midnight air — the Angelus bell of the Hospice — turned the conversation to the Benedictines who live on Mont Cenis. We went back to the great St. Benedict, whose famous Holy Rule was said to contain the maxims of perfect government; that system which Cosmo di Medici, and all those great rulers of men, studied reverentially. Those Benedictines, his followers, were great people at every period of their history, either as sturdy forest-clearers, tillers of the soil, or scholarly gentlemen copying with clerkly skill, and protecting, with cultured reverence, the treasures of Greek and Latin poesy.

Guizot says of them, "The monks of St. Benedict were the great land-clearers of Europe"; and Mignet calls them, "Those great republics of agricultural and literary industry of the Order of St. Benedict."

"*Scienter nesciens, et sapienter indoctus*, (learnedly ignorant and wisely learned,) St. Gregory, his biographer, called this wonderful man," said Janet; "and these Benedictines on Mont Cenis are living quite in accordance with their holy founder's rule, but that cannot be said of every Benedictine order; they have fallen many times sadly away from his rigid self-denying practice. Why, to become a member of the very community St. Benedict established at Monte Casino, near the frontier or line between the Roman States and Naples, the applicant has to be not only a person of high birth, but also of independent fortune. At one time the Abbot of Monte Casino held the rank of Baron of the kingdom, and drove his coach and six."

"So soft is flesh of mortals, that on earth
A good beginning doth no longer last
Than while an oak may bring its fruit to birth," *

* Cary's Dante, *Paradise*, Canto XXII.

I quoted. "But you must remember, Janet, even in their days of backsliding the gentlemen of that convent were not idle men. To them you lovers of the classics are indebted for a great deal that you now enjoy. That very monastery of Monte Casino was a sanctuary for Greek and Latin treasures which otherwise would have been lost. You would never have had even those six *Fasti* of Ovid which you prize so highly, nor the great Englishman Fox, his beloved Idylls of Theocritus, but for these scholarly Benedictines of Monte Casino."

We dwelt on the life of the great founder of the Order, of whom Montalembert says, "At a season of universal desolation and gloom, when the whole world was steeped in heresy, schism, and divisions, a solitary monk created a centre of supernatural virtue, and illuminated it with a splendor which shone during ten ages over regenerated Europe." *

The beautiful love which existed between St Benedict and his sister St. Scholastica, and the touching story told by St. Gregory of their last interview, interested Venitia deeply. St. Scholastica's convent was five miles distant from Monte Casino, and once a year she always visited her brother. He would not let her visit the monastery, but went out to meet her at a place appointed, and there they passed the day in sweet talk on their mutual faith and great hope.

When she knew she was dying she made her people carry her to the place of meeting, and her brother came to her. The day seemed short to the dying woman; and as the setting sun sank behind the beautiful hills, she clung with mortal yearning to her dearly loved brother, whose blessed words of comfort during the day had given

* *Les Moines d'Occident*, par Montalembert.

her so much healing strength. She besought him to stay until morning with her, and talk again to her of the happiness of that other life which lay beyond the dread, dark sea of anguish, called Death, — that sea which she was so soon to cross alone.

But the rule of his Order, established by himself, forbade a monk to pass the night away from his monastery. He knew it was his beloved sister's last request, but he steadfastly, though sorrowfully, refused.

Then the poor, expiring woman, seeing her entreaties were in vain, lay her trembling hands on a table, rested her face in them, weeping bitterly, and besought Almighty God to interpose in her behalf. Straightway the heavens seemed opened, and there came pouring down such a flood of rain with fierce thunder and sharp lightning, that no man or beast dare venture out in it.

"God forgive you, sister!" said St. Benedict. "What have you done?"

"I asked a favor of you," she replied, with reproachful tenderness, "and you refused me. I asked it of God, and he has granted it to me."

All night long the holy brother and sister held solemn vigil together, and his strong words became as an armor of might to the feeble woman whose soul and body were having their last great battle. At dawn they parted, not in tears, but with faces that shone like angels; and as St. Benedict kissed his sister, she said, —

"My brother, the parting will not be long. We shall soon meet again."

Three days after, she breathed her last breath in great mortal anguish, but in holy peace of spirit; and her sorrowing brother, who was praying at the time in his tower at Monte Casino, believed he saw her pure soul ascend to heaven in the form of a dove.

Only a few weeks passed and it was as St. Scholastica had said; the parting was not long, for the monks of Monte Casino were mourning their great founder's death.

Brother and sister sleep together under the magnificent high altar, rich in precious marbles, of the superb Church of Monte Casino; and the tender beauty of their love steals gently down through thirteen centuries with a light as pure as their great virtue.

"Ah yes," said Janet, as I finished this sweet old story; "and St. Gregory, their biographer, gives a beautiful reason for the granting of St. Scholastica's prayer, *Justo valde judicio illa plus potuit quæ amplius amavit,* —'By a just judgment, indeed, she who was the more loving was the more powerful.'"

"Was St. Bernard, the stern judge of poor Abelard, a Benedictine?" asked Venitia.

"The great Abbot of Clairvaux," I answered, "belonged to a reformed Benedictine order, the Cistercians, but his followers were sometimes called Bernardins. He lived six hundred years after St. Benedict. St. Benedict's period was 480 to 543; while the apostle of the ill-fated Second Crusade, St. Bernard, flourished from 1091 to 1153."

"St. Bernard's period," said Janet, "was also famous for many new religious orders. The mendicant friars sprang up then. St. Dominic, and St. Francis of Assissium, the founders of the Dominican and Franciscan brotherhoods, were contemporaries of the all-powerful St. Bernard."

"Lord Lindsay, in his Christian Art," I remarked, "says that during this period, extending from St. Benedict's death up even so far as 1400, Christianity found its chief expression in architecture; the spirit of Faith, reigning supreme, gave utterance to its grandest voice, its symphonies in stone." *

We talked all night, and Janet told us of quite an exciting adventure she once had when crossing this same Mont Cenis with Venitia and a young brother, when they were children.

* Lord Lindsay's Christian Art, Letter I. Vol. II.

JANET'S STORY.

ATE one afternoon in January, about fifteen years ago, said Janet, "I received a letter telling me of my sister Mary's dangerous illness. I was at Geneva and she at Turin. The letter was from her physician; it bade me come immediately; even then I might not find her alive.

"I had the two youngest children with me, — my poor little brother Ernst, a child of seven, and Venitia, who was not more than five; they could not be left in Geneva, for I knew no one there to trust them with, therefore they had to go with me. I had only just time to hurry down to the Diligence Bureau to see what seats I could get. Of course, I found the *coupé* engaged; for when one is in a disagreeable position, the difficulties that spring up on all sides can be named Legion. There were only two seats to be had in the whole diligence, and they were in the interior.

"I could not help hesitating, used as I was to facing disagreeable things; for it is so unpleasant for a woman to travel alone in such a place. But what alternative had I? 'Go,' said Courage, 'and trust to the children for protection.'

"The diligence was being arranged while I stood in the office talking about the seats with the courteous clerk, who very good naturedly sympathized with my annoyance; in fifteen minutes the coach would start. My hesitation was ended by the arrival of the commissionaire whom I had employed to have my passport *visèd* by the Sardinian consul. I lost no more time, paid for the seats, lifted the children into the interior, and followed them; it was soon crowded with men. All nations seemed to be represented, and, until midnight, their conversation was very animated, — a perfect Babel of tongues.

"On entering the diligence I put Ernst in the corner, taking the seat next him, holding Venitia on my lap. My next neighbor was a German, and soon he showed a disposition to be friendly. At the Sardinian frontier he handed out my passport officiously, as if I belonged to him; offered repeatedly to relieve me of my child, and evidently desired to make himself agreeable, but, in such a manner as to cause all the hedgehog in my nature to put out its quills; besides, at that time I had so much trouble that there was, as is apt to be with energetic women under such influences, more harshness about me than anything else, — it was just at 'the darkest hour before day' in my life.

"I was no longer in my first youth, and it would have been quite a figure of speech to have called me pretty; nevertheless I found I was more attractive to my German neighbor than was pleasant. He sat very near, saying once in a while, with vulgar familiarity, in German, 'Nahe zusammen sitzen macht gute Gesellschaft.'*

"Such a night as I passed! But the interior being crowded was some little protection. Pressing Venitia close to my breast, whilst Ernst slept soundly, leaning

* "Close sitting makes good company."

against me, I turned a deaf ear to the impertinent remarks of the German. At last he also slept, and had the insolence to rest his head on my shoulder. I had anticipated some such proceeding from his manner, and accordingly had put a few pins there, points outward; he quickly raised his head, muttering angrily, 'Vermaledeites Weib.'*

"I was too alarmed to laugh, I assure you; moreover my heart was too full of apprehension for dear Mary; she might at that moment be dead! Memories of our youth swept up before me. Hours of joy and hours of sorrow we had had together; for we were the eldest of that large family, and very near of an age. Then she was my only counsellor and friend in the bringing up of the whole little flock; and though her health had been failing for some time, and she was almost a penniless widow with two little girls of her own, adding to, as she would mournfully say, instead of relieving the family burden; still she was of great value to me in many, many ways, — most of all to a woman in trouble, she was one, near my own age, who could love and be loved. The other children were my charges and responsibilities: she was my only earthly luxury and consolation.

"Be merciful, O God!" I inwardly groaned, resting my burning, dry, aching eyes on Venitia's soft curls; for she, like my little brother, was sleeping soundly that blessed child-sleep 'that the thunder cannot break.' Looking at them I envied their unconsciousness of danger, their freedom from apprehensions and care, their sweet trust and faith in me as the living present providence of a mother, which is 'the heaven that hangs around' a child.

* "Confound the woman!"

"Mary and I had once been young and tolerably happy; more cared for in the way of luxury than they, but not more loved. Now what were we? Solitary wrecks on life's sandy shore. If God's angel of death had come then, and shielded us all three with his dark wing, very sweet would have been the sleep to me! But still I ejaculated 'Be merciful, O God!' and the prayer for Mary's life went on.

"Towards morning the diligence rumbled into Chambèry. The first thing that struck my eyes when I looked from the window in the dim morning light was that large monumental fountain you were so struck with to-day, ornamented with huge elephants standing in the middle of the street. Some day we must go over together the history of General de Boigne, his eventful life in India, his romantic but unhappy marriage with Madame Récamier's friend, and his return to his native town far up in the Sardinian Alps, where he sought consolation for his disappointed domestic hopes in charities. After his death his grateful townsmen raised this curious and costly fountain to his memory, and gave his name to the street in the centre of which the fountain stands.

"We drove through Rue de Boigne to the bureau. When the diligence stopped I roused the sleeping children, pushing aside hastily my offensive German neighbor, who, notwithstanding his experience of pin-points, was ready with disgusting freedom to assist me. Two or three of the men talked with him of me, as I handed out the children to the guard. I took occasion to address the children in English, which we seldom used; for French, as the language of the country we lived in, was easier; but I did so, because the best protection to a lone woman on the European continent is our good, brave

Anglo-Saxon tongue; the woman who speaks it as if born to it is supposed to know how to do, to be, and to suffer, — and most especially not to suffer any impertinence. Their conversation was in German.

"'Engländerin,' said one.

"'Nein,' replied my meddling neighbor, 'nein, sie sprecht nicht wie eine Engländerin.' *

"Another suggested 'Russian,' for cultivated Russians speak, as Berlioz drolly says, 'all known and unknown tongues' with the greatest facility, almost without accent; they speak English too, in the monotone manner of Americans, quite free from British emphasis.

"Taking the children by the hand I went into the diligence office to secure the *coupé* if possible for the rest of the journey, but to my dismay found it engaged all the way through to Turin. The morning sun shot a little bright ray through the office window and seemed to give me fresh courage. One rarely feels timid in broad daylight. After inquiring the time of starting, finding I had seven or eight hours for rest, I went to the hotel.

"A pleasant chambermaid gave me a nice room and brought us a good breakfast. I undressed the children, bathed them, and put them to bed, where they soon fell into a sound sleep. I did the same for myself, but it was in vain that I tried to sleep. My uneasiness about Mary tortured me; the painful tension of my nerves during the night caused them to throb fiercely. I crept quietly out of bed and dressed myself. Ernst opened his full brown eyes on me, as I stooped down by the bedside to get my walking boots.

"'Dear child,' I said, as the affectionate little fellow

* "An Englishwoman."—"No, she does not speak like an Englishwoman."

held up his arms to clasp around my neck, 'Jennie is feverish and needs air. Ernst will take good care of his little sister, will he not, while Jennie is out?'

"The self-sacrificing child assented with a bright smile, and whispered good by. I hurried out of the hotel. I wished to see something of this town in which De Maistre was born, to ramble through its streets, and up the mountain roads where he had roamed in his youth, and dreamed visions, strange to say, more than realized in his eventful life. Military renown, successful authorship, a long married love, were his; he was a soldier, a philosopher, — 'studied all things and yet knew nothing,' as he said in the light, graceful epitaph which he wrote for himself a few years before his death. Do you remember it? No? I will try to repeat it, it is so well turned.

'Ci-git, sous cette pierre grise,
Xavier, qui de tout étonnait,
Demandant d'où venait la bise
Et pourquoi Jupiter tonnait.
Il etudiat maint grimoire,
Il lut du matin jusqu 'au soir,
Et but à la fin l'onde noire,
Tout surpris de ne rien savoir.' *

"I went out of the Faubourg de Montmeillan, and followed the left bank of the Leysse for some distance. First I came to a village; then seeing the ruins of a

* Here lies under this gray stone,
Xavier, who, quite astonished,
Asked whence came the north wind,
And why Jupiter thundered?
He studied many a gramarye,
He read from morning until night,
And drank at last the black wave,
Quite surprised at knowing nothing.

castle on the other side of the stream, I crossed it, and soon after entered a beautiful mountain gorge, completely shut in. High steep rocks swept up, seeming like the pedestal of the serrated mountain in the distance. A peasant woman guided me around a paper-mill to see a cascade, which came tumbling down the cliffs, and spouted out in jets through fissures in the rock, while all around hung brilliant icicles glittering and sparkling in the sunlight superbly.

"'*C'est bien* "*Le Bout du Monde*"'* said the peasant woman naively, and I afterwards found it was the actual name of the place.

"I gave her some money and dismissed her. My watch told me I had only been a little over an hour and a half walking there, thus leaving me at least two hours more for my ramble; so I gave myself up freely to the luxury of a silent revery in this beautiful spot.

"I returned to the gorge, where I paced rapidly up and down the snow-covered path. The shadows of the fir-trees rested on the ground as firm and still as if inlaid; the glittering snow flashed in the morning sunlight a million of facets, — a sheet of diamonds; and the sharp peaks of the mountain lay white and icy against the blue sky. My fancy, morbid from the influence of sorrow, drew a sad contrast between those cutting ice-peaks, the soft clouds of the heavens, and my own broken life; I thought of Mary's lot and mine with something like bitterness.

"I could not feel disheartened with that strong fresh mountain air, washing like waves over my hot brow and cheeks. Nor could I, when I thought

* It is indeed "The End of the World."

> 'o'er loss of days no more to be,
> Of actions dropped to dreams, and dreams to Death,
> And then Eternity,' *

feel what is called resignation. Like you, Ottilie, I have no such grace given me. I think I am more submissive than you, — certainly not more enduring, my friend, — but not one whit more resigned. I may meet with a hundred rebuffs and disappointments and be desperate; but still I stand with armor buckled on ready for fresh action.

"I planted my feet strongly and firmly on that rocky, icy road, as I paced rapidly to and fro, looking up at the cliffs and the shut-in gorge, which doubtless was 'the end of the world' to the innocent inhabitants of the place. It was a solemn, sublime spot, where fancy might readily weave woof and web of sombre but grand contrasts, filling memory's storehouse with material for the use of the imagination at more healthy seasons. I seemed surrounded with

> 'Fragments of a crystal world
> Long shattered from its skyey course.'

"Does it seem strange to you, Ottilie, that I should be able to recall the very detail of emotions felt so many years ago? It was just at the turning-point of my life, when the load of trouble had grown so heavy as to be near that perilous toppling over which is apt to carry the sufferer with it in its fall. Thus my memory retains the impression of the keen cutting left by those sad experiences.

"Poverty, 'that sorrowful human poison,' as some one has called it, had added itself to our other trials, giving to my soul little nervous tremblings, exaggerated apprehensions and timidities, quite foreign to my character,

* Read's "Doomed and Forgotten."

paralyzing every power and desire of happiness. O, it is a terrible poison of pride, that same poverty, for it distorts and chills the heart, making one believe in the existence of a sea of ice between ourselves and others. I felt like shutting the book of life forever, so hopeless seemed our future, without even the memory of a happy past to relieve it, — and yet so soon life was to open up to me, for the first time in my existence, a real, true, unalloyed joy! That very spring it was I first met Paul."

Janet stopped. The night was too dark for me to see her face; but there was an agitation in the rich tones of her voice, which showed she was deeply moved. After a few moments, she continued, —

"Noonday approaching, warned me of the necessity of returning towards the town, and I retraced the road on the border of the Leysse, which had led me to this beautiful spot in the morning. I found the children up, dressed, and the maid spreading a nice dinner for us in the anteroom of our apartment.

"'How fresh and rosy you look, dear Jennie,' they cried, leaping into my arms, and almost smothering me with kisses.

"As my walk had sharpened my appetite as well as brightened my cheeks and eyes, I hastened to our dinner. That through, we went to the diligence, in order to be seated before the other passengers arrived. When I stepped in after Ernst, the boy made an outcry, and my foot pressed something hard which had just fallen from his hand.

"'O, my knife, my knife!' he exclaimed.

"'Here it is,' I said; and stooping down I picked it up from the straw where he had dropped it. I slipped it into my pocket, intending to put it in the travelling-bag after we should be seated, for it was a heavy, troublesome thing. It had been sent to Ernst a little while before from the United States,—a real Western bowie-knife, which he wished with boy pride to show to our little nieces at Turin. We had just taken our seats when in trooped the other passengers. There were not so many as the night before, and most of them were new comers. An old peasant woman was among them. I made room for her beside Ernst, having taken the corner seat myself. My German neighbor, I observed with great satisfaction, had left also.

"Toward sunset we reached St. Jean. The children wished to look out of the window, so I stood up with Venitia, while Ernst left his seat to see something on the roadside which had attracted his sister's attention. When the diligence was ready to start, to my surprise and dissatisfaction I found Ernst's seat occupied; I looked at the person and recognized the officious German. He had been travelling from Chambèry in some other part of the diligence. I observed also that every one had left the interior but the old woman, who had settled herself to sleep in the farthest corner.

"My heart seemed to stand still for an instant. The man said nothing, but as my eye met his I fancied in its expression that he observed my annoyance and exulted in it. I went over to the opposite bench and put one of the children on either side of me. The German taking no other notice of the change than by stretching himself out on the unoccupied seats, I began to think I had been foolishly alarming myself; so gradually dismissing him from my mind, I became absorbed in thinking of Mary and the desolation of life her death would cause me.

"Night came on very cold and dark. I listened to

the heavy breathing of the sleepers. The dull hoarse snoring of the old woman proved how leaden was her slumber. The diligence wheels groaned through the hard, stony snow, grinding it with sharp harsh creaks into powder. The wind blew high, moaning in soughs and gusts around the desolate place. The voice of the driver, the cries of the postillion to his horses, all sounded as if coming from a great distance.

" While I was observing this, the helplessness and loneliness of my position again presented themselves to me. No cry of mine thrown out from this shut-up box of a place on that surging, roaring wind could possibly be heard, or, if heard, probably no attention would be paid to it; for, according to European notions, I had no business to be travelling in such a place unprotected.

" Ernst had crept down on the large tin foot-warmer, his head rested on my lap, one dear soft cheek nestled lovingly in the palm of my hand. I listened to the sweet rise and fall of the breath of the sleeping children ; so loud did my own heart throb, that I could plainly distinguish its anxious troubled beat from the peaceful measure of their childish slumbers. Suddenly I heard a slight rustling in the corner occupied by the German, and I thought I saw in the dim light a figure moving.

" My anxiety is making a baby of me," I said to myself, while I strained my eyes forward, watching closely. I was not mistaken, — he was coming stealthily over to my side of the coach.

" ' Wir sind besonders glücklich, so allein zu sein in dünkler Nacht, und um eine solche gute Gelegenheit zu benützen setze beiseite äuserliche Besheidenheit,' * said

* " We are very lucky to be all alone this dark night; we ought to use such a good opportunity, and not be too modest."

he, taking his seat beside me, and resting his arm on my neck.

"I sprang to my feet, snatched the knife out of my pocket, the recollection of which came to me as if by inspiration, touched its spring, and flashed the broad, bright blade in his face; there was just light enough from the dim lantern to show the glimmer of the steel. I am sure if he had touched me I should have killed him.

"I never saw a human being so alarmed in my life. He was struck dumb, cowered down, and gradually crept off, farther and farther from me, until he had reached the end of the coach. I did not speak a word, nor cease looking at him; I was afraid of breaking the fascination. I sat down with assumed calmness, but continued snapping the blade with leisurely beats to and fro. I do not know how long I sat watching him; the time seemed interminable. About midnight the diligence stopped at one of the relay houses, or houses of refuge. There my German admirer stepped out, and I saw him no more. Just before the diligence started, I heard one of the guards bantering him, evidently urging him to return to the interior.

"'Verdammit, nein,' he muttered, sullenly, 'da drinnen ist eine Bärin.' *

"'Sie ist eine Americanerin,' † said the guard, laughing.

"The German's teeth fairly chattered with fright, as he cried, 'Americanerin! was sie nicht sagen! Mein Gott! lieber ginge ich in die Höhle einer Bärin als einer solchen Americanerin zu nahe zu kommen!' ‡

* "Curse it, no! There is a she-bear in there!"

† "She's an American woman."

‡ "An American woman! You don't say so! My God, I had rather go into a she-bear's den than come too near such an American woman."

"The other men laughed heartily as he clambered up to some other part of the coach, grumbling angrily, while the diligence rolled on to Susa. My journey after that passed without incident; and when I reached Turin I had the great happiness of finding Mary not only alive, but relieved from immediate danger. In a fortnight she was well enough to enjoy my description of the journey, and laugh with me over the fright caused by my German admirer, as well as the good use I had made of Ernst's bowie-knife."

This story led Janet and Venitia to recall many old memories, while I fell into a troubled, disturbed sleep of fatigue which caused me the loss of the fine sunrise at Susa. I remember trying to arouse myself to look at the mountain outlines of the Plains of Piedmont as the keen-eyed Janet pointed them out on our approach to Susa, but I was growing so weary with the twelve hours' confinement in the *coupé* as to feel really ill and long for the sight of Turin.

At Susa, our diligence was raised upon the railway again, but we did not reach Turin until ten o'clock in the morning. I have a dim recollection of being lifted to a carriage, carried to a room, laid on a bed, and in the midst of much suffering, feeling Janet's dear hand-touches, with once in a while a soft, cool kiss on my hot brow, and a short, eager, loving press of her cheek against mine, which tender nursing at last quieted the mortal pain, soothing me into a heavy sleep, filled with mysterious magnetic dreams. Of course we could not continue our journey; but I am so much better this morning that we shall leave at two o'clock, as we wish to be in Genoa before Carnival closes.

Janet and Venitia have gone out to refresh old memories. Years ago this was one of the tarrying places of their curious nomadic life. I should have liked to go with them, but I did not think it prudent, as the streets are covered with snow. It disappoints me, too, for I wished to visit the Turin Royal Gallery, which has a fine collection of pictures of the old German school. Viardot says, in his *Musées d'Italie*, that no museum in Italy is so rich as this in German paintings. There are Albert Durer's, some fine Holbein portraits, — one of my historical heroine, Marguerite de Valois,—Rubens's, Rembrandt's, Van-Dyck's, and, above all, one of the tender pictures of that devoted observer of "the beautiful laws of Catholic symbolism and religious painting, who united the deep symbolism of devotion and holy beauty with a German abundance of feeling and expression";* Henling, whose touching picture of the "Passion," is in this collection.

But I only tease myself by naming them over. Here come Janet and Venitia, full of eager, earnest, pleasant talk. Venitia has turned over the leaves of my journal, crying out with surprise at the number of pages I have written during their absence. Janet scolded me tenderly. But it would have been greater fatigue to have lain on a sofa with hands folded over the aching heart, feeling the biting tooth of resentful, bitter memory eating in and in!

* F. Schlegel.

RAILWAY TALK AND CARNIVAL STUDIES.

GENOA.

E arrived last evening at eight o'clock, having left Turin at two in the afternoon. Although there was snow at Turin, the country lost its wintry look very soon, and the air grew soft and balmy.

Piedmont — *Pied de monte,* foot of the mountain — lay spread out before us; we almost fancied we could see these vast plains between the Alps and Apennines, stretching from their mountain frontiers far across Lombardy to the Adriatic, their mistress; for though the western and southwestern shores are washed by the Mediterranean, their waters are all sent to the Venetian Sea.

The journey between Turin and Genoa was very pleasant. The rest which I had taken in Turin refreshed me, and made me strong enough to notice and enjoy this new landscape, which differs very much in all its points from Swiss scenery. The color of the sky first struck me. Its mellow amber hue is so unlike the cold transparent stony blue of the Alpine heavens. Then the buildings are novel. I had grown familiar in Switzerland with the heavy turreted tops of the grim Middle Age chateaux and the gray stone churches, whose massive, four-sided spires, with ogive openings, seemed part and parcel of the mountains from whose sides they jutted out.

The Italian campaniles, or bell towers, are the first buildings which attract attention on these Plains of Piedmont. The Lombards, in adopting the Basilica of Latin architecture, did not lose sight of this graceful accessory. They seemed to have enjoyed the picturesque effect these campaniles and the baptisteries produced when grouped around their churches; for they displayed so much architectural taste in them. These beautiful towers run gracefully up against the soft sky, several stories in height, each story often bearing a different order of architecture; the rich-hued heavens peep through the many-arched, airy-looking belfry-tops, these sweet warders and gentle guards of the churches, beside which they stand, and they differ widely as well as pleasantly from the frowning towers of old Lombardy castles, which bristle out from many an Alpine crest, whose heavy machicolations and sharp turrets of inverted triangles tell of the fierce times when Guelph and Ghibelline warred hotly against each other.

"This landscape is very gentle and gracious," remarked Venitia. "It is quite a relief to my eyes, after having looked so long on rugged Alps, with their torrents and glaciers and dense forests."

"The garden of Europe," I said, half to myself, as I leaned back in the comfortably stuffed seat of the railway carriage.

"A garden it is truly," answered Janet, "but one that has been nourished with precious human blood. This little kingdom of Piedmont, or Sardinia, has grown on what kills other and larger governments, — politics and war; in this it resembles Prussia. Two great men erected their inheritances into kingdoms through the force of their individual will and courage about the same period. Frederick the Great, of Prussia, that prosaic, wondrous hero, as Heine calls him, and Victor Amadeus II. of Savoy, — both princes, too, struggling against one common enemy, — Austria. This very north of Italy was then the scene of the same struggle which is now going on, Piedmont against Austria, with France for her ally and kinsman; for a royal marriage then sealed the treaty between Louis XIV. and Victor Amadeus, as it is going to do now between the French Emperor and Victor Emanuel. Louis's grandson, the Duc de Bourgogne, you know, married a daughter of the aspiring Savoisien Duke-King.

"France her kinsman!" I repeated. "Yes, you are right. The questionable fidelity and friendly tyranny which France has always shown Savoy and Piedmont is very like that which a strong and powerful kinsman is apt to show a weaker relative. But the first part of your remarks recalls to me a fine expression of De Mazade, — you will remember it. He says, 'this Plain of Piedmont has had the fatal privilege of being the *champ-clos* * of European duels.'"

"That is very true," assented Janet. "Every spot here has been trampled under foot with war-steeds; every clump of grass and every leaf on the trees should be blood-red instead of green. All these towns we have been travelling through during the last two or three days have names which bristle with warlike memories as with spears. Conquered and reconquered Susa, besieged Turin, both tell the same old story of European antagonisms, rival struggles, and Italian yearnings after liberty."

"Which yearnings," I added, "generally resolve themselves, so far as true national or governmental liberty is

* *Champ-clos*, field for single combat, — lists.

concerned, into a sonnet, a written tragedy, or an epic. From Dante to the present day, all their poets have moaned over, 'in deathless verse,' the oppressions and wrongs endured by this 'geographical expression,' as Metternich pertly called Italy."

"The Italians, it is true," replied Janet, laughing, "have always believed everything could be said in verse, and, as I think of it, I remember that one of the noted Italian poets of the present day, a Piedmontese, too, by the way, has actually written a poem, in which he has celebrated the Piedmontese statutes, the two Chambers of Deputies, and the Constitutional laws, —just fancy the droll air of such an epic!"

We sat silent for a little while, when suddenly Venitia exclaimed, —

"O Jennie, do you remember that famous journey we made last year, coming from Paris to Switzerland, when we passed through the vast plains of Franche Comté, that golden Burgundy, the rich Côte d'Or, with its sweet flowering vineyards which filled the air with fragrance? for it was in early June, you know. You remind me of that delightful journey, for, just as you have been doing now, you and Ottilie mingled with the subtle odor of the grape-flower your memories of the past. You showered down a flood of names and a stream of historic story as brilliant in its flow as the precious Burgundian wine. But I remember it poured black and dark with that bad Philip, 'the greatest duke in all the world,' the one whom history calls 'Good,' notwithstanding the cruel wrong he did to his poor orphan niece, Jacqueline of Holland, —

'She whom they called queen
In Brabant once.'"

"Yes," answered Janet, smiling, "we went over the whole Burgundian line from Philip the Bold down to Charles the Bold, and his chronicler De Commines; then when we came to that great struggle of ducal pride and state ambition warring with the general power, that never-ending sphinx riddle for countries, Ottilie and I had a grand argument, I remember."

"But I did not follow you through those political historical disputes," said Venitia. I got no further than poor Jacqueline, — as Owen Meredith sings: —

> 'Alas, it was a piteous history,
> The life of thát poor countess! —
> Wrongs, insults, treacheries,
> Hopes broken down, and memory which sighed
> In, like a night-wind.' "

"It is very hard," said Janet, laughing, "to make you enthusiastic young persons accept those great facts which history establishes; namely, that there are some rights which are perfectly just in themselves and yet seem *politically impossible*, and some concessions which are not only humiliating, but cruel, that seem *politically necessary*."

"Venitia must accept them," I remarked. "If she does not now, her life experience, I fancy, will teach them to her; for they are proved, not only in the history of nations, but in the history of every woman."

"It is not so pleasant to learn them from experience," said Janet, pressing my hand tenderly. "There is a sort of aerial perspective hanging around historical wrongs which makes them less painful to regard than personal ones. The distance of time prevents us from seeing and feeling all the detail of suffering caused by these wicked political necessities and impossibilities; it enables us also to distinguish the whole great plan and note the divine balance made in the end, the holy compensation which equalizes all at last. This very Jacqueline of Holland story, for example; we who look at it now may feel like Venitia, indignant for the unfortunate young countess's sake, but our indignation is tempered quickly; the eye has only to run down a few sentences, as it were, on the page of history, to find the injustice meeting its punishment. Forty years after the sad period when poor Jacqueline

> 'in Holland night and day
> Watched those long lines of siege, and fought at bay
> Along her broken army,'

the Burgundian line ended in one fair girl, who, like her grandfather's niece, stood alone in life, an orphan, and had her duchy, that beautiful Burgundy for whose advancement Philip had sinned, wrested from her by Louis XI. Jacqueline's wrongs were resented, just where Philip would have felt them most, on his granddaughter, Mary of Burgundy; and yet the innocent young duchess was compensated too, for she was bride to a great emperor, Maximilian of Austria."

"What a sweet opium for private griefs is contained in this journeying over European lands," I remarked, after a little pause. "These 'majestical steam-horses' carry us swiftly through countries whose history revives pleasant home studies of our youth, the quiet library readings when we pored over books night and day, the printed page setting our young brains to thinking earnestly of great events which seemed to us

> "Dust and ashes, dead and done with,"

but which here take living form and shape. Memory forgets to dwell on her own little tale of sorrows while making these glorious sweeps over thousands of years filled with great incidents, many of which, too, are draped with the glowing, sparkling tissue of rich old 'poesy and romance.'"

"Heine says so touchingly," replied Janet, "in his Pictures of Travel, that the study of history led his soul to calmer paths, and he talks of 'those historical consolations enabling him to bear the painful events of his after life.' Then add to this study, Ottilie, the visiting and living in countries which are famous in history, the very 'breathing the spirit of the place,' and we gain from it, not only a consolation and enjoyment, but a refinement of character, a mental culture, which cannot be obtained in any other pursuit or study."

"But to reap the full benefit of it, Janet," said Venetia, "what years of study and thought are required. And not only these, but vivid memory and quick fancy must be united to the past labor. I wonder if I shall ever arrive at the time when I can be able to allow my mind to lie still and simply drink the rich draught which this European journeying offers me without the everlasting hard study I now have to keep up, like a difficult accompaniment running underneath some divine melody."

We could not help laughing, though the dear girl was in very sober earnest. She joined in our laugh good-humoredly; but, shaking her head, she added, a little sorrowfully, "I am sure I should do or be something if that time should ever come, for I am taking in all the while Art's very nutriment, not only the spirit of beauty, but knowledge itself from its glorious fountain-heads."

"Poor child!" said Janet, "and are you troubled with that naughty

'Canker of ambitious thoughts?'

You will never find sweet, quiet paths in Europe or anywhere else so long as your spirit travels that hot, dusty, high-road. But here we are at Genoa la Superba. Genoa and a Carnival! Think of that, Ottilie! One would be enough for common mortals, but we must have both glories showered down on us."

The cars stopped, and then followed the usual bustle. We were soon through the confusion, however, and nicely accommodated in the Hotel Féder, which was formerly the Palace of the Admiralty. It is a grand old building, with noble halls, broad spacious flights of stone stairways, rooms of palatial height, size, and adornments too, for our apartments are beautifully frescoed and luxuriously furnished.

At last I find myself really in Italy; it seems like living awake a beautiful dream. Snowy Turin discouraged me and I looked longingly, hoping to see what Heine calls "the variegated tangled life of Italy come leaping towards me; real, warm, and humming." Here I have it in its fullest force, for added to the native exuberance of life is the Carnival. Then the weather is delicious. We are just stepping on the flowery lintel of this blessed land

"Where summer sings and never dies,"

and are already breathing its divine atmosphere.

Carnival is near its close, for Ash-Wednesday is at hand, and the people are on their maddest height of fun and frolic. I see the same exhibitions I have read of hundreds of times in books of travel; but, as it is my first Carnival, the festival strikes me not exactly as a new thing might, but with greater power, I fancy. When I read the descriptions of others I often tried to imagine these scenes; thus I have now in my mind their impressions, the feeble pictures of my fancy, and the wonderful reality which is indeed hard to represent in words, or even on canvas, for it is such a motley, changeable, emotional thing.

I find myself recalling the various instrumental Carnivals of musicians with greater satisfaction than those given in books. To read aloud the finest written description here in its presence would sound tame and insipid; but Venitia goes from the window to the piano every little while to play passages recalled or suggested to her memory by something in the street from some musical composer's Carnival, and the music, instead of sounding out of place, seems to give even a richer color to the fête.

I have drawn my writing-table into the large balcony on the outside of the window, and as I write I can look down on the thronged strada beneath, and sketch from nature as a painter painting a picture. Barouches filled with gayly dressed people, some in grotesque costumes, are driving slowly along. One barouche has just passed by, in which was a merry party of children dressed superbly in the magnificent costume of the time of Louis XIV. Two little girls represented, one a marquise and the other a duchess; they wore paint, powder, and patches, and robes of the richest satins and velvets, but all their fine clothes could not take the child out of them, for the carriage scarcely held them in their frolic mirth.

From these carriages come showers of confetti; the occupants throw them at each other, on the crowd and even up into the balconies, for Venitia has just received a shower of very nice ones from the carriage load of children.

Now a clown dashes through the crowd, and the people scatter on each side, as if his bursts of reckless fun and droll somersets were handfuls of sharp missiles; he jingles his bells, leaps up in air, making the eyes dance as his mantle of brilliant zigzag figures waves about, and his Joseph garment of many colors flashes to and fro from his rapid movements.

The people give a fresh shout, and out from a strada at the east comes trotting a troop of asses; the clown is forgotten; he has dashed off to amuse another crowd, while we gaze at the gay feathered trappings of the asses, and laugh ourselves almost sick over the droll devices of the various riders; each one carries an absurd bâton, whose ends are surmounted by heads of geese and pigs, &c.; and the faces of the donkey-riders are hidden by ludicrous, huge-nosed, broad, grinning-mouthed masks.

"O look!" cries Venitia; and the crowd stop laughing to gaze, as we do, admiringly at a party of young gentlemen, who pass by with stately tread, masked and richly dressed. Their glittering spurs clank against the stones of the strada, their swords ring in the scabbards, and the gay hat-plumes nod with a gracious wave. Behind them are their horses superbly caparisoned, and each is led by a servant in an Oriental dress. It is just sunset; and although the golden rays cannot enter the narrow street, still the air is made bright, and we feel the sunlight, if we do not see it.

As the graceful cavaliers disappear, we hear music approaching. A band of singers are turning that corner of Piazzi Bianchi, and their chorus is as mellow and golden as the atmosphere. They pass on, and from another point a crowd of motley-hued maskers come pouring tumultuously into our already crowded strada; but they all mingle together as quick blending figures in a kaleidoscope, or like the circles and eddies in a stream, where a fast-flowing downward current meets a bubbling up spring; they form bewildering mazes, and yet there seems some curious tangled harmony of figure in the whole variegated mass.

There are shrill ear-piercing fifes and whistles, while real Pulcinellas squeak and brandish their wooden swords. A glorious peal of the merriest laughter mounts up like the foam on a goblet of new wine. Every moment there is a fresh absurdity, and each absurdity is sometimes graceful, but never vulgar. The mingling, blending crowds grow more noisy as night comes on; there is, however, no fighting, brutality, or coarseness; they sweep on in one endless flow of gayety.

Opposite our window, on the other side of the strada, is a shop where masks and dominos are sold; they hang around the door and windows, flapping about in the evening wind, as if longing to leap off their hooks and dance along in the merry crowd. Every rank and condition of costume is swaying there, from costly corn color or pink satin, bordered with this delicate silver lace of Genoa manufacture, down to common red and black muslin. Then the masks are as various. There are strings of lovely Venetian ones, made of black velvet with falls of rich lace, looking most bewitchingly and entreatingly out of their almond-shaped eye-hollows, while hob-nobbing beside them are absurd Pulcinella masks, with huge noses and hideous mouths.

We saw a living picture this afternoon at the corner of the Piazza dell' Annunziata, such a one as would have set an old painter half beside himself. A handsome Genoese woman, one of the lower class, sat in a chair in the open street, having her fine hair dressed by a girl almost as pretty as herself. Two or three men stood near her, "assisting," (as the French say,) and seemed really to enjoy the plaiting and trailing out of those rich long tresses as much as we did. The work also exhibited to advantage the fine arms and well-formed person of the pretty hair-dresser.

One of the men held in his hands a long veil with gay flowers stamped on its border. It was the *mezzaro*, as it is called, the costume of every woman in Genoa; for even those of the highest rank wear it to church. In most Catholic countries a French-shaped bonnet, such as all women wear elsewhere, is considered bold and irreverent at a place of worship. Italian and Spanish women, who delight in the costliest and gayest bonnets for a promenade or visit, will shroud their heads meekly and devoutly in a simple veil when going to their devotions.

But to return to the Genoese *mezzaro*. It is worn like the Spanish *rebosa*, thrown over and covering the head, and extending nearly to the waist; the ends are gathered up on the arms, and crossed over the breast, making one of the most bewitching costumes imaginable, combining the gracefulness of the scarf with the pretty coquetry of the veil.

I must not forget our street picture, however. Another lucky dog literally "assisted" the pretty hair-dresser, for he smoothed out awkwardly, but softly and tenderly, one of the long thick braids of hair. The girl, who was the fortunate possessor of the luxuriant tresses, sat leaning lazily back in her low wooden chair, twirling a gilt hair-pin between her fingers, laughing and looking up at her friend in high glee. Both were evidently "belles in their own circle," and, if rivals, were friendly ones, or wise enough to know they were most powerful united. According to Janet's and Venitia's report, — for they understand this Genoese dialect, — the girls were saying all manner of saucy things to their beaux.

Their brilliant eyes shot out sparkling jets of fire, their lips were as red as the coral beads encircling their proud, well-formed throats, — throats which looked like bits of fine columns, — and the skin! O that was delicious, "Phœbus had loved it and kissed it brown," and the genial warm blood mounted up in a rich glow on their cheeks.

"Ah!" I exclaimed, "if an artist would only deign to copy such pieces of nature from these street corners of Italian towns, his pictures would be ravishing before he hardly knew it. As Stendhal says, 'Filippo Lippi and Frère Angelico da Fiesole, when they had the good luck to meet with a fine bit in nature, copied it with conscientious fidelity. It was this close study of real life in its most perfect form which makes the works of the painters of the last half of the fifteenth century so enchanting.'"

"But those old Italian artists," said Janet, "were something more than mere painters. When you come to see the numberless walls, ceilings, and altars in South Italy, covered with fine decorative frescoes and paintings, you will say they were the works of men possessing more than ordinary mind, and higher, purer culture than we see now. Their creations must have cost them vigils of meditation, days of labor, and concentrated thought; then, added to this, they had a gift of conception, such as great poets or famous writers possess."

"Lord Lindsay," I remarked, "after giving the first period, from the sixth century to the fifteenth, to architecture, as the voice of the simple, pure faith of the age, devotes the fifteenth century to sculpture, as the expression of Christianity battling with Intellect; the third, however, extending from the latter half of the fifteenth to the middle of the sixteenth century, he says witnessed the successive triumphs of that struggle, and Painting became then the handmaid and exponent of Christianity." *

"There is something very earnest and true in architecture," responded Janet, "I mean that architecture of the early ages of the Church. Jean Paul was right, or felt right, when he said, 'the giant stood out of it and close before the soul.' The men who built those great works were nourished on 'plain living and high thought'; they must have had a faith, not childlike, but godlike. The painters who followed them — those marvellous men I was just speaking of — seem to me to have been earnest believers too; but they had become poets, and were as little children in their expression of the new gift. They looked up into the throbbing heavens, and saw adoring cherub heads crowding in to behold the glory of the Infant God; and on the long, cool, level clouds beautiful Madonnas stood, crowned with the glory of the setting sun of old Heathenism beaming on them, while the long folds of their chaste garments swept above the young crescent moon of Christ's faith, which was just rising. These men had hearts running over with love, bodies brimming up with rich exuberant life, and minds not so full of learning as of heavenly inspiration. A great Word was given to mankind in each one of those periods; but we do not seem to possess, now-a-days, organs capable of hearing or comprehending the language. Even the few of us who fondly think we possess them, grope as children at twilight or see as 'through a glass darkly.'"

* Lord Lindsay's Christian Art, Vol. II. p. 4.

— The night has closed in completely; the turmoil still goes on in the strada, but as a sea-breeze is blowing, and it is cool, I have come in and closed the window. Venitia is playing mad wild bursts of music, broken bits of conception suggested by these Carnival sights. She is more than clever, but her thoughts to-night are disjointed and rugged.

Here comes our refreshing nine o'clock tea; for we Americans, like the English, never lose our home habits, whatever part of the world we may float to. We shall have a little pleasant talk over the teacups, and then we shall part for the night, as the confusion of the Carnival has wearied us sadly.

PRIDE, PIETY, AND AMBITION.

E have spent the day in church-visiting. First we went to the Cathedral of San Lorenzo, one of the oldest churches in Italy, built in the beginning of the eleventh century; but only one of its towers was ever completed. It remains unfinished, as do so many of these old churches on the Continent, notwithstanding the early date of its foundation.

The traveller soon grows accustomed, however, to these half-completed works of Europe; and, indeed, to so much that might seem to be hinderances to enjoyment;—to ruins that are not even sublime; to all the surroundings of rugged footpaths, and the rude makeshifts of an indolent population, such as hovels and ignoble buildings, crowding close in against these vast piles of architecture.

But these drawbacks are no more noticed than the withered branches, dead leaves, unsightly bugs, or woody paths made muddy by the trickling of a wandering rivulet in a vast forest. The unfinished towers and spires, too, are like some forest-trees that have shot out one complete branch to its full and perfect height, and quite forgotten, through stress of storm, or some other forest trial of earth, or air, or sky, the rest of the branches belonging to the original tree-plan.

The exterior of the Cathedral of San Lorenzo is curiously ornamented with blocks of white and black marble, a Saracenic fashion of decoration. In the interior, the nave has sixteen columns of black and white Parian marble. The architecture is of no particular style, and ineffective, the church having evidently undergone those alterations which the architects of the Renaissance saw fit to make.

San Lorenzo has a number of side chapels, into one of which Venitia was obstinately bent on entering, and had quite a playful, coaxing talk with the Sacristan, endeavoring to bribe him, not only with silver *lira*, but with her own bewitching smiles and beguiling words; — all in vain.

It was the Chapel of St. John the Baptist; and Innocent VIII. having been attacked with a fit of anger against the memory of the pretty dancing daughter of the cruel Herodias, resented her sin on her sex, by forbidding all women to step foot over the threshold of this Chapel, except one day in the year, the fête day, which does not fall during our stay.

"Your church, Ottilie," said Janet, "has always been sadly wanting in gallantry to our sex."

"On the contrary, my dear," I replied, "it has always acknowledged our great power."

"Not in very courteous terms or ways. But do listen to that witch, Venitia. How well she remembers this Genoese dialect! Dear child! She makes me think of those old days. Her born tongue is that caressing, childlike Venitian; but she was always very quick in catching these peculiarities of speech which make up the different dialects of a language. Hear! how she rings out this Gallicized Genoese, as good, I assure you, as any of the people might speak it themselves."

But all Venitia's sacrifice in the way of pronunciation had no affect on the Sacristan, who was quite willing to show us the rest of the church, the Queen of Shéba's Emerald Vase, — the famous "Sacre Catino," — all the wonders, in fine, but not this Chapel; and wound up his refusal with a compliment that made us laugh heartily.

"The Signorine was so charming and dangerous, that he now saw how necessary it was for the poor men to guard themselves against such perils."

Before leaving the Cathedral we held the "Sacre Catino" in our hands, and reverenced it for its great legendary history.

"What if it is not a real emerald," said Janet, "and suppose the Queen of Sheba never did present it to her beloved Solomon, human faith has rested on it; it is a relic of those blessed, childlike days, when belief was what doubt and unbelief are now, a credit and a virtue. Seven hundred and odd years, little vase, you have lived, to our knowledge; — Heaven only knows how much older you may be; — and so great was your success at one time, that you grew tyrannical, and punished with death any one who should doubt your regal and holy history. That was a mistake, — a mistake of pride, — a poison which lies at the root of all errors. 'A haughty spirit goeth before a fall,' dear emerald, and, as high as was your pride, so great has been your ruin; shattered and valueless you remain now, except to some dreamy believers, like Ottilie here, or, charitable, indulgent legend-loving heretics, such as I. You are very dear to me, little vase, and I shall kiss you to show my reverence."

We had to laugh at Janet's droll apostrophe to the "Sacre Catino"; and the Sacristan, who did not understand a word of her English, stared, as he well might;

but when he saw her lift the famous old crystal to her lips and kiss it reverentially, then hand it to us for a like show of respect, he nodded his head approvingly.

From San Lorenzo we drove up La Strada Nuovo, which is bordered on either side with fine palaces; while looking at and admiring this grand *réunion* of lordly buildings, we understood well why people called this city "La Superba." We went also through Stradas Balbi, Carlo Felice, Carlo Alberti, Giulia Carrettiera, and several other streets, enjoying the Italian appearance of the place.

It was high noon; the magnificent architecture of this gay, southern city, which lay inundated with golden sunlight, looking so regal and opulent, running over with exuberant life and action, the merry, mad Carnival mood of the population, their beautiful costumes, — all affected me deeply. It reminded me of the delicious dreams I used to have of a summer's day, when I was a girl, and would fall asleep in a hammock, under the shade of an old walnut-tree, after having read myself luxuriously full of fancies over Arabian Nights or Spenser's Faëry Queen. It being the hour of luncheon, we returned to our hotel; after that meal was over and we had rested a while, we started out

"To fresh woods and pastures new."

"Oh Jennie," said Venitia, after we were seated in the barouche, and the courier stood at the door to receive his orders, "let us go look at that brilliant Church of L'Annunziata. You cannot tell, Ottilie, how much I adored its gold and purple splendors when I was a child."

So to the Church of the Annunciation we went. It is one mass of gold-leaf and frescoes, brilliant-hued silk,

Genoese crimson velvet drapery, and cloth of silver and gold. The effect is not only dazzling but bewildering, every part glittering with costly adornments. It was built by Della Porta, and is a true church of the Renaissance style.

At the intersection of the cross — that is, where the transept and nave meet — there is a gilded cupola, supported by caryatides, also blazing with gold-leaf. This superb and costly church was built for the Lomellini, a great old Italian house, the heads of which counted themselves sovereigns, and reigned over a little island kingdom, about a mile and a quarter long and a few furlongs wide, with five hundred subjects, out in the lovely Mediterranean. Kings of Tabarca! Half Spanish, and half African; no wonder, when fashion required every noble family to own at least one church, as part of the appointments of their establishment, these island sovereigns displayed such barbaric splendor. As I was talking of this old custom of family church-building, Janet said: —

"Let us leave this place; I wish to show you a church which was really built to gratify family pride; and, not only that, to heal wounded vanity, a superb palace was demolished, in order to make room for a house of religious worship. It has a curious history, which I will tell you when we are in one of its chapels."

We left L'Annunziata, and, driving through the Carnival crowd to the other end of the city, came to a hill on the eastern side, which overlooks the gulf and a great part of the town. On this hill stands a fine church, Santa Marie de Carignan. We entered it, and finding seats near Luca Cambiaso's "Pietà," placed so that we could look at the picture leisurely, — the standing figure in which, to the right of the spectator, is supposed to be the portrait of the church founder, — I sat and listened to Janet's account of the cause of the building of the church.

"Near the middle of the sixteenth century the Marquis de Sauli was one of Genoa's richest and most esteemed noblemen. He owned, among other delightful things, a number of city palaces; and the one in which he loved best to live was a magnificent building standing high and lordly on the Hill de Carignan.

"Although the Marquis was so passing rich, strange to say, he had no chapel nor church of his own. He was in the habit of going to hear Mass in the church belonging to his old friend, Count Fieschi, — the Santa Marie in Vie Lata; and he continued doing this even when his old brother nobleman died and the haughty eighteen-year-old heir succeeded to the title and vast estates of the Fieschi family. It never entered into his head that he might not be as welcome to the young Count; for we middle-aged people are very apt to think lightly, and often not at all, of the likes and dislikes of young folk. It was only yesterday they were children, and had to obey; it is hard to step aside and give them our path, while we fall off into the shadowy one of the elders; and this stepping aside to make way for the young comes to almost every one of us unawares; we suddenly awaken and find not only the old gone, but ourselves lifted into their places.

"To return to the Marquis de Sauli.

"Every church-day the good nobleman went, as he had done all his life, taking his family with him, to the Fieschi church. Now 'family,' in those days, did not simply mean one's children and grandchildren, but also retainers, a household guard of soldiers it might be, or something of the kind, which made an addition to one's congregation not always agreeable to a nobleman, who wished to worship God as he lived with man, in solitary grandeur. The young Count Fieschi, I fancy, was one of these same social, pious aristocrats, for one day he advanced the hour of celebration, so that when the Marquis de Sauli and his suite arrived, Mass was over, the church empty. The first time the Marquis met his young friend, Count Fieschi, after this occurred, he complained good-naturedly about it.

"'My dear Marquis,' said Fieschi, in a stately way, 'if a gentleman wishes to hear Mass he should have a church of his own.'

"'So he should,' replied the Marquis curtly, and, turning on his ringing heel, he gave orders to have his superb palace on the Carignan Hill, the grandest he owned, razed to the ground; and after some years of patient and costly labor, the handsome Church of St. Marie de Carignan rose in its place. He wished to show the haughty, churlish young nobleman that a gentleman could indeed have a church of his own, and at the same time destroy a superb palace if he pleased."

This story being told, we looked up at the sorrowful "Pietà" of Luca di Cambiaso (Luchetto da Genova), that natural, unaffected artist of a period when nature had nearly died out in art, — the mannerist era of the sixteenth century. We thought of the poor, gifted painter's sorrowful life, and talked of him and his lovely sister-in-law, whom he has painted in this picture as the woman who weeps, and has wept silently there for near three hundred years! Luca is kneeling hopelessly beside his dead Lord; the two have brought their mortal love and anguish to that Sacred Presence of Immortal Life in

Death,— that passionate human love which man forbade, and which sent the great artist to his grave and the woman he adored to the cloister, when they found nor man nor God could help them.

I looked at the portrait of the stately founder of the church, and then upon the fine well-proportioned building, which had been raised to display wealth, to gratify family pride, and heal wounded vanity, — not for the love of God. O no! piety was as dead as that painted Christ of the heart-broken painter, for

"'T is the substance that wanes ever, 't is the symbol that exceeds."

This church is a specimen of fine architectural unity. It is built on a square of a hundred and fifty feet, without including the absis, and was erected on the original plan of Michael Angelo for St. Peter's at Rome. Three naves divide the interior, and a Greek cross is formed by the intersections. In the centre is a grand cupola, supported by four massive pillars; at the four angles of the cross are four smaller cupolas. We went up into the large central dome to see the magnificent view it commands of the gulf and part of the city.

On the left of us were the ramparts, with the whole length of the picturesque wharves bordered by the fishermens' huts, and the petty gulfs of the harbor making graceful indentations in the shore. The peaks of the Apennines rose behind the town, the west was gorgeous with light, the blue waters of the harbor tossed up the sun's rays playfully, then seemed to rush off with frolicsome glee out of the clasping arms of the Mole into the green sea beyond. Towards the west the beautiful shore stretched out, looking like strips of lapis lazuli, the headlands were so blue, resting on

"The waters crystalline ;
And before that chasm of light,
As within a furnace bright,
Column, tower, and dome, and spire
Shone like obelisks of fire."

We sat silent for sometime, feeling that it was quite impossible to point out to each other the quick succeeding beauties which were causing us such sweet, unutterable rapture. But gradually our eyes, as if satisfied with the first eager sweep over the distance, rested on the objects nearer at hand, and at last upon the church itself.

Then we felt that need of expression which comes to us when some strong emotion has been roused and gratified on the instant. We do not care to talk of the cause of our joy precisely, but talk we must, of something, or deep sadness will ensue.

The beautiful church made one common subject for us, and was a pleasant theme, as it satisfied our yearning for social communion. Venitia was the first to speak; for the young are always restless and impatient when fronting these silent, invisible barriers which stand between the world of emotion and this outside life.

"These great 'symphonies in stone,'" she repeated, "that expression is very beautiful."

"There is a fitness in comparisons made between architecture and music, Venitia," I said, "that is seldom thought of. Goëthe called architecture 'frozen music,' and remarked that the influence which flows upon us from it is as that from music. Lord Lindsay, too, from whom we have been quoting so much lately, says, *apropos* to this very subject, 'as symbolical and expressive of emotion, not of definite ideas, Music and Architecture are identical in principle, and distinct, the one from

Painting and Sculpture, the other from Poetry or verse,—and not only distinct, but independent of them to such a degree that, in proportion as they rise to absolute perfection, the addition of words to the one, or of subsidiary design to the other, becomes not only unnecessary, but obtrusive.'"*

I then gave her a short and rapid outline of the deep symbolic meaning contained in the construction of a church when architects were the great poets and wrote their epics in stone. The position of the church had to be first considered. It was placed towards the east in memory of the birth of our blessed Lord. It was built on a hill or elevated place if possible as an emblem of divine superiority, and also as an intermediate place between heaven and earth.

These two points obtained, then rose the church. Four parts were essential to it, the porch, the nave, the choir, and the sanctuary, as emblems of the life of the penitent, of the Christian, the saint, and the angel. Thus in the early ages of the Church, the penitents, called *audientes* and *prostrati*, prostrated themselves in the porch during the offering of the Sacrament, not being considered pure enough to be present during the holiest part of the celebration.

In the nave were the *consistentes* or members. In the *ambo*, or choir, which was always elevated a step or two above the nave, the clergy or *participantes* sat: while at the sanctuary stood the representative of our blessed Lord offering the Holy Sacrifice.

The church sometimes had four doors, two symbolical of earthly life, *speciorœ portœ;* two of celestial life, *portœ sanctœ.* The sanctuary, which could be entered only by

* Lord Lindsay's Christian Art, Vol. II. p. 13.

the clergy, was separated from the choir and nave by a chancel or balustrade, which prevented the laity from intruding, expressing in a mystical form the barrier which separates heaven from earth, and opens only to one who is dead to the world, such as the priest consecrated to the service of the altar.

In the representations which decorated the church those on the left side were subjects taken from this life, those on the right side from the future life. The form of the cross in the ground plan of the church was in memory of the crucifixion of our blessed Lord: the absis indicated the place where his head rested. The absis, or apsis, as it is sometimes spelled, is the termination of the choir; the altar was often placed there, although in many churches of Italy the altar will be found in front of the choir, especially in churches which have religious brotherhoods attached to them. The chapels, which were placed often around the absis, were symbols of the glory or *aureole*. The transepts were the arms of the cross.

In some churches there were three doors and three gable-ends; these signified the Trinity. The beautiful Catharine-wheel window meant also the Unity as consecrated in Christ, the Light of the Church, from whose Greek monogram its shape was probably taken, — the well-known monogram formed of the initial of the name of Christ in Greek.

The monsters that supported the pillars of the church, or placed on the roof as gargoyle heads, had various meanings; they were talismans to frighten off evil spirits, or indicated evil spirits driven out of the Church by the Sacred Presence within. The crypt which is to be found under some Basilicas, and which is often almost a subterranean church, signified the moral death of man. The cruciform shape of the church recalled also the Atonement; the cupola, heaven.*

"I love Gothic architecture best of all," Janet remarked; "and yet the Lombard style, so much of which we shall see in Italy, has its own peculiar beauty."

"Before I came to Europe," I answered, "I was sure I should never be content with anything but the pure Gothic; my opinion, however, has changed very much. I now find more repose and calm beauty in the circular arches, horizontal lines, and expanding cupola of the Lombard architecture. The Gothic, with its pointed arches, springing vaults, and elaborate tracery, fatigues me beyond expression. There is infinite rest and peacefulness in the beautiful Basilica. The Lombard church, with its octagonal baptistery and the graceful campanile or bell tower grouped around it, seems to me just the perfection of religious architecture. It is so complete and satisfying, while the Gothic is more like human life, yearning, aspiring, incomplete."

"The Gothic is an emblem of the unapproachable ideal," said Janet. "However, I will not argue with you, for, like all new converts, you are of course bigoted. Your excellent author, Lord Lindsay, says, you may possibly remember, that the mind capable of comprehending the Gothic would be likely to appreciate the Classic more justly than the devotee of the Classic would the Gothic."

The Sacristan, just at this moment, told us, with many civil excuses, that the hour for closing the church had arrived; so we left our fine cupola seat on the Santa

* *Essai Sur les Legendes Pienses du Moyen Age*, par M. Alfred Maury.

Marie de Carignan, though very loath to do so, and thus put an end to our pleasant talk on the calm Greek Basilica and the restless Teuton Church.

On returning to our carriage we found we had nearly an hour at our disposal, for we had given orders that dinner should not be served until after sunset, that we might have all the daylight for sight-seeing. We drove again through the Strada Carlo Alberti, which fronts the harbor.

When we reached the Douane we alighted and walked on the marble-floored promenade, which extends from the Douane, or Custom-House, to the Darsena, or Water Dock, and Marine Arsenal. This walk or terrace is supported on fine porticos, and is one of the beauties of the city; from it the whole port can be seen.

We looked up at the Douane very earnestly, when Janet told us that in it were the rooms which had been formerly used for the famous Bank of St. George, which had begun to receive deposits and make loans before Columbus crossed the Atlantic; it was the India House of the Middle Ages.

Our courier, a quiet, intelligent person, showed us a heavy iron chain, which hangs over the principal entrance door; it was formerly the chain with which the Pisans closed their gates, and which the Genoese, after the fatal battle of Meloria, in 1290, broke and carried off in triumph to Genoa, nearly six hundred years ago!

It was the hour of sunset, and, though a mid-winter month, the air was soft and balmy. We returned to the carriage, and drove slowly, enjoying the lovely sight of the sunrise and sunset shores of the Genoese Gulf, as they are called, — Riviera di Levante, where the coast stretches out towards Tuscany in the east; and Riviera di Ponente, where the shore leads off towards Nice in the west. We examined the distance with our glasses. The long western coast, with its Lantern, or Lighthouse, at Cape St. Benigne, was brilliantly illuminated with the twilight glories, for the sky was

"Robed in flames and amber light,
The clouds in thousand liveries dight."

Nearer to us, on a rocky terrace projecting out on the water, almost in front of the port, we observed a group of ilex-trees; and back of them, the palace of Genoa's great Admiral, Andrea Doria, who gave his state a Constitution which lasted near three hundred years.

As we talked of this Palazzo Doria, its famous master, and the regal banquet he had given to Charles V. on that ilex-shaded terrace, we were very naturally led to the memory of his unfortunate young rival, Count Fieschi.

"In these very waters of the Darsena," I remarked, "the unhappy young man perished. It was just touch and go with Admiral Doria's power then; but for that fatal midnight mistep of the young Count, history might have had a different tale to tell. At the moment Fieschi was treating the Marquis di Sauli so haughtily, he was probably planning his conspiracy; therefore, was it, that he did not like being approached as an equal when dreaming of sovereignty.

"'Madam,' he said to his startled wife, on that sorrowful night three hundred years ago, when he disclosed to her his intended revolt, 'you shall never see me again, or you shall see everything in Genoa under your feet.'

"She never did see him again! He left his palace; one short hour after, when he was stepping on board the captain galley, which lay here in this Darsena, to take command, and bring his masterly-planned conspiracy to a successful conclusion, the plank broke on which he strode.

Nothing could be seen, for it was dark midnight; but a plash of heavy armor falling on the sullen waters was heard, a plunge, a short gurgle, that was all! The Fieschi pride had met its fall; and the long line of popes, cardinals, and great generals ended in this young nobleman of twenty-two, while his ill-fated ambition became a mere fact for history to mention and people to forget, until, three centuries after, a bold young German poet made it into a famous play; for although Schiller's Conspiracy of Fieschi may not be equal in literary merit to his other historical dramas, it is more popular on the German stage than anything he wrote, except the Robbers."

"It was the old political quarrel between Guelph and Ghibelline," observed Janet, "that struggle which had then been raging five hundred years. Doria was a Guelph or Papal adherent; Fieschi, a Ghibelline or Imperialist. You should not be sympathizing with young Fieschi, Ottilie; he did not belong to your side of the question at all."

"No; that is very true," I replied; "but Fieschi was bold, young, aimed high, — and failed! Nine times out of ten that is the side on which women will be found, utterly regardless of all reason, principle, or opinion, simply from admiration for that which she does not possess, — high courageous daring; and tender, loving pity for that which is so often her own fate, — failure!"

The twilight deepened; the driver turned his horses' heads towards the hotel, and quickened their gait. In a short while after, we were enjoying a capital dinner, and a merry talk on the trifles of the present moment, quite forgetting for the while history's tales of mingled luck and wanluck.

PLANTING ROOTS.

NAPLES, — Strada Mergellina.

HAVE no visit to Pisa or Civita Vecchia to tell of, — no sweet raptures over the voyage from Genoa to this place, on the beautiful Mediterranean, with historical memories aroused at every turn. During the whole period I was ill, — ill in body and mind, heart and soul.

Apprehension stalked beside me like an evil genius, stretching out its long, spectral finger to deaden every pleasure. A crowd of forms surrounded me, all the shadowy beings that people the lands of presentiment and memory; and there arose before me "those towering gates of the Past which seem to stand forever open." Once in a while the eager, hot breath of love and longing sweeps aside the sombre curtain, and discloses for one brief instant joys, hopes, and aspirations forever gone; then the black folds fall with dumb, appalling weight, and we move onward oppressed with the dreary thought, that forever in this life our hands are unclasped from the loved one's neck, our lips forever parted, our confidences forever stilled, for the ear of the fond, indulgent friend is filled with the dust and ashes of death!

But these sorrowful thoughts are quite out of place here; they sound like harsh dissonances in a beautiful melody. It seems impossible to be sad under such a sky and breathing such an atmosphere. The simple play of light and shade over the heavens, and on the beautiful land and sea, produces on me the effect of sweet succeeding harmonies in some musical creations, — Mozartian, for it is joyful and fresh.

We are enchanted with this city; with its picturesque streets paved with lava; its beautiful surroundings; its buildings, telling so many legends of olden times; and its lovely bay, whose shores, from one arm to the other, are crowded with memories of poetic myths and historic facts.

I never shall forget the effect produced by the first sight of Vesuvius, — "that stall of the incessant stamping thunder-steeds." In front of us lies Capri, where Tiberius sinned, — and suffered. Farther off to the right, a little hidden by those beautiful elm-crowned heights of Posilippo, lie "the heavenly hills," true mountains of azure, Ischia and Procida, each bearing a chaplet of memories; and Nisida too, where Brutus and Portia parted to meet no more.

Then follows Baiæ, with its ruins, telling of those old voluptuous days when Romans came to its baths in the gay season, "to enact the Greek," as they said. They had in their language one short word, *Græcari*, *græcatus*, *græcanicus*, which meant something pleasant but wrong, and this word they applied to the lives they led at Baiæ. They put aside with business all the stern personal habits of Rome, they loosened their robes, took off their sandals, and indulged in recreations which Roman eyes could hardly distinguish from vices.*

But Baiæ has another memory, a buried tomb, the earthly trace of which is lost; but not the tradition, for a

* Merivale's Rome.

poet has made it immortal. Petrarch visited the grave of the great Scipio Africanus at Baiæ, and leaning over read, "*Ingrate patrie*," chiselled on the stone which has now crumbled to dust.

Between us and Baiæ, however, at Posilippo, stands a poet's grave, which is not yet levelled and lost in the bosom of mother earth. Though some antiquarians may call it a mere *columbarium*, Petrarch believed it to be Virgil's tomb, and planted a laurel on its green summit.

Naples, beautiful Naples, beneath whose burning breast sleeps the siren Parthenope! Here Virgil lived, drank deep of poesy, and gave "imp feathers to the wings of his fancy from harsher, stronger studies." Here Tasso was born, and held consoling converse with his demon. Here Petrarch feasted, and Boccaccio loved. Naples, the golden, the glorious, whose chalice of beauty is filled to overflowing!

"No more, no more
The worldly shore
Upbraids me with its loud uproar;
With dreamful eyes
My spirit lies
Under the walls of Paradise!" *

Our lodgings are pleasantly situated on the Mergellina, which is the western branch of the Riviera di Chiaja extension, — that part which fronts this beautiful Vesuvian Bay, — just on the hem of the great city. We are in an old palazzo, a square solid mass of white stone several stories in height; its different floors run off irregularly, so as to form terraces for the various suites of apartments contained in it.

This palazzo, like all other buildings of the kind, has

* Read's Drifting.

in its centre an open square, called a court-yard, opening on the street with a huge gateway. This gateway is flanked on either side by the porteress's lodge and her dwelling rooms. At the window of the lodge is hung a large frame containing the cards of the different occupants of the palazzo. We amused ourselves looking over it this morning, when the porteress, a pretty, civil-spoken woman, put into it our cards. We found there a principezza and an excellenza, among other notorieties.

When we enter the court-yard we find a motley group and strange occupants, according to American ideas of the entrance to a palace containing an ambassador and a princess. The place is as crowded and probably more noisy than it was in those "grand old times," when the count or baron to whom the palace belonged assembled in it his retainers. There are poultry, yelping curs, and dirty children rolling in the mud-puddles, — for our court-yard is an untidy place, as are most of them, — and noisy men and women screaming out this shrill Neapolitan dialect.

The place is so novel to us that we often stop a few moments in the morning, as we are stepping into our carriage from the broad white marble slab at the foot of the handsome stone stairway leading to our suite of apartments. There are the men hard at work, and the women busy gossiping. These Neapolitan women of the lower class are a lazy, listless set, and remind us of what Thackeray said of "every Irish gentleman needing another Irish gentleman to wait on him," for every Neapolitan woman seems to have at least one man, if not more, to wait on her; and they are not a pretty race either, but show their mixed blood of Moor and Spaniard, making an ugly, mongrel Italian.

The first floor of all these palazzos has, beside the porter's home, the stables and coach-houses. Carriages and horses consequently take up a good part of the place. In one corner a coach will be receiving its daily cleaning and the horses their rubbing down; in another part of the yard a fine establishment will be waiting on its owner, who is paying a visit to some friend in one of the numberless apartments of the palazzo, while the tired coachman sleeps on the box.

In the early morning, and at sunset, our court-yard is a much more curious place: it becomes a sort of farm-yard, and is filled with cows and goats, which are brought in to supply the different occupants of the palazzo with milk; once in a while a goat clatters its little pan-like heels, up the stone steps of one of the various passage-ways, to the apartment of some invalid, who must drink goat's milk fresh and warm.

This lowing of cattle and tinkle of cow-bells has a sweet pastoral sound, and pleasing too, making us think of green meadows and rich pastures while living in a large, crowded city. At sunset, when the Riviera di Chiaja is crowded with brilliant equipages dashing along, filled with the rank and fashion of this Paris of Italy, the eye is struck with the curious appearance these flocks of goats and herds of cattle present, pouring down from the hills of Posilippo into the broad, gay thoroughfare, to spread themselves throughout the various streets, as if going into farms and dairies.

Virgil's Bucolics and Georgics rise to Janet's lips from her well-stored memory; and this evening, as I sat on the terrace listening to these rural sounds and gazing dreamily over the Posilippean hills, bathed in the gold and purple of the sunset, their beautiful bases washed by the glittering waters of this Vesuvian Bay, placing her hand on my shoulder, she repeated, with her pretty, earnest enjoyment of the memory, which took all air of pedantry from it, even supposing any one could have been so ungenerous as to imply its presence, —

"Thus of the culture of fields and flocks and of trees I sung, whilst great Cæsar at the deep Euphrates was thundering in war, was victoriously dispensing laws among the willing nations, and pursuing the path to Olympus. At that time me, Virgil, sweet Parthenope nourished, flourishing in the studies of inglorious ease; who warbled pastoral songs, and, adventurous through youth, sung thee, O Tityrus, under the covert of a spreading beech."

The third floor of this palazzo, according to our counting, is, nevertheless, the *premier piano* with Italians, — that is, the first lodging-floor for gentlefolk. On this floor are our rooms, — a charming suite, consisting of parlor, dining-rooms, and bedrooms; part of them opening on a terrace; the parlor and dining-room are on the west side; from them we can look over to the glorious hills of Posilippo, while from my bedroom window

"Ischia smiles
O'er liquid miles;
And yonder bluest of the isles,
Calm Capri waits,
Her sapphire gates
Beguiling to her bright estates." *

The view from the terrace is ravishing. In front is the beautiful bay; to the right are the heights of Posilippo; and on the left the town seems to draw back, to give us a full view of the Sorrentine promontory and

* Read's Drifting.

that great altar Mount Vesuvius, which is forever sending up its incense into the high heavens.

Behind our palazzo rise graceful hills, crowned with fair villas and "clad with greenery." Beside it is a tufa-hill, in which are hollowed out huge picturesque arches, half in ruins, with vines and the tender-hued, feathery-leafed, maiden-hair fern clambering up around the stones. Above this tufa-hill, houses seemed piled on houses; and, if I lean over the terrace side and stretch my neck a little, I can see on another hill far above us a carouba-tree, whose round, cauliflower-shaped top brings back to me my earliest ideas of Italy; for, ever since I can remember, one of these trees was as necessary in my mind to the making up of an Italian as poplars and willows for a French landscape.

We were very lucky in obtaining these apartments; and this pleasant good fortune came to us through a social connection which Janet and I have, with one of the foreign ministers and his wife, both charming accomplished persons.

All the morning we have been out "planting our roots," as Janet says. We have called on our minister and his wife, Mr. and Mrs. Rochester; opened our accounts with the pleasant English banker, Mr. Iggulden; and established ourselves as subscribers and good customers at "Detken's," the "Foreign Book Store and Circulating Library," where they speak all manner of known and unknown tongues, and keep a most attractive collection of new books, photographs, and journals.

Venitia's piano is under the tuner's hands, and she is busy sorting her music. Janet is making our apartments look habitable. The only coquetry Janet shows is in the arranging of furniture and the effective display of attractive room-ornaments.

She is placing piles of pleasant books about; stereoscopic stands, with fine views just at hand's grasp; neat *portefeuilles* of engravings and fine photographs; and diminutive easels, with beautiful little pictures on them, standing on the tables and *consoles.* A few costly ornaments are here and there, not many; a small Sevres vase or two, and tapering amber, and ruby-hued Bohemian, and old Venetian glasses; some rare bronzes, — just enough to touch the rich, high tone of luxury, without having the artistic freshness overpowered. Then, as if scattered by a Flora's hand, there are delicious bouquets; clusters of rich purple violets; anemones, whose deep scarlet is softened by the cool neutral tint of heliotrope sprays; and delicate mignonette.

And I? What am I doing? Filling up my journal; trying to remember some of the clever information which the intelligent minister gave us this morning. He has certainly one of the freshest, most attractive minds I have ever met with. His description of the topography of this place was not only graphic and clear, but also very interesting.

The town is divided by a ridge of hills into two parts, the old and the new town. The different elevations of this ridge take the names of Capo di Monte, St. Elmo, and Pizzofalcone; the termination of it is the promontory on which stands that Castel del' Ovo, considered by Froissart one of the strongest forts in the world, "which only could be taken by necromancy or the help of the Devil," but which has a sweeter memory to us than all Froissart's mystical accounts. In this Castel del' Ovo, Robert the Wise, and the happy, light-hearted artist Giotto, had many a merry hour together, when the father of modern painting was decorating its walls with those wonderful frescoes which have unfortunately disappeared, — gone, doubtless, as Mr. Rochester, our minister, observed, to that land of fantasy Gautier whimsically imagined, which contains all the divine lost landscapes ever painted, and whose inhabitants are the lovely figures created by art, "in granite, marble, or wood, on walls, canvas, or crystal," which have perished.

But, to return to our real living land. The ridge of hills of which I speak, united to the graceful indentations of the bay, forms two crescents in the outline of the town. The beautiful bosom of hills on which the town is built slopes down gracefully, stretching out into the superb, arm-like promontories of Misenum and Sorrento, which seem to embrace tenderly the Mediterranean.

On this central ridge stands St. Elmo's Castle, the next great feature, after Vesuvius, in all pictures of Naples, — another of those fortified palaces of Robert the Wise. This St. Elmo height explained to me the reason of the beautiful bridge which spans one of the most thronged streets of the old town, Strada Chiaja, and which arrested my attention yesterday when we were walking. It is called the Ponte di Chiaja, and is a viaduct, connecting St. Elmo with Pizzofalcone, the hill which terminates in the promontory of Castel del' Ovo.

To the east of this ridge lies the old town. In it are the Royal Palace, and a superb city artery, called Strada di Toledo, which sweeps from the bay at the Santa Lucia coast, or wharf, clear through the great throbbing heart of this tumultuous city, for the distance of a mile and a half. In the Middle Ages this street, which is now the centre of modern Naples, was out on the very edge of the suburbs, having been built on the fosses of the old city (1540), by Don Pedro di Toledo, that wise Viceroy of a wise Emperor, whose government is remembered as a precious legend to this day, both by the presence of good works and the memory of good acts.

This morning we stood at the foot of this grand street, on the fine, spacious square called Largo del Palazzo, Reale, with the Royal Palace on one side of us, and a modern Pantheon, San Francesca di Paolo, on the other. In front of us was Canova's equestrian statue, which has contrived, like Goldsmith's chest of drawers, not only a double, but a treble debt to pay; — first it was Napoleon, then Murat, now Charles III.! What shall it be next? Louis Napoleon, Victor Emmanuel, or —— Garibaldi? Poor statue and poor Italy!

We laughed over this history of changes, and made many speculations on its future; then grew silent, as we gazed up into this noisiest street of Europe, with its sea of human beings surging to and fro, and its wave-crests of carriages. The noise that arose from it, like the alternate come and go of an ocean's grand pulse, made us feel a little bewildered, and very still.

To the west of this central ridge lies the second crescent, or new city, called Chiaja, on the outskirts of which we live.

After the Toledo, which it surpasses in beauty, the next great street of Naples is the one running around the bay, skirting gracefully the little indentations of the coast from one end of the city to the other, and bearing as many names as any Spanish viceroy might.

This street starts from the Sebeto, on the very outer edge of the old city, at the Ponte della Maddelena, where the road to Portici leads off. First it is called La Marinella, which used to be the old head-quarters of the Lazzaroni; but the Cantastorie have now taken possession of it, those marvellous public street-singers of Naples, who, as Mr. Rochester told us, sing at this day the old mediæval poem of Rinaldo and his Paladins.

Passing by the Castel del Carmine, Masaniello's stronghold, it becomes Stradas Nuova and Carlito; then it reaches Porto Piccolo, the port of old Palæpolis, the conquering of which Greek town (323 B. C.) gave a Roman prætor a triumph. The Molo follows, which is now the rendezvous of the dying-out race of the Lazzaroni.

This brings us to the Castel Nuovo, built in that Italian morn of Dante and Giotto (1283), by the brother of St. Louis, Charles of Anjou. A little farther on is the Royal Palace, from whose Largo, or Square, springs the Toledo, at which place this coast-street comes out to the famous wharf of Santa Lucia, the great fish market of Naples, where "fruits of the sea," — "*frutto di mare*," — as they call them, are sold in great abundance.

Now we have arrived at the little promontory which lies at the base of the Pizzofalcone Hill, on which stands the Castel del' Ovo; and the road, as it sweeps around this place between the foot of the hills and the little jutting-out bit of land, is called Chiatamone.

After this central point is passed, there comes another pretty sweep around an indentation of the shore, which is named Vittoria; then the street opens fairly into the new town quarter, called Chiaja, at which place this graceful coast-road, or street, bears the name of Riviera di Chiaja, Chiaja Shore; this part of it is the celebrated promenade of Naples, and has on it the narrow strip of a park, called Villa Reale.

Mr. Rochester traced out the whole route of this street for us on a map this morning; then, when he reached this point, he rolled the map-table to the balcony of his library window, and pointed across the broad Riviera di Chiaja, on which his palazzo fronts, to a villa, or park, filled with a variety of shade-trees.

"There," said he, "is the Villa Reale. It is about five thousand feet long by two hundred in width, and on the sea side it has a fine wall and parapet. You see sentinels standing at the gates of the iron railing which separates it from the Riviera di Chiaja. Only the gentry and nobility are allowed to use it. It is the only spot in Naples into which the lower classes are not permitted to enter. They may invade your court-yard, and even the steps of your palazzo; keep house literally out on the sidewalks of the finest streets; cook, eat, wash, live, and sleep in front of the noblest palace; but into the Villa Reale they cannot enter, except one day in the year, the eighth of September, at the great festival of Santa Maria di Piedigrotta. It is an agreeable lounging-place, with pleasant winding paths and fine broad walks, a terrace running out into the sea, some grottos with statuary, two small handsome temples to Virgil and Tasso, and pleasant fountains. The trees are mostly acacias and oaks, with some few Oriental shrubs.

"Now we will come back to the Riviera di Chiaja. After you pass the Villa Reale, you will observe that it divides into two branches; the left, or lower one, running by the sea-shore, is called Strada Mergellina, — that is where your palazzo stands. The right, or upper branch, is the Strada di Piedigrotta; follow it some distance, and you will arrive at Virgil's tomb, which stands at the entrance of the celebrated Grotto of Posilippo, the one Petrarch and Corinne made famous, — called also Grotto di Pozzuoli. This is a tunnel, over two thousand feet long, and twenty-one feet wide. In the after part of the day this Grotto is lighted by the western sun, but during the morning and midday, you will find it pretty much as Seneca describes it, 'Darkness made visible'; and to foot-passengers it seems a terrifying place, for it is nearly always crowded with two streams of people going and coming, screaming donkey-drivers, carriages, and peasants. But once through the Grotto, the road leads off to Pozzuoli, where it finds the little bit of Mergellina that has been straying gracefully around by the sea. At Pozzuoli the two join, and then, as the old song sings, it goes,

'Over the hills and far away';

out, if you please to follow it, Mrs. Dale, to that Eubœan coast of Cumæ, where 'the anchor with tenacious fluke moored the ships of Æneas, and the bending sterns fringed the margin of the shore.'"

When we returned to the carriage, on leaving the palazzo of the embassy, Venitia, with a playful, knowing air, directed the driver to take us to "Detkens," as if quite at home in this new city.

"The truth is," she said, "that although I cannot help feeling as Goethe did in Sicily, when you and Ottilie will persist, like the Sicilian guide, in 'marring, by your ill-timed erudition, my refreshing feelings of peace, calling up departed spectres, and reviving tumults and horrors,' I must, in self-defence, do as the contradictory German poet did at Palermo, rush off to purchase a Homer and Virgil; for I find I am to be persecuted with learned allusions on all sides, in these eternally classic heights of the ancient world. So, while you and Mr. Rochester were dancing stately tongue *minuets à la cour*, I learned from his agreeable wife that this place,—'Detkens,'—

to which we are now driving, is where bookish strangers most do congregate, finding there all manner of nice things."

To "Detkens" accordingly we drove, and Venitia — who has not Janet's cleverness in old tongues, never having been willing to study any but modern languages and music, which have needed but little application on her part — supplied herself with translations of all the old poets and historians she could find.

ELECTRA.

ENITIA is playing fugues. How positive the dear girl is, but very clever and original. She has just finished a fugue of Bach, with a throbbing beat in it like a full heart. It is the one in the Chromatic Fantasia, — that Fantasia so soft and tender and flowing in its modulations, that one would scarcely imagine a single deviation had been made from its fundamental harmony. He was, indeed, a great master, this same John Sebastian Bach. While listening to his fugues I forget that they are exercises of deep thought, great intellectual power, and profound knowledge, — mental musical feats, — for he throws into them a rhythmical life that is full of freedom; they are not mere themes transposed into different keys, one hand following the other slavishly, but independent, reasoning poems.

Of a totally different nature are Handel's fugues, and yet, to my ears and taste, not less masterly. They are not so self-contained or persistent, but quite as free and strong. Some few of them give me more pleasure than Bach's even, especially the one Venitia has just commenced, the superb fugue in E minor (mi); it sounds like the concentrated roll of mid-ocean.

But I do not like her execution of fugues. She thinks

they must be rigid, because they are exact. While she executes other compositions freely, stamping them with the sharp impress of her unmistakable genius, she shows the student in these; you can hear the beat of the metronome through every measure. She needs emancipating, as it were, in almost everything. Not that she is bound by Janet, or me, or any one; on the contrary, her opinions are independent enough. She is a little dogmatical and obstinate once in a while; at such times we combat her, but are very careful not to repress her in any way. But she is angular, and hard, and too devoted to technical minutiæ. I feel discouraged sometimes, and fancy that this enchantment results from the fairy-like spell which extreme culture and exquisite surroundings of social refinement exercise over some natures. There have never been any rough points in her life since her recollection; no heavy shadows to bring out rich, strong lights; it is this smoothness of existence which deprives her of comprehending some things in Art as well as in Life, seeing only the cold, bald, matter-of-fact side of the crystal, entirely losing sight of the beautiful prismatic play of Fancy and Poesy. She would fain touch, hold, weigh, and measure all things, never dreaming that the sweetest, dearest, loveliest emotions in this existence are but the shadows of a dream,—intangible, inexpressible, like the faint odor of a rare fruit or flower, the delicate droplet of a luscious grape, the perishable down on Psyche's wing.

But to return to Handel's fugue.

There are some creations of Art which can never be comprehended until one has been anchored as far out in the deep waters of sorrow as the master who created them; therefore I will not complain that Venitia is not capable of seizing the meaning of this great E minor fugue. God forbid that she should ever have her ears, eyes, and taste sharpened into consciousness on such a brackish wave of grief as is contained in it! As I read over the notes of the music lying near me on my writing-table, I think of the composer, and of his life, which was so void of love and tenderness. The solitary suffering of Handel is betrayed in such passages as "He was despised and rejected of men," in the Messiah, — which he is said to have written with hot tears raining down on his manuscript, mingling with the ink, — and this fugue, which makes every fibre in one's being vibrate with emotion.

Poor, passionate Handel! A haughty pride, almost Satanic, made his life what it was. In his youth he loved a beautiful young girl, and she adored him. Her parents looking upon him as an inferior, insulted him. He never forgave them. So keen was the wound that even when at last they consented to the marriage to save her life, he refused; and the poor girl died of a broken heart, — of the harshness of her lover, not of her family.

Now go play that fugue in E minor, and think of this opening theme in his life-fugue, — of his haughty reiterated anger, which, like that thrice-repeated B in the music, led through all the stormy modulations of his fierce, contentious existence. In every measure of it you will hear the passionate love and passionate anger which combated together, resulting in a life of sullen loneliness for him, and death for the woman he loved.

We were talking of *Vêpres Siciliennes*, after sunset, "over our Hyson," as Lamb says, "which we are old-fashioned enough to drink unmixed still of an evening." For we all love our tea; and Janet quotes with great satisfaction DeQuincey's approving declaration, that "Tea will always be the favorite beverage of the intellectual." I had been singing the *Bolero* of Helène, in the fifth act of the *Vêpres*. After I had finished it, I came out on the terrace, humming the sparkling *motivo* of this enchanting passage, while I took my cup from Janet's hand, she of course being tea-maker.

We drink our tea on the terrace, where we can look over on Vesuvius, down on the gay-thronged Mergellina, out on the sparkling bay, and up on the beautiful hills and soft heavens. This glorious view, the delicious atmosphere, and this bewitching bit of melody combined, touched Venitia unconsciously; for a few moments her little silvery thread of a voice united gayly with mine, in the passionate bursts of the short-lived joy which this Bolero expresses.

"Bigoted as you think I am," she said, "I like the *Vêpres;* it has the French *élan* in it. It might have been an early effort of Meyerbeer, when he was under the influence of the golden Capri wine of *Tancrede*, in those gay *Romildo e Costanza* and *Crocciato* days; and I am giving it great praise when I say this. I know we do not agree about Meyerbeer, but I think one cause of your opinion is, that you have never heard his music as I have."

"You may be right, Venitia, for I have never heard a Meyerbeer opera to advantage."

"And I," she exclaimed, with enthusiasm,—"I have heard the finest of them in Paris, where they were brought out superbly. Think of seeing and hearing that grand creature, Viardot-Garcia, in 'The Huguenots'!"

"She whose ugliness," interrupted Janet, with a laugh, "is, according to Heine, noble; and 'when she opened her great mouth, with its white, sparkling teeth, and smiled with a horrible sweetness and gracious *grincement*,' made the poor nervous poet think of leopards, giraffes, and young elephants."

"Yes, that same Pauline Garcia, whose ugliness is beauty to my eyes," answered Venitia, seriously. "But we were talking of Meyerbeer," she continued. "You say he sounds labored, Ottilie; now, I enjoy his *effets d'industrie*, because they result in such a marvellous control and power of harmony. And yet the labor is not without inspiration, for a divine unity of thought exists throughout his compositions. His orchestra is one grand whole; it is like a huge heart, palpitating and bounding with every varying emotion, from the '*Piff-paff del fuoco*,' in the first act of 'The Huguenots,' to that solemn and grand fourth act of the same opera; or that heart-rending Andante of Fidés, in the famous fifth act of *Le Prophète*. Wait until you hear this great master's gorgeous instrumentation, before you call him labored, and wanting in clearness of thought. His music is not sensational, like that of Verdi; it thrills me, not to the heart, that would be momentary, but to the very centre of my brain. It is impossible to talk while hearing one of his operas. You may take Verdi for *flânering*, but never Meyerbeer."

She was in one of her most dogmatical moods, so she continued extolling Meyerbeer, his rich and powerful sonorousness, his melodies so full of dignity. She expressed herself so prettily, too, that I liked to listen to her, while my silence seemed to pique her on to a further assertion of opinion.

"The melodic tissue of Meyerbeer's music," she said, "is sown with seed-pearls; and rubies, diamonds, and emeralds are strung and hung in glittering chaplets all over it, flashing out their various brilliant rays, each one struggling with playful splendor for superiority. Then his *nuances* are not shades; they are tints, for light mixes with the normal color, as painters say, not black. His broad German manner, too, is softened by the modern poetical fire which he possesses, and which gives lyric effect to his superb instrumentation, thus satisfying both mind and heart."

I could have overthrown her enthusiastic praise in two or three weak parts; and Janet and I had exchanged glances upon noticing the slips made by her youthful earnestness. But it would have done no good; on the contrary, chilled and mortified her. So I contented myself with stating a few instrumental facts by way of answer, first saying, as introduction, —

"My dear, the very sonorousness which you admire is as painful to my ears as too high and brilliant coloring in a painting is to my eyes. His power does not lie, to my seeming, where we are told it should, in the idea, but in rich instrumentation —"

I was about continuing, when she interrupted me hastily.

"The coloring of modern instrumentation is not a defect, Ottilie. A composer like Meyerbeer knows how to use with masterly power the fine full palette of sounds gained from modern orchestral improvements; his imagination finds new resources in them; and as to the idea, how can you say that is feeble because it is decorated with greater beauties? He has a right to use these fine extensive powers of musical coloring; they are the natural elements of art."

"But the greatest masters, my dear, produced greater effects without all this instrumentation. Let us run over some of the masterpieces of Beethoven, Mozart, and Haydn, for example. There is the grand Symphony in A (La) of Beethoven; it has nothing but two horns and two trumpets. The famous Symphony in C (Do) of Mozart has no more, and yet on account of its power and splendor it is called the Jupiter Symphony. Then I have read somewhere — I cannot give you my authorities now, but I can hunt them up for you — that only fifteen of Haydn's one hundred and seventeen Symphonies have two trumpets; the remaining one hundred and twelve have only two horns. Venitia, if those old masters produced so fine an effect with such simple coloring, how far superior must they have been to our Meyerbeers and Verdis."

Janet here interposed, —

"'When we drive out, from the cloud of steam, majestical white horses,
Are we greater than the first men, who led black ones by the mane?'

"O ye fanatics in music! Why cannot you both be more truly catholic? These different masters are like the various colors of the rainbow; some delicate, some gorgeous, some delicious; celestial blue, golden, and purple, with soft violet and the green of nature's garb, each lovely in itself."

"You are right, dear Janet; your comparison is just. The rainbow is a perfect type of Art, — manifold gifts working resolutely and harmoniously for a great unity, an everlasting and beautiful truth. Whenever I look at a rainbow, I shall hereafter remember your art-type. To me, as to all expectant souls, it should also prefigure the mystery of the true life, and the longings of the many-colored instincts of our varying hearts, which shall arrive in the end — but not in this world — at that Unity, that great Light, which is divine."

"But the music-rainbow," said Venitia, "let me divide it. Mozart shall be the celestial blue of promise; Verdi the soft, rich purple, appealing to our senses; Bellini and Donizetti many-tinted, with the tender violet hanging like a sweet atmospheric haze over them, as Capri looked an hour ago; but to Meyerbeer shall be given the glory that hung around the hills of Posilippo, gorgeous crimson and gold. And now, Ottilie, I shall gratify you by my last comparison: to Beethoven belongs the whole rainbow of beauty."

She turned to leave the terrace, intending to go into the salon, to the piano; suddenly she came back to the window, and said, —

"O Ottilie, Mrs. Rochester told me to-day she has heard Schroeder-Devrient in 'Fidelio.' Just fancy what a treat it must have been, listening to 'Fidelio'—this Comus of epic music, as 'Adelaïde' is the sorrowful Lycidas Idyl — from the lips of such an actress and singer. Remembering this has put me in the humor of playing it."

She then went to the piano, and commenced at the Introduction, or opening of the third act of "Fidelio." She rendered it finely. It is a touching scene, that *mélodrame*, where Rocco and Leonore are digging in the subterranean prison of Florestan. I leaned on the iron balustrade of the terrace while I listened, and looked up at the slender line of smoke ascending from Vesuvius, observing the faint, sudden fire-glow which pulsated from time to time at the base of this waving column of vapor. I drew a fanciful comparison between this vapor and fire-glow and the effect produced by the violoncello and double bass in this passage of "Fidelio."

The double bass has an isolated part, broken by rests, which throws the harmony, as it were, on the violoncello; but the real bass remains, notwithstanding these interruptions, with the double bass. Thus this vapor, rising from "Vesuvius's misty brim," continues forever streaming and floating off into the heavens, as if it was the real flame; but ever and anon, broken by rests, as it were, comes in the gloomy, deep throb of true fire, — short, dull even, but unmistakable, like the reiterated recurrence of this passage, —

in all its various pathetic forms, broken and detached though it may be, but showing that the true throb of the volcanic heart of the music is there.

Venitia then modulated into some improvised studies of curious bass passages, undoubtedly suggested to her by this remarkable one; and Janet and I had a little talk, which sent me to my room somewhat sad and dispirited, although it was far from her intention to produce any such effect on what she calls my "too easily impressed nature." The talk was something after this fashion. I have been trying to forget it, by recalling the Meyerbeer argument, but in vain, and perhaps if I write it down I may "lay the torturing demon." I have often found my journal good for such purposes. Many a morbid evil spirit lies safe locked up in its various volumes.

As Venitia concluded the "Fidelio" passage of the *mélodrame*, Janet turned to me, and, resting her beautiful little hand half playfully, half caressingly, on my cheek, quoted, —

> "I loved Ophelia. Forty thousand brothers
> Could not, with all their quantity of love,
> Make up my sum."

"I was thinking of the burial of poor Ophelia, Ottilie, during all that passage, and yet cheerful Shakespeare's 'jocund wood-note wild' should not be recalled by Beethoven's music. It is another Hamlet, — a religious one. Pascal I think of most often when listening to Beethoven. Who was it, my friend, by the way, that called Pascal a religious Hamlet?"

"Indeed, I do not remember; but Pascal was what Goethe called Hamlet, — 'a being possessed with a great action, and incapable of accomplishing it.'"

"Both had such delicate organizations," continued Janet, "as to be almost feminine, and both were called upon to perform duties too strong even for the ruggedest masculine natures."

"Hamlet's nature is indeed like that of some women," I said, half to myself, as if thinking aloud. "So many women seem to be introverted as he was, and also, like him, possess too great a sense of their own individuality, which, if unaccompanied by great energy, is apt to create morbidity, if not something worse."

Then, rousing myself, for I felt to what a painful end the conversation was tending, I tried to divert it a little.

"I have been thinking lately, Janet, of Shakespeare's skilful use of the supernatural in expressing to the reader or the audience the secret workings of the mind. By means of the Ghost in Hamlet, we are shown the struggle which takes place in a young heart filled with a craving for enjoyment of life, — a life of love and courtly pleasure, — and the stern duty of avenging the death of a father. The supernatural part gives us the key to the sorrowful and strange transformation of a dreamy, pleasure-loving youth, tortured, like Orestes, by the furies of his own imagination into a fitful, capricious monomaniac. Hamlet, by the way, is a sort of Shakespearian Orestes."

"Yes, in some points; but there is this distinction to be made between Greek tragedy and the romantic tragedy of Shakespeare, — one is the classic Ideal, the other is pure Nature. Greek tragedy is like sculpture, — one idea, and that carried straight without deviation to the end; no vagueness, no doubt. The sin may have arisen from Destiny; still it is sin, and must be punished by Death. You hear the tramp of the guards from the opening scene; you see the instrument of Fate ready to make the blow; its shadow falls sharp and dark on the victim from the first moment. But in Shakespeare how different! How like nature, — like that mysterious web which we see woven in real life! With picturesque and sometimes sorrowful fidelity, he throws in the mingled weft of joy and grief; we have the same strange triumph of the guilty, the incomprehensible suffering of the innocent, the tangled braid of light and shadow, the whole weary, complicated life-knot, — all is shown in its utter hopelessness, until we feel at last, as we often do in life, that Death is indeed gracious in unknotting the tangle, and that the peace and rest of the tomb is very sweet."

"Shakespeare was so great, Janet, that I am not surprised posterity has doubted his individual existence. His plays display gifts and wisdom never before or since combined in one human being."

"That is true; but you must remember his advantages were greater than any other writer who ever existed. United to his own superiority, the period in which he lived was singularly adapted to a Prophet of the New

Word. It was an age advanced in science and arts, and still retaining all the picturesque character of the Middle Ages; the very soil and atmosphere were ready for the planting and growth of the romantic drama."

"The modern school of music, Janet, is like the romantic drama," I added, with a forced attempt at continuing the conversation, for I felt my sadness increasing beyond my control. "I mean the music commencing with Beethoven; not the gay, joy-loving, Athenian Mozart, but from Beethoven, the sad old giant, up to poor Schubert and Schumann and Chopin. There is a whole lifetime of woe, sometimes, in one of their shortest creations. I wonder, Janet, if the Greeks ever suffered and sorrowed as we moderns do? They seem to have been exempt from our curse; they worshipped the beautiful, and raised it to their altars, — made of it God."

"Their drama, my friend, was the voice of their ideal, not of their real life. The moderns have indeed bowed down before sorrow and pain, lifted them up to their most holy of holies, and there they will remain so long as the quick pulse of anguish throbs in man's and woman's heart. But why are you going? It is not late. Are you not well, dear?"

"Quite well, thank you; only I wish to have a little chat with myself in my journal, while I can have the benefit of Venitia's music as an inspiring accompaniment. Good night."

So here I came, and have been all this while striving to write myself quiet, but in vain. The inward unrest still remains. Venitia has stopped the fugue, and is now playing a passage which sounds at times like poor Florestan's delirium, that grand air in "Fidelio" which is "filled with such immeasurable grief." No, it sounds like the short Adagio in the Beethoven Sonate, which is twin sister to the "Lauben Sonate" of the Countess Juliette (Opus 2, No. 1, E flat). De Lenz says, "It is a distant echo of this great air of 'Fidelio'; it is not the rhythm or the tonality which establishes the analogy, it is the soul of this Adagio which is identical with Florestan's aria."

Yes, it is that Sonate she is playing; and, as I listen to her, my conversation with Janet comes up in my memory, like that mounting, syncopated passage of octaves which Venitia has just grasped so finely; and I think of Hamlet, and of Janet's likening him to a woman. I recall his sensitive, delicate feelings, his truthfulness, honor, chivalric romance, deep love, high moral code, and noble nature, quite feminine in its elevation and tender purity. All this might well be likened, as it was by the great German poet, to a frail porcelain vase, for to put such a nature to stern uses is to shatter it.

And thus can we say of woman. Our code is nobler, our moral nature higher than man's. In intellect he may be stronger, — he is. We can freely cede him the intellect, so long as we possess the other. We show this difference thus: when a man feels he is wronged by his brother man, resentment is natural; and not only that, to right himself, even at the bitter expense of his enemy, is a duty. It is admitted by the world's practice that "society can justly be harsh upon a man for being tame under insult or injury." But a woman cannot right herself as a man does, and preserve her interior peace. No matter how just may be her cause, if she violates the high code of her nature by leaping down from her pure, still atmosphere into the hot, crowded arena, to seize on or wrest justice from the hands of her oppressors, she comes out of the fray fatally wounded. Justice for her is as Prince Adeb's Imam,* — she must forego all hope of it, and yield "the Imam for her own soul's sake."

Characters of delicate make and subtile stamp should not, cannot contend; they must endure with patience and courage, and look with sorrow and pity, not scorn and anger, on their oppressors. Truly unto woman were the words of Gospel law addressed: "Resist not evil, but whosoever shall smite thee on thy right cheek, turn to him the other also."

Woe unto that feminine nature that is forced by necessity, as was Hamlet, to right a great wrong. Intense mental anguish must result; and even when the assistance of the Most High seems vouchsafed by the gift of courage and the mysterious power of holding the poor bewildered mind well balanced, — even then she is fated, as Electra, to a solemn state, dedicate as it were to sadness. All glad, joyful feelings are hushed, and she will be as "an angel who has lost its way from heaven, and its wings also, looking perpetually up, with a sigh and a longing to return."

Why did I touch on this nerve, and set it to aching so fiercely? Venitia's music is ended. She and Janet have gone to their calm, quiet sleep. On the still, soft spring air comes the noisy throb of a steamer passing near the coast, sounding like the throes of some huge animal in mortal anguish. But physical pain is weak when compared with this agony of the lonely heart stung with the necessity to perform a stern duty, and filled with wild, passionate memories of a past forever gone, — a past which planted no seed for a future in this life!

Beat, beat, beat, comes that sorrowful steam-throb on my ears, and to its melancholy sough my heart replies

* Boker's "Prince Adeb."

sullenly back a dull, slow pulse. Poor heart! It sits, like Electra, mourning rebelliously over its griefs.

The steamer has passed, and I now hear the cool, passionless ripple of this tideless sea breaking on a shore strewn with mysterious fragments of a long lost past!

> " And the stately ships go on
> To the haven under the hill;
> But O for the touch of a vanished hand,
> And the sound of a voice that is still!
>
> " Break, break, break
> On thy cold gray stones, O Sea!
> But the tender grace of a day that is dead
> Will never come back to me."

THE TITAN'S CHILDREN AND CAPRI THE SPHINX.

THIS delicious climate of Naples is to work wonders upon me ; — so says Mrs. Rochester, the agreeable wife of the Minister. She paid us a visit last evening, and gave us much clever information on the character of the atmosphere, and the various winds that blow over and around this beautiful boot-like promontory of Europe. The climate, from its lively action on the skin, and the variety of impressions it makes on the body and mind, is capitally suited for alleviating the suffering arising from all sorts of melancholy, and every kind of neurotic intermittent produced by mental causes.

Naples, more than any other place in Italy, is strongly influenced by two great powers, — the volcanic soil and the wind. The atmosphere is constantly filled with various gaseous emanations, sulphuric and the like, and carbonic acid is spread throughout the air.

The account Mrs. Rochester gave me of the winds of Naples interested me exceedingly. The gulf or bay is open to the west and southwest. The hills of Posilippo, extending around to Capodimonte, protect the city from the north wind, and Monte Somma is a shelter against the east; but the northeast, southeast, west, southwest, and south meet with little obstruction, especially the west and southwest, which come in from the sea. The south and southeast winds, called mezzogiorno and scirocco by Italians, are the most disagreeable and injurious, especially to the natives; they are hot and damp, favorable to vegetation, but enervating and exhausting.

"They are, in truth, 'winds of idleness' in every sense of the word," said Mrs. Rochester. "You can feel them most sensibly at the entrance of the Toledo, and near the Royal Palace. I have often stood there during the blowing of a scirocco, and noticed with curiosity the warm, half-visible vapor which seemed to bathe everything; it permeated, like a subtile fluid, not only my whole physical nature, but also my mental, — prostrating muscular energy, and even vivacity of thought. I have often believed that this wind might be the unrecognized cause of Neapolitan indolence and Oriental fatalism, for these people are much more affected by it than we *forestieri*, or strangers. During its blowing the sky is of a dark leaden hue."

"This scirocco, which is so overwhelming here," remarked Janet, "is our old friend the *föhn* of Switzerland. There, however, it is of great service."

"Yes," said Venitia, "I remember, when I was a little girl, and we were living for a season or two in the Grisons, hearing the peasants there saying, 'that without the *föhn* neither the good God nor a golden sun could do anything.'"

"This scirocco of Italy, and *föhn* of Switzerland," continued Janet, "is the same thing as the simoom of Africa; it springs up in those immense sand-plains of the Sahara, which lie exposed to the rays of a tropical sun, and are easily heated. Just opposite Sicily and Italy the Atlas Mountains of Africa lower their peaks, and through this passage the simoom reaches the Mediterranean; then, after pouring its hot breath on the Peninsula, it sweeps up the Rhone valley as through a tunnel, and spreads over Switzerland. It is the saving wind of the Suisse; for, without its gracious presence, the snows on the Alps would never melt, and the glaciers, constantly increasing, would in time invade the valleys, and make an ice kingdom as fearful as Dante's description of Lucifer's abode in the lowest depth of Hell, —

> 'Where all the shades beneath the frozen tide
> Transparent shone, like straws in crystal clear.' "

After this little episode on the scirocco's wanderings, its good and evil doings, we returned to the other children of the Titan who visit Naples. The notus, or mezzogiorno, south wind, first cousin to the scirocco, blows oftenest in autumn. It is gentle, but oppressive. The libeccio, or southwest wind, is stormy. The northwest, or maestro, is not a pleasant wind in Naples: its passage over the sea makes it damp. Our palazzo is so situated on the Mergellina that we shall not feel it, nor do those suffer who live near the Villa Reale; but around the Chiatamone this wind is very unpleasant, and causes such a lively effect on the skin and nerves as to prevent some persons from living there. It is a noisy, glacial, squally wind, which makes *dolce Napoli* as disagreeable as any "common vulgar town"; in autumn and winter it visits this place about one day in four.

The tramontana, or north wind, is cold, but dry and invigorating, and serves as an antidote to the scirocco (southeast) and mezzogiorno (south). But the most pleasant wind in Naples is the west, or ponente. It is the conciliatory one, for it softens the cold and tempers the hot blasts; under its sweet influences the Cantastorie, or street-singers, pour out their mediæval melodies, the women dance the Tarantella, and everything goes as merry as a marriage bell. It is blowing now, making the bright, sunshiny morning delicious; and Venitia is standing at my room window informing me of it, repeating at the same time snatches of Owen Meredith's "Seaside Song."

Now she walks away, paying the sweetest compliment to this young poet that he could receive, — reciting his beautiful poetry in the soft morning air, and she as lovely as the poetry. I wish she had a lover for whom she felt, as this song says, "this joy of life." She is walking with all the gentle dignity of a graceful young empress up and down the terrace; her step is queenly, and yet without any affectation of dignity or consciousness of its fine air; it is a simple, natural motion, resulting from her well-formed limbs and perfectly proportioned body. She is just pronouncing these words, with a sweet beat and rhythm as musical as her gait: —

"For o'er faint tracks of fragrance wide
A rapture pouring up the tide, —
A freshness through the heat, — a sweet
Uncertain sound, like fairy feet, —
The west wind blows my love to me."

We spent a day at Capri last week, in company with the Rochesters and some other friends. On reaching the island, we visited first the far-famed Grotto Azzurra, or Blue Grotto, one of the old haunts of Roman luxury. Who does not remember Hans Christian Andersen's lovely story of the "Improvvisatore," with its Blue Grotto episode? Venitia, who had never read this book, sat up all the preceding night to finish it; but brows never ache, nor eyes grow heavy, at twenty, so she looked nearly as fresh as usual, the next day at noon, when we entered the Grotto.

The opening of the cavern is so low and narrow that we had to lie flat in the boat to enter. It is to the form and peculiar position of this opening that some heliographers attribute the faëry-like atmosphere of the Grotto. They say the sea is deeply imbued with light at this entrance, and emits it at every flow inside the cavern. The best hour for seeing the cave is "at silent midday,"

"The hush of noontide quiet";

then the waters are sapphire-hued, the walls of the purest blue, — that India shade which the Chinese call "the blue of the heavens after a rain," — and the ceiling is like the empyrean. It was at this hour we went, and seemed suddenly transported to a land of dreams.

We dipped our hands in the magic stream, and they became as alabaster, with a blue light playing through them. With these spectre-like fingers we dashed up the waters playfully; we seemed to be tossing up liquid gems, sapphires, and bluish pearls.

There was a sparkle on everything, as if a blue flame was lighting up and playing upon the glittering surface of crystal. The whole atmosphere seemed charged with blue, and the vaulted ceiling looked as if made of some azure-hued, transparent substance as clear as crystal, lighted by fire-rays from above, shining down on it.

After leaving the Grotto, we loitered up the steep walk to the hotel, stopping from time to time to enjoy the divine bits of landscape which came in at the spaces made by the lowering of vineyard walls. After luncheon, I did not accompany the rest of the party to Lo Capo, where are to be seen the remains of the famous twelve palaces of Tiberius. The noon-day visit to that enchanted Grotto, followed by the long walk, had caused total physical prostration; but the repose which I took while they were gone, and the full goblet of amber-hued, fragrant Capri wine,

> "With beaded bubbles winking at the brim,"

which I drank, restored me so completely, that I was able to be up and walking on the terrace of the hotel, when they came back from their sight-seeing.

The party returned full of the subject of Tiberius and his history, each one with a learned speculation. As I sat listening to their various opinions, I remembered Jean Paul's words, — "Sphinx-like Capri, lying on the broad plain of the Mediterranean, as a beautiful sphinx, forever offering up to man the solving of her Tiberius and Blue-Grotto riddles."

"It is a beautiful spot," said Mr. Rochester, leaning on the terrace-rail, and looking off into the distance. "From the heights of this island, on a clear day, can be taken in at one view the whole Italian coast, from the promontory of Circe to the temple of Pæstum. There, on one side, stretch out the Apennines, away back to the Lucanian Mountains, while Vesuvius stands fronting the eye, an ever-smoking altar. Here to the south lies the Mediterranean, and, with a little exertion of the imagination, one can almost see the fair coast of Sicily. I was reading yesterday a glowing description of Capri in Merivale's 'Rome.' He speaks of the island as fronting the Sorrentine promontory with bold beauty, advancing forward, as some lovely nymph proud of her charms."

"Yes," replied Janet, "I remember the passage. I recalled it as I stood at Lo Capo, and the same associations he writes of came to my memory. On these exquisite heights the pedantic but scholarly Tiberius must have thought over many a grand old heathen legend, as he gazed on the various points in the landscape which told of Circe and Ulysses, the old poem of the 'Odyssey,' and the new one of his uncle's laureate, Virgil, the 'Æneid,' which sang the works and exploits of his own fabled ancestor, Æneas. Recalling all these tales, he could well perplex his parasites with his favorite insoluble questions on the subjects of the sirens' songs and the name of Hecuba's mother."

This beautiful island of Capri — so called from the wild goats which inhabit it, *capreæ* — produces many excellent things. Its olives and white figs are far-famed; its wines, both red and white, are luscious, — the red smells and tastes of raspberries, but the white wine has the taste and aroma of violets, and is a drink fit for the gods and goddesses of Hellas. While talking of the productions of the island, Mr. Rochester observed, —

"In our frigid climates we can form no conception of the delight of simple living and breathing in this part of Europe. The earth yields its fruits a hundred-fold: for example, there are three vintages a year, in December, March, and August; a very little suffices for existence, even for the poorest, and such an existence as cannot be found elsewhere."

"In our Northern countries," I said, "physical necessities being great, we have to throw out all our strength to meet them, and the superfluous force spends itself on those painful and fatiguing subjects, human liberty and human progress. Here the people trouble themselves little, and purchase pleasure, or rather accept it. What do they care for freedom and the march of mind? Happy souls! they leave that illusion, that Sisyphus labor of life, eternal progress, to nations whose rugged, inhospitable soils force them to advance."

"I hardly agree with you," replied Mrs. Rochester; "or, rather, with that which your words imply. Little is done here, it is true, for those great life-works, human liberty and human progress, because the people are lying fallow. They may need a *red* fallow of blood yet to clear out the weeds; but I believe Italy will some time in the future revive her past; and surely, when we recall that past, we, who are only beginners, have need to be patient."

Janet looked triumphant at this earnest reply to my heresy. I shrugged my shoulders, laughed, and remained silent; while Mr. Rochester, with the pretty, attractive gallantry of a husband, came to his wife's aid.

"This little peninsula," he said, "and its surrounding shores have produced more eminent men than any other country on the face of the globe. Art and love of Nature were earliest and best developed here; and history can prove that it was the leading country in all civic and political activity in the early and middle ages of our era. Its history is the base, and gives the key-note to all æsthetical and philosophical study. It is the intellectual home of all artists, where they can best commence true study, and develop themselves most satisfactorily. Many nations have often governed the world by fraud, or force of arms; but only twice in the range of ages has the gentle rule of the Fine Arts held sway. Here in this little quarter of the globe the fair throne of Parnassus was raised; and the world shall ever remember those two epochs, the age of Pericles and the age of the Medici."

Just then some Italian gentlemen passed beneath the terrace, conversing earnestly, pouring out, like rich oil, their beautiful language.

"Listen!" said Venitia, in a low voice; "listen to the

music of this tongue. Notice its rhythm. Its very prose sounds like poesy."

This reminded me of a fine description I had heard of the Italian tongue, and I repeated it to them. "It is by turns royal as the Eridan, boiling like Vesuvius, but always harmonious as the voice of the wind in the great pines on the shores of the Chiassi."

Mr. Rochester quoted to us passages from the Greek poets, to prove to us the analogy between these two tongues in sound. The spoken Greek sounded no more satisfactory to my ears than its tantalizing hieroglyphics appear to my unlearned eyes. But I am as Uncle Miramont, in Fletcher's "Elder Brother,"

> "Though I can speak no Greek, I like the sound on 't,
> It goes so thundering as it conjured devils."

No signs of the word tongue are so despairingly provoking to me as Greek characters. They have a mysterious beauty too. Those eternities of ο's; those λ's, looking, with their tails upturned, like frolicsome dolphins in the waves of a Grecian archipelago; the prim ω's, with their various accents, seeming to hold a great secret as Lara's nodding steward; busy spider ε's, weaving, Arachne-like, interminable webs of mystery; incomplete Δ's, like Schumann's mute, questioning chords; Π's, silent as the weird columns of the Serapeön; the subtle, serpent-like forms, ς, θ, φ, and those reflective η, μ, ρ, with "their tenacious flukes mooring them to the shore" of some mighty thought.

I made Mr. Rochester laugh by telling him this, and his wife added, —

"Yes, you are right; these word-symbols are as lovely and deceptive as 'those ivory gates of sleep, through which come false dreams to mortals.' Whenever I meet with a Greek passage in my reading, it seems as if it intended to resolve itself, just for me alone, into full and perfect meaning; and the sparkling and pretty-winged accents, that hover over the hieroglyphics, wink with seductive familiarity, wooing me on, — in vain; the vision passes, and it all remains as incomprehensible as the great stone sphinx which gazes out alone over the desert so silently, — and looking almost scornfully too, for every passage seems to resolve itself into those ominous characters pointed at my vulgar ignorance, *οἱ πολλοί!*"

"But luckily a path for deliverance remains, ladies," said Mr. Rochester. "Being women, you are not expected to understand Greek. Remember what that great master of our strong Anglo-Saxon tongue, De Quincey, says: — 'Fair reader, our sex enjoys the office and privilege of standing counsel to yours, on all questions of Greek. We are, under favor, perpetual and hereditary dragomans to you; so that if by accident you know the meaning of a Greek word, yet by courtesy to us, your counsel, learned in that matter, you will always seem not to know.'"

And thus passed away this lovely day. We returned by moonlight, and the stars and the sea-ripples shone with a golden sparkle; even the pure moon-rays, as they fell on the tideless Mediterranean, broke into a flood of gold. Part of the company walked the deck of the steamer, chatting gayly; the rest of us remained at the upper part of the boat, and fell into a sweet silence. I passed off into a reverie that was too full of fine visions to be called ordinary slumber, unless it was as Endymion's magic sleep, —

"Great key
To golden palaces, strange minstrelsy,
Fountains grotesque, new trees, bespangled caves,
Echoing grottos, full of tumbling waves
And moonlight; ay, to all the mazy world
Of silvery enchantment!"

NEW FRIENDS.

ENITIA is reading Pope's Homer with great interest, and her remarks afford us much amusement. She laid down the book just now, and, walking across the terrace to the window where I am at my writing, said: "Ottilie, in the Iliad I notice, more than in anything I ever read, the great power, the irresistible influence, exercised by beauty, breeding, grace, and gentleness. Before these the haughty rage of Hector bows, and Priam's afflicted anger melts. Even Troy's matrons accept the naughty, unchaste Helen, won by her unassuming loveliness and lowly grace. Paris, so courtly, gentle, and beautiful, disarms all attacks, however well merited, and yet he shows so much dignity in his meekness as to maintain his position as a gentleman."

I had to laugh at this conclusion.

"Why, listen," she continued earnestly, half joining in my laugh, and taking up her Homer. "You remember, in the sixth Book, the stern, stormy Hector gives the naughty 'Phrygian boy' a sound berating, which it must be admitted the lazy, but charming, young fellow had richly deserved; but how ashamed the Trojan chief and the reader feel of his violent epithets, when the graceful Paris answers:

'Brother, 't is just.
Thy free remonstrance proves thy worth and truth;
Yet charge my absence less, O generous chief!
On hate to Troy, than conscious shame and grief.
Here, hid from human eyes, thy brother sat
And mourned in secret his and Ilion's fate.'

Now pray what reply could be made to such a gentlemanly waiving aside of well-merited reproaches?"

"Look out on the terrace, both of you," cries Janet, "and admire my sweet flowers. You can quote your Pope's Homer over them."

She is watering her pot-plants and flower-beds, for she has quite a hanging garden on this lovely terrace. The morning sun is peeping around on them, and the air is filled with their fresh fragrance. I look up at her, and acknowledge the loving thoughtfulness she displays by having a huge box of blooming mignonette, violets, and hyacinths placed beside my window; and after Andrea, our waiter, has arranged it to her perfect satisfaction, she strikes a pretty attitude before it, and repeats, with playful emphasis, —

"Thick new-born violets a soft carpet spread,
And clustering lotos swells the rising bed,
And sudden hyacinths the turf bestrow,
And flaming crocus makes the mountain glow."

* * * * *

We have formed and renewed some pleasant acquaintances. I say renewed, because Janet has met some English friends whose acquaintance she made during her husband's life. Among them is a Mrs. Folham, who, like ourselves, is making a tarrying-place of Naples. She has a daughter, Florence, with whom we were very much pleased the few times we saw her. She has gone on a journey of a few weeks through the Abruzzi, with an uncle and aunt. When she returns, we hope to have much pleasure in her society, as, added to her being an agreeable, pretty, and well-bred girl, she is something of a musician. We found her a pleasing singer, with a soft, delicious voice, just a little veiled and well-trained.

Mrs. Folham had a *thé musicale* — as her pretty little note of invitation called it — just before Florence left, a few evenings since. At it we met Tito Mattei, a young Neapolitan *pianiste*, whose execution, when he was a boy, attracted the attention and praises of Thalberg and his father-in-law Lablache. Mattei is about three or four and twenty, quite youthful in appearance; his face has a frank, boyish expression, with more simplicity and good nature than deep feeling or vivacity.

During the evening, being asked to play, he executed a fragment which puzzled us, for the accessories of execution created a contest with, and partly veiled, the musical thought. The idea contained in the piece was masterly, and provokingly familiar to us, but we could not seize it as a whole, so as to give it its proper name. This happens to me often, however, for I have a curious difficulty in commanding the names of pieces when I hear them unexpectedly, which is very tantalizing to one who has studied music so closely as I have.

Venitia is never at a loss. Her musical information is not packed, labelled, and docketed as mine is; it lies out near at hand. Thus, when the unexpected or unknown comes suddenly upon her, she is quite ready to encounter either. This exact memory and quick reading on the keys which she possesses, and is naturally so proud of, arise, I think, partly, if not entirely, from her being so fine an *executante;* she applies everything she studies in music instantly to the piano, — indeed, studies through it and through her ear. I, on the contrary, am an indifferent performer, and have enjoyed music for many years, as I do books, in silence and to myself, independent of all instruments; thus, the notes appeal more forcibly to my mind and fancy than to my ear, and when I hear the full battery of sounds I am a little bewildered. But on this occasion Venitia could not name the fragment either, and it vexed her, for she felt all the pride of an *executante*, and did not like to find herself as confused as a mere carpet knight, such as she regards me.

The passage was brief, breathless, and full of vigor, and Mattei played it well; but, just as it would be putting aside its mask, like a sprightly Venitienne at a carnival *fête*, in order to show its bewitching self, he would throw over it a gorgeous mantle, studded with brilliant octaves, and embroidered with graceful arabesque scale forms, while his thumb flashed like a little demon Ariel from one end of the piano to the other, just in the most difficult and unexpected places, and the curious but beautiful fragment would peep through here and there with a mocking smile, then dance off in bewildering zigzags in company with chasing scales, showing itself only in sparkling bits. After a while, the first and second passages of the opening gleamed out again, and, melting together in sorrowful minor, closed in the most fragmentary doubt. When Mattei arose from the piano, some one asked him the name of it.

"The *motivo* was a passage from Beethoven," he answered, with a frank smile.

"O, to be sure!" exclaimed Venitia, impulsively, to me, as if provoked with herself for not recognizing her old friend. It was the *finale* to the first Sonate in Opus 10, C minor, the Prestissimo, you remember."

He started, for he had overheard her, and turning half towards us, said to Mrs. Folham and her daughter, "Mademoiselle is a musician."

Mrs. Folham presented him to us, and we entered into conversation.

"You have of course read De Lenz?" I remarked to him.

"*Plait-il?*" he replied, with that blank expression of countenance a person has when he does not comprehend even your words, much less your thought.

"The man never read anything in his life, my dear, I'll wager a bright golden guinea," whispered Janet in English, "except probably his Book of Prayers. His music *nascitur non fit*, of course."

Choking down a laugh, I extricated myself in a few words of explanation, telling him as simply and concisely as possible, that De Lenz was a clever German musical writer, who had published a useful book on Beethoven's Sonates, and had said some nice and suggestive things about this very Sonate, the finale of which he had been playing. He listened to me as a person looks in the dark, and, when I had finished, shook his head wistfully, as if just understanding my words, and no more. Then he turned to Venitia, and they talked about different piano-forte compositions.

While they were talking, I seemed to be listening to them, but I was really thinking of what a different thing music was to each of us. To him it was innate, and seemed to require no mental nourishment, nor give rise to any ideas or feelings out of and beyond it; he was not a creator, but a gifted executant, who controlled the instrument as a member of his body, and bent and moulded the musical ideas of masters at will into numberless forms of beauty, like the Florentine artist-goldsmiths of the fifteenth century, who took precious ore, and worked it into beautiful and graceful garlands for fair women.

But music to me is a language, and though, so far as my own fingers are concerned, it may be a dead one, it is like the ancient tongues to a classical scholar, — the beautiful

> "fluent Greek, a vowel'd under-song";

and tells me through my eyes and my mind of diviner thoughts and things than any living spoken words can breathe.

> "Heard melodies are sweet, but those unheard
> Are sweeter; therefore, ye soft pipes, play on,
> Not to the sensual ear, but, more endeared,
> Pipe to the spirit ditties of no tone." *

We found Mattei intelligent enough about everyday musical matters, and tolerably posted in the history of his noble old Conservatoire. I made his inexpressive dark eyes glow with something like emotion, when I told him of the younger Trajetta dying in indigence and obscurity, at an advanced age, some years before, in America, and he listened, as if deeply interested, to my account of Trajetta's mode of training the voice, and the beautiful Solfeggi he had given me to study. When I ended, he said, in a pretty, tender, half sad tone, —

"He was one of our holy men in art, and he died far away there, unknown and poor. Mais que voulez-vous, Mesdames? We poor artists! So we go!"

He shrugged his shoulders, threw up his hands with the palms outward, raised his eyebrows, and pouted his lips in the true Neapolitan sign-language, indicating, even

* Keats's Ode on a Grecian Urn.

stronger than words could, sympathy with the master's sad fate, reverence for his memory, all united to a calm acceptance amounting to fatalism; which last, I have no doubt, he inherited from nature, for his face bore that half vague, half indifferent look which is entirely distinct from the dreamy expression of the poet, or the hopeless look of the discouraged: it is the unmistakable sign of the born fatalist.

Venitia talked with him about Thalberg, Liszt, Mendelssohn, and Chopin, but it was difficult to get his individual opinions about any one of them, though he was quite willing to tell what other persons thought. We asked him if he played Chopin much. Then came again his expressive shrug, and another motion of the hands, with a smiling elevation of the lips, meaning, as we translated it, that however he might admire Chopin, he was not his own master as to what he should play for the public; indeed, the remark he made a few moments after these graphic gestures had finished, confirmed us in the truth of our interpretation.

"Chopin's music," he said, "is not popular in Naples. After all, it is the music for the virtuoso, Mesdames, not the multitude."

Some one addressed him, and he turned away from us, which gave us an opportunity to speak of what we cannot help noticing constantly in Naples, this curious sign-language. All the lower classes, especially, use it with great skill. One of our anteroom windows looks over into the court-yard. I often stand there, watching, through the blinds, with great interest, the coachman, grooms, servants, and porteress, engaged at their various occupations, talking together, and I have observed closely their use of this mysterious means of communication. They seem to have certain gestures for a whole phrase. Indeed, I have often seen one of them stop when half-way through an animated sentence, as if words were powerless, and finish his meaning by a few rapid, fierce gestures, which seemed to be perfectly comprehended by his companions, and much more effective too than the words had been, judging from the flashing of their keen eyes. Thus, when Mattei left us, we talked about it, and Janet said,—

"This sign-language is not original with these modern Neapolitans. I have no doubt it is a descendant of the sign-language of ancient Italy."

"I wish I understood it better," I remarked, "for I am sure a knowledge of it would make the symbolism of the old painters much plainer to us."

"The other evening at Mr. Rochester's," said Venitia, "a gentleman told me that when Ferdinand I. returned to Naples, after the downfall of Murat, he addressed the people from a terrace or balcony of the Royal Palace entirely by signs; he gesticulated furiously and rapidly; conveyed his reproaches, promises, and reconciliation entirely by these motions of the hands and muscles of the face; and although he did not speak one word, they perfectly understood him, and gave him shouts of applause expressive of their satisfaction and admiration."

"That was what made him so popular with the lower classes," observed Janet; "you remember it was said the lazzaroni were faithful subjects of a king who made a lazzarone of himself, meaning this Ferdinand I.; but they obeyed grudgingly a lazzarone who had been made a king, meaning Murat."

"But what a droll sight that must have been," I remarked, "that royal pantomime! Their replies, however, should also have been mute. Fancy, my dears,

H

how excessively funny it would be to see such a town-meeting, with the *vox populi* having no *vox* at all, and speech and applause going on by gestures. I should think a great deal of violence might be spared, if all popular assemblages had orator and audience limited to motions and gestures."

"Not at all," said Janet; "noise might be prevented probably, but not violence, judging from these Italians; for you know very well that here the blow can come, and does, without the word."

Just then our hostess asked Venitia for some music; and I noticed with pleasure that Mattei stopped his conversation in the anteroom where supper was served, and came into the salon to listen to her. Notwithstanding he had said Chopin was not popular in Naples, all the company appeared charmed with her execution of the Romance from the Concerto dedicated to Kalkbrenner by this composer. Her beauty and calm self-possession increased very much the effect her music produced. She looked like a young Sibyl as she sat at the piano, still and fair as a piece of sculptured marble, her glorious full eyes gazing out into the beyond, while her fingers seemed to draw from the instrument this charming passage. Her playing makes me understand what Heine felt when he said of Chopin's own execution: "Whilst Chopin is playing I forget entirely that it is the performance of a *pianiste* whose reputation is that of a master, and I bury myself in the sweet abysses of his music, in its sad delights, which are as exquisite as profound. Chopin is the great musical poet, the artist of genius, that can only be named in company with Mozart and Beethoven."

As Venitia finished, a gentleman came in, who was received by the family and musical circle with great friendliness, and kind reproaches for his coming so late.

"Our friend, Mr. Luini," said Mrs. Folham, coming to Janet and me. "I was afraid we should not have the pleasure of seeing him this evening. An exceedingly nice person, I do assure you. Yes, Mr. Luini."

Mrs. Folham has a droll way of repeating the *motivo* of her remark, as a sort of refrain, looking around the room as she does it, as if driving four-in-hand, and watching her leaders.

"Luini!" I repeated, in a stupid way I have of thinking aloud; "Luini, I wonder if he is a descendant of the Milanese Raphael!" for in Italy we are constantly startled at hearing names used familiarly, and applied to living, breathing human beings, no better than ourselves, which we have been accustomed to seeing only in books, and there applied to the great landmarks in history and art, setting such brains as mine to work in the most absurd manner, framing imaginary genealogies.

"Milanese?" asked Mrs. Folham, in the most ridiculously practical manner; "quite likely, my dear." (She had lost the word "Raphael," and, if she had not, I do not know that it would have been of much use to her.) "Mr. Luini is a Milanese by birth; probably he knows the family to which you allude, and may be a kinsman. Let me present him to you, and you can ask him."

And to my intense amusement and embarrassment she bustled off to fetch her friend. Mrs. Folham is a very intelligent woman, so far as all ordinary practical subjects go. But it must be confessed that everything relating to what she calls, with amusing emphasis, "the Fine Arts," is about as clear to her comprehension as "Shakespeare and the musical glasses." She looks upon "the Continent" — another English expression of hers, as if there was but one continent on the globe — as a vastly agreeable place for persons of failing health or invalid income, a capital place indeed for educating children, and I sometimes think she hopes to make it an available place for picking up a count or a baron for her pretty blonde, Florence. Galleries of pictures and statuary, ancient ruins, and old churches, she regards as accessories to the country, like bowling-alleys, the shows, and exhibitions of a watering-place, gotten up by the natives as amusements and attractions, and quite likely she shrewdly suspects them of being speculations on the easily-gulled travellers, who are not as clever about those sort of things as she is. Thus, my allusion to the celebrated pupil of the great Leonardo da Vinci, Bernardino Luini, was Greek and Latin to her ears. As Mrs. Folham left us, I looked at Janet dismayed, and yet the mistake was so absurd we had to laugh. While we were in the height of our merriment, imagining what possible explanation I could make to the strange man about the mythical Luinis in question, we saw Mrs. Folham approaching, leaning on the arm of her friend.

"He is very handsome, at all events," whispered Janet.

Mrs. Folham presented him; and just as she was about speaking of my unfortunate Mrs.-Harris-of-a-Luini, that Providence who watches so kindly over the halt and the blind of good society, interposed in my favor, in the shape of her youngest boy, *un vrai enfant terrible*, and she disappeared hastily with him, saying, as she did so, in the best satisfied manner imaginable, — "Now, my love, ask Mr. Luini all about your friends. Yes, your friends." And she nodded her head encouragingly.

As our ridiculous position presented itself to us, good breeding, self-control, every discipline of courtesy and Mrs. Grundyism, which keeps us poor human beings in check and good order when we meet together in those crowds called "society," was forgotten, — no, not forgotten, but completely swept aside by the torrent of fun which rushed over us both, and Janet and I astounded our new acquaintance by the merriest peal of laughter he surely had ever heard.

He opened wide his cold blue eyes on us; but I saw creeping around his handsome mouth quiverings which showed he should like to know the cause of our mirth, that he might enjoy it also. This encouraged me, for I had been afraid of encountering an Italian, not only as innocent of "the Fine Arts" as poor Mrs. Folham, — no uncommon thing, by the way, — but equally innocent of appreciation of humor. After the first burst of laughter had subsided, I controlled myself sufficiently to speak, and said, — "Really, we must appear very rude. You must excuse us. I am almost sure the same cause would make you behave just as badly."

"I have not the slightest doubt of it," he answered, with a cordial laugh and the loveliest voice I ever heard in man or woman; then he added, "Permit me to take this seat beside you, and pray let me into the secret of this merriment. Food for fun, you know, is not to be found every day."

In a few moments he was laughing as heartily as we, and our rather noisy laughter attracted Venitia's attention. She was standing at the piano with Florence and her mamma, and she reports that Mrs. Folham said, "Yes, my dear, your friend knows some relatives of Mr. Luini. How lucky, to be sure, for he is an exceedingly nice person. We have known him these two or three years. In Rome we first met him, was it not, Florence? Yes, my dear, — Mr. Luini, — in Rome, — a Milanese by birth, I am pretty certain. A very proper person, I do assure you. What did you say, Florence? An artist? Beg pardon, my love, you are entirely in error"; then she added, in a solemn and reproachful tone, as if Florence had accused him of some sin or dishonor, "An artist! no, indeed; on the contrary, comfortable means, lives very handsomely, quite the gentleman. Plays finely, to be sure, but only *en amateur*. I have heard," here she lowered her voice confidentially, "that he is noble"; and, with a little nervous laugh, like Toots's "no consequence," she added, "He may be a prince in disguise, or something of the sort, who knows? But, at all events," here she resumed her ordinary hearty English tone, "he is a very nice person, — very; — yes, — Mr. Luini, — O no, not an artist at all. By no means; — quite the gentleman, on the contrary; — amateur, that 's all."

Mr. Luini and we were capital friends from the start. When we bade him good night, we invited him with sincere cordiality to visit us.

"Yes, my dears," interrupted Mrs. Folham, "Mr. Luini shall fetch me some time very soon to see you. Pray, what evenings are you receiving?"

The kind, pleasant woman had all the proper feeling of an English person about it, and by offering to have him "fetch" her, as she expressed it, she wished frankly to assume any responsibility there might appear in the sudden acquaintanceship. The next day, when we returned from our morning drive in the Toledo, where we love to see the motley crowd, we found his card.

SPIRITISM AND DREAMS.

E have been having a strange and interesting conversation this evening, arising out of our meeting to-day with Mr. H——, the celebrated Spiritist. This gentleman has lately arrived in Naples, and his sayings, doings, and movements are so freely talked upon, that he seems to be the public property of the English and American society collected in this city. We hear more of him than others, because he is very intimate with our friends the Rochesters.

He is not in full possession of his powers at the present moment, they say. He has held only two or three *séances* since he came, and these have been strictly private, at Mr. Rochester's palazzo, at which no one has been present but the immediate family of the Minister and the King's brother, Prince Luigi, for whose gratification they have been held.

The reports of these *séances* have made us curious to meet this spiritual lion; but although he told Mrs. Rochester he would call on us with her some day, *sans cérémonie*, his promised visit has been deferred from time to time, for he is as the man in the parable, "marrying a wife and cannot come." His intended bride and her family, with whom he is travelling, — wealthy Russians, — are making excursions to Amalfi and Pæstum, Sorrento and Capri, Pozzuoli and Baiæ; thus every moment of his time is occupied.

This morning Mrs. Rochester called and told us that Mr. H—— had asked Mr. Rochester to present him to Mr. B——, the distinguished American poet, now also in Naples; that he was to call on this gentleman and his family this afternoon, and that she had come to invite us, in their name and hers, to be present at the interview. Accordingly, at three o'clock we went to Mr. B——'s apartments at the Hotel de l'Europe, where we were received cordially by him and his ladies. We arrived a little before the expected visitor, but a few moments after Mr. H—— and Mr. Rochester were announced.

When Mr. H—— was presented to Mr. B——, I noticed that he took a rapid, keen survey of the poet, — who has as distinguished a presence as name, — just as if he were weighing and measuring him mentally. "You are very cunning and clever, young Aureolus, doubtless," I thought, "but you cannot measure that man."

Only a few moments passed during the presentation, and no one seemed to notice, as I did, the sharp weight-and-measure glance that flashed out of the bright, blue eye of the young Spiritist, as he scanned the patriarchal-looking poet, who received his boyish guest with simplicity and loyalty of manner, as if he respected himself and his surroundings, and was willing to extend the same feeling to all who approached him; but short as the moments were, this look made a strong impression on me. As I noted the young man's expression, there rose to my lips the words which Browning puts into the mouth of Paracelsus, when he first sees Aprile the poet, —

> "Art thou the sage I only seem to be,
> Myself of after time, my very self,

With sight a little clearer, strength more firm,
Who robs me of my prize, who takes my place,
For just a fault, a weakness, a neglect?
I scarcely trusted God with the surmise
That such might come."

During the first part of the interview I examined the personal appearance of the young man. He seemed about five or six and twenty; had light brown hair and blonde complexion; a frank, boyish countenance; and a quick, bright, blue eye, clear as the waters that wash the base of a granite mountain. His voice was ringing, and had a cordial tone in it; and his laugh was the fresh, throaty one of youth, as if no care or sorrow had sent the laugh lower down for springs to feed it.

A genial, merry manner, an egotistical freedom in talking of himself, which had the appearance of hearty, innocent candor, also struck me; but for the sharp expression which I had observed on his face when first looking at him, I probably should not have examined him closer, but have listened to, and regarded him as an imaginative person, possessing a great deal of this mysterious magnetic power of which so little is known, and using it with the unconsciousness of a real childlike nature.

But the recollection of that look remained; and after the first survey of his person and manner, I returned to the examination of his face, to find out where lay the sharpness and shrewdness. At last they were discovered in those glancing blue eyes, and frank, laughing mouth;—there, around the eye and mouth-setting were numberless little foxy lines, which gave a curious, cunning, knowing expression to the face, strangely at variance with its surface-character. They were the marks left by the constant use of a subtile and intuitive power of penetration into the characters of others, — that strange, bland, and noiseless gift, the practice of which is called shrewdness by some, dissimulation by others, but is, after all, best named tact.

"Has for genius no mercy,
  For speeches no heed;
It lurks in the eyebeam,
  It leaps to its deed.

Church, market, and tavern,
  Bed and board it will sway;
It has no to-morrow,
  It ends with to-day." *

How curious is the history that each human face tells! No matter how hidden the labor, how strong the will, how stern the self-control, the murder will out in some little leaf of the countenance.

I looked from the Spiritist to our Minister, from him to the Poet, and contrasted the three remarkable men. Mr. Rochester's face is dreamy, speculative, and almost poetical; but there are certain hard lines about the mouth and square wrinkles on the brow which tell of the struggle that may have gone on in his nature between wild, Utopian visions and sober common sense. This struggle has transformed a vague, youthful dreamer, who would have spent his life in trying to carry out impossible schemes, into the practical, acting man, fit to be what Madame de Staël said his great preceptor, M. Fellenberg, desired his educational system to produce: "A liberal bond between the inferior and superior classes; a bond which should not be founded only on the pecuniary interests of the rich and the poor." †

Mr. B——'s face and head are as satisfactory as any admirer of the great poet could wish. He has a fine, high

* Emerson. † Madame de Staël's "L'Allemagne."

brow; a head as classic in its outline as an antique; a calm, reflective eye, so serious that but for its serenity it would be stern; inquiring in its expression at times, not so much of outward things, but as if communing with the high and beyond; a mouth expressing sensitiveness and purity. Gray hair clusters around his fine head, and he has a patriarchal beard, which is as oddly at variance with the fire of his eye as Richelieu's eye and voice were with his tottering gait. His manner is calm, simple, and plain; but the simplicity and plainness arise from high breeding and culture, and an inherent self-respect, which is unobtrusive but none the less felt. I have heard him described as cold, stern, and exclusive; to me he always seems serene, self-poised, and just.

From his quiet face, expressive of that perfect wisdom which results from a constant communion with good, true thoughts, I shifted my eyes again to the young Scotchman, whose success in Spiritism has made him famous enough to be mentioned hereafter, in the history of this unknown, magnetic human atmosphere, when future discoveries have made it as "*natural*" and "*easy to believe*" as steam and electricity.

While the young man's tongue was running with voluble facility, his eyes were scanning closely and keenly his audience; the graceful form of the poet's invalid wife, who lay upon the sofa, her delicate, lady-like features and exquisite little hand and foot, which peeped out from the folds of the soft, silken dressing-robe, — all these attractions, I felt certain, were noted, as that sharp, blue eye swept over her.

One by one he took in each member of the company, and I observed that he remembered exactly which lady among us was the great poet's daughter. He had a word for each and all; in proportion to our ranks, however, for intellect sat on that American throne, — a B——, not a Bourbon.

He talked of a living *double* he had, with frank fun, as if he heartily enjoyed the thing, — some charlatan who was pretending to be Mr. H——. This person had played numberless pranks, which were even rascally and dishonest, — such as introducing himself into families, getting invitations to stay all night, and decamping before daybreak with the plate and other valuables. This *double* had visited Florence, Marseilles, and various other places.

"And so droll!" said the young man, with a burst of innocent surprise, as if all the world should be familiar with his personal appearance; "so odd! the descriptions given of this person show him to be totally unlike me, for they all say he is a middle-aged, large, dark-haired man."

He talked of his matrimonial engagement with delicious *naïveté;* said, with a merry laugh, that he had only known the lady six weeks. "Although," he added, with a little dash of the chin up, and toss of the head, "we had known each other by reputation long before." It was inimitable. He said he was born in Scotland, had been taken to the United States in early childhood, then returned, while yet young, to his native country.

There was none of the accepted notion of a magician about him. Indeed, it seemed strange, while looking at this eager, boyish, apparently enthusiastic youth, to think of him as the man who had been consulted seriously by the long-headed Louis Napoleon, and had been invited by persons of the highest rank in Europe to visit them, all treating him and his faith and powers with respect.

He did not, during the whole interview, say one word about Spiritism. He spoke of himself as well known, not with offensive conceit or presumptuous vanity, but with the frankness of a youth. Notwithstanding all this openness, he impressed me with the thought that he was sharper and cleverer than this air implied. There was certainly method in his *manner*.

He made the conversation as general as possible, for he held the reins in his own hands. He seemed to possess, among his other gifts, that *art de causer*, which De Tocqueville defined as that charming science which consists in touching upon and agitating a crowd of ideas, without dwelling in tiresome detail on any one; with this difference, that Mr. H——'s talk touched on personalities, not ideas, — things, not thoughts. He kept the ball rolling swiftly, and even when speaking of himself left no room for suggestions, or the natural remarks or questions that might have arisen from such a personal style.

After talking an hour or so, Mr. Rochester reminded Mr. H—— of the time. He arose with a quick, alert movement, which was quite in keeping, and took leave of Mr. B—— and us with the fresh, eager manner of a very young man, who had not been long enough in society to grow conscious or affected, but entirely free from awkwardness or shyness.

Of course, we "talked him over" after he left, and among other things that were said and told of him was this pretty story: —

One evening in Florence Mr. H—— was visiting two distinguished English authors, husband and wife. While talking with them, he played idly with some fresh leaves that were lying near him, forming them into a wreath, which, after he had finished, he threw carelessly on the table, and turned to play with something else; for this thoughtless, unconscious handling of cards or little table ornaments and trifles while he is talking is said to be one of his peculiarities. A low exclamation from the one

> "who mutely sits
> Musing by the firelight, that great brow
> And the spirit small hand propping it,"

attracted the attention of each one present to the little leafy wreath. It was rising in the air without the help of any visible hands. It rose gently, swayed an instant to and fro, as if a soft breeze half lifted, half impelled it. It moved slowly along, each one watching it earnestly, until it hung directly over the head of the lady he was visiting; then it fell eddying down, like the leaf commemorated in the beautiful poem "By the Fireside," and rested on "that great brow," mingling its soft, green leaves with the hair,

> "So dark and dear, how worth
> That a man should strive and agonize,
> And taste a very hell on earth
> For the hope of such a prize."

We all united in the opinion that Mr. H——'s powers had never been better employed than in making his "unseen spirits of the air" crown

> "My perfect wife, my Leonor."

This evening Mrs. Rochester came to talk over with us the visit of the day; and while we were drinking tea on the terrace, she told us of some strange things which had occurred in her drawing-room during the late *séances* held there for Prince Luigi. Shapes like baby hands had appeared under the table-covering, supposed to be spirits of children Mrs. Rochester had lost by death twenty years before! Their small clenched fists had played in the silk flounces of the mother's dress, their little unseen forms had nestled down beside her. 'Kerchiefs had been snatched up by invisible hands, and knots were tied in them with unseen fingers. An accordion was held beneath the table, and the little invisible spirits played on it a broken but sweet minor melody, — only a few measures; then the instrument trembled, as if held by tiny hands too weak to bear its weight, and fell to the ground.

After Mrs. Rochester left us we remained on the terrace talking. Janet said: "Spiritism has its root in the imagination, and this root is as old as humanity itself. In every age a new shoot comes up in some form or other, but the root remains the same, — the same burning desire to know and determine the future. It is but a repetition of that old longing which impelled the astrologists 'on the mooned plains of Chaldea, and by the dark waters of Egypt, to penetrate into the womb of Event.'"

"But this Spiritism," I replied, "does not seem to be a very poetical repetition of that glorious astrology, and its evidences are more positive and tangible, while they are not so elevated as those which the learned philosophers of old exhibited. The greatest charm in the supernatural for me, however, lies in losing sight of the Before and After. I long to soar into a realm of eternal Present, where I can be free from the goading sting of the snake Memory, and the delusive dream of Hope."

"Wait patiently," said Janet, with serious tenderness, "and that great Present will come. When the undetermined hour strikes, our Past and Future will be shown to us as one divine Whole!"

We talked of Life and Death with sweet solemnity.

"Dissolution, Ottilie dear, is not death nor birth," said Janet. "Life — that is, what we call Life in this world — is a transient division from the creative power, and Death is simply a reunion with it." Then, in her pleasing, speculative way, she rambled on something after this fashion: — "Life, real, true life, is like a beautiful tree bearing one matchless flower. It takes ages to perfect root and tree-stem, branch and leafage, and, in fine, the blessed blossom. Each being is a contribution towards this purpose, and the warmth of countless suns is needed for its glorious ripening, for

'I doubt not through the ages one increasing purpose runs,
And the thoughts of men are widened with the process of the suns.'

Each earnest life-labor goes towards this increasing purpose, and each complete existence is as a snowy petal opening in perfect whiteness to help the expanding of the one great thought-flower."

We talked of dreams and the inexplicable influence arising from them, which constitutes what Lewes calls "the atmosphere of life." I remarked that in dreams we seem to be completely disengaged from the distractions of common life; nothing exists but ourselves, our very spirits, without contact or mixture. "*La bête,*" as De Maistre wittily called the body, lies senseless and helpless, while "*l'autre*" is free and soaring.

"Some physiologists think," said Janet, "that dreams, instead of being a reflection of spontaneous will, uninfluenced by the narrow experiences of the hour and surrounding circumstances, are simply an organic action, a reflex movement of the nerves, an automatic operation of the brain."

"It may be," I replied, "a sentiment of the difficult or easy, strong or languishing, course of organic life. I have noticed that trouble often makes the sleep as heavy as if it resulted from an opium draught; petty annoyances, on the contrary, cause wakefulness, and so does gayety; but deep grief, after it has had its full sweep, mercifully turns and spreads the dense covering of a leaden sleep over the prostrated mind and body."

"Descartes said that sorrow and danger, or disagreeable business, made him both hungry and sleepy," remarked Janet.

"Have you ever noticed," I asked, "the sensations following sleep? Sometimes I awaken with the current of life flowing abundantly and with facility. I seem to be hearing the inspiring murmurs of a far-off ocean, and the mysterious sounds fill me with a strange gladness, an unaccountable light-heartedness."

"As if," responded Janet, resting her hand affectionately on my shoulder,—

"'Though inland far we be,
Our souls have sight of that immortal sea
Which brought us hither;
Can in a moment travel thither,—
And see the children sport upon the shore,
And hear the mighty waters rolling evermore.'"

"Then at other times," I continued, "I awaken with lead in every little organ-pipe of nerves, the current of life flows languidly, and I seem plunged into a state of insurmountable melancholy. I am apt to fancy that only the body has awakened, and the soul is still lingering in that home, where Rahel Levin said 'it goes in sleep to recruit,' and that the animal spirits are waiting in sadness for their Prospero, to relieve them from the gnarled oak-like prison-house of matter."

"Do you remember, Ottilie," asked Venitia, "old Volktman in Bulwer's Godolphin? He talked of 'girdling our sleep with dreams,' and when the wished for dream glided into us, our souls walked with the Spirit of the Vision. I cannot help indulging in a little fanciful superstition about dreams, it is so pleasant. In the morning I often find myself thinking if the last night's visions are of good or evil omen. Indeed, I have never removed this ruby ring at night since I heard that the ruby gave pleasant dreams."

"But, Venitia, if you observe yourself closely, you will find that you rarely admit any dream to be positively ill-omened. Cunning Hope always contrives some little loophole to let in on it a bright glimmer of good meaning."

"Let me tell you a strange dream I had once," said Janet. "The clock is striking midnight; it is the very hour for a weird story, and this terrace has a ghostly look, with the phantom-like vapor of Vesuvius flashing out on us its fierce fire-eye. One evening, some years ago, I sat alone at bedtime, thinking how happy I was, how well in mind and body. I was leading a comparatively solitary life, for we were at Paul's country home in England, and my days and hours were flowing by silently and sweetly. I went to bed and fell asleep.

"I dreamed I was standing on the door-sill of a strange house, looking out into a garden which I had never seen before, but I did not feel any surprise at being there. A servant told me that a certain woman, who was in some way associated with me, I cannot tell how, — for, of course, you have observed how vaguely information is conveyed in dreams — we accept everything without any of the 'whys and wherefores' of waking life, — that this woman had just passed out with a strange-looking snake following her. I ran into an adjoining arbor, or summer-house, and looked after this person.

"I saw her very near where I was standing. She was walking slowly away, and beside her, as if listening to and following her, was a horrible little Cobra de Capello! It was about two feet in length, and it leaped along with a bold, agile movement, that had a strange fascinating grace in it. It stood half upright, the slight undulatory body supported on the foot-like tail, the hood dilated, showing plainly the black curved line and spots, and they had the mysterious expression that is seen on a mask. The yellow color of the serpent's body glowed like fiery gold, and the delicate black stripes and spots on it flashed and glimmered as if each possessed individual fiendish life. As I looked at this fearful creature, I heard distinctly a faint stridulous sound, resembling the staccato note of a treble hautboy, and I remember saying to myself, 'That is the voice of the serpent! It is answering the woman, and they are talking about me!' I was seized with a feeling of insurmountable terror, and an apprehension of coming evil.

"I returned to the house. Soon after, this same woman entered the room where I was. She looked like some one very different in character, for she had taken the form and manner of my dead mother; but I was not deceived, and kept myself on my guard. She came up to me with the tenderness of a mother. I tried to avoid her, but my precautions were all vain! She succeeded in resting her hands on my forehead, then passed out of the room silently, looking back at me with an air of sly triumph.

"Something seemed to inform me that this touch had put me in great peril, for by it the serpent could recognize me. I was almost beside myself with terror. Just then I heard the Angelus bell of a neighboring church. On the instant I resolved to go and put myself under the protection of the sacred roof.

"In olden times, I said, the sanctuary was a safeguard, the very Spirit of Evil itself falling powerless at its threshold; and although no Catholic, I seemed to have unwavering faith.

"I went to the church and became a resident, for there was a religious order attached to it, and also many buildings. This order seemed to have secular as well as religious occupations; it was a large community.

"Soon after, I was standing in one of the reception or business rooms. A strange woman, looking like a traveller, entered, and asked to rent one of their halls; she wished to exhibit to the towns-people some curious things she had for show. The business arrangements were concluded. As the woman was leaving the hall, one of the members of the community came to me, holding in his hand a placard, printed in gay colors, saying, 'There is to be quite a curious show to-morrow evening,' and handed me the placard.

"It was an advertisement or bill of the woman's exhibition. To my horror, I saw at the head of it, in red letters, that seemed to scintillate, these words: 'A very curious Cobra de Capello, that is perfectly tame; so docile that it will perform anything its mistress bids it, as an intelligent dog would.'

"I let the placard drop, and, trembling in every fibre, looked towards the woman. She was just leaving the room, and her eyes rested on me with a smiling, triumphant expression. She was dressed not only plainly, but commonly; her face was perfectly unknown to me, *yet I knew it was* SHE! She had on her arm a small wicker-basket with lids, but both lids were thrown back, and I saw that the basket was empty. She left the room.

"Just as I was trying to command my agitation, I felt a sharp, stinging bite on the back of the upper part of my left arm. I groaned, for I knew on the instant the cause. The Cobra had found me. And lo! out from the thin mull sleeve of my gown crept the horrible snake; and before we could recover presence of mind, it had glided out of the half-open doorway, and disappeared, no one knew whither. We heard very plainly, however, the clear, treble, hautboy note of its voice, which sounded to me like the exultant cry of a fiend. This strange sound passed through the building as a swift wind, then died away, with a faint wail, into utter stillness.

"Death seemed inevitable. I felt the bite burning and aching intensely. I plucked off my sleeve, and there upon my arm was a yellow spot as large as a pea, with skin and flesh bitten out, and the hollow filled with the angry poison of the serpent. I was taken to the infirmary of the establishment. Two members of the community said I must have a place two inches square cut out, and a hot iron applied; this must be done immediately, otherwise I had only thirty minutes to live.

"I was stretched on a bed; and watched them as they sharpened their instruments for the excision, and heated the iron for searing. The serpent poison was beginning to act upon me; this, added to the dread of the approaching suffering, overpowered me, and I fainted.

"When I recovered my senses, I learned that the operation had been performed successfully, the poison completely extracted, and I was safe; for they told me that some days had elapsed during my insensibility.

"Soon after, I awakened, trembling from head to foot.

I was unable to arise, and was ill for some days; indeed many weeks passed before I recovered my usual health and elasticity; and, strange to say, for a long while after I felt a pain in my left arm, and a sensitiveness to the touch in the spot where the dream-bite had been, though there was no mark or bruise perceptible.

"My physician, to whom I told my dream, said my whole nervous system was as much prostrated as though I had really suffered the terrible serpent bite, excision, and cauterization which I had imagined with such vivid power in my dream. So, Venitia, my rubies did not save me from that dream trouble, you see."

"Ah," answered the girl, with a pretty look of half superstition, half playfulness, "but in your ring the rubies surround the ill-omened opal, — that unlucky gem that brings the wearer disappointment and fallacious hope."

And thus closed our midnight talk.

HUMAN FAME.

ALKING of the Toledo crowd, "what a sight it is to be sure," as Mrs. Folham says. Every clear morning we drive through it, getting out of the carriage occasionally to hunt up old buildings, or spend an hour or two looking at the wonderful things contained in the Museo Borbonico. The bronzes, and marbles, and pictures, and precious relics of "those palimpsests of Nature,"—as Heine so finely called Herculaneum and Pompeii,—"where the original old stone text is brought out,"—these are all safely deposited in the fine halls of this building, and displayed there with striking effect.

But most often we go and study in the churches; for study indeed it is, to hunt up the old tombs and monumental marbles contained in them, and link correctly together the double and treble chain of the artist who carved the story, of the man who lived it, and the full period of history which rounded it into a whole.

Persons who visit Naples are hardly aware of the vast amount of sepulchral wealth contained in her churches. They are lined and floored and almost roofed with tombs, sarcophagi, statues, bas-reliefs, and stone chests, covered with fine old monumental sculpture, the works of the artists of the fourteenth and fifteenth centuries. We go again and again to certain favorite ones. Santa Chiara, for example, is an unexplored mine of curious beauty and wealth. The old pulpit and bas-reliefs overhanging the western entrance are fine leaves, as it were, in the history of Middle-Age sculpture, for they are the works of the elder Masuccio, who died on the threshold of the fourteenth century (1308).

By means of ladders and glasses we examined both of these old relics. The bas-reliefs contain the whole of the beautiful legend of that learned and saintly woman, St. Catharine of Alexandria, — she whose history has inspired so many great artists. The daughter of a king, and renowned for her beauty, her learning, and her pride, when a mighty prince asked her in marriage, she refused him, saying she would take no one as her husband unless as noble, as rich, and as wise as herself.

Some time after, her mother, the queen, sent her to see a holy hermit, who, having promised her a spouse that should be not only her equal, but far exceeding her in rank and all beauty of mind and body, then showed her a tablet on which was traced an image of the Mother of God, holding her Son in her arms. The princess returned home, and dreamed that the figures she had seen on the tablet came to her, as if alive; and when she went to receive the lovely Child, he turned from her, saying she was not beautiful enough.

Through her mother's prayers, and the intercession of the hermit, she was secretly converted to Christianity; then again she had a vision, and in it Christ's Mother came to her with her Holy Infant, who held a ring in his little hand, and the royal maiden was wedded to him with that ring, which the Child put on her finger.

All the principal passages in her life are told with

touching simplicity in these bas-reliefs. Her first visit to the hermit, her visions, her mystic marriage, her great dispute with the learned heathen doctors, her scourging, exposure to the wheel, and the angel of God breaking it to pieces, her martyrdom, — each one is sculptured with curious grace. They seem uncouth and rude to some eyes. Venitia, for example, sees no beauty in them; on the contrary, she considers them barbarous and frightful. But to Janet and me they unveil all the lovely thought and feeling which lie folded up in them, as the many-hued petals of the flower in the green bud-sheath.

The secret is, we love the old masters who lived in the early ages of art; we reverence their labors and their memory. These are the master-keys of entrance into the closed chambers of Art's mansion. Some one has beautifully said: "These old sculptures and frescoes remind one of the beneficent fairies, who appear disguised as withered hags, and bestow diamonds and pearls on the discreet maidens who accost them with reverence."

These bas-reliefs of Masuccio I., rude and unattractive as they may seem to modern eyes, have served, as Spenser said of Chaucer, as a "well of *sculpture* undefiled"* for great artists. The famous Florentine painter, Masaccio (1402 – 1443), one of the great founders of a dynasty in art, whose age was an epoch, who had his successors hailing from him like a mighty emperor, and whose frescoes greatly influenced Leonardo da Vinci, Raphael, and Michael Angelo, not only studied, but borrowed freely from them for his frescoes at Rome in San Clemente. When we go from such old works to a church filled with modern sculpture, such as the Santa Maria della Pieta de' Sangri, with its figures covered

* "Well of English undefiled."

with veils and nets, — feats of skill rather than fruits of genius, — it is like passing from fresh, pure, mountain air, into the oppressive atmosphere of a conservatory.

After seeing these bas-reliefs, we never rested until we had hunted up all we could find of Masuccio's works. We left Santa Chiara without examining the beautiful royal tombs sculptured by his nephew, Masuccio II.; they must take another day of study, we said, and we drove off to the cathedral to find his labors there.

The cathedral or Duomo building was designed by him for Charles of Anjou, in 1272. The troubles arising out of the "Sicilian Vespers" (1282), which cost Charles the central gem of his newly-acquired crown, Sicily, prevented both king and architect from seeing it completed; it was finished, however, by his nephew, the younger Masuccio, during the reign of Robert the Wise, grandson of Charles of Anjou (1316).

Several earthquakes damaged the original edifice so much as to require frequent rebuildings; thus its original character is nearly destroyed, little remaining of Masuccio's work except the four lofty towers in the centre of which the architect placed the church. It is a Latin cross, with a nave and two aisles. There are one hundred and eighteen columns in these aisles, of Oriental or Egyptian granite, and African and Cipollino marble, taken by Masuccio I. from the ruins of the temples of Neptune and Apollo, on whose site the cathedral was built. The baptismal font at the entrance, over which we lingered, is a beautiful antique vase, of Egyptian basalt, with a porphyry pedestal, and sculptured with Bacchanalian masks, thyrsus, and festoons of ivy, showing that it must have been a lustral basin in one of the old temples.

Not wishing to have our chains of dates hopelessly tangled, we did not stop to look at the numberless points of attraction which beckoned to us at every footstep, but proceeded to the Minutoli chapel, to see the tribune, or Gothic altar, and crucifix, with its statues of the Virgin and St. John, which are said to be by Masuccio I., though Lord Lindsay attributes these statues to his friend Pietro de' Stefani.

Under the tribune of this chapel is inserted the tomb of the Archbishop Filippo Minutoli, by another of Masuccio's pupils, Bamboccio. I should not have noticed it, but Janet, with roguish eyes dancing merrily, said, pointing to it: —

"O, those naughty, wicked poets! How their bright fun intrudes into these sacred places! Look, Ottilie. This is the very sarcophagus Boccaccio describes in his story of the Jockey of Perugia.* This fellow, Andreuccio by name, came here with two robbers, the night after the Archbishop was buried, to steal a ruby ring of great value which was said to be on his finger. They made a cat's-paw of Andreuccio; but he was more cunning than puss in the fable, for although they frightened him into entering the sarcophagus while they lifted the lid, they could not make him give up the ring. After he found it, he secreted it, and declared it was not there. They did not believe him, of course, and became so provoked that they let the lid fall, and left him, half dead with fright, shut up with the dead body. But they had scarcely gone, when another set of robbers, headed by a naughty priest, entered this chapel on the same errand. They lifted the lid, propped it up, and the priest entered the sarcophagus boldly. Andreuccio said not a word, but gave a furious

* Decam, Giorn. II. Nov. V.

gripe on his leg, and the priest, being suddenly seized with faith, howled from terror. Making a desperate effort, he broke loose from the Evil One, as he supposed, and rushed off, with his three companions, as if demons were pursuing them. Andreuccio quietly stepped out of the sarcophagus with the ring, left the chapel and the cathedral, and walked straight out of Naples; the next day he was hard on his way to Perugia. Are you shocked, my dear? Well, never mind, I will stop remembering these wild, wicked, witty stories; though, I assure you, your half-serious, half-amused look is very provocative. You know you enjoy them."

Of course I laughed heartily at the Boccaccio interlude, and replied: —

"I do not object to hearing it. Boccaccio, with all his naughtiness, was, I fancy, a better believer than many more straight-laced persons. In his day, faith had a living, breathing existence. The poet loved his Church so dearly, and believed it to be so true a thing, that he dared to take liberties with its objectionable accessories. He did not feel afraid of hurting that which he held as immortal, and above all harm. But let us go see the crucifix in the Caracciole Pesquizi chapel; that is another work of Masuccio II."

While looking at it, a longing took possession of us to see the miraculous crucifix that spoke to St. Thomas Aquinas, and which is preserved in the Church of San Domenico Maggiore; supposed by many to have been made by Masuccio I., and by others to be the work of his unknown master, that aged artist of the semi-Byzantine succession, whose fame, but not his name, is faintly whispered down through Time's long, dark corridor. We drove to San Domenico Maggiore, and had a long and patient search for it; at last we found it, hanging over the main altar of the Capellone del Crocifisso, — Chapel of the Crucifix, — a small side church attached to the main building.

"Now I am no Catholic," said Janet, as we stood in reverential silence before this wonderful old painting, "but I can never look unmoved on such relics as these; they stir up my whole being; mind and fancy both begin to work. How beautiful the story of this crucifix is, Ottilie. Before it the learned monk St. Thomas Aquinas studied and prayed; and after he had finished his great theological work, the *Summa*, he fell down humbly before this, offering up himself and his labors to the Lord. The scene took place on this identical spot, the sacristan says; at all events, it could not have been far off. While the 'Angelic Doctor,' as men called him, lay prostrate in prayer, one of the brethren entering, Dominick Caserte, beheld the holy man lifted from the ground in ecstasy, and heard a voice from the crucifix saying tenderly and soothingly, 'Bene scripsisti de me, Thoma; quam mercedem accipies?' And the great Father of the Thomists answered meekly, 'Non aliam nisi te, Domine.'" *

After a little pause, Janet, who was bubbling over with Montaigne's sparkling *folle de logis*, — "bright nonsense and humor full of wisdom," as some one has prettily translated this quaint old expression, — said: —

"I must tell you another droll story, Ottilie; not a naughty one, but very *apropos*. Let us leave this sacred old place, and go into that long hall of the sacristy we passed so hurriedly through a little while ago. We can sit down in those old oaken stalls, under the crimson

* "Thou hast written well of me, Thomas; what recompense wilt thou receive?" — "No other than thyself, O Lord."

chests in which rest the dust and ashes of the Aragonese dynasty."

Three sides of this sacristy corridor to which Janet alluded have rows of coffins on narrow shelves, near the ceiling, covered with faded crimson velvet; on them are the effigies of a sceptre and crown, telling us of the high birth and royal rank of those who were laid away there to sleep, before our western continent was discovered.

It was the third royal burial-place we had been in that morning. Two were of the Anjou family, which governed Naples from 1266 to 1435. Over the principal entrance of the cathedral we had seen the marble chest or tomb of Charles of Anjou, the founder of the house, the brother of St. Louis of France (1266 – 1285). At Santa Chiara we had left abruptly the famous and beautiful monumental tomb of his grandson, Robert the Wise (1309 – 1343). Now we seated ourselves under the remains of the poor descendants, as they claimed to be, of that Manfred Dante sang,* and of those glorious Hohenstaufen Barbarossas whose deeds in the Middle Ages history loves to dwell on (1194 – 1266).

With the last one of these unhappy Aragonese princes the romantic Middle Ages ended. Naples, too, ceased to be a kingdom, and for nearly three hundred years swung back into the humble state of a Spanish and German possession (1496).

These wooden coffins, with their shabby velvet and tarnished gilt ornaments, tell as well as history does of the ruin of the house. In Sicily, costly sculptured marbles and precious porphyry columns commemorate the resting-places of the Suabian Hohenstaufens, from whom these illegitimate Aragonese were descended. Crumbling

* Dante's Purgatorio, III. 112.

wood and decaying finery point out gloomily the end of the reigning Neapolitan branch. Illegitimate and unfortunate, it was time for it to cease.

The sacristan demurred a little when we seated ourselves in the oaken stalls for a comfortable chat; but, telling him we wished to rest awhile, and giving him "that metall," as old Froissart says, "whereby love is attayned both of gentlemen and poor soldiers," he left us undisturbed, and Janet told her story: —

"After I repeated that dear old legend of St. Thomas Aquinas and the miraculous crucifix, and was thinking how many persons would laugh at it, an anecdote flashed into my mind. The winter after the war with Mexico was over, I met an American gentleman in Paris, who told it to me, and vouched for its truth. This is it. In one of the battles during the war, a colonel was severely and dangerously wounded; he was taken to a neighboring hacienda to be nursed. This hacienda, or plantation, was some distance up in the country, and its master, a wealthy Mexican, had lived on it all his days. He was a gentlemanly, pleasant person, and did all he could to make the stranger comfortable. After some delay and doubt, the colonel was pronounced out of danger, but his convalescence was slow. The Mexican showed him every courtesy. As the invalid grew better, and as the host was a tolerably intelligent man, the two gentlemen naturally fell into conversation over their wine and cigars.

"The Mexican loved to hear his guest tell of the various improvements modern science had made in the machines and engines used for manufactures and commerce by men in that outer world of which he knew so little. Born and brought up on his hacienda, quite out of the reach of modern books and journals, he was entirely in the dark as to all these things. So the American officer, being a fluent and graphic talker, described, agreeably to his host, the steam-engine and its various uses, and many other wonders, which sounded to the Mexican as marvellous and much more exciting than his holy legends and church miracles. He listened to his guest with a childlike faith that was interesting, never doubting a word he said.

"One beautiful moonlight evening, they were walking the full length of the long gallery surrounding the house, smoking, and enjoying the freshness of the air after a heavy thunder-shower. The lightning still played in some clouds along the horizon, and, as the colonel looked at it, he commenced describing to the Mexican the electric telegraph. The profound silence of his host made him more earnest; he grew even eloquent, and gave a glowing account of its discovery, application, and use. When he arrived at the close, noticing that his host did not ask the usual questions, he said, 'Is it not wonderful?'

"'Yes,' answered the Mexican coldly, taking his cigar from his mouth, and leaning his back against a pillar of the high gallery. 'It is very wonderful. Everything you have been relating to me, Colonel, is wonderful. But I will tell you what is more wonderful still, your powers of invention. I have been listening to you now for some time, not only enjoying your fine conversation, but believing with the innocence of a child all the great things you have been describing. I might have known they were fables, but I did not; nor should I have suspected you, if you had not created this last story. Now I know that they are all untrue.'

"It was useless for the colonel to assure his incredulous

host; he never gained any credence after that last great demand on his faith. I often think of this story when I hear the marvellous old legends which have come down to us from that saintly age when sweet Faith was what Science is now, the sovereign ruler of men's minds and hearts. The world was benighted then, according to modern views, — the Dark Ages! And yet that blessed sun of Faith must have thrown lovely lights. Now it is twilight; and our lamps of Science show us that the branches, and leaves, and ground are not pure gold, as those beautiful rays made them appear; but it seems we walk darkly, notwithstanding all our lamps and all our knowledge."

Before leaving the sacristy, we stopped to look at one of the coffin-chests resting on a balustrade against the wall. Above it was a portrait of a fine soldierly-looking man, in a Franciscan habit, with a banner and a sword. As with one thought, we both exclaimed, "Francis Pescara, O unconquered peer!"* It was the tomb and portrait of the celebrated Ferdinando Francesco d' Avalos, Marchese di Pescara, who died, in the flower of his age, of the wounds received at the battle of Pavia (1525), after contributing greatly to the capture of Francis I. He was the husband of Vittoria Colonna, the woman who was adored by Michael Angelo, and reverenced by Ariosto, and all the great men of her day. The conjugal love between Francesco d' Avalos and Vittoria has always been a subject of comment and admiration. When he was taken prisoner at Ravenna (1512) by the French, he addressed to her a beautiful dialogue on love.

Vittoria was only thirty-three when she lost him; and though living many years after, and wooed and wor-

* Ariosto's Orlando Furioso, Cant. 37, Stan. 20, Rose's trans.

shipped by poets, artists, and famous men, she remained true to her husband's memory. She was a gifted poetess, as well as a beautiful and virtuous woman; and sung her love, her loss, and her sorrow, over on that island of Ischia, in lines that won not only Ariosto's praise,* but gained her the title of "Divine" from her contemporaries.

It is true Aretino calumniated the wife, and Guicciardini said very harsh things of the husband; but the historian must have been blinded by political prejudice; and as for the infamous Aretino, as a witty Italian said, "he satirized every one except God, whom he spared only because he did not know him."

So we stood a little while before the coffin-chest and portrait, remembering only the beautiful things which had been said and believed of this great general and his noble wife; for the woman graced with Michael Angelo's love and reverence, and the man adorned with Ariosto's praise and friendship, could not have been wanting in honor and excellence.

The next day we returned to Santa Chiara to look at the royal tombs which we had left so abruptly the day before. They were sculptured by the nephew and successor of Masuccio I. This Masuccio the younger was patronized by Robert the Wise, Charles of Anjou's grandson, he who afterwards gave royal favor and reception to Giotto and Dante, Petrarch and Boccaccio, for he had a long and a prosperous reign.

When the king and the architect were young, they labored together for God's and Art's service, in completing the cathedral, which had been commenced by the grandfather of the one and the uncle of the other, as I have

* Ariosto's Orlando Furioso, Cant. 37, Stan. 16 *et seq.*

mentioned before. Then when the young king had passed early manhood, and reached his first grief, — the death of his only son, the Duke of Calabria, — Robert sent for his favorite artist to come and sculpture a fitting monument for this beloved child, who had lain down to sleep just as manhood was beginning.

Masuccio sculptured a beautiful sarcophagus to the memory of the prince, and laid the stone image of the young man on top of it, clothed in royal robes, which are spotted with *fleurs de lis.* On his head is a crown, and two angels draw aside the veil from the body. A bas-relief in front represents the young Duke as a sovereign, surrounded by his court; at his feet are a wolf and a lamb drinking together at a fountain, emblematical of the peace and good-will which would have resulted from his justice. Columns supported by lions uphold the sarcophagus, and the whole is placed in a recess to the right of the main altar, which recess is a lofty Gothic arch.

After Masuccio II. had finished this work, he showed to the king a design which he had made for a monument to be placed over Robert when he lay down to rest beside his child. The king was pleased with it, but said "it was too magnificent for a man of little merit in the sight of God." But after some years the good king died, and his lovely but unfortunate granddaughter, Joanna I., commanded the sculptor to erect it to the memory of that beloved grandfather who had reared her so tenderly, as the only child of his darling son, and left her such a perilous inheritance as a kingdom. Poor queen! All the sorrow which her young father escaped by his early death must have been held back in store for her, as she had more than double the anguish that falls to the lot of mortals, even when grievously afflicted.

On approaching the church, we tarried awhile in the close, to look at the Campanile, also said to be a work of Masuccio II. It remains unfinished, as Robert the Wise died before its third story was completed. Masuccio's design gave it five stories, each bearing one of the five orders. The arrangement of the capitals on the third or Ionic story is attributed to Michael Angelo.

Upon entering the church, to our vexation we found the place around the high altar and tombs filled with persons preparing for a grand fête. There were ladders leaning near the gaudy modern altar, which stands in front of one of the tombs, and upholsterers on scaffolding, hanging rich draperies of crimson, sewn with gold. We feared we were to be baffled, but Janet and I are equally pertinacious; so, by a judicious and generous application of old Froissart's "rare metall," we secured even a better view than we could have had on any other day, for they allowed us to mount the ladders and walk on the scaffolding; thus we got so close to the upper parts of the sculpture, that we stood face to face with the marble effigies, and touched them with our hands.

They are fine specimens of Gothic beauty, when we remember the early age in which they were done (1350). The modern altar stands in front of and hides King Robert's tomb. It is a stately pile of marble, full thirty-five feet high. The king is seated on his throne, clad in royal robes; he lies extended also on the sarcophagus, wrapped in the monkish habit which he assumed a few weeks before his death, — the Franciscan gown. There are apostles, saints, and various other emblematical figures distributed around the tomb. Every part is conscientiously worked; the back, which is far away from sight, is just as perfect as the front; and, as I stood on a swaying ladder, I passed my hands around the decorations of the royal chair and upper part of the monument, and found that nothing was left incomplete, all was as perfect as if intended for the most exposed part of the tomb. The artist had worked for himself and Art's holy service. On the tomb is this line, which is said to be by Petrarch: —

CERNITE . ROBERTVM . REGEM . VIRTVTE . REFERTVM.

On our return home, we stopped at Detken's, and were lucky enough to find a copy of Cicognara's Revival of Arts in Italy, in the first volume of which is an engraving of the tomb of the Duke of Calabria, Robert's son. I cannot pretend to do justice to either of these stately and beautiful tombs; but if ever monumental art should revive, become again a living work, and there should be Pre-Angelites in sculpture as there are now Pre-Raphaelites in painting, Naples will be their Mecca.

While at Detken's, I purchased a book, which I am reading with great interest, — General Colletta's History of Naples, which is the popular one of the day, especially among liberalists. It was recommended to us by "that vigorous-minded little person, Mrs. Rochester," as Mrs. Folham, with true English expression, calls our agreeable Ambassadress. Indeed, it was through her husband's kindness that I obtained the work, as it is, of course, a forbidden book; he ordered it for me from Paris, through Detken; and, being for the American Ambassador, no questions were asked.

Mrs. Rochester, by the way, is really full of intelligence and *esprit;* as clever in mind as a man, and naïve as a gay girl. Her social position, with its attendant duties, she being "La Doyenne," or eldest resident of the diplomatic circle, separates her a little from our daily course; but she loves nothing better than to throw off the trammels of her position once in a while, and enjoy what she calls "true life" with us. She has lived in Naples several years, and is quite familiar with the country and its history in its various remarkable phases, — its classic, mediæval, and modern, — so that with her assistance, added to our own previous and continued studies, we find out nearly all we wish to know.

She told me a curious story about this Colletta book. General Colletta, its author, was an officer in the Engineers, who served under Murat, and distinguished himself. In 1820, after the return of Ferdinand I., he was banished from Naples. He went to Florence, and soon found his way into the literary and political society of the Palazzo Buondalmonte.

Now I must make a little digression to explain what this Palazzo Buondalmonte was. It was literally a great literary workshop, belonging to a Genevese, Jean Pierre Viesseaux. In 1820 he took this palazzo, and divided it off to suit his purposes. On the ground-floor he put his printing-presses; on the next was a circulating library, of great extent, with magazines, reviews, and journals from every part of Europe spread out on the tables, — a public reading-room. The upper stories were devoted to his editors, press-correctors, secretaries, clerks, in short all the staff of an extensive publishing business. The *Anthologie*, a review something like the *Revue des Deux Mondes*, was published by him. When it had reached its thirteenth year, it was suppressed to gratify the Czar of Russia, who thought it had treated him and his affairs too familiarly in one of its numbers. Cavour was one of its contributors, when Predari was its editor, somewhere near 1846 or 1847.

But to return to the Palazzo. Its reading-saloon has always been the rendezvous of the literary and political men of the day. Giordani, Nicolini, Leopardi, Pœrio, and many other Italian notorieties, could be found there. A gentleman carrying a letter of introduction to M. Viesseaux would always receive an invitation to his Thursday *réunion* of artists and savants. He was a generous and intelligent publisher, not only helping authors to means, but to fame.* His encouragement and good advice developed General Colletta into an historian, for he felt a great sympathy as well as friendship for the old man.

* Viesseaux had some happy days at the close of his long life. In 1859 he completed his eightieth year, on which occasion his friends presented him with a gold medal, bearing his profile and this simple legend: —

Per quarant' anni benemerito
Dell' Italiana Civiltà
Compriva l' Oltantesimo della Vita
Il 29 Settembre 1859.

Before he died the old man had the satisfaction of seeing his friends who had been disgraced and persecuted for politics' sake high in favor, and foremost in rank, — Peruzzi twice in power, Ricasoli at the summit. The great work was accomplished, the dream verified, and Viesseaux could sing the canticle of old Simeon, and go to sleep in triumph.

One morning in 1863, Victor Emmanuel arrived in Florence, and Viesseaux seemed to have grown sixty years younger. His serene joy burst out into youthful gayety. He invited relatives and friends to reunite at his house the next day, and rejoice with him over the attainment of National Unity. But on that very evening the old man was stricken down with apoplexy, from which blow he never arose, and the 30th of the same month a funeral procession from a mourning city followed the remains of this great publisher to the Protestant cemetery of Florence.

Up to his last moments he retained his faculties and mental strength. His correspondence extended over two hemispheres, and was with high and low. M. Marc-Monnier, from whose article in the *Revue Germanique*, 1 July, 1863, the facts in this note are taken, mentions that he has upwards of twenty letters from Viesseaux, written just before his death, the handwriting of which is firm and clear.

Soon after Colletta became a *habitué* of the Palazzo Buondalmonte, finding his companions were all great authors, a natural spirit of emulation made him desire to be one also. And two greater reasons than mere ambition impelled him, — a need of support, and an earnest desire to tell his country's story, which he felt he knew by heart better than any one else. The brave old soldier had never read a book in his life but Tacitus. This was nothing. He resolved to write his nation's history, taking up the thread where Giannone had stopped, and continuing it up to 1825; for, he thought, in that period the causes of many present evils could be found, the palliation of many sins discovered, and, from them, future help and improvement be obtained. So he set to work boldly.

When he brought the manuscript of his first volume to his literary friends at the Palazzo Buondalmonte, to his extreme mortification they condemned it. Leopardi, it is said, even discouraged him from continuing. The style was stiff and diffuse, the stories prolix and dull.

But the kind, good publisher would not listen to his giving up the work. He encouraged him, and roused anew the old man's flagging energy. Accordingly, the brave soldier set to work again courageously from the very beginning.

"Write your story as you tell it; that 's all," said the practical Viesseaux.

And he did. He tore up the stilted pages of the first volume, and put down on paper his own simple, but fiery and rapid words. He recast the whole work, and grouped facts with soldierly precision together. The result was a striking, well-written narrative, that was applauded highly by the very ones who had condemned the first attempt.

Viesseaux did not think it prudent to publish the book

in Florence, so he sent it to Geneva to be brought out. The good old man, like Byron, awoke one fine day and found himself famous. The free tone of the work delighted the large body of Liberalists throughout reading Europe; and the book was gladly received, as it contained just the information everybody wished to know. But its stern condemnation of the poor Bourbons created a great alarm and enmity. The good-natured Grand Duke found himself forced to banish the author from Florence, even before his work had appeared in the city.

But the order of exile, and the fame, and the worldly prosperity arrived nearly too late. When the officer came to deliver the Grand Duke's message, he found the poor old man in bed, dying.

"Ask his Highness," said Colletta, "to grant me the delay of a few hours. In that time I shall have departed for an exile where no police will trouble me again."

A little while after, the stout-hearted old soldier lay stiff and dead. He never had the gratification of seeing his fine History in print; but the coming sound of its future fame reached his dying ears, and, I hope, it gave him much peace and content.

"NOBILE OZIO."

APLES is the very place in which one can best enjoy Machiavelli's *nobile ozio,* — "a noble idleness of delightful society, with classical associations, under a heaven of beauty."

The weather is delicious just on the threshold of May, — a pleasant season in most countries, but in this paradise particularly lovely.

> "Soft, silken hours,
> Open suns, shady bowers;
> 'Bove all, nothing which lowers."

I have already told how we spend our mornings. Late in the afternoon we drive on the Chiaja, and out to Posilippo, or loiter through the long alleys of the Villa Reale, which, "with its ever green groups of holm-oaks and laurels, its fountains and sculptures, its temples sacred to Virgil and Tasso, lies along the shore of the Mediterranean like a string of emeralds." *

Sometimes the morning's occupation keeps us out so late that we feel indifferent about the drive to the Posilippean hills; then we meet on the terrace, to enjoy the sunset, and watch the stream of elegant equipages rolling along the smooth lava pavement of the Chiaja and Mergellina, and look at the groups of idlers lying down or

* De Reumont.

sauntering about, — the thriftless, do-nothing Neapolitan masses.

Over on the Mergellina bank are crowds of fishermen and boatmen, preparing for a sail or row, either to take a party of pleasure or to follow their fishing trade. This Mergellina beach is their only home; they know no other; here are their children playing in the pebbles and shells, their wives lounging and gossiping, and their gray-headed grandmothers spinning with the old distaff of Clotho, looking as if they were grim Fates, attending the coming destiny of this doomed land, — the fulfilment of that fearful old oracle,

"Some day, around the Siren's stony tomb,
A mighty multitude shall meet their doom."

These common people of Naples are a strange race; full of contradictions; lawless, demanding liberty even to license, and yet king-loving; a religious nation, full of faith and devotion, but quite devoid of piety. They can no longer be called Lazzaroni, for they are losing fast all claim to that title. Indeed, on a grand fête-day there is not a *lazzaro* to be found in all Naples; every man is dressed, and going as swiftly as he can on his road to the *tiers état*, or Third Estate; that is, so far as decent appearance is concerned.

General Colletta, in his History, speaks very bitterly of the origin of the name of these "Sons of Lazarus." "They," he says, meaning the Spaniards, "called them '*lazzari*' (for *lazzaroni* is only an augmentative), a word borrowed from the language of these superb tyrants of ours who insulted a misery of which they were the authors, and made its memory eternal by this name.

"A man was not born a *lazzaro*. The *lazzaro* who applied himself to a trade lost his name; and the man who lived like a beast, became a *lazzaro*. These Lazzaroni increased to an innumerable swarm; for how was it possible to take the census of such a semi-savage, vagabond population? At one time, it was believed they amounted to thirty thousand; poor, audacious, eager and greedy in robbery, and ready for every sort of disorder."

Under the Spanish vice-regal rule (1502 – 1700), which was the period of time when the Lazzaroni flourished in fullest force and vigor, this wild set had a species of government, an organization as strict as that of the thieves in the Paris *Cour de Miracles*, during the reign of Louis XI.*

Every year a chief (*capo lazzaro*) was elected, charged with the duty of defending their interests before the viceroy. One of the most famous of these *capo lazzari* was the fisherman of Amalfi, Massaniello, the chief of the great revolution in 1647.

"By the fruit judge ye the tree," says a French author, alluding to this curious clan of people. "The Lazzaroni were the fruit of the Spanish vice-regal government. Naples has often been reproached with the shame of having produced this race of white negroes. This reproach is unjust. The plant flowered and bore fruit at Naples, it is true, but the seed came from Spain. The Spaniards carried it into Italy as their garrisons and vessels have so often taken the plague there."

This Spanish vice-regal government was the saddest and most injurious rule in its effect that could have been inflicted upon a people; it lasted two hundred years (1500 – 1700). Spain held Naples all this time by virtue of a right derived from Ferdinand the Catholic, who was the legitimate representative of that Aragonese house which

* *Notre Dame de Paris*, of Victor Hugo.

traced its genealogy back to Constance, the daughter of the great Roger of Sicily, daughter-in-law, wife, and mother of the three famous Barbarossas of the "splendid Suabian house of Hohenstaufen" (1194 - 1250), — she whom history and poesy has contributed to make immortal.

> "quest' è la luce della gran Gostanza
> Che del secondo vento di Soave
> Generò il terzo, e l' ultima possanza." *

I will turn back the pages of history rapidly to repeat over the story of the kings of Naples deposed by Ferdinand the Catholic in 1500. Those poor crumbling coffin-chests, covered with faded velvet and adorned with tarnished tinsel, which we saw the other day in the Sacristy of San Domenico Maggiore, hold the remains, as I mentioned then, of the illegitimate branch of the family which came in possession of the throne in this way.

Joanna II. (1414 - 1435), great-great-granddaughter of Charles of Anjou, left as one of her heirs Alfonso, king of Sicily, the descendant of that Hohenstaufen family just alluded to, from whom her ancestor, Charles of Anjou, had wrested the kingdom of Naples (1266).

This king of Sicily, called in history the Magnanimous, reigned in Naples until 1458. When he died, Sicily reverted to his brother, John II., king of Aragon and Navarre, father of Ferdinand the Catholic; and Naples also should have gone to him, but Alfonso had a natural son, Ferdinand, who had been legitimated by Pope Calixtus III., fourteen years before his father's death, and to him Alfonso left the crown of Naples.

* "Great Constance' light is this; who to the blast
Which second came from Suabia's kingdom, bore
The mighty power that proved the third and last."
Dante's *Paradiso*, III. 118, Wright's trans.

From 1458 to 1490 this illegitimate branch held Naples, when the last one, Ferdinand, Prince of Almatura, was expelled by the son of John II., king of Aragon and Navarre, who had succeeded to his father's dominions and claims. This son is well known in history; he was Ferdinand the Catholic, husband of Isabella of Castile, — Columbus's queen, — representative of the old Suabian Hohenstaufens, and grandfather of the Emperor Charles V.

After some contests between Ferdinand and Louis XII. of France, arising out of the Partition Treaty of Granada (November 11, 1500), in 1504 the kingdom of Naples became, like Sicily, a Spanish province or possession.

The "Great Captain," Gonsalvo de Cordova, whose military skill and success had secured this rich kingdom to his royal master, Ferdinand of Aragon and Castile, was the first Spanish viceroy (1504). With him commenced this unhappy rule of Spanish viceroys in Naples, the injurious effect of which can be seen to this day, for they oppressed the people with taxes, and degraded the nobility by encouraging them in vice and extravagance.

Among these viceroys, however, some honorable exceptions can be found; for instance, Don Pedro de Toledo, who was the father-in-law of Cosmo de' Medici, first Grand Duke of Tuscany, and representative of Charles V. (1532 - 1552). Over three centuries have passed since this vice-regal sovereign held rule in Naples, and yet the impression remains sharper in its outline and deeper in its stamp than the rule of any later governor or king, except Don Carlos, the founder of the present Spanish Bourbon family (Charles VII., son of Philip V. of Spain, and his queen, Elizabetta Farnese of Parma, 1734).

In walking through the streets of Naples, and visiting its public buildings, we find that these two men, Don Pedro and Don Carlos, stand out prominent as almost fathers and founders of the place. Their respective eras are two hundred years apart; but the traveller unites the two in his mind, and wishes this beautiful place could have been blessed with a long line of such wise and just rulers; then would the peninsula have been a governmental reality instead of a mere "geographical expression."

"No ruler," says De Reumont,* "ever had such despotic power, or exercised as great an influence over the fate of Italy as this first Toledo. He governed the Neapolitans for their own benefit, and not for the king of Spain only. He treated the people with so much favor, and the depraved nobility with such severity, that the barons offered the Emperor a million and a half of ducats to relieve them from his *surveillance*."

But that Emperor was Charles V., who, although he was one of those "great royal devourers of the people," ate them after a generous, soldierly fashion. He was a wise prince, so far as kingcraft was concerned; he knew Toledo's value, his fitness for his place, and paid no attention to the complaints urged against him.

So Don Pedro reigned twenty years, and steadily built up for himself and his descendants fame and fortune, as he thought. In the most enviable and beautiful principality in all Italy, — Tuscany, — he placed one of his daughters, the unhappy wife and mother, Eleanor de Toledo, Duchess of Cosmo de' Medici, first Grand Duke (1537 - 1574). But what matter if sin and sorrow and

* "Carafas of Maddaloni, Naples under Spanish Dominion," by Alfred de Reumont.

fearful tragedies did flow in a thick-clotted red current around this Grand Duchess's daughter; the golden and purple drapery of rank and royal station enveloped her and her griefs in their gorgeous folds; was not that recompense? — Heart-breaking anguish, enough to shake her reason from its balance, crimes that make the reader of history shiver and close his eyes in disgust, and shut the chronicle with a sickening loathing, whether it be that fearful scene in the hall of the Ducal Palace, at hot noontide, which the painter Vasari saw from his scaffolding where he lay half asleep, after his ceiling fresco labors of the morning, or that of the fratricidal son clinging to the robe of his mother, — poor Eleanor de Toledo, — for protection against the uplifted and relentless dagger of his crime-stained father! O no, these were nothing when weighed in the balance with success and power!

Don Pedro neither saw nor thought of any of these sorrowful attendants on his firm, granite built grandeur. He gave this beautiful daughter a rank which was almost equal with a queen, and saw his son viceroy of Sicily; resisted Pope Paul III.; put haughty Neapolitan nobles to the torture; reformed the laws; remodelled the town; built castles and fortresses and watch-towers on all the coast around, in order to protect the country from the ravages of the Turks; opposed and prevented the establishment of the Inquisition in Naples; and this, too, in the very teeth of his royal master, Charles V., a monarch that not many men dared brave or oppose; and, through all his stern, iron, but just rule, kept the confidence and favor of this master, and held also his almost kingly office from middle age up to his death.

Full of years, honor, and success was this great Don Pedro when they brought him to the palace of his daughter at Florence to die. As commander-in-chief of the emperor's forces, with his ducal son-in-law, Cosmo di Medici, serving under him, he had been enforcing submission on the Republic of Siena, the brave old man! Though threescore years and ten, he was taken from the battle-field to his death-bed, dying with the harness on (1553).

Mrs. Rochester loves this grand old Viceroy's history and memory. The other morning she took me to the Church of San Giacomo degli Spagnuoli, in the Largo del Castello, to see his tomb. This church was built by Don Pedro, in 1540, as a church for the use of Spanish soldiers. The architect was Manlio, pupil of Giovanni Merliani, or da Nola (as he was called, from his birthplace). This church, and Santa Chiara, are under the jurisdiction of the Papal Nuncio.

The tomb is the masterpiece of Giovanni da Nola, who is called also the Neapolitan Michael Angelo (1478–1559); it is covered with fine sculpturing, and surmounted by kneeling statues, full life size, of Don Pedro and his wife. It is behind the grand high altar of the church, in the place called the choir. We sat for some time in the beautifully carved stalls, and examined leisurely this fine work of monumental sculpture, while we talked together about Don Pedro's eventful, successful life.

"Soon after I came to Naples," said Mrs. Rochester, "becoming interested in this great Spaniard's history, I searched out faithfully every trace of his career. I found this tomb by chance.

"One day my friend A—— and I had been groping about down in the old quarters of the town near the sea. We had been hunting up the cloisters of Mont' Oliveto, that old garden where Tasso had mourned and held mysterious intercourse with the unseen spirit who visited him in those last sorrowful years while he was waiting for the peace and rest of death to come.

"I love to recall the morning of which I speak. A—— and I had heavy loads of trouble weighing us down at the time; but we shook them off, and were as gay as girls, while we hunted up the old gardens and cloisters. At last we found them; but they were wofully changed into a fruit and vegetable market, filthy and muddy of course. We bought apricots, figs, and green almonds; leaned against the columns of the cloisters while we ate our fruit, and listened to the screaming, shrill talk of the people around us.

"A—— contrasted these unmusical tones with the sweet sounds which had filled the place when the dying poet found tranquillity under the shadows of the trees long since dead. We bought some flowers, too, I remember, — for it was only a little later than this in spring, — June roses, in memory of those famous white and red ones which had grown in Tasso's time in this now crowded and dirty market-place, where nothing thrives but petty trade and vile dirt. Very different in that time was it, indeed, — not only for this market-place, but for everything; grand old tyrannical days were they, when, as you and A—— say, if great wrongs and great sins were committed, the acts and works of Poesy and Art were correspondingly magnificent.

"But to come back to my story, — what little I have to tell. After leaving the desecrated garden of Mont' Oliveto, we rambled through one or two of the old quarters of the town, which you know bear this day the names of the callings or trades to which they were formerly devoted, — the Guantai or Glove quarter, and the like.

About midday, we came out on this Largo del Castello, hot and tired enough, I assure you; the air from the Mole was very pleasant, and the sparkling water in the Fountain Medina was refreshing to look at. I think the jets darting up from the stone trident of Neptune, and the spouting tritons on the sea-horses in the centre of the fountain shell, never looked so beautiful to me as they did on that hot June noonday.

"On our way into the Toledo, where we intended going to rest at the nice cake-shop on the corner of the Strada Chiaja, we stumbled on this church. We were attracted by those sarcophagi in the entrance-way. A—— asked a man the name of the church. 'San Giacomo degli Spagnuoli,' was the reply.

"We were just linking Don Pedro's history together; and, tired as we were, we could not resist the temptation, like children reading a fairy-tale at bedtime, to turn over just one leaf more.

"'Here is where Don Pedro is buried,' I said. 'This is the very church we have been intending to search for. Come, let us go in for one minute at least.'

"We entered, and spent a full hour feasting on this huge sarcophagus. Look at the grand old Viceroy, — the Imperial Commander! There he kneels, opposite his young wife, — not the beautiful heiress bride of his boyhood, the one he wedded when he was only thirteen, and who brought to the favorite little page of King Ferdinand the Catholic — this second son of the ducal house of Alva — a title, a fortune, and fair sons and daughters who were born to reign and sorrow. No, not that wife: she had been dead some years, not only before her Tuscan duchess daughter wept tears of blood over incest, and fratricide, and all those shivering sins, — but also in time to give her husband another fair young wife to cheer his martial old age.

"Very meek this second wife, Donna Vicenza Spinelli, looks in that sculptured image of her. See, she is bending over her book of devotion. And then the old soldier Viceroy, bold and resolute is his air; he leans on the hilt of his sword, and gazes around with pride, as if he tasted and loved his power, — while the young wife prays. Great need for prayer there, Ottilie. For, powerful and successful as was this Don Pedro, ruin and disgrace flew fleet as hounds on the heels of his posterity. It is a superb monument, is it not?"

Mrs. Rochester then pointed out to me the bas-reliefs on its base, and read to me from her active brain and memory the sculptured history. All Toledo's proudest deeds are there recorded in stone, — his enterprise against the Turks at Otranto, his victory over Chayreddin Barbarossa, and his triumph over his enemies, after the Inquisition insurrection, when the Emperor Charles V. made his grand entry into Naples, leaning on his proud Viceroy, and saying, with grim pleasantry, "Don Pedro, you are not the fierce tyrant they have described you."

Neither of these two men indulged in pleasantry often; when they did, it was for a more serious purpose than mere mirth. Both were solemn, stern, warlike, and full of unwearying activity. Life was no holiday for them, no merry fête, but a strife for dominion and success, — a season for the planting of that sorrowful vine, climbing ambition, which yields a sad vintage, and did for the posterity of both these men, — imperial master and viceregal servant, — for their second generation drank the bitterest draughts of the blackest sorrow; from the golden cup of high station, it is true, but so bitter and black as to make the most ambitious recoil from rank and high estate, if such penalties must come with them.

Just two hundred years this vice-regal government lasted, during which time Naples was treated by Spain as another Mexico or Peru, — used and abused. Her nobles sacrificed their fortunes, and sometimes their lives, in foreign wars, — in the military service of a foreign government, — or remained at home, in idleness, deprived of all political employment and influence. The people were oppressed by taxes and degraded by the bad example set by their rulers, — the example of loose morals, not only in politics, but in their daily domestic and social life; and all that Naples gained, by having established the political succession of the Spanish house of Aragon, in 1490, were humiliations, misery, and a demoralizing servitude of two centuries, the corroding marks of which chains can be seen festering at this very day.

During these two hundred years of Spanish tyranny, two great insurrections broke out, which were remarkable for two curious things; they took place exactly a century apart, and were each headed by a popular leader bearing almost the same name.

The first one was the Inquisition revolt during the viceroyalty of Don Pedro in 1547, — the insurrection that set Tasso's father on his wanderings, by ruining his patron Ferrante Sanseverino, Prince of Salerno, teaching the poet and his father Dante's bitter experience, —

> "how salt a stranger's bread,
> How hard a path still up and down to tread
> A stranger's stairs."

The leader of the Inquisition insurrection was Tommaso Annello of Sorrento, who had not, however, the ruinous success and unhappy fate which attended the leader of the great second rebellion a hundred years after, Tomaso Anniello of Amalfi, so well known as Massaniello, a name formed by a union of the diminutive of the first name with the surname.

This second insurrection, headed by Massaniello, broke out in 1647, under the viceroyalty of the Duke d'Arcos, and was caused by the heavy weight of taxes, which had grown to be so painful a load as to make restive even the patient, good-natured Neapolitan human mule. "Everything was taxed," says De Reumont, "even the light of the sun."

This last Massaniello insurrection is famous also for having had among its rebellious numbers a little group of artists, whose names, especially one, Salvatòr Rosa, are associated more with fine works of art than patriotic street-fights. They banded together, and called themselves by the murderous name of "Compagnia della Morte," Company of the Dead. Salvator Rosa's master, Aniello Falcone, the great battle-painter, headed this little band; he was a relation of Massaniello; the cavalier Calabrese (Mattia Preti) and Mico Spadaro were also members of this company. These artists were all friends and boon companions of the unfortunate fisherman of Amalfi. Mico Spadaro's fearfully graphic pictures of this insurrection and the plague which ravaged Naples ten years later can be seen in the first room of the "Early Neapolitan School," in the Musée Borbonique; also a life-like portrait of Massaniello, smoking his pipe.

We were talking of this fearful insurrection to-day at dinner; and Janet suggested that the sudden and mysterious madness of this ill-fated *capo di Lazzari* might have been caused by that subtle power, so well known, and employed with such fearful *sang-froid* by the rulers of that day, — poison!

At last an end came to this vice-regal rule. In 1700 the Spanish or elder branch of the house of Austria ended with Charles II. of Spain. By the will of this monarch, the Spanish kingdom, with all its possessions, went to Philip, Duke of Anjou, who was his grandson and the son of Louis XIV. Philip's mother was Louis XIV.'s queen, the Spanish Infanta, Maria Theresa, daughter of Charles II. This prince ascended the Spanish throne as Philip V., the first of the Spanish house of Anjou. But, when he proceeded to continue possession of the Neapolitan part of his dominions, Leopold I. of Austria, who had married a younger daughter of Charles II., disputed his claim, presenting his son the Archduke Charles as the rightful heir, under a will of Philip IV., father of Charles II.

Then came a long war, called in history the "War of the Spanish Succession," in which figured "the crafty, uncertain, fascinating hero," Marlborough, and the high-minded, noble Prince Eugene; it lasted until 1713, when it was partially terminated by the Peace of Utrecht; but only partially, because neither of the two leading governments engaged in the war would yield its pretensions. Austria continued, however, to hold Naples until 1734, under a succession of German viceroys. Then a gallant, bold young paladin of a prince, scarcely eighteen years of age, conquered, by his sword, what he considered his birthright, the Neapolitan throne. This was the great "Don Carlos," Charles de Bourbon, founder of the Neapolitan Bourbon family, son of Philip V., by his beautiful second wife, the ambitious and clever Elizabetta Farnese of Parma.

In this chivalric young prince the Bourbon blood of France and the Aragon blood of Spain were centred.

He was one of those great breakwaters in history which seem to rise up suddenly while the waves of political events are sweeping noisily and confusingly on, as if created for the occasion, either to stem and check the tide of some overwhelming chaos of rebellion run riot, or to establish a new dynasty.

There was no reason why this young Bourbon prince should not have been one of the same royal figure-heads that had preceded him in the Spanish family. In his veins ran the same *sang azur*, and he had fed on the same white bread. But Nature needed a man, and it suited her waywardness and caprice just then to toss the soul of a conqueror and a hero into a royal cradle, instead of a *bourgeoise* bed.

His life was one of those military romances common to the close of the eighteenth and opening of the nineteenth centuries; since then Europe has relapsed into the old way of statecraft and policy, and has more heroes of tools and protocols than heroes of the sword. While reading his dazzling career we seem to be transported to mediæval times, even to that far-off Norman era of his ancestors, commemorated by the Monk of Monte Cassino,* when the "forty valiant pilgrims appeared in the world, a thousand years after our Saviour's death"; — the Boemond and Tancred of Tasso's song, and Robert of Guiscard, and the great King Roger of Sicily, who conquered the fair Neapolitan dominions from "Paynim dog," just by way of employing their swords, for "they were on their road home from Jerusalem," says the old cloistered chronicler, "where they had been to worship Jesus Christ"; and, as their vessels came up the Tyrrhenian sea, and

* *L' Ystoire de Normant, etc.; par Aimé, Moine du Mont Cassin, publiée par M. Champollion-Figeac.* Paris, 1835.

they neared the lovely coast of Salerno, they found their old enemy the "Paynim dog" at his favorite work of oppressing Christians; so they tarried, and unsheathed their swords, delivered their brother Christians from "horrid heathen rule," and gave them, in lieu of it, their own adventuring selves for masters.

One of these heroes, King Roger, was an ancestor of the young Don Carlos de Bourbon; and it may be, his ambitious, beautiful young mother had fed his mind, in boyhood, with these stories from old historic legend,—monkish chronicle and poet's song,—for surely no ordinary mental food had nourished such a youth. At eighteen years of age the boy-conqueror was crowned at Palermo; ten years after, in 1744, when only twenty-eight, he routed the Austrians at Velletri, and expelled them from his kingdom; and, at the Congress of Aix-la-Chapelle (1748), Europe acknowledged him as Charles VII.,* King of the Two Sicilies.

For twenty-five years Don Carlos reigned wisely over Naples. But the romance was not ended then.

> "Glamis, and thane of Cawdor:
> The greatest is behind."

When only a little over forty, he succeeded to the Spanish throne of his ancestor, Charles V., by the death of his half-brother, Ferdinand VI. This succession requiring that the king should reside in Spain, Don Carlos gave up the Neapolitan part of his dominions to his third son, Ferdinand I.,—as he is counted in the Neapolitan Bourbon house,—who was only eight years old at the

* He was Charles VII. of Naples, in order of succession, and by the Bull of Investiture of Pope Clement XII.; but he is generally called Charles III. by the Neapolitans, because that was his title on the Spanish throne.

time (1759). Don Carlos had commenced life so early himself, I fancy he did not think the boy too young; but Nature had stopped her grand work in that quarter, and the succeeding Ferdinands of Naples have relapsed into the old mould of royal figure-heads.

A succession of such kings as Charles III. would have ameliorated many of the national ills; but this lovely peninsula seems to have been born in that unlucky day-dawn of nations just as

"Pale Hecate, star of the sorceress,"

was flying before the spirits of the new revelation, and her angry eye of malediction fell upon this fated land; for, as we look back upon its history, we see but a succession of short-lived promises of good, followed by long seasons of misrule and misfortune.

During Charles III.'s reign a new element entered political life, — the Bourgeois, or *Tiers État*, — which then took position and rank. To be sure, under the Spanish vice-regal government, the throb of this great social pulse could be seen by the appearance of such men as the lawyer and historian Giannone, the jurisconsult Gravina, — Metastasio's beloved patron and friend, — and the professor and rhetorician Vico; but these were exceptions, and not a class, as now. The effect of this new element, which has been steadily working for years, is now showing itself, not only in Naples, but all over the peninsula, and will cause material changes both in the governments and the people before long. In the present day, however, this same *Tiers État* is a very necessary element in all European states. As Janet said to-day: "It gives the backbone to all the new governments of this old continent."

The history of Naples since the reign of "Don Carlos"

is short and inglorious. During the minority of the young king, the government was directed by that wise minister of Charles III., Bernard Tanucci; but, though he ruled well over the country, he left one duty unperformed, the proper training of his royal ward.

When this young Ferdinand I. reached the age of seventeen, — a year younger than his great father was at the period of his crowning at Palermo, — he completed his minority, and the following year married an Austrian archduchess. This archduchess, Maria Carolina, was the unworthy daughter of Maria Theresa, the unwomanly sister of Maria Antoinette, the fit friend of the infamous Lady Hamilton, and the bad queen of a weak husband.

Ferdinand allowed her to assume the control, for she had the same desire for rule which characterized her mother, but she lacked Maria Theresa's ability. Her first exercise of power was the dismissing of Tanucci; and the result of her ill management was not only injurious to the kingdom, but to her own interests, for, when the terrific political European earthquake of 1789 burst out, Naples was in a weak and unprotected state. Nature had played truant then; there was no "Don Carlos," no Vanucci, to hold the government firm when the revolutionary tide swept over the peninsula; and the feeble king, with his unwise queen, had to fly from Naples for their lives.

Then followed the Parthenopian republic, established by the French General Championnet, which failed, for Naples is essentially a king-loving place. After its downfall, Ferdinand returned for a little while, but was soon driven out again, to make room for Napoleon's brother Joseph. When Joseph was transferred to Spain, Murat succeeded him; then came Napoleon's downfall, and with him his little family of sovereigns.

At the Treaty of Vienna, in 1816, Ferdinand recovered his throne. To him succeeded his son, Francis I., who reigned only five years; then Ferdinand II. ascended the throne (1830).

There have been short-lived rebellions in the mean while, and it is said there is no stability now.* The Bourgeois, and even the nobility, are tired of the Bourbons; and "the innovation-loving, excitable, loquacious, and unsteady Neapolitan people" are also quite ready for any change. But look,

> "What envious streaks
> Do lace the severing clouds in yonder east.
> Night's candles are burnt out, and jocund day
> Stands tiptoe on the misty mountain-tops."

I have been so interested in my *nobile ozio* as to write all night, a poor preparation for to-morrow's — nay, to-day's — sight-seeing.

* 1858.

STONE TONGUE.

HAVE received great assistance lately in this examination of Neapolitan churches from our new friend Mr. Luini. New friend? He does not seem new to me. It is not more than two months since I first met him at the Folhams, and yet I feel as if I had known him years instead of weeks. There are many reasons to be offered for the close intimacy which is fast growing up between us. We are of the same faith, and hold similar views about our grand old religion. Then we are travellers, not residents, and acquaintances ripen into friendships on journeys much more quickly than by firesides.

Janet rallies me playfully on my enthusiasm about him once in a while, although she also likes him very much; but I retort quite good-humoredly by quoting Jean Paul to her.

"There is a sacred fault noble maidens have of forming too enthusiastic conceptions of their friends. Married women rarely do this, because ordinary men check and discourage all feminine enthusiasm which is not for themselves, and sometimes they weary of that."

Mrs. Rochester teasingly says, "Are you not afraid of spoiling Mr. Luini?"

And I reply, with one of my strong human faiths, —

"It is the way to test him. Great natures are never injured by appreciation and preference, even when frankly and openly expressed; on the contrary, they are encouraged by it, and grow nobler, nor do they ever misunderstand it. It is only the petty, inferior mind which puts a wrong construction on such regard, and wounds us by its vanity and conceit."

He appears to have made Naples his home, for the present, at least. He has a pleasant suite of apartments in a palazzo on the Chiaja, near the Church of San Pasquale, not far from our friends the Rochesters. He has a very fine library, judging from the nice works he lends me: indeed I cannot mention a book of reference, without receiving it from him immediately, — handsomely illustrated old folios, such as St. Non and Montfaucon, together with modern works like Cicognara, and all the standard histories, Guicciardini, Giannone, and the like.

He is very intimate with that excellent man, the Saint Charles Borromeo of the present day, the Archbishop of Naples, Cardinal Duke Sforza; and when any surprise is felt by his acquaintances at his perfect independence of life and opinions, his intimacy with this prelate seems to be the satisfying reason. I fancy, however, that the intimacy has no more power than this; the Cardinal knows him to be a prudent, wise, good man, and such men command independence of mind and action everywhere.

There is some mystery, I believe, about his "antecedents," as we Americans say; and, although an Italian by birth, he has very little intercourse with resident Neapolitans. His intimacies are mostly with foreigners, especially the English. This arises, I suppose, from the fact of his mother's having been an Englishwoman. She must have been a person of high culture and great loveliness, for he has spoken of her to me with an affection amounting to veneration. She died while he was quite young; for he has passed the age of early manhood, being now about thirty, or may be a little older.

There is a rumor that he was interested in the Milanese political troubles of 1848, and this same rumor makes the story complete by supposing him to be one of the discontented noblemen, who preferred withdrawing from a rule they could not endure to keeping up a disturbed condition of affairs in the present unripe state of the times. Whatever may have been his past, it is shrouded in impenetrable silence, which in him is not at all melodramatic. I suppose — nay, I know — that rumor has some foundation for its stories about him. He has tasted of the enchanted plant of our day, Liberty, and, like the Chevalier of the Saint Esprit in the old legend, has dreamed of finding the lost Grayle, and bestowing on all humanity the blessed draught of Love, Fraternity, and Equality.

After his political disappointments he retired from the world for some time, and found peace and consolation in meditation and books. Like Kenelm Digby, Montalembert, and De Broglie, he is a thoroughly educated, devoted Catholic, but unlike them, he has no desire, it may be he has no power, to express himself to the world. He has by degrees passed into the *rôle* of an intelligent spectator, and has lost all taste for action, while he has gained more capability for, and pleasure in, thought. He often quotes Goethe's expression, "Thought expands, action narrows."

His study of, and belief in, human individual liberty, have led him to prefer almost the tyranny of the masses, sooner than accept the old rule of the privileged. Only certain urgent circumstances, I am sure, could make a prominent political man of Luigi Luini. It may be he is deficient in political instinct. But I think, under different and happier circumstances, he might have been useful to his kind, and covered himself with distinction, for he has the calm, self-poised, honorable nature of a wise ruler.

He began life as a politician, — that is, in the highest sense of the word, — he devoted himself to the study of governing. While analyzing men and making himself familiar with the general laws which rule their mobile natures, his far-seeing mind displayed to him a higher, wider scope of thought and labor: it showed to him

"The very pulse of the machine."

Gradually as his pure nature has soared aloft from one range of mighty thoughts to another, he has become indifferent to the passing struggles of the day. He sees a mighty moral law which is unceasingly governing Nature.

"Beautiful, careless, ever fertile Nature!" he exclaims sometimes in our conversations. "She is like a lovely Undine. She displays her exquisite resources under a million of forms. She feels in herself unexhaustible powers, and therefore throws off failures and successes with the same bewitching indifference; sometimes it seems she loves the fascinating wrong the best. But, my friend, her vagaries are all divinely corrected. There is a power which follows her as a loving mother does a charming child, purifying, governing her, directing even her follies to good, and in some blessed future she will possess herself and gain her soul, as did the lovely creation of the German."

But such speculations, while they enrich his mind and

heart, take from him the desire for action or creation. He loves to hear all great acts and doings in the world, to gather from all sources the works of men in every quarter of the globe, having some sublime consolatory word to offer for the fearfulest human folly; but he no longer thinks of playing a part in the life-drama, — his work seems ended, — he only *remains*, as he says, in the present existence.

Luigi, — for this is his beautiful first name, — viewing thus all things from an elevated point, is happily relieved from that curse of clever men, — ambition. There is a calm, tranquil look from his blue eyes which is as limpid and smooth as the surface of deep waters. His moderation is not timidity or caution, but a quiet consciousness of interior strength too deeply felt to need assertion. He is enthusiastic too, quite enough so to satisfy even me; but his enthusiasm has no feverishness, and his fine imagination, quick taste, and keen appreciation of the beautiful are tempered by that rare gift, — good sense. He is practical without being narrow, and self-contained without being cold or selfish. In society he must always command the love as well as respect of his associates. He startles the most artificial, and even the most doubtful and desponding into human faith. He possesses that powerful magnetism which enables some persons to pierce through the cold surface with which society, like the globe, is enveloped; and he touches the warm current which flows burning in every one's heart, though covered over as with a lava crust, by the conventionalities of out-door existence.

I have known him but a little while, to be sure; the instincts of a woman, however, are as quick as they are keen in action, and stand her in lieu of reason, which is slower in its judgment; thus she is enabled to discern character much more speedily than man can. Besides, the calm Janet, who is almost his feminine counterpart, agrees with me in my opinion of him.

During one of our first conversations he discovered my interest in the history of Naples, written so marvellously in stone, as Dumas says of Florence, — "on its palaces, its statues, and its tombs, and we jostle against these stone leaves at every step we take in the streets and public places." Since then he has gone with me to several old churches and palazzos.

During Holy Week, at the close of Lent, he kindly gave me opportunities of not only enjoying the ceremonies of our church at that solemn period, but also of seeing many things which, as a stranger, I could not have seen or known. Every evening of the week I went with him to the old Celestin Church of San Pietro a Maiella, adjoining the Musical College, to hear the scholars of the Conservatoire sing the music appropriate to the season.

One evening they executed a most unmistakable *Stabat Mater* of Mercadante. I say unmistakable, because Rossini's, though a fine thrilling composition, is the song of a triumphant Christian describing imaginary sorrows; some of its passages are almost exultant, they are so full and rich; while this of Mercadante, though cold and scholarly, is solemn and religious in its character. How different both are from the *Stabat* of Pergolesi, which is simple and tender, and yet the grief it expresses is as mild and intense in some of its bursts as a woman or young child might utter under the sting of deep anguish.

Another evening they sang a *Miserere* of Zingarelli, the Master of the Conservatoire, who preceded Saverio Mercadante. The accompanying ceremonies, the darkening of the chapel, and the extinguishing of the cruciform tapers, were very effective; then, added to these, was a harp accompaniment of Mercadante, which sounded like what I suppose persons mean when they speak of "the music of the spheres," but I should have rather listened to the *Miserere* without it, although I have no doubt the harp accompaniment is more popular.

At the present day persons will not inquire into the whys and wherefores of certain traditions in art, and by demanding that which is superficially pleasing, they are fast losing the true spirit. By this means art is ceasing to be a revelation; it may produce fruit after its present nature and be a willing handmaiden to us, but it is no longer an inspiration.

But to return to Naples "sight-seeing." It is an "*embarras de richesses*" here. One grows stunned, as it were, with the fast-thronging memories that crowd the brain at every turn. Greek, Roman, Barbarian, Mediæval, and modern traditions and remains jostle each other, mingling dates, incidents, and names in the most bewildering manner.

One morning in Easter Week, which is just over, I stood on the grand stone platform leading into the Church of San Paolo in the Strada Tribunali, and resting my hand on one of two old blackened and broken columns, I gazed up at the architrave, and then down at the crowd of Christians pouring like a stream up and down the spacious broad stone steps, sweeping a living tide every little while against those pillars. Then there arose in my brain a "sweet pain of mental wilderment" as I recalled that on this very spot where we were worshipping the despised, crucified Nazarene, had stood in olden, olden times, a temple of Castor and Pollux, and these shattered columns and remnant of an architrave remained to tell us, in their mysterious stone tongue, which thrills every fibre of our being, the tradition of that heathen faith and that heathen day. Then, mingling with the crowd of visible mortals, in my fancy arose a ghostly multitude, fleeting fast along, like the water-shadows racing swiftly over the bushes beside a running stream, and there sounded a dim distant chant which uttered,

"There to the Great Twin Brethren
Vow thou thy vows and pray,
That they in tempest and in fight
Will keep thy head alway." *

I went afterwards into the cloister, looked at its twenty-four granite pillars, and remembered that there had stood the Theatre, on the stage of which Nero had played. Three hundred years my memory had swiftly stepped over in passing from the platform of the great entrance of the church into the cloister. I leaned dreamily against one of the columns, imagining the scene so graphically described by the historian, — Nero, the poor crazy Emperor, — "mounting the stage, tuning his lute with much care, and flourishing before he began his part. About him were his companions; the cohort of guards was also there, with tribunes and centurions, and Burrus, praising his master, but grieving for him." †

After lingering some time in the cloister we were taken into the Sacristy to see some pictures and frescoes. We found it thronged with clergymen, not priests of Castor and Pollux, "clad in purple and crowned with olive," but

* "Battle of Lake Regillus. Lay sung at the Feast of Castor and Pollux on the Ides of Quintilis, in the year of the City CCCCLI." — *Macaulay's Lays of Ancient Rome.*

† Tacitus, Book XIV.

simply dressed men, whose long closely-buttoned black cassocks clung to their bodies from the throat to the foot, servants of that New Faith now near two thousand years old.

On a stand was a superb church vestment of cloth of gold, embroidered and studded with precious stones; little sapphires, rubies, emeralds, and diamonds flashed out from the gorgeous mass of work; over one corner of it had been flung a magnificent worked white linen alb, with a heavy broad fall of rich antique lace, whose creamy-hued Spanish point told out well as it lay on the gold of the vestment.

At the head of the room some of the clergy, with some gentlemen, were assembled together admiring an exquisitely wrought gold chalice. Luigi was among them. Seeing us he stepped forward to show us the costly and beautiful thing, worthy in workmanship to have come from the skilful fingers of a Cellini. I held it in my hands while they told me its history, not one word of which did I hear; for I was thinking of the old worship of the proud Ides of Quintilis, and ringing in my ears came the verses, —

> "While flows the Yellow River,
> While stands the Sacred Hill,
> The proud Ides of Quintilis
> Shall have honor still.
> Gay are the Martian Kalends:
> December's Trones are gay;
> But the proud Ides, when the squadron rides,
> Shall be Rome's whitest day."

And then flitted again before me the sorrowful Imperial displays of the poor degraded grandson of that proud, but pure, good Agrippina, Germanicus's wife, surrounded by his Rosencrantzes and Guildensterns, with poor mortified Burrus, applauding but grieving for his royal master's shame, — and I wondered what new faith shall be worshipped here after the tide of two thousand years to come had swept over this spot.

Now how can one return home and sit down leisurely, and in cold blood to hunt up dates and parcel out historical information from books to fit this church, or that statue, this palazzo or that fountain? The labor would be wearying in the extreme; moreover, I should not enjoy as I do now this delightful half-dreamy feeling which steals over me while listening to the conversation of such a man as Luigi Luini. In nervous, picturesque language he tells me the history of each spot or work of art which attracts my notice or admiration, and much better, too, than I could find it in books. Then he revives, as by a magical touch, all my own knowledge, and has that happy faculty, not often possessed by clever men, of drawing out from his companion, by his own suggestive remarks, the most delightful talk.

This is a feminine gift, by the way. Men generally are monologists, they deal only in large bills and notes of language. Some witty Frenchman has said that an intelligent woman can always seize the thoughts of a man, and give him back immediately the small change. Blessed little word-brokers it makes of us to be sure, but how could society get on without such bewitching bankers?

The streets of Naples are becoming so thickly thronged to me with old historical memories that sometimes, as I lean back in the barouche and gaze up at the palazzos or churches, I fancifully compare them, as the carriages sweep by, to the rapidly turning leaves of a gorgeously illuminated missal, or some brilliantly decorated Pugin Glossary, whose vivid colorings of old diaperings and monograms flash on the eye with a painful pleasure; therefore it is a luxurious relief to have such a person as Luigi Luini beside me, to hold down as it were, one of these stone pages, and shade its brilliant past by the calm recital of its history, so that I can look and learn, or remember without bewilderment or confusion.

"CASA DELLA SIRENA."

JUST as we were starting out on our afternoon drive to-day, Luigi entered the court-yard. He helped us into the barouche, then stood for a few moments talking, and resting his delicate, graceful hand on the low door of the coach; for he is not large, nor is he under size, but he is slender, and has all the patrician marks of form, — small hands and feet, suppleness of limb, and grace of motion.

"Why cannot you go with us, Mr. Luini?" asked Janet, as he bid us good day, wishing us a pleasant drive, for, Janet attends to all the inviting and etiquette business of our little community, Venitia being too young, and I now-a-days am too dreamy and forgetful.

"Should you really like to have me?" he answered, with a bright smile, which lighted up finely his handsome face.

"I should not ask you, I am sure, if I did not," replied Janet, with a natural abruptness, which is always softened by her musical laugh and cultured voice; "and as for Ottilie, I know I can answer for her gratification."

He opened the door of the coach without saying another word, and took his seat beside Venitia, thus giving me a chance of enjoying the good looks of both, for he is as handsome for a man as she for a woman. I repeated to myself his name as I looked at him, and recalled what Poe had written of a beautiful Italian woman's name, —

> "Two words, two foreign soft dissyllables,
> Italian tones made only to be murmured
> By angels dreaming in the moonlit dew."

But I thought "Luigi Luini" sounded best when pronounced by waking, loving, human beings, in their sincerest, most cordial tones.

Our carriage swept out the Strada Nuova along the fine, broad road that skirts this picturesque coast, in and out its various little indentations, which shows the skill that has been displayed in the making of this grand route, the broad pathway of which has been gained in many places from the rocks themselves. High up in air, on our right, rose gracefully the green hills of Posilippo, crowned with elms and beautiful villas; and as we came around the Punta di Posilippo, the setting sun shot brilliant rays on the beautiful old ruins of the Palazzo della Regina Giovanni, as it is called, which lay to our left. The sparkling sea flowed into its marble-paved court, and plashed restlessly up against the foundations.

"Casa della Sirena," said Luigi, "should be its name. It is not known certainly that it ever belonged to either of the Queen Joannas, although both were unhappy and unlucky enough."

This led us to talking of the beautiful unfortunate granddaughter of Robert the Wise, Joanna I., the tombs of whose father and grandfather in Santa Chiara I have already mentioned. She was also great-great-granddaughter of that bold adventuring brother of St. Louis of France, Charles of Anjou, Count of Provence, and is the Mary, Queen of Scots, of Neapolitan history (1343 – 1345). No matter what may have been the shortcomings of this unhappy queen, one thing should be remembered of her. When her bitter enemy, Charles of Durazzo, her cousin, was besieging the poor lady, she shut herself up in one of the fortified palaces of her city. The people came clamoring at its gates for admittance, praying for protection and food.

"Open the gates," said the weeping, beautiful woman.

"No, your Majesty!" replied her counsellors, "that cannot be done, for, added to our having only enough food for ourselves, barely sufficient to last until aid comes, if we open the gates the enemy may also force an entrance."

"And they are to suffer and starve!" she cried. "O no, there are women and young children among them; open the gates and let them enter! I cannot leave my people in danger to preserve my own safety."

The gates were opened, and while the populace rushed in, clinging with tears around their beloved queen, the enemy did indeed force an entrance; the poor woman was seized by her cruel kinsman and brutally murdered. But the mangled remains of that once lovely form, the queenly presence of which glows down upon us from the ceiling of the Church of L' Incoronata, made immortal by Giotto's pencil, found rest at last in the same stone coffin where lay her dead mother beside the high altar of the Church of Santa Chiara.

After we had dwelt on her history tenderly and charitably, we talked of the second Joanna, the weak, vain daughter of this cruel Charles Durazzo, almost as beautiful and almost as wretched as the first one, for fate seemed to wish to avenge on her the wrongs and cruelties her father had inflicted on her predecessor (1414–1435).

This occupied us while our carriage rolled around the promontory of Posilippo, and we came out on a full view of Cape Miseno, Procida, and Ischia, with the pretty little Nisita close in shore.

Nisita, with its sweet, sad memories! Joanna II. had a gay villa there, in the days of her prosperity; but far, far back, fourteen centuries before that, the stern Brutus did there fulfil his tender promise to his Portia, on the eve of their final parting before the battle of Philippi (42 B. C).

> "And by and by thy bosom shall partake
> The secrets of my heart,
> All my engagements I will construe to thee,
> All the charactery of my sad brows."

The sun gilded every tree that lay against the western horizon, giving them a true leaf-glory. Janet of course quoted Virgil.

"See!" she cried, "'the gold sprouting forth on the shady holm-oaks, and the metallic leaves tinkling with the gentle gale.' The decorations of the hero's tomb are gone, — the sculptured oar and trumpet, — but, as the Mantuan poet said, 'the lofty promontory, which from him is called Misenus, shall retain eternal through ages the memory of the son of Eolus, whom none excelled in rousing warriors by the brazen trump, and kindling the rage of war by its blast.'"

"I wonder," said Venitia, with a shy playfulness quite new in her manners, but very becoming, "whether the trumpeter, if he has lain under that lofty cape all these long ages, has made the acquaintance of old Typhon, — poor, oppressed giant, with all these burning loads of the Crater Bay resting on his shaggy breast!"

We talked of old myths awhile, then, looking over at

Ischia, recalled some of its pleasant, historical memories, and dwelt longest on that part of its history which relates to the three beautiful women, whose names will hang forever over it as a halo, — Costanza d' Avalos, the sister of the hero of Pavia Francesco d' Avalos, Marquis of Pescara; Vittoria Colonna, his wife; and Mary of Aragon, his cousin.

First, Costanza, who so valiantly defended the Castle of Ischia against the army of Louis XII., preserving thus a home for Frederick of Aragon when the Partition Treaty of Granada, between Louis XII. and Ferdinand the Catholic, left this poor Prince of Altamura homeless (1500). Her famous brother, the hero of Pavia, was born at this Castle (1489), and the government of the island remained in the family nearly three hundred years after Costanza's display of valor and fidelity.

Twenty-five years after, her beautiful young sister-in-law sought a home of consolation in the island. When I described the Marquis of Pescara's coffin, and banner, and sword, which we saw in San Domenico Maggiore, I told then of Vittoria Colonna's going to Ischia to mourn her youthful wedded lover, and how she sang, like "the nightingale with its breast against a thorn," her husband's virtues and valor, in verses which a famous poet said should give her so much honor that they should

> ". . . . burst the tomb and live through every age." *

We dwelt again on the sweet story of this lovely woman, quoting Ariosto, and talking of Buonarotti's pure love, and of the great sculptor's presence at her death-bed, watching with reverential tenderness for her last sigh and last breath.

Then we had a merry laugh over the third beautiful

* Orlando Furioso, Canto XXXVII. St. 16.

widow whose memory is connected with Ischia; the lovely Mary of Aragon, Marchese del Vasto, who followed Vittoria's example when left a widow in 1548. She went to this island to grow old gracefully, and succeeded so well that Brantome said, "her autumn surpassed the spring of other women." It was she, who at sixty was so irresistibly attractive, as to charm the heart out of a grand Prior of France, who should have been thinking of other things than of delectable feminine amaranths.

Yes, we talked of all these pleasant memories, sweeping over the first three quarters of a century, which followed the termination of the Middle Ages (1490–1560), and which saw the firm establishment of Spanish rule in the Land of the Sirens, the age of Ariosto, and Angelo, and Raphael.

"Casa della Sirena, House of the Sirens," exclaimed Luigi as the coach, whose horses' heads were now turned homewards, came near again to the beautiful ruin outside of Punta di Posilippo, and we listened to the history of this ill-fated Palazzo in the Sea, which looked gray as the shades of evening gathered around it, and solemn sounds of warning seemed to breathe through its ruined halls as the sullen plash of the waters of the Crater Bay could be heard against the Siren rocks of the foundation.

The lofty arched windows and empty niches, the heavy projections and peculiarities which it displays of that seventeenth-century architecture, — grand and splendid like Genoa's magnificence, but not equal to Venitian glory and beauty, — were all noticed as though we had looked on it for the first time, and might never see it again. We gazed earnestly, too, at the "various desert and rocky little islands which are called the Sirenusæ," on which this ill-fated palace stands.

As far back as anything is known of this castle, the tradition tells of ill luck. It might seem that those transformed Sirens possessed power to harm, though stilled into solid rocks. Every owner of the place has had ruin to track him to his doom. Outlawry, death, and disgrace have steadily followed its various masters and their descendants, even more relentlessly than sorrow attacks other mortals. At last, by some chance, it came into a family whose name is more frequent and continuous than any other in Neapolitan history, — the Carafa.

These Carafas were a grand old set of people; generation after generation made their mark on history faithfully. Nature never forgot them, through ages of change and extinction of other families. The last "Duke of Naples," who in the year 1130, after a long and heroic defence, yielded to the superior strength of the Normans, and delivered the last Grecian free state of Italy up to King Roger of Sicily, was a Carafa, — Duke Sergius Carafa.

Then in 1435, a Lord Malizia Carafa was sent by the poor childish Joanna II. — the last queen of Naples, indeed the last of the Anjou-Durazzo family — to summon her cousin Alfonso of Aragon, king of Sicily, to be her heir and protector. His monument, with other fine ones of the family, is in the Carafa Chapel at San Domenico Maggiore, a sculptured knight under a canopy, with a sepulchral urn, and his arms folded quietly over the cross he loved and served.

The Carafas swept grandly along through the Aragonese dynasties, both legitimate and illegitimate, and also in the hard iron Spanish times, managing to be loyal through all changes, — that is, faithful to the reigning power, but never failing to give history in each generation a landmark.

One of this great family was so famous, he must have more than a mere mention of his name. This was the austere friend of St. Cajetan of Thiene, Gian Pietro Carafa, Cardinal Archbishop of Naples, who, with his holy and dear companion, founded the order of the Theatine Monks (1524), that great and noble "Seminary of Bishops," formed "of men of noble birth who might have revelled in the enjoyments of life, but who began to seek out the sick in their habitations and in hospitals, and administer the last consolations to the dying."* They lived in profound solitude and extreme poverty, never asked alms, and studied closely the Gospels, then went down in the cities to preach.

Cardinal Carafa himself appeared with cap and cross and clerical habit in the pulpit, and "poured forth that copious and vehement eloquence which distinguished him till his death." He did not produce mere excitement and ebullitions of feeling in his auditors, but a deep impression. He was "tall and thin, moved quickly, appeared to be all nerve," had an iron will, "was never known to have made a concession or compromise, and always acted on his opinions with the utmost vehemence." Men said he led a strange and austere life, he slept by day and studied by night, and, what is rare with such solemn, stern men, he was gifted with a flow of words that was filled with earnestness and freshness, and which poured out in a powerful stream, influencing every one who came within his reach. Of course Charles V. hated him, for Cardinal Carafa was a man free from selfish ambition, but full of holy zeal and ardor for the restoration of the Church to its original purity; therefore he felt a contempt for the double-dealings of the ambitious Emperor,

* Ranke's History of the Popes.

and despised the game of fast and loose with Protestants which Charles played so skilfully to suit his kingcraft and policy. But notwithstanding this, Cardinal Carafa was elected Pope in the very teeth of Charles V.'s power and disapprobation, and will be known to all ages as Paul IV. When the Imperial Ambassadors warned him that their master would never consent to his election, the bold prelate answered, — "If God wishes me to be Pope, no emperor can hinder me from being so; but for myself his opposition will be so much the better, for then I shall owe my elevation to no human power."

Stout words these for an old man of seventy-nine. Whatever may have been the influence, human or divine, he was elected Pope; and the same life and death struggle which the haughty Hildebrand, Gregory VII., had fought nearly five centuries before with the Hohenstaufens, was renewed by this Pope with the Hapsburgs.

That grand old Pope, Paul IV., with his strong Italian nationality, religious fervor and zeal, and Brutus-like severity to his unworthy kinsman, stands out in bold relief, even in the sharply-chiselled history of that day, and for three things shall he be remembered; as the undaunted opponent of Charles V., the dear and loving friend of St. Cajetan and St. Charles Borromeo, and one of the leading, indeed most active, spirits of that great Council which was intended by the wise, earnest, and pious churchmen of the day to assist in the reviving of a true catholic and apostolic spirit, — the Council of Trent.

Like all great Popes who have ever been at the head of the Church, he was an earnest opposer of foreign rule, whether French, Spanish, or German, and a warm advocate of Italian union and nationality. He called "Italy an harmonious instrument with four strings,—Rome, Venice, Milan, and Naples," and looked upon Lodovico Sforza, the Duke of Milan, —"Il Moro," as he was called, — and Alfonso of Aragon, as eternally lost for having destroyed the harmony of this beautiful instrument by their divisions. "*Infelice quelle anime di Alfonsa d' Aragona e Ludovico duca di Milano che furono li primi che quastorono cosi nobil instrumento d' Italia.*" *

He said of the French, what will apply to them at this day, "The French break off in the middle of their work, and do not stop even where they are tightly bound."

Only a little over four years did this resolute, strong-willed old man hold the Papacy, but in that time he made a stamp on history which will remain deep and clear for ages. He died in 1559.

Along through succeeding generations came this rich old Carafa blood, until in the second quarter of the seventeenth century, — at that period when Vandyke, and Poussin, and Domenichino were painting, and Calderon singing, and Richelieu governing, and Charles I. and his beautiful Henrietta losing a fair kingdom, while Queen Christina of Sweden was receiving one to play with as a toy, — in 1630, the Carafas, Princes of Stigliano, the main branch of the family, brought short up in the presence of a young, golded-haired, beautiful girl, Anna Carafa, who was not only a Carafa, but a granddaughter of Vespasian Gonzaga, one of the most illustrions men of his day; her mother was Elena Aldobrandini, niece of Clement VIII., and she was the richest heiress of all South Italy.

She was sought in marriage by a nephew of a Pope; an Austrian Archduke; a Prince of Poland; a reigning

* Navagero.

Duke of Modena; a son of a Spanish viceroy; and her own handsome cousin, the brilliant, dashing Diomed Carafa. But she married none of these. After much stormy wooing, in 1637, the heiress beauty was at last wedded to the Duke of Medina de las Torres, and became Vice-Queen of Naples.

Whom the gods wish to ruin, they first drive mad, and so it was with this beautiful young girl and her Viceroy husband. Their immense wealth and dazzling position bewildered them. They made all Naples even, so accustomed to Spanish display, stare at their magnificence, which was more than regal, and to this day their extortion and dishonesty are remembered.

Into the hands of this young vice-regal Duchess had come, with her other possessions, the sorrowful Casa della Sirena. A Ravaschieri, too prudent to defy destiny, had sold it to Donna Anna's grandfather, Prince of Stigliano, and straightway commenced that "waywardness of fate which baffles all human calculations." His son, the father of Donna Anna, a prosperous, brilliant man, with fair sons and daughters clustering around like strengthening young branches to the Carafa house-tree, was soon after snatched from him by death, and also every child except this young girl Anna, felling the poor old Prince Stigliano to the earth with grief, just in the very hour of his brightest prosperity; he left the world and his great possessions and went into a Jesuit monastery to die. I remember the other day standing by his monument, which is also in the Carafa chapel at St. Domenico Maggiore. He was buried in the ground under the chapel.

But the daring young Vice-Queen would not see ill-fortune in the beautiful ruin; nor would she hear the song of the mysterious Fate, who, it was said, could be seen sitting on those rocks spinning, through the long watches of the night, like the fearful vision of false Sextus: —

"A woman fair and stately
  But pale as are the dead.

"And as she plied her distaff,
  In a sweet voice and low,
 She sang of great old houses,
  And fights fought long ago.
 So spun she and so sang she,
  Until the east was gray,
 Then pointed to her bleeding breast
  And shrieked and fled away."

Donna Anna commanded a goodly palace to be built on the foundations of that fearful place, in which she vowed she would dwell in royal splendor. She sent for the great architect, Cosimo Fanzaga, and made him sketch a fine plan for her daring castle. Then four hundred workmen were set to work at its stately arches; and Naples was robbed of ancient statues to fill the niches, and of rare pictures to adorn the walls.

The beautiful, golden-haired young girl developed rapidly into a covetous, tyrannical woman. She oppressed her subjects, and joined with her husband in every scheme of selfish exaction and extravagance that could be thought of. Only seven years ran their brilliant, comet-like course; then the Duke of Medina was recalled to Spain in disgrace, and his vice-regal office taken from him.

This disgrace was keenly felt by his haughty young wife. Not that she had ever loved her husband, nor had their marriage been a happy one. She had loved her brilliant cousin Diomed, — he who had wooed her, so like a knight of old romance, — with his painted felucca sailing up and down the lovely coast, a Cleopatra's barge in luxurious magnificence, dedicated to her honor, whose music and songs in her praises came wafting over sea and land, — the gallant young Carafa of Maddaloni, who, to win her hand, out-rode, out-feasted, and out-fought the princely foreign competitors.

But in an evil hour she had listened to the voice of ambition rather than love. Probably there was some pique, some lover's quarrel, which, instead of ending in a wild, keen joy of reconciliation, had snapt off suddenly in eternal silence. Whatever may have been the cause, she, instead of being the happy, loving wife of Diomed, and probably a better woman, had become a Vice-queen, and sought bitter remedies for the stinging pain of her heart, in the fierce, dangerous game of selfish ambition. But how could it be otherwise?

"So spun she and so sang she,"

that Siren fate, who sat invisible to mortal eyes by the rocky foundations of the Palace in the Sea.

Thus when her husband's sudden downfall and ruin came, she had nothing, — not even poor despised love to sustain her. A few months after the Viceroy was recalled, and while he was standing his trial at Madrid, the lovely Anna Carafa, whose beauty poets had sung, and dukes and princes had wooed, and in whose veins flowed the richest Italian and Spanish blood, was lying in a villa at Portici, dying, almost alone! For if the unprosperous, even when good, are apt to be deserted, how can the wicked, when sorrow comes to them, expect to reap that which they never sowed, — grateful, devoted friendship?

On the Christmas-eve of that year, 1645, at midnight, Donna Anna Carafa, Duchess of Medina de las Torres, Ex-Vice-Queen of Naples, was buried privately, and without honor, in the church of the barefooted Augustinian monks, at Resina, at the foot of Mount Vesuvius.

"And the Casa della Sirena?" asked Venitia of Luigi, who was telling us this sad story, whose tragic fatality, aided by the melody of his rich voice, touched us deeply.

"It remained unfinished of course," he replied. "The earthquake of 1688 made a complete ruin of it. It stood a long while unappropriated. At last, as years went by, the Mirelli, Princess of Teora, bought it, tempted by its small price. The same ill-fortune attended them that has visited every owner of this 'House of the Sirens,' — rapid prosperity and sudden ruin. Then it remained unclaimed for a time, and was afterwards used as a glass-manufactory, — a fitting use surely to put it to, — the fabrication of that frail, glittering substance which has been compared to successful ambition. Now the report is that the ruin belongs to the king."

"Alas!" I said sadly, "he, poor man, does not need the possession of any tangible Casa della Sirena to bring him ill luck, for he is a Bourbon, and his family have been playthings of Fate for ages."

Luigi returned home with us, and drank of our "Hyson" on the terrace; then we spent a charming evening of music and talk. After he left, I threw some fresh pastilles into a little bronze pastille-brazier of beautiful antique form, and sat inhaling the delicious vapor, playing idly with the graceful little folds of smoke drapery, as they rose up and floated off into the air.

"Now," said Venitia, "I shall place candles in those alabaster vases; have all the other lights put out, and, while you continue burning pastilles, I will play."

I have never seen the girl look so lovely as she has the past week or so; and to-night, as she said this, I noticed again the indescribable charm which is beginning to breathe softly through and over her beauty, as the faint, subtile odor of some rare flower creeps out of the half-opening bud.

She did not observe my look, but with a preoccupied, unconscious air, which is peculiar to her and Janet, and which is uncommon in a young girl, she lighted the vases, put some flowers on the piano, near the key-board, then drew two little easels forward, under the vases, so that the pictures on them might be seen in the picturesque pearly brightness which streamed down from the illuminated alabaster.

These two pictures are fine copies Janet has lately purchased of Di Napoli; they are of two Correggios, the originals of which are in the Musée Bourbonique; one the famous small "Marriage of St. Catharine," in which, as Schlegel says, "smiling grace is exalted and refined into almost unsullied beauty"; the other that bewitching "Zingarella," the sleeping "Madonna del Coniglio," or Madonna of the Rabbit, called so because of the cunning little rabbit which peeps its head out of the bushes with droll inquiry at the sleeping Mother and Child, and points up his long ears, as if it indeed heard the low songs of the little angels who are floating over head, bearing rushes to make a shelter for the Divine Mother and Son. It is the loveliest of his pictures, to my fancy.

The expression of fatigue in this picture is not at all repulsive, as physical suffering of any kind is apt to be; and yet the poor Virgin is so very tired that it can be seen in every part of her form. She has thrown herself down beside, not on, a bank; every muscle relaxed, every limb drooping; she presses her child close to her from instinct, for her sleep is very, very leaden; and the poor baby, like its mother, is so weary, too, that it sleeps despite its uncomfortable position; one of her hands has fallen down from the little feet which it had wished to support, and the arm is held in position by a tight fold of drapery, which is bound around it, while the other hand is clasped in clinging fondness by the child.

Love, divine love, of the purest, tenderest nature, is the exquisite *motivo* of this melodious picture. It shows itself in all the details, which are as so many modulations and workings of the theme. The expression of the faces — breathless exhaustion, beautified and mellowed by the deep happiness which both mother and child feel in sleeping close, close to each other — is almost voluptuous.

There is a sort of sensible sonorousness in the works of such painters as Titian, and all rich, warm colorists; the effect is like that of fine, satisfactory passages of orchestration; but Correggio and Raphael are like delightful executants on a single instrument, — fine solo players.

"There," said Venitia, leaning back, with a sweet air of languor and content, looking around the room, and drawing a long, full, happy sigh. "Now for the music, — for Chopin. I was thinking this evening, Ottilie, that Chopin should be listened to by shaded lights, in air filled with fragrant incense, flowers, and a few Correggios and Raphaels, with two or three darlings like you and Janet for the audience."

I wished to exclaim, "Venitia growing sentimental!" but I would not, for I should give a great deal to see the sweet birth of what she calls, mockingly, *sensiblerie* — but which I call true feeling — in her heart.

Her fingers rambled over the piano-keys, letting drop

sweet chords, but nothing connected, not the shadow of a modulation; at last the combinations of sounds took form and shape, although she still played dreamily. It was that Prelude in E flat of Chopin, in which

> "Thought and memory ring, like a funeral peal,
> Weary changes on one dirge-like note."

After she had finished it, she said, as if thinking aloud, —

"What a gift Chopin had of phrasing in music whole volumes of unexpected joys, and dim, mystical senses of loving; not love, — not tangible, practical, housekeeping love, such as you and Janet believe in, and which is good enough, I have no doubt, for those who like it, — but it is a vague, poetical expression of this 'joy of life,' as you call it, Ottilie. And he seemed to know, too, that for him his Psyche could never take form or shape; for just as his previsions approach positive resolutions in the music, what a flood of misgivings pour out in the fast-succeeding chords!"

She played again for a little while, and I leaned back on the sofa, with half-closed eyes, listening to the music. Janet was walking up and down the room, half hearing, half thinking. Venitia suddenly stopped, and leaning forward, looked earnestly at the "Zingarella."

"Venitia, Stendhal says," — I commenced.

"Bah! The scoffing wretch!" interrupted Venitia.

"'Strike, but hear me,' as Themistocles said," I replied.

"That 's right, Ottilie," said Janet, laughing, "never give up your quotation."

"*Et tu, Brute?*" I answered with playful reproach; but, true to the persistency of my nature, in little things at least, I repeated the same words, and at my obstinate reiteration of "Stendhal says," both women burst into a contagious fit of laughter, in which of course I joined; but, never daunted, I carried my point.

"Stendhal says, 'Is there anything true in this life, but the tender pleasure we feel while listening to Mozart and looking at the creations of Correggio?'"

"That is so like him," responded Venitia; "he could not enjoy with hope and faith, but must wither everything with his doubt and unbelief."

"I like his appreciation of Mozart," remarked Janet. "Mozart is one of those 'sweet men,' as old Chaucer says, 'who giveth absolution to his grieving listeners.' His glorious draught of joy is of a

> 'vintage, that hath been
> Cool'd a long age in the deep-delvèd earth,
> Tasting of Flora and the country-green,
> Dance, and Provençal song, and sunburnt mirth!
> . . . . a beaker full of the warm South,
> Full of the true, the blushful Hippocrene,
> With beaded bubbles winking at the brim
> And purple-stainèd mouth.'

His happiness is sparkling and clear as the note of Shelley's Skylark, and seems as 'free from sad satiety.' His love, too, if it was what you, Venitia, saucily call practical, housekeeping love, is beautiful; much more charming to my ears, certainly more healthy, than poor Chopin's sad misgivings, and wayward, doubting tenderness."

"But Figaro was gay, Janet," I remarked, with a malicious laugh.

"Yes, and so was Mozart, I admit; but happy would it be if the women who possess the real love of such men as Mozart could do as Constance Weber, his wife, — shut their eyes to the shortcomings, and receive in return for their generous faith adoring love; for to her he was, no matter what were his errors, true as the needle to the Pole —"

"North Pole, Janet," I interrupted, teasingly; "rather a cold atmosphere, but I fear the true one of many loving women."

"Heaven forbid," said Venitia, in a low voice, and with a shudder, "that I should ever be the North Pole to any man's heart."

"Or like Fancy," continued Janet, pleased with her comparison, and not hearing Venitia's half-whispered remark, "which

'like the finger of a clock,
Runs the great circuit and is still at home.'"

I shook my head with laughing doubt, and Venitia commenced playing the "*Voi che sapete*," Cherubino's delicious air in Figaro, of which Scudo says: "The world may grow old, a great many miracles may be performed, the very surface of the earth may be changed, but the sentiment which Mozart has expressed in this divine passage is eternal, and can never be said in any other way."

I left her playing, and came to my room, thinking I could sleep, as I felt a little weary; but as usual I have written until not only the whole Palazzo, but even the great city, are stilled in slumber, indeed are almost ready to burst out into the daily Babel of sounds.

PHILIP.

HILIP has come. No need of telling any one who Philip is. Every journal I have kept since my girlhood has Philip in it, in some form or shape, with his mother, his father, his wife, or himself.

His father was my sworn defender and friend from childhood. There was a chivalric tone in Mr. Edelhertz's regard for me, which was like that love which an enthusiastic, highly cultivated man feels for a daughter, born to him in his young manhood, and who, as she grows up, is more friend and companion than child to him. It is a feeling totally different from that which he could have for any other woman, and is one of the sweetest, tenderest emotions of which a man's heart is capable. Yes, of all masculine loves, this one is to be preferred by a woman, the tender, protecting regard of a father near enough to mid-age to have enthusiasm and appreciation, and old enough to have grown generous and indulgent, and to command obedience and reverence.

Thus Gaspard Edelhertz, Philip's father, loved me, and I gave back to him the trusting, adoring love of a daughter in full measure. Ah, if he had lived, I should not be what I am! But let that pass, and

> "Upon the heat and flame of my distemper
> Sprinkle cool patience."

Mr. Edelhertz was a German of high birth and culture. He had come to America in his youth in the diplomatic service of his government, had married an American, and settled in the States. He had only one son, the possession of whom had cost him his wife; and poor Philip bid fair to be not only a costly but grievous possession to his father.

Brilliant, gifted, erratic, he was exposed to numberless temptations, and just on the outer lintel of manhood he returned home from Europe, where he had been sent for his education, almost a disgraced boy. I say almost, for I never knew the details of his errors, as I was too near a friend of the family. It is the curious, prying outsider, the malicious or inquisitive acquaintance, who knows "everything" in a disgraceful family trouble, — knows more, indeed, than ever happened. I needed no further information than that which I saw, the silent sorrow of my honored friend, Mr. Edelhertz, his proud anguish that but for me would have been solitary.

Philip came amongst us haughty, handsome, and with a recklessness that amounted almost to insolence; had his father been a reproachful, wordy, fretful man, he would have gone to ruin. I was only a few years his senior, but having been early settled in life, and moreover a woman, I seemed much older than he. I fancied I discovered under this recklessness resentment at injustice, and in this pride promise of future reparation.

Society, that capricious, fitful goddess, who is quite ready to cry "Fie!" at vices which, at another moment or under other other circumstances, she will adore, had prepared herself to let down the grate against Philip, and he was just as willing to throw the scabbard aside, and wage perpetual war for life on this power which he has now made his slave.

All the Scandinavian in his blood seemed to surge up, an indomitable pride of will, an appetite for struggle and contest, a craving for danger, a species of inner exaltation which I think would have almost gloried in destruction. Revolt and battle appeared to be his ruling tastes. His father was a man for whom nature, education, and society had done everything towards producing in him the true gentleman; he never noticed this mental and spiritual fever; he avoided all causes and chances of collision with his son; never watched him, nor uttered a syllable of warning or remonstrance, never showed that he even noticed his savage predispositions. With admirable philosophy and prudence he must have resolved to allow time and nature to cure this disorder, feeling sure that no mortal means could be applied.

Philip's little ocean of passion washed up with fierce will on the shores of his petty social continent, and finding no obstacles, lashed out all its impotent fury on the dry sands of his egotism and selfishness; but at last the good in him grew weary with this useless and unopposed violence, and Love, that grand and potent power, also aided him.

My cousin Ellen came to live with us after the death of her grandparents. She was, of course, the exact opposite of that which many supposed would please Philip, and yet she had in her the very qualities to suit him. She was beautiful, graceful, intelligent, and had the culture and breeding of a gentlewoman. "She was still as a mountain," he would say of her, drolly, "and gentle as a lamb." At any rate she quelled the lion in him and held him as another Una.

When Philip first returned home, I luckily was in possession of sufficient position to influence the society in which we mingled. I received Philip with as much earnest friendship and attention as if he had come to us covered with honor instead of disgrace. I ignored his affairs; treated him with the confidence and respect of a valued friend; and I did more, I smoothed the road to his love, and helped to make Ellen his wife.

Only once has Philip Edelhertz spoken to me of his youthful trouble. It was a year or so after his return, when our little world and his then happy father seemed to have forgotten the past, so brilliantly was the future opening to the gifted young man. With the enthusiastic exaggeration of a warm-hearted youth, he was thanking me for my friendship, and overrating, with that imprudent but natural generosity in such dispositions, its worldly value and effect.

Alas! how often in life are such costly acknowledgments made to the selfish, who take advantage of them cruelly, and wring and pierce the heart that would have adored them, with instruments forged out of the very abnegation and self-sacrifice of this generous nature, to which they should have bowed down in reverence!

"O Ottilie!" he cried, "but for you I should have gone to ruin. You knew all, and yet —"

"I knew nothing, Philip, and never wish to know. Nor should you ever speak of this past in confidence to me or any one. Whatever your errors may have been, my friend, they rest between your conscience, your father, and your God."

"Three very disagreeable individuals to face, Ottilie, under certain circumstances," he answered, in his own peculiar frolicsome way, which meant no irreverence. "But you are right," he continued earnestly, "and I thank you now, not only for your frank, confiding friendship, but for your wise counsel. If anything can make me forget the past and believe in a future, it will be your kindness and regard."

"Errors repented of, Philip, have no past, only a future of atonement and amendment."

"And mine shall have a future, Ottilie, a future that neither you nor I shall be ashamed of, so help me God, my dear, dear friend," he added solemnly.

He has kept his word, with God's help. His errors have had a golden future, for Fortune is now as prodigal of fame and good gifts, so far as worldly success is concerned, as she seemed disposed on the other hand to be churlish and frowning in his youth. But, if Fortune is gracious, Fate resents it, and poor Philip has had two great sorrows, which have made him hold lightly his more material blessings.

Formerly his happy artistic nature enabled him to slide easily over the ordinary trials of existence; but when we parted, three years ago, it was with him, as "if life were worn threadbare, and he had got to the end of things, as if indeed he had worked his way through the upper coats of existence down to what Bossuet calls the 'inexorable ennui which forms the basis of human life.'"

First, Mr. Edelhertz was taken from us; then, shortly after, Philip's young, beautiful wife, Ellen. Poor Philip! How bitter sorrow made him! Such visitations are apt to bear thorny fruit, when grafted on the enthusiastic and deep-loving human soul. The calm nature, that never loves unwisely, or suffers immoderately, bows to the very first blow of sorrow, with a meek patience that is called beautiful; but the quick throbbing heart and active brain bound fiercely and resentfully against such trials as lost love and death. It is wrong, I know, but it is nature, the wickedness of which we all admit, and this rebellious nature can only be subdued and stilled by God's loving patience, not man's futile, irritating reasoning.

"Poor heart! — what bitter words we speak,
When God speaks of resigning."

Resentful and wretched as Philip's grief had made him, it did not separate him from me; on the contrary, we seemed to be closer and nearer than ever before, for sorrow, too, had laid its heavy, dull hand on me, and we stood unveiled by those two events which show us poor human creatures, not only to ourselves, but to each other, — Love and Death. They are the apples of our tree of knowledge, of good and evil, — the supremest joy and the supremest suffering; they tear away all false coverings and leave us naked.

Of this sweet and bitter fruit we had eaten, both after our kind; and after the awakening we had met on the outside of our lost Edens, and sitting down sternly in our desert, gazed with stony looks at each other, and said, "Friend, can we ever again make anything out of this life?"

There was nothing of what is called resignation in our stunning, blinding grief; nothing of that deadening condition in which one loses all memory of past good and evil, all apprehension of future suffering, and is in a state of almost nothingness and moral death. No, there was passion, and morose melancholy, and bitter despair in our anguish; but notwithstanding our hearts were convulsed with such sad feelings, courage breathed in the despair, and love in the melancholy, — courage, which in time would help us to battle bravely to the end, and love, which warmed our hearts to each other, and thus kept alive that divine spark of true life, human tenderness.

First, Philip's destiny lifted him up from his cold, bleak wayside, and he journeyed far, far off from me. I remember how longingly I looked after him as he faded from my sight, and I sat there outside my Eden too feeble and powerless to move on. Life was a distracting burden to me; all my individual existence seemed suspended, or crushed out by the force and weight of my surroundings. The social atmosphere I breathed was suffocating and stifling. I struggled for mental breath, then fell lifeless, and should have sunk into moral inanity had I not been emancipated. And yet, so weakened had I grown from the effect of the influences surrounding me, that the very emancipation was a pain. I said, hopelessly, "My grief can never rise, take up its bed and walk." But it did, and now we two meet again after these three long years in the most unlooked for way and place. He has been travelling in the East, in Egypt and Syria.

"In the wilds
Of fiery climes, he made himself a home,
And his soul drank their sunbeams."

Philip is a poet, not only a skilful and graceful versemaker, but a true singer, and the world acknowledges him as such. He is a perfect master of this curious modern instrument of word-music. His style is throbbing; its passionate beats fall on one's heart like the hammer on the anvil, each stroke driving out the brilliant spark of keen enjoyment and appreciation.

As Listz says of Heine, Philip's poetry tells us of enchanted atmospheres and celestial marvels, inaccessible and unknown to those mortals who have not for a godmother that marvellous fairy who during life counterbalances bad fortunes by being prodigal of her treasures.

He grasps the fullest and most difficult chords of emotion; makes the most curious and weird application of words; weaving sound and thought together in such a mysterious combination, as to play upon the hearts and ears of his listeners or readers as cunningly and cleverly as he does upon his word-instrument.

His poetry is essentially modern, the passionate lyric beat; the half acknowledged mysticism; superb and glowing images, keen in their effect as the taste and odor of a tropical fruit or flower, — dazzling lights on this word-coloring, whose brilliancy is at white-heat from very intensity, like Dante's

> "Bianca aspetto di cielo,"

— all characteristic peculiarities of modern poetry, which arise from the restless emotional nature of the times. It is as many-hued as the dying dolphin's back, and is filled with vague sounds

> "of that mysterious sea
> Which brought us hither,"

giving it an inexplicable charm. It is like some of those weird, musical poems in the tone language, whose mystic modulations suggest to the listener glorious aspirations or happy hopes, while it may be that the creator of them saw in their waving, changing hieroglyphics a meaning totally different. Chopin's sad Preludes, for example, written during his Promethean sufferings in Majorca, chained fast to the rock of solitude, with the fierce vulture of his exacting nature, not only eating out his own heart, but wounding mortally with its sharp beak the love as necessary to his existence as breath. These Preludes were soul-cries of anguish and rebellion as he uttered them; to my ears they sweep over a higher range of thought. They are sublime poems filled with previsions and promises of hope and faith, which sing out as clearly as a seraph's note in the turmoil of all the despair.

And yet these masters of this wondrous gift, inspired utterers of all these deep suggestive thoughts of beauty, are sometimes unconscious of the power their productions possess. They sing, as the Sibyl of old, words not their own; while to us, mute worshippers before the tripod, hearing and understanding are given. Philip is most provokingly unconscious, not only of the curious suggestions his poems convey to me and others, but in music also, although he is a clever vocal *executant*, and possesses that quick, exact taste which is near akin to genius, he seems to have only the comprehension of a half-developed nature.

He will write a poem that thrills the hearts of multitudes, and when he reads some fine criticism on it, which tells of this hidden spark of deep thought that lies under the gray haze of outward meaning, he laughs and quotes teazingly to me,

> " Shakespeare's critics bring to view
> More than Shakespeare ever knew."

It is the only point on which our minds and sympathies do not touch, and it would grieve me, but for some reasons. I can see that it is wisely ordered so. We cannot all be singers. Then, moreover, it may be that the men and women to whom is given this great power of presenting to us the incarnation of the Ideal of Beauty, — " this pure note of celestial reason and the fiery energy of the simple spirit," — must have this free, unconscious nature, into which " the prophetic god of Delos can breathe an enlarged mind and spirit, and disclose the future " with greater ease.

It is a divine mystery, and like all such spiritual mysteries, beautiful. Therefore, though Philip and I often have playful arguments, he teasing me for my enthusiastic fancies and imaginings, and I reproaching him for the unworthiness of such an unconscious nature, still I do not take it really to heart, but find comfort in the balance made by the division of gifts. Mereover, we should remember that the instrument cannot hear its own divine effects, nor can the *executant* judge of the power and beauty of his work, being all too near.

Philip is looking very well now. His health, which was so shattered by his fierce troubles, has become invigorated by travel and change of scene. He has a strong physique; and I was thinking to-day, as I contrasted him with Luigi, while the two were sitting together smoking on our terrace, after they had dined with us, that if I were a stranger, I should take Luigi for the great poet sooner than Philip, Luigi being more spiritual-looking.

In Philip there is a pretty fair balance between soul and body, indeed just now his fine robust body seems to have the preponderance. He has broad, rather high shoulders, is a tall, large man, has a fine, massive head, square, full brow, and the outline of the nose is sharp and firm. The expression of the upper part of his face is stern and reflective, but this look is softened by the full mouth and rich curve of the chin and cheek, and fine lines flowing off into the well-set neck and throat. His lips have almost a voluptuous beauty, not at all sensual, but full of deep passionate feeling, which, added to the rich color on the cheeks, gives a tenderness to the face.

His manners are also as opposite to those of Luigi as his personal appearance, being abrupt, and at times unsympathizing. There is more self-consciousness about him than self-possession; not at all conceited, for he is too proud a man for that; but he has the air of a successful word-wrestler, who has tried well the sinews of language, and felt, tasted, and gloried in his power over his brother men.

But he can be tender and almost womanly at times, especially to me, for he knows I value these rare revelations of his feelings too highly to desecrate them by alluding to them afterwards. I believe he loves to indulge himself in thinking aloud to me. This evening, after tea, the moon shone brilliantly; a little lull fell over us all, for we had been talking in a perfect gale of pleasant social excitement. Philip leaned over to me and said,— "Cousin Ottilie, throw a shawl over your shoulders, and come stroll with me on the terrace of the Villa Reale."

I went with him, and we stood on the beautiful terrace which juts out into the sea, watching the vapor and spark on the summit of Vesuvius, and noticing the golden glitter of the moonlight on the waves, as they shivered into watery atoms against the shining shells and pebbles on the beach, and the fishing boats rocking softly to and fro on the waters, while the blazing torches in their sterns streamed out a fiery splendor over the sea. We were entirely alone, for almost every one had left even the Villa walks. Philip remained silent for a while, sitting on one of the benches, leaning his arm on the iron railing of the terrace, his large white hand buried in his thick light brown hair.

"My God! it is beautiful, Ottilie!" he exclaimed, at last; then after a few moments he continued, in his rapid, earnest manner, "What a fierce thrill of appreciation a great thing of beauty creates in us! Have you ever analyzed it? Have you never noticed that hot tears spring to the eyes, and the heart throbs petulantly and impatiently? I am not now speaking of the mere gratification which some lovely things bestow, like a rich odor, or the sight of remarkable physical beauty, but that deeper feeling you talked of this evening, when, as you said,

> "one's nature is cloven
> To its depths within depths by the stroke of Beethoven,"

when the bliss is agony, and the rapture keen pain. Yes, Ottilie, you know this feeling well. Indeed, to-day, in the Musée Bourbonique, when we were looking at the divine Psyche torso of Praxiteles together, you must have felt thus, for you turned to me, with a crimson spot on each cheek, and your eyes swimming in tears, saying, 'Come, my friend, let us go. I have seen enough to-day; my heart is full.'

"I have often tried to discover the secret springs of this feeling, and in failing to find them, I have analyzed its varying emotions, hoping to see what is its real nature. I used to think it was envy, — but — and I dare be conceited to you — I have a feeling strongly akin to it, whenever I write anything over which the enthusiasm attendant on creation flings the halo of illusive beauty, satisfying my craving ideal, but only for a brief instant. It is as if a door had opened, disclosing to me a view of the most ravishing things, and then suddenly closed again; or, like a flash of lightning, that in a dark midnight shows glorious outlines of beautiful forms in the sky and earth, then night's solemn inky pall obliterates them in an instant."

"A shivering delight, — 'Divine despair,'" I said, not in answer, but half thinking aloud. Philip's quick responsive memory replied on the instant to my thoughts,

> "'Tears, idle tears, I know not what they mean,
> Tears from the depths of some divine despair.'

That delicious poem!"

And as we paced up and down the solitary terrace, he repeated in his clarion-like voice the whole of that etherial lyric of Tennyson, which, I know not why, had suddenly presented itself to my memory. I suppose because the feelings he had described, and which are as the soul's longing for the lost home, reminded me of the sorrow for "the loved and gone," which always comes to me in the presence of the beautiful.

> "Deep as first love, and wild with all regret;
> O Death in Life, the days that are no more."

Then he "discoursed me," in his most eloquent style, for Philip is an inspired rhapsodist under some influences; and what could there be more potent than the divine Nature by which we were surrounded, and the presence of a friend he loved tenderly, who understood him as a second self, and who is moreover connected with all that his memory holds dear!

It is very strange that we can never remember anything but the shadow of the beautiful; and so it is with Philip's brilliant talks, they leave only a faint representation of their superb outlines on my memory, and my meagre sketches of them are simply suggestive to me of the glorious reality. I wish I could recall the sparkling words he uttered, when he broke out with something like this: —

"Life is but the reflection of a remembrance, Ottilie." His light hair was thrown off his high, fair temples, and his keen gray eyes shone resplendent. "There is nothing real in it," he continued, his voice growing deeper than its usual key-note, — which is high, — from intense feeling. "There is nothing real in it, my dear, dear friend, but faith in God, which purifies and strengthens it, and the pursuit and accomplishment of some mental triumph. The only thing, too, a man really owns in this existence is a creation of that which is immortal in him, — his mind. The sovereign, the rich man, lose forever their possessions when they die, even though it be a great king who may have carved out his kingdom with his sword, or a rich man who may have earned with his own head and hands his vast possessions; death takes these forever from them; and could they return, after the lapse of centuries, to claim their rights, they would find them in the hands of others who had also earned them. But the poet, painter, or sculptor, on whom this rich man or sovereign may have bestowed his haughty patronage, own their creations forever; Dante's Divina Commedia, Michael Angelo's 'suspended Pantheon in air,' his fresco world of giants on the Sistine ceiling, and Raphael's Madonnas, remain intact, — they can never pass away from their creators."

Then we talked of Philip's last poem, which came out a few months ago, and has added another circlet to the diadem of his fame. It was written in Egypt, and is marked by all the peculiarities of his style and genius. It has "deep poetic intention and noble harmonious conception"; that which we call accent in music is in it, the pulse, the life-throb, which is one of his strong characteristics, combined with profound thought; satisfying thus the two demands of the world-audience on Art, — pleasure for the eye and ear, and what Poussin calls "delectation" for the mind.

He had been under the influence of his great grief during its creation, and this had given it the rich soul-hues and profound shadows, and also "that mysterious harmony between the personality of the poet and his creation," which is, after all, the great secret of artistic success, the magnet which attracts the hearts of our fellow-beings, the true divining-rod which sounds to the depths of human hearts grown cold, unhappily, in

"The dreary intercourse of daily life,"

and shows the hidden treasure of human tenderness, on which Custom indeed lies

"with a weight
Heavy as frost, and deep almost as life."

While talking of the state of mind and feeling he had been in during its composition, he said: "Sorrow may surely be compared to opium, Ottilie, — that delicate black droplet: dusky amber, with the dumb flash of the spirit-gold in it, such as one hears in what you call 'a mute chord' in some wildering music. Yes, this opium of grief, like the mysterious Oriental drug, increases the activity of the mind in such a way as to enable us to construct out of palpitating feelings and emotions curious and delightful intellectual pleasures."

We walked up and down the terrace, talking, quite forgetting that the Villa was locked at nine o'clock. When we turned to leave the grounds we found it was eleven o'clock. The gates were fastened we felt certain, and we might be exposed to disagreeable trouble by asking any of the sentries to open them for us. To be sure, Mr. Rochester lived in the palazzo directly opposite the corner entrance; and by sending for him as the American Ambassador, we could be relieved instantly from all annoyance. But there was an awkwardness in this which I did not like.

We had no business to be there at that hour; it had arisen from our thoughtlessness, our habit of personal independence of action as well as thought, which had been encouraged in us almost as a virtue, — certainly as a charm in our childhood, — but which has plunged both of us into many sad scrapes since we have grown up; and we have learned, that when we do thus innocently and unconsciously outrage the world's *dicta* and laws, which are wise and should be observed for many reasons, the best plan is to extricate ourselves from the penalties and dilemmas as quietly and with as little help from others as possible.

"Can you clamber down a wall, Ottilie?"

"We shall have to try it, at all events, Philip."

"Suppose a sharp sentinel shoots at us? But I remember, you, like most nervous persons, are as brave as Julius Cæsar, — especially under the spur of excitement. You will neither halloo nor faint, if he does; so come, let us make the attempt."

If I was as brave as Philip gave me credit for being, I was feeling a most cowardly repentance for having allowed myself to be placed in such a position. As we walked to the parapet wall, near the terrace, I was actually shivering and trembling with fear, — not at being shot at, — I would willingly have faced a battery of shots, — but I was dreading the appearance that the whole affair would present, in case some sentinel, seeing us, should take it into his dull head to defend the fancy ducks and other public park property of his sovereign. Suppose Philip should be killed, or I maimed!

As this absurd proposition loomed down in all its gigantic proportions upon me, I said to myself, "If they would only pitch us into the sea after they had shot us, I should not care so much; for all idle talk and gossip would be silenced in the presence of perfect ignorance of our fate."

But no such tragic and terrific event happened. While Philip was clambering down the wall, a fisherman in his boat passed near the beach. We called to him, and explained our difficulty. The man went in search of a ladder, and soon returned, giving me a chance of descending the wall safely and easily.

We had a merry walk up the beach to the Mergellina, and quite an adventure to relate on our return, magnifying it of course, and dwelling on the imaginary danger of sentinel shooting and the like; for, once relieved from the immediate presence of peril, my repentance, like that of most cowards, had passed away, and I was quite as ready to enjoy the whole affair as if I had indeed shown what Philip calls "game" through the dilemma.

PSYCHE.

HILIP and Luigi are becoming close friends. They had met before in Paris, but only in general society and among men. Their intercourse through us places them on a different footing with each other. Intelligent, frank women, with generous natures, bring truly superior men very closely together; and the influence they exercise on each other is beneficial to all.

A new period of life appears to be opening to Philip. A free interchange of thought passes between him and Luigi, and the poet seems to gain new strength while talking with this pure young high-priest of nature, who has been called so early away from life's turmoils and placed in the sanctuary.

Philip, like all truly superior persons, is free from petty jealousies and selfish uneasiness in the presence of an equal; his fine, broad-chested, healthy mind has no wretched diseases, no sad maladies of morbidity to contend with: therefore he is capable of doing full justice to Luigi. He makes me very happy by coming to me with his enthusiastic expressions of delight at their intimacy, and his frank admiration of his new friend. This morning he said to me, "Luini is a very superior man, Ottilie. His calm, observing mind, his just intuitions, almost feminine in their delicacy, his pure unspotted heart, make him a being totally apart from the rest of men. He does me infinite service. He is a draught of old Grecian to my thirsty, half-savage Teuton spirit, — very cool and refreshing. His reason is strong and yet so enlarged, that while it holds firm the folds of his character, it does not cramp or dwarf them. Now that is my trouble, you know; my imagination controls me more than my reason, and, being less firm, lets the folds fly loose, and the character therefore shows great inconsistencies."

Luigi responds frankly to Philip's friendship, and shows to me the same kind brotherly manner he has from the beginning of our acquaintance; but if I am not very much mistaken, I think he is finding in our trio "metal more attractive" than either the famous poet or his friend Ottilie. I am almost sure he is fast falling deep in love with Venitia, and yet I do not think he admits it, even to himself.

From the commencement of our intimacy he has expressed an artist's rapturous admiration for her rare beauty. As they have grown better acquainted, his attention has been attracted by the charms of her mind and the striking originality of her genius, toned down by exquisite culture and refinement, — which are to intellect and genius what the polish is to the diamond's brilliant light and the haze to the opal's fire. His sudden intimacy with me brought him first into our little circle free of ceremony; and since Philip has been here, he has seemed as one of our family circle.

Gradually Venitia has thrown aside her girlish shyness, allows her playful, piquant ways to sparkle out as she used to when we were alone, and completely enchants the poor man.

And Venitia?—Dear girl, she is beginning to be beautifully affected by this new element which is operating on her. Her playfulness and piquancy remain, but her hardness is fast disappearing. She is growing tender and gentle. All those positive points of manner, which were so difficult to come at for correction, but which I have always felt keenly and wished to have removed, are being completely transmuted into charms, by the magical influence of this true philosopher's stone of life, — love!

> " D'un moment qu'on aime,
> On devient si doux."

Love is showing itself in a deliciously naïve manner in her. She thinks she is not in love with Luigi, I am certain, — that is, if she thinks about it at all. She makes a show of talking about him frankly; greets him cordially; and asks and receives help from him in her musical studies as if he were a relative; but she shows a graceful hurry and pretty eager interest in everything, which most becomingly replaces the former imperiousness and self-contained manner, that was unnatural in so young a girl.

It takes very little to make these two unconscious lovers happy; neither is demonstrative by nature; both are highly intellectual; and a look, a tone of voice, the slightest movement, contains more food for quiet rapture and love dreams, during the hours of absence, than positive caresses could scarcely bestow on more tangible lovers, especially at this stage of their intimacy.

Luigi shows no impatience to be with her, rarely talks of her. I suppose his calm, quiet nature keeps him from all unrest. He is more with me than with the others; we walk and ride on horseback together; for neither Venitia nor Janet is fond of the persistent, almost violent exercise my restless body needs. This craving for motion in the open air is an appetite like hunger with me, and must be gratified or I suffer; therefore we are a great deal with each other, even now that Philip is here; for Philip is more fond of his cigar and lounging on the terrace over a book, than of walking.

But when we meet, as we do almost every evening, Janet, Philip, and I seem to be resolved into pleasant accessories to their beautiful vision. We are the golden *fond*, on which this intangible, unacknowledged love traces its throbbing, delicate, arabesque designs. After I return from a long walk or horseback ride, I love to lie on the lounge near the window, and look across the orange leaves and blossoms which border our beautiful terrace, on this subtle, delicate love-growth, which no one else is noticing. It is so spiritual, free from all earthly soil or rustle; only one avenue, the eye, between them; there, on that bounding, brilliant beam, their souls meet and hearts blend.

It seems to be a beautiful hour-plant, blooming in each succeeding present. I never think of a future for it. The two are floating along happily together on their enchanted life-stream, bathed in the sweet delirium of a love, which seems to need no words of acknowledgment, no vows, no troth-plighting, as vague and indefinable as one of Venitia's own wildering music-poems.

We all lounged to-day for three or four hours in the Musée Bourbonique. Philip and I went early after breakfast, as we have been doing ever since his arrival, for he is very fond of looking at these ancient marbles with me. I grow bewildered among them, they are such a vast crowd, — upwards of fifteen hundred. I am always wishing that I might have the power to select a few and have them set apart in a private gallery, that I might gaze my full, and in sweet leisure at them.

First should come the Psyche torso, of course. I cannot express in words my reverential admiration of its beauty; they are all too poor. I stand spell-bound before this great creation, and find myself listening for the tender, low words, which it seems should come from those almost speaking lips. But Cupid is flown, Psyche's wings are broken, and she stands there, stilled into cold marble, — this lovely heathen thought, — telling of the sweet faith of those old Greeks in the power of love to bestow a soul, even though it might be a soul for suffering, — still for love!

That strange myth of Psyche! The ancients were forever representing it tenderly, as if throwing "the shadow before" of what the moderns are living so fiercely. The human soul, aspiring after the divine, loses the sweet, childlike confidence in the first mysterious presence of happiness, and seeks to make this happiness tangible and positive. This was the antique thought; but it exists actively in the spirit of the present age. Everything must be tasted, held, and possessed. Nature is forever punishing this bold, rash curiosity; for penances and expiations must continue, until the human soul perfected will enter into full possession of the divine, and all the lovely foreshadowing of ancient myths and modern faiths and hopes, Eden and Psyche, Prometheus, and that Holy Sorrow, which, like the Jews' Jehovah, must be nameless, shall be made manifest.

The frolicsome young Cupid, tangled in the Dolphin's folds; his graceful limbs tossed playfully up in air with the dolphin's tail lashing in mad glee, — this group should come next, to brighten me after the solemn, stilling suggestions of that deserted, wingless Psyche.

What debtors we are to the Greeks! They have left

behind them deathless images of the beautiful. Their statues speak eloquently to those of us who listen understandingly; they are petrified poems, sweet emotions and sentiments, earnest expressions in stone. But this ancient Greek sculpture tells very plainly that it appealed to a candid, frank race of people, who required a visible lan guage of beauty. Less sensitive, less nervous than the people of the present day, they found their æsthetical food and pleasure in the simple beauty of form. They loved best the nude too; for there is a flowing beauty, a cadence, so to say, in the soft lines of that human form which is perfectly but delicately developed, that produces true sculptural harmony. The fulness and richness of drapery, which adds so much to painting and is such a powerful accessory in all modern sculpture, had no place in antique art; it seems not only to have been an interference to the chisel, but to the poetical freedom of thought and expression of their idea of sculptural beauty.

I often see persons smile when they hear us talk of "the language of art," — of different forms of art having a tongue, so to speak, by which they express the sentiments and feelings of the age producing them. They think it fanciful, and some very practical ones call it affected to use such expressions. A building is a building they say, a statue a simple stone figure, and a picture nothing but a copy on canvas of nature. But I never grow impatient with such persons; rather feel sorry that this sweet æsthetic sense, which endows us with so much capacity for enjoyment, is denied to them.

We can read these dead languages of the ancients and the Middle Ages with so much pleasure, seeing that the Beautiful has had its full rich voice in every day. The Greeks had their sculpture and architecture; the Middle Ages, their architecture and monumental sculpture and painting; and now the voice of this nineteenth century, we music lovers fondly believe, is the tone tongue. This is the true art language of a race which combines the positive, fiery character of the semi-barbarian with the poetic imaginative nature of the old Greeks, and which, too proud to show its emotions, its sufferings, its keen enjoyments in visible forms, gladly seizes on a tongue that will express its whole moral history discreetly.

"*La langue de la musique est la seule qui permette à la pensée de garder ses voiles.*" The tone tongue alone permits thought to remain veiled. Psyche can fold her beautiful wings over her throbbing heart, and floating on the sonorous wave of harmony, feel, suffer, rejoice, grieve, hope, and fear in secret.

But I have wandered far away from my gallery. The next piece of sculpture I would select should be the work of a day many centuries later than these lovely old Greek groups. The sitting figure of Agrippina — this piece of statuary so very full of feeling and tenderness — should have the next place in my collection. That great, good woman, against whom Tiberius could urge nothing but that she had "haughty looks and a turbulent spirit!" How these words tell of the struggle this granddaughter of Augustus made to obey her dying husband's conjurations: —

"By her remembrance of him, by their common children, to divest herself of her unyielding spirit and humble to fortune in the storm of her displeasure; and on her return to the city not to irritate those who were more than a match for her by a competition for the mastery." *

In this representation of her which Winckelmann pre-

* Tacitus.

ferred before all other statues of this great woman, she is seated in a chair of exquisite form, her hands are clasped in her lap, her head droops on her breast, and her face, though expressing deep anguish, has a resolute look, showing that she had courage enough to face her great griefs. Some French writer has said finely of this statue, "She seems manacled by Fate, but still unable to give up the superb thoughts which filled her soul in happy days."

Thus might she have looked when, as the historian tells us, "on her return from the perils and rigors of a sea voyage, in winter, carrying the funeral ashes of her husband, uncertain of vengeance and alarmed for herself, she stopped at the island of Corcyra, situated over against Calabria. Unable to moderate her grief, and impatient from inexperience of affliction, she spent a few days there to tranquillize her troubled spirit.

"Philip," I asked, "why does not some modern sculptor give us a representation of Tacitus's touching description of her landing at Corcyra?"

Philip repeated the passage with all his thrilling accent of expression: —

"The fleet came slowly in, not as usual, in sprightly trim, but all wearing the impress of sadness. When she descended from the ship, accompanied by her two infants, and bearing in her hand the funeral-urn, her eyes fixed steadfastly on the earth, one simultaneous groan burst from the assemblage." *

Then he added: "But, Ottilie, sculpture is not a need of the present day. These grand epics in stone are no longer really loved. The remains of the past are regarded with reverence as the great epics of Dante, Ariosto,

* Tacitus.

Tasso, and Milton are read and revered; but they are all traditions, not living things. This sensation-loving age has a stronger taste for prose than poetry of the higher order, for rhetorical, eloquent, highly decorated prose or passionate lyric poetry. The calm quiet of simple beauty and the severe thoughtfulness of ancient art are no longer demanded. The human heart now asks to be cloven, not touched; to be made to shiver with keen tingling pleasure, or pain. Then imagine how fiercely dramatic, how emotional, must be the creation which can produce the desired sensation on this nineteenth-century heart, which has grown callous from its exacting inventions, making lightning a messenger and fire a slave."

I reminded him of what Hegel says in his *Cours d' Æsthétique*, that the character of antique art is the perfect equilibrium between the idea and the sensible form, its purity, serenity, sweetness, and calm, tranquil majesty; a rhythmic beat or measured cadence, which affects us as a piece of musical sonorousness, and which makes up the charm of all its creations, whether in marble or verse, by a Phidias, a Sophocles, or a Plato.

Since Christianity appeared, the equilibrium is broken, the sentiment of the Infinite has spread itself throughout the human soul, and the idea is profoundly agitating. Humanity feels impatient at seeing itself at once free and a slave, — immortality and mortal life forever struggling, — the soul forever manifesting itself under a form which compresses and restrains it, — hence arises in Christian art a new style of the pathetic, entirely unknown to the ancients.

"O, that is all very plausible," replied Philip, "and may probably apply to the works of the Middle Ages, but not to the present day. It is not so much Christianity with us now as the positive nature of our people. The truth is, we are like the Romans. Their relics are as true to their character as are those of the Greeks to theirs. One was a poetical people; the other, like us, a practical race. In the place of statues that seem like transfixed souls, and temples which are the very ideal of beauty itself in marble, we see relics of great roads, superb aqueducts, huge excavations, noble bridges, just as at present, everything to help on the actual material life of man, not his soul."

We walked up and down the silent gallery, peopled with these still, cold creations, that stood around us, like some world of fancy or fairy tale, waiting in expectant attitude the power who should give motion and speech to their "life breathed into stone," and held there in magic death. Philip's clear voice rung out, undaunted by the weird stillness and strange solitude which awed me. Undaunted? Indeed he seemed inspired, and continued pouring out earnestly his fine rhapsodical talk, of which this is only a faint shadow.

"Sculpture is now purely a decorative thing," he said, "not an expression of thought and of worship, as in those old Greek days. The cities of the New World demand its portrait works for public adornments; the *nouveaux riches*, its prettinesses for their salons and gardens; but the faith of the present day has no saints to represent, no sweet or solemn allegories to put life into marble. Sculpture is no longer an expression of any leading thought or feeling of the times, or representation of the great schemes and plans of progress. The love and appreciation for the pure ideal is gone from the crowd. Man's great poems, which he used to ask to have sung and painted and chiselled, he now seeks for in practical, tangible objects, which he calls creations, — in tubular bridges, spanning, with a keen, gratified sense of danger escaped, some perilous abyss; the tunnelling of a mighty strait through which the waters of an ocean rush; or a magnetic chain, which comes thrilling across the great sea, seizing on the hearts of distant continents, and binding them in one thrall of positive materiality."

For a while he remained silent, and we returned to the Agrippina statue. I looked at it for some time, and then walked over to the famous one of her son Caligula. The Romans hated this unfortunate child of Germanicus so fiercely that they strove, after his death, to blot out every record of him in existence. But, notwithstanding, this statue remains, even after such treatment as might be supposed to have destroyed it forever. It was broken into fragments; and on its head can be seen the marks left by the ferrymen of the Garigliano, as they used it to steady the wheels of chariots which crossed the river in their boats. Low, mean, and degraded is the expression of the face, — very unlike that of his sister Julia, to a bust of which I then went, and after that to a bust of her son Nero.

Nero's head is, as some one has said, a biography in itself, — inflated nostrils, sensual eyes, thin lips; the whole expression of the face showing a mere enjoyer of art, not a creator. But for the possession of supreme power he would probably never have been a monster, simply a selfish egotist. Added to his evil propensities, he had mental capacities which were more than respectable, and much artistic skill and cleverness; but when able, clever men give loose to their animal passions, they do not become simply brutal, as ordinary men do, but demoniacal, — for the best idea we can form of a demon is an immortal brute.

Philip followed me in silence as I went from one marble head to the other, and I saw him smiling as I returned from Nero abruptly to Agrippina.

"I am thinking," I said, "how strange it was that the great and wise Germanicus and this virtuous Agrippina could have had such children. There must have been bad blood beyond which crept out in that pretty creature yonder, Julia, and then came to a culminating point in her son, that terrible man-devil, Nero.

"Beautiful woman she is, truly," I continued, going again to the lovely head of Julia Agrippina; "ambition scarcely shows itself in that girlish face. Her mother's resolute countenance might have ambition in it, but there is no sign of persistency, no steadiness of purpose, in these soft, mobile lines. This delicious mouth and rounding chin, and the very eyes, look as if they loved and coveted ease, pleasure, and freedom from all care. I cannot imagine such a woman replying to the Chaldeans whom she consulted on the fortune of her son, and hearing that he would certainly reign and kill his mother, 'Let him kill me, so that he reigns.'"

"Follow me," said Philip, taking my hand abruptly, and leading me across the building to the "Gallery of Large Bronzes," saying, as we walked there, "You believe in blood. So do I. And we can find proof for our belief in this very family."

On entering the hall he took me to a fine bust of Julia Augusta, as Tacitus calls Livia Drusilla.

"There is the answer to your mystery," he said. "Leave the brave, good Germanicus, and his excellent wife Agrippina, and step back another generation. Here you find the bad blood in this woman; for do you not remember she was the adulterous wife of Augustus, mother of Drusus, grandmother of the excellent Germanicus, great-grandmother of the vain, sensual beauty, Julia Agrippina, and, consequently, great-great-grandmother to Nero. The bad blood you talk of held back these descents, to gather fresh force and sweep on to a flood-tide in a Caligula and a Nero." *

While he was talking we were very much surprised at seeing Janet, Venitia, and Luigi enter the hall.

"We have been searching for you," said Janet. "Florence Folham has returned. She and her mother came to see us this morning, and Mr. Luini and I took the liberty of making an engagement for you with her, which I will leave him to explain."

"Miss Folham expressed a great liking for riding on horseback," added Luigi. "Trusting to your approval, and encouraged by Mrs. Dale, I invited her to go with us this afternoon."

"By all means. You did right. The pretty creature will be a delightful addition."

"Is she pretty?" asked Philip. "But I forgot," he added saucily, "all Ottilie's men and women — that is, those she likes — are Venuses and Sapphos, Apollos and Adonises. Luini, you and I stand a fine chance of being made demigods, I assure you, in her imagination, which is a veritable hallucination."

* The bad blood might also be attributed to Nero's great-grandmother, Julia, daughter of the Emperor Octavius Augustus, by his first wife, Scribonia. This Julia was the wife, first, of her cousin Marcellus (Octavia's son, commemorated by Virgil), afterward wife of Agrippa; by Agrippa she had a daughter, Agrippina, wife of Germanicus, and mother of Nero's mother, Julia Agrippina. This elder Julia is represented by history as a shameless, bad woman.

"Go on with your historical lecture, my learned professor," I interrupted; "you are most eloquent on that subject."

So we continued talking of Livia.

"But, Mr. Edelhertz," said Janet, with her troublesome exactitude of memory, which upsets provokingly all poetical jumping to conclusions, "do you not remember what Tacitus says of this Julia Augusta, as he calls her? 'In her domestic deportment she was formed after the model of primitive sanctity, but with more affability than was allowed by ladies of old; as a mother, zealous and determined; as a wife, kind and indulgent, well adapted to the fastidious and complex character of her husband and the subtle nature of her son.'"

"Yes, madam, I remember all that; but I remember also, that, to gratify her ambition, she married the enemy of her husband, while her husband was still living; then, to satisfy it still further, she plotted the ruin of every one who could stand in the way of her son Tiberius; and, to make this same Tiberius emperor, she murdered the very man whose blind adoration for her had placed her on the throne. No, despite the loose praise of Tacitus, she was a bad woman. Look at her, Ottilie. Here you see the same beauty which her granddaughter, Julia, inherited from her, and, added to it, is all the persistency of purpose you looked for in vain in the pretty Julia's face."

"I am always disposed," urged Janet, "to take the part of women who are abused in history; nine times out of ten, they are innocent."

"I have a capital answer to make you, Mrs. Dale," said Philip, with a laugh. "Thackeray supplies me, luckily. 'So was Helen of Greece innocent. She never ran away with Paris, the dangerous young Trojan. Menelaus, her husband, ill used her, and there never was any siege of Troy at all. So was Bluebeard's wife innocent. She never peeped into the closet where the other wives were with their heads off. She never dropped the key, or stained it with blood; and her brothers were quite right in finishing Bluebeard, the cowardly brute.' Yes, this Livia was innocent, I shall interpolate. She never poisoned her husband, not she; and Mary of Scotland never blew up hers; nor this Joanna of Naples, whom Ottilie defends, never murdered hers; nor, as Thackeray winds up drolly, Eve never took the apple, — it was a cowardly fabrication of the serpent."

Of course we laughed heartily, and dropped the argument; then went across the room to look at a Sappho head which Luigi and Venitia were admiring. We noticed every detail of this charming bust; the cheek and chin full of feeling, the tender, tearful mouth, the chaste style of head-dress, — consisting of two simple fillets, one banding the temples, and both holding up the hair, which is rolled in a rich, loose knot almost on the back of the neck, — and the poise of the head, and form of the throat, which are very fine. I looked for some time at this lovely face, and as I dwelt on its divine beauty, and recalled her genius, and sorrowful, tragic love, I thought of what that strange Frenchwoman, Madame de Staël, said, — she on whom "hunger of the heart" acted as "love on the Psyche": — "Man gives homage to woman according to the affection with which she inspires him, but all that woman grants is almost always a sacrifice."

After leaving the Sappho, we united in one burst of admiration over a bust of Plato, which might serve for a head of our Blessed Lord. There are in it majesty, dignity, and sweetness. The head is bent a little forward, and the face expresses deep thought, and a sublimity which is divine; but for its gentleness and softness, the character of the countenance would be stern. I remarked this, and Philip replied: "'As sad as Plato,' was a Greek proverb. He always walked with his head bent downward."

Some little bronze figures attracted our attention: a Venus Anadyomene, which is beautiful; it has an exquisite back, and perfect loveliness is displayed in the form and play of the limbs: also a Fortune, poised tiptoe on a globe; this last airy and delicate thing is considered one of the most curious relics from Herculaneum. Like the Venus Anadyomene, it has delicate inlayings of silver in the bronze.

Then we shook the huge key of a water-pipe, and listened, with light, trifling words, but strange, unavowed feelings of awe, to the noise of the water inside, which has been shut up there for nearly two thousand years, almost ever since that fearful night when God said "No!"

"To the pulse's magnificent come and go"

of those gay cities.

We loitered awhile by the "Drunken Faun," and laughed merrily; for Philip said all manner of droll things to the tipsy creature, who sits jollily on the empty liquor-skin, snapping his fingers in air with the maddest sort of fun. The "Mercury in Repose," by Polyclete or Lysippus, or some other great artist of those grand old Greek times, took our fancy next. The mouth is so full of life, that one listens for short breath-pants to be heard; for he seems spent with a long flight, and every muscle is relaxed and trembling with fatigue.

We noticed the bird-of-prey look in the face of Tiberius's bust, the wilful, cruel, Napoleon shape of the head, and curiously projecting ears. But the face is handsome, there being a bold, courageous strength in the fine outlines that is almost noble. The mouth, however, that sad, tell-tale feature of the face, reveals the cruelty and cold depravity, — thin, hard, dry-looking lips, utterly devoid of feeling or refinement. He resembles his mother, Livia; the same patrician features, quiet, secret brow which tells nothing, and composed expression, free even from the hate and selfishness which lay like a snake coiled around their hearts in withering folds. Dissimulation and cruelty were a necessity with both, and both were too brave and capable to show either in outward ordinary signs.

As we stood in the centre of the room, near a beautiful bronze gazelle, and looked around to see if we had missed any striking or beautiful creation, Luigi said, —

"But for that sorrowful covering up of Herculaneum and Pompeii we should have had but few and imperfect specimens of antique bronzes. The Saracen and other barbarian hordes which overran Italy melted all the metal they could find into money and arms. The Juno of Samos, you remember, was made into money. Therefore this little collection of one hundred and fifteen bronzes is now the most remarkable in the world."

"Look at this Seneca, Luini," cried Philip. "I never saw such a face in inanimate substance before. Every feature seems quivering with life. It is not remarkable for good looks, Heaven knows, nor for elevation of thought, but for life itself, — the thing almost speaks."

"The lips have a painful expression, and there is a restless feverishness about the whole face," said Venitia.

"It does not give one an elevated impression of the philosopher, that is true," remarked Janet. "He looks mean, hard, worldly, and selfish. I remember hearing

Ampère say, however, that the numerous busts of Seneca he had seen represented him always without nobleness, almost pitiful in expression; beard and hair badly kept, an affectation of exterior stoicism, a lying severity, which would deceive us if we were ignorant of Seneca's life; but that being known, they describe well the hypocritical pretensions of this Tartuffe of the Portico."

"Poor man," said Luigi; "he at least knew how to die."

The cicerone of the hall stepped up, and set us off on a peal of laughter, by informing us, with great earnestness, that all Americans said that bust resembled "a great American warrior," he had forgotten his name.

"Monsieur le Général — le Général — le Général" — and the man meditated, tapped his forehead, while we suggested every living and dead American lion we could think of. Suddenly the President hero of the Mexican war flashed across my memory. "The very one, that was the name."

We looked again and again, to see if we could discern the slightest resemblance to the effigies of General Taylor.

"The upper part of the face does look like his pictures, a little," said Janet.

"It looks a great deal more like some weather-beaten old Yankee sea-captain," remarked Philip.

Then we examined the face closely to see where the meanness lay, and where we could trace the marks of the philosopher; and we agreed that thought was expressed in the brow and head, the meanness can be seen in the mouth and chin.

"I am like old Montaigne about Seneca," said Luigi. "I do not like to hear him abused. You remember how modestly the French philosopher gives his reasons for defending both Plutarch and Seneca: — 'La familiarité que i 'ay avecques ces personnages icy, et l'assistance qu'ils font à ma vieillesse, et à mon livre massonné purement de leurs despouilles, m' oblige à espouser leur honneur.' " *

"Diderot," remarked Philip, "said his veritable image — that which will strike you with admiration, which will inspire you with respect — is in his writings; it is there you must go to seek Seneca."

"I am disposed," said Janet, "to hold your men in history to the same harsh, exact judgment you display to the women. Macaulay's summing up of Seneca's claims to the name of a philosopher is more true, to my fancy, than Diderot's opinion, or Montaigne's defence. He says, according to Seneca's views, 'the business of a philosopher was to declaim in praise of poverty, with two millions sterling out at usury; to meditate epigrammatic conceits about the evils of luxury, in gardens which moved the envy of sovereigns; to rant about liberty, while fawning on the insolent and pampered freedmen of a tyrant; to celebrate the divine beauty of virtue with the same pen which had just before written a defence of the murder of a mother by a son.' "

"I yield," replied Philip, bowing. "You took my severe judgment of women so quietly, Mrs. Dale, that, in the presence of this bust and you ladies, I am willing to accept anything you urge against the poor philosopher; but when Luini and I are alone in his library, enjoying that fine old Amsterdam Montaigne of his, over

* "The familiarity I have had with these two authors, and the assistance they have lent to my age, and to my book, wholly built up of what I have taken from them, oblige me to stand up for their honor." — *Hazlitt's translation of Montaigne*, Chap. 32, Book II.

his equally fine cigars, I shall return to my manly allegiance, and repeat what the charming old Frenchman says of his favorite author, who is, as he expresses it so quaintly, 'full of notable commodity for his humor.'"

"Ampère," remarked Janet, "said that one of the Seneca busts in the Vatican seemed to say, 'Alas! I can do nothing more.' What is this bust saying to you, Ottilie? You are looking as if you were holding a parley with it."

I started, for I was indeed, although listening to the conversation, giving speech to that almost quivering mouth, and living thought to that frowning brow, so I answered promptly in the philosopher's own words, — "Life, my dear Lucilius, is a battle."

"Vivere, mi Lucili, militare est," repeated Philip musingly, as he passed his fingers with a sort of tender sympathy over the haggard, wrinkled face of the great old Spaniard; "and this face surely tells of a fierce internal war. If this countenance be a true index of his inner man, no wonder he thought death the best part of life."

"Here is a bust of Scipio Africanus we have forgotten," said Luigi. "Look what a fine, benignant face it has."

Again we analyzed features, and were well content to read in this bust the character of that great man. The strong, heavy jaw and firm mouth are those of an energetic, resolute, intrepid general; the rapt, vague eye, and intelligent, but dreamy brow, told of that strange, half-comprehended faith which his contemporaries called mysticism, — of that elevation or enthusiasm which impelled him to hold those long, solitary conversations in the temple with Jupiter, whose son he said he was. Yes, to that grand old Roman in that far-off heathen day were given the glimmerings of a Divine light,—the belief in one living God, who was his Father.

On the left side of the fine, high, bald head we found the sacred marks, — the scars of those twenty-seven wounds which he received when he was a boy of only eighteen years of age, in defending his father, the elder Scipio. There is capability and energy in this face, but no adroitness or world-wisdom. One can well understand, while looking at it, that such a man could never maintain a hold over a mobile, capricious people as the Romans were.

"Like all leading republicans in stirring times," said Philip, "he was unconsciously a fine actor, and he played his part well. Look at that simple, wise face, and imagine it lighted up with the fire of wounded pride and indignation when, on the day of his trial before the Roman Senate, he rose up superbly, and made no other answer to his accusers but this grand one: 'Tribunes and citizens, on this very day did I conquer Hannibal and the Carthaginians. Come, Romans, let us all go to the Capitol and render thanks to the gods for our victories.'

"And, gathering his mantle around him, he strode out of the Senate, followed by the whole assembly, who forgot the trial, the charges, everything, in the effect produced on them by this fine, telling point. Great Jove, but it must have been sublime."

"There was no play-acting, however," remarked Janet, "in his retirement to this Campania; there was an honest, indignant contempt and a sorrowful, true feeling in his words, 'My ungrateful country shall not have my bones.'"

"There is no bust of Cato here," I said. "What a pity! I should like to contrast it with this of Scipio. He was the one who drove him to Liternum."

"How unhappy our enemies would be," said Luigi, "if they could only know how often their persecutions and hatred turn out to be benefits to us. Scipio was happier away from Rome. Such a man as that, after the heated life of youth and action was over, with his fine tastes and culture, showed himself in a much better and more dignified light in retirement."

"His life here must have been a very agreeable one after all," cried Philip, laughing. "A charming villa, in a delightful region of country, leisure, taste, comfortable means, and the 'best society,' with the rather pleasant sting of a little martyrdom, a little unjust persecution to make him comfortably pharisaical and self-complacent. No, old Scipio, I do not think you need our sympathy in your afflictions. I shall give all my heart holds to that sorrowful old Spaniard, Seneca, who, supposing that the cruel things the relentless Mrs. Dale urges against him were true, is so much the more to be sorrowed with; for he had to live hourly and instantly with that divine inner man, who thought and wrote such sublime words, and whose reproaches must have been fearful if he was disloyal to himself."

A MIRACLE.

E have been devoting the greater part of this first week in May to the famous spring festival of Naples, — the "standing miracle," as Baronius calls it, — the liquefaction of Saint Januarius's blood.

We have seen the miracle performed almost every day this week; but the most interesting ceremonies were those which took place the first day of the festival, last Saturday, — which was the Saturday preceding the Sunday that falls next to the calends of May, — the anniversary of the translation of the Saint's relics from Pozzuoli to Naples (400 A. D.).

Luigi had told me, some weeks ago, that he should make arrangements for me to see this miracle satisfactorily. When he learned that Mrs. Rochester and Janet also wished to be present, he kindly included them in the party; I say kindly, as it is an uncommon thing for Italian Catholics, no matter how intimate they may be with Protestants, to give them opportunities for seeing the most sacred services of their Church. They will show their galleries, their palaces, their works of art, with courteous freedom, but they jealously guard the solemn festivals of their religion from the curious and unbelieving spectator.

Through Luigi's intimacy with the Archbishop, permission was readily obtained for us to go behind the High Altar of Santa Chiara, into the space between it and those great mediæval treasures of the church, Masaccio's Royal Tombs, which I have already described. This recess was made private by heavy crimson curtains hung at each side; and eight or ten comfortable seats were placed there, for a few persons as favored as ourselves. It was a most desirable situation, for between the altar pillars and drapery we commanded a fine *coup d'œil* of the grand religious pageant which always takes place in the church the first day of the Miracle festival.

On entering the church, a little after midday, we placed ourselves in front of the altar, as we wished to see the bust of the Saint, the decorations, and, above all, the curious attendants on the ceremony; these are "the relations of Saint Januarius," as they are called, the oldest and poorest women in Naples, who are always seated within the altar balustrade, and form one of the most remarkable features of the spectacle. Seats are placed for them on the right of the altar, and from time immemorial they have literally "assisted" at these services. They were already assembled, filling up four or five benches, looking like the witches in Macbeth, clothed in grotesque costume, with horribly ugly faces, and chanting a rude, wild invocation; it was a Litany, which they repeated and repeated, unbroken and undisturbed, through the whole long ceremony. Neither the superb music of the orchestra, the interest excited by the procession, nor the intense emotion created by the slow performance of the miracle, interrupted their rude chanting; on the contrary, every interference only made them shriek the shriller, and louder; and, wild as the chanting was, there was a curious melody in it.

The costly High Altar, of fine marbles and *lapis lazuli* inlayings, was draped with crimson velvet, whose rich folds hung down beside and around the massive silver bust of the Neapolitan Saint. This bust, which was placed on the right of the altar (to the left of the spectator), holds in its interior Saint Januarius's skull.

The sunbeams streamed in on the jewelled mitre, gorgeous necklaces, and crosses adorning the bust, breaking into dazzling fragments of light as they fell on the four thousand rubies, sapphires, and diamonds there collected. One of the crosses alone had sixty-three handsome diamonds in it. Another superb one was composed of alternate large diamonds and sapphires; and still another, of fine-sized diamonds and emeralds, — all gifts from various Catholic sovereigns.

We looked at these splendors leisurely, and the Catholic members of the party had time to perform their devotions; for we were not to take our places behind the altar until the procession came near the church; and the warning for our removal was to be the martial music accompanying it.

The plan of that day's celebration was this. In the morning, the silver bust containing the Saint's head had been brought to Santa Chiara from its home, the Chapel of Saint Januarius, which is in the right aisle of the Cathedral, — a beautiful little Greek cross building, that cost half a million of ducats, and is filled with exquisite works of art, such as Zampieri's, Giordano's, and Domenichino's paintings, Fiorelli's bronzes, and Vinaccia's marvellous silver *basso-rilievos* and sculpture.

After the bust departed, a procession formed in the Cathedral, consisting of the Cardinal-Archbishop, his clergy, and the municipal authorities; which after forming proceeded to the Chapel, to obtain the sacred relics. These relics are always kept in a place called the Tabernacle, which is a large aperture behind the altar of the Saint Januarius Chapel. This Tabernacle is closed up by a massive iron door, with two strong locks; one key is kept by the municipal authorities, the other by the Cardinal-Archbishop, and both possessors must always be present at the opening of the door. The Tabernacle contains the *châsse*, or shrine, of richly chased silver and cut-glass; in it are the sacred vials holding the relics.

The Cardinal, after entering the Chapel, unlocked the Tabernacle door, took the shrine carefully in his hands, and left the Chapel and Cathedral at the head of a most stately procession, composed of his canons, the municipal authorities, men carrying the costly silver busts and statues of the forty-eight saints, protectors of Naples, — which superb works belong also to the Chapel of the Treasury of Saint Januarius, — accompanied by soldiers, and military bands playing all the while the most inspiring music.

This procession, with its fine gilt state coaches and statues; superb uniforms, glittering banners, and rich canopies; burning incense, rising up from beautifully-wrought silver censers, tossed high aloft in the air, and gay music, — formed a sight well worth witnessing; and if we are here another year, we shall select it for the first day's view. It proceeded along the Anticaglia and through various streets until it reached Santa Chiara, followed by crowds of people; and an hour or so after midday, while we were sitting in silence before that superbly decorated altar, we heard the music first faintly, and then approaching nearer.

I had noticed a little group of gentlemen standing half

within the archway of a side entrance to the sacristy, composed of Church dignitaries, among whom was the Pope's Nuncio. As the procession music drew nearer the church, one of these clergymen stepped forward, and made a friendly sign with his head to Luigi, who arose and told us to follow him.

This gentleman was a fine, soldierly looking man; he walked in front of us with a courteous air, managing his long purple robe with much grace. He wore on his shoulders a small red silk cape, — cape and robe were buttoned from throat-band to shoe-buckle with very small buttons, no larger than peas, placed as close as possible. He held aside one of the curtains of the space where we were to be seated with the most courtly reverence, while we passed in, then entered and assisted Luigi with much interest in placing us in the best position for seeing both the procession and the ceremony. This accomplished, he bowed gracefully to us, and resting his hand on Luigi's shoulder, looked into his face with a pleasant, friendly smile, said a few words in a low tone, and disappeared behind the curtains.

"That is one of the canons of Saint Restituta," said Luigi, as he took his seat behind us. "He belongs to the Chapter of the Metropolitan Church, and enjoys many of those distinctions you admire so much, Ottilie; he can wear the ermine cape and the mitre, — can bear the crosier and cross. One of your favorite Popes, Paul IV., — Cardinal Carafa, — was a Neapolitan canon, like this gentleman; also Urban VI. and Boniface IX. There are thirty of these canons officiating in the Duomo, or Cathedral; but the church belonging to them is Saint Restituta, that ancient building adjoining the Cathedral, in the aisle leading off on the left, as you enter the Duomo. It is the oldest church in Naples, I believe, for it was founded by Constantine the Great, in 334 A. D., and has always been independent of the Archbishop, who can only visit it in the character of apostolical delegate. You will see this canon taking part in the ceremonies of to-day. He has been detailed for some special duty at this church, probably to assist the Nuncio, who always has jurisdiction over Santa Chiara."

Just then the Pope's Nuncio entered with a party of ladies, for we had found the space unoccupied. This dignitary is rather a handsome, smooth-faced, smooth-mannered man, not at all priestly or grave-looking, rather gay and mundane. Luigi and Mrs. Rochester told us the rank of the ladies accompanying him, two of whom were diplomatic associates of the American Ambassadress.

One was a pretty young Roman princess, as tender and lovely looking as About's "Tolla"; there was a regal-looking Russian duchess; and besides the two Ambassadresses, a graceful German countess, full of unconscious and bewitching coquetry, evidently the belle and popular woman of the party; for although the lowest in rank, she was the one to whom the Nuncio paid the most attention and the others showed the most courtesy; all of which she accepted in the prettiest manner, generously insisting on seating them before she took her own place. To this unselfish disposition, probably, she owed her popularity, for she was not so very pretty, I think. Her face, however, had one great charm; it was, as Emerson says, "fluid with expression," and so rippled all over with happy smiles and pleasing looks, as to make us unmindful of its features.

We have often spoken of her since, and not one of us has been able to tell Venitia and Philip the color of her eyes, the shade of her hair, or the tint of her skin; we simply say, "She was lovely and charming."

Very soon the procession arrived at the Basilica. The statues and busts were carried in first. As they entered the large door, glorious music poured out from the choir, filling every part of the grand old church with its rich, subtle fluid. It was a fine orchestral symphony, composed for the occasion by Mercadante. Luigi told us the great old master was there in person; but not to lead his beautiful work, for, alas! the poor old man is becoming hopelessly blind.

The procession was very imposing. The eight-and-forty silver statues and busts, each one on a gilt pedestal, placed on a crimson-covered platform, with rich silken canopy, and carried by golden rails on the shoulders of superbly-formed Neapolitans, filed up one side of the large Basilica, and after a gracious, reverential obeisance to the bust of San Januarius at the altar, swept grandly around and moved, with their accompanying banners, down the other side of the church, leaving ample room in the centre for the immense crowd of spectators and soldiery collected there.

This finished, the crowd separated as if by magic or machinery; and far down this long aisle of human beings, near the door of the church, appeared the Archbishop and clergy, robed in full canonicals, blazing in the afternoon sun with purple, and gold, and precious stones.

The music pealed out still more grandly. Every neck was stretched forward eagerly, each one was anxious to see Cardinal Duke Sforza — who was holding the sacred relics — approach the High Altar. Clouds of incense arose. The old women shrieked out their witchlike plain-song in still shriller tones, some striking the key-note of the symphony, while others, with the unconscious ear for musical harmony which these Neapolitans possess by nature, kept their wild chant in curious, grotesque union with the scholarly composition of the maestro; the effect produced reminded me of the demon supporters to old altars, or the impish gargoyle heads on the roof-spouts of some superb cathedral.

The clergy, on reaching the altar, ranged themselves on either side, according to their functions; among them, I recognized the gentleman who had so kindly placed us in our seats. His keen, dark eyes flashed in for an instant through the pillars; I fancy he wished to see if he had been successful; a half-look of recognition passed between us as our eyes met.

The Archbishop placed the shrine in front of the altar, on the broad slab, a little to the right of himself, directly opposite me, and so near that by reaching out my hands I could have touched it. The shrine was hollow on the side towards us, and the two bottles, which looked like old-fashioned vinegar-cruets, stood on its small silver shelf. There was nothing under or above, and the illuminations of the altar were not near enough to affect them.

We examined these bottles with curiosity as well as great interest. They contained a substance which in hardening had adhered to the sides, resembling dark red sealing-wax. The Archbishop took them in his hands, — one and then the other, — held them up by the top and bottom with his thumbs and middle fingers; turned them around and upside down, showing that the substance inside was hard and immovable; then he returned them to the shrine, and began the solemn services.

The belief in relation to this miracle is, that the solution and ebullition of the blood are caused by the approach of the vials and head to each other; while waiting for this to be accomplished, solemn religious ceremonies are performed, and devout prayers and litanies offered up to God.

Saint Januarius was a Bishop of Benevento in the early part of Diocletian's persecution of the Christians. This was the tenth and most bloody one, continuing from 286 A. D. until the time of Constantine, 312 A. D. The good Bishop of Benevento had a dear friend whom he loved tenderly, Sozius, Deacon of Miseno. This Sozius, with several other men, was seized, by an order of Dracontius, Governor of Campania, and thrown into prison at Pozzuoli.

When Saint Januarius heard this sorrowful news, instead of caring for his own safety, and keeping himself in seclusion, he travelled in all haste to comfort and encourage his friend. The Governor, learning that an eminent person had come to visit the prisoners, gave orders to have him also seized. The Saint was thrown into the same prison with his friend and companions, and soon after an order arrived from the Emperor condemning them to be torn in pieces by wild beasts.

But when they were taken to the amphitheatre at Pozzuoli and exposed to the half-famished lions, the savage animals crouched tamely and even kindly at their feet; nothing could provoke them to touch the holy men. This exasperated the Governor so much, that he ordered them to be beheaded. They were executed and buried near Pozzuoli, as Bede testifies.

When Christianity triumphed, about 400 A. D., the relics of these holy men were disinterred and distributed. Miseno obtained Sozius, and Naples was fortunate enough to secure Saint Januarius. The Neapolitan faithful believe that his relics preserve their city, not only from volcanic destruction, but many other dangers.

At the time of the Saint's martyrdom there was a holy woman present, who collected some of his blood in two bottles. The tradition tells that she took it to a Bishop of Naples, Saint Severus, and when he touched it, the blood liquefied and bubbled up, and continued doing so, on the annual feast of the Saint, 19th September, and on various other occasions.

Thus it can be seen that this miracle is of very ancient date, counting back as far as 400 A. D.; and besides, many holy, learned, and venerable men have believed in it. Cardinal Lambertini, afterwards Benedict XIV., published a famous defence of the liquefaction of San Januarius's blood.* Baronius, Ribadeneira, and Bollandus also wrote in its favor. Indeed, the list of the great and learned men who have examined this miracle, not only attentively, but with reverential, jealous suspicion, would be too long to copy.

Then, on the other side, many distinguished and equally learned German and English Protestants have attributed this ancient and wonderful fact to the heat of the officiating priest's hands, the steam or vapor of the altar tapers and lamps, or some unknown chemical influence.

Cardinal Sforza's hands did not touch the bottles on the parts where the blood is congealed. There was no lamp or candle flame near them. And as for "chemical influence," what a marvellous discovery would that chemi-

* *De Canoniz*, C. IV. par. 1, c. 81; also Alban Butler's Lives of the Saints, Vol. III. p. 501.

cal secret be, which has been so strangely kept for fourteen hundred years!

Scripture miracles are objects of faith, and never questioned by orthodox Protestant or Catholic Christians. Other miracles are not regarded in the same light, nor does our faith rest on them as on the revealed ones of the Gospel. It is prudent and wise to examine such miracles closely, and be thoroughly convinced that they are supernatural; but it is well, at the same time, however, to bear in mind, that the glorification of God is the great thing contained in a miracle; that its main intention is, to excite in us more lively sentiments of humble adoration, love, and praise; not to obtain any worldly gift or advantage.

Such a miracle as this of Saint Januarius illustrates and confirms the faith of the devout Catholic Christian, while the doubting brother is not condemned for withholding his belief, but treated patiently and tenderly, as our Blessed Lord bore with St. Thomas.

Janet said, after we returned home that day, — and it was the only remark made on the subject, for we all felt too serious to talk much about it, — "Admitting that there is a fraud or juggle, that may be discovered by some person cleverer than all the great and good men who have examined the matter, this one thing is certain, that pure and holy man, Cardinal Sforza, has never lent himself to it. The strange work is accomplished without any help from him. I was sufficiently convinced of this fact by the sight of his calm, beautiful, saintly face and devout expression during the holy invocations. There was something inexpressibly effective in the simple earnestness and childlike faith he displayed, when the miracle seemed delayed, and he chanted aloud, independent of the service apparently, '*Amen, dico vobis, quidquid orantes petitis, credite quia accipietis, et fiet vobis.*' " *

I do not know how long the services lasted. While I was lost in deep thought over such faith and its power, I was aroused by a shrieking chant which burst from the old women shriller and more impatient than any of their preceding cries; just then, too, the symphony pealed out in strange dissonances, and a discordant passage from the wind instruments followed, reminding me of the weird incantation scene in Weber's *Der Freyschutz.* The Archbishop recited a litany, in concert with his canons, and each one seemed overflowing with holy fervor.

I turned and looked at the vials; as I did so, I felt thrilled to my heart. I could hardly credit my senses, for on that very instant I saw the hard substance suddenly change! Red blood trickled down the sides of the bottles, and, as the liquid accumulated, it looked warm and bubbling.

The Archbishop held the sacred vials aloft, that the multitude might see, and his face seemed radiant and glowing with a divine exultation. A cannon thundered forth from the close outside the church, a peal of thanksgiving burst from the people and mingled with the wild melody of the symphony. The Archbishop descended from the altar, carrying in his hands one of the bottles, and, followed by the canons, went around the full length of the Basilica to share his joy with the people.

When he had finished the circuit, instead of returning to the altar, to our surprise he approached the place where we were seated. I never dreamed of the high

* "Verily I say unto you, whatsoever ye seek, praying, believe that you will receive, and it shall be done for you." — St. Mark.

favor which was coming to me, obtained by Luigi's kindness.

The curtains were held aside, the Archbishop entered, and as he drew near us I saw him exchange a look with Luigi, who took my hand in his for a moment. The Cardinal-Archbishop stopped in front of me, and smiled kindly. With a half-bewildered feeling I knelt down and received the sacred vial in my trembling hands; he aided me in holding it to my lips, and gave me his blessing; then he left the recess, accompanied by the few clergymen who had entered with him, and returned to the altar.

The military bands began beating their drums. The Cardinal, holding the silver shrine high before him, in which were the bottles and the warm, flowing blood, and followed by his canons, went in solemn procession down through the centre of the crowd, leaving the building as he had entered it.

The intense excitement which pervaded the dense mass of human beings thronging the Basilica made them surge to and fro like a high sea. We reached our barouche, which was waiting for us in the close, by a private passage-way through the back part of the church, and drove home in serious, respectful silence.

A DINNER AT BAIÆ.

HAVE had so little time to write in my journal, that I have allowed many pleasant occurrences to pass unnoticed. Florence Folham and Philip have been riding on horseback with Luigi and me, for Philip says he is captivated with the exercise; I shrewdly suspect he is more captivated with Florence. He tries to be very bold about this sudden fancy for riding, desiring to deceive either himself or me, and I say not a word except to tease him a little about wishing to rid himself of some of his superfluous corpulency.

"How perfidious and cruel you women are," he cries; "I can call all the world to witness that you have for years, Ottilie, admired what you called my 'superb proportions.'"

"But when they cease to be proportions, and become dimensions, dear Philip, you cannot expect me to remain true to what no longer exists."

I do not wonder, however, that he admires Florence. She is a charming creature, — "*si gentille et blonde comme les blès*," as a French lady said very prettily of her the other evening; an alliterative comparison which loses half its point when translated into "fair as the wheat," and yet it is strongly suggestive of just such beauty as hers. She has golden hair hanging in loose, floating curls which let the light in over her soft red-and-white skin in the most delicious flecks; and blue eyes with the hue of the *Viola pedata*,—the bright little flower found in early spring on the margins of wheat-fields,—eyes that are as cold as the hardy little *Viola pedata* itself, but which at times have a strange misty expression when she is deeply moved, either by Venitia's playing, or when singing one of her own operatic passages; this sweet mistiness seems as a sort of prevision of future "trouble, love, and poesy."

> "Such mystic lore is in her eyes
> And light of other worlds than ours,
> She looked as she had fed on flowers,
> And drunk the dews of Paradise."

Although "English from top to toe," so far as blood and birth go, foreign education has made her a complete Parisienne in manner and appearance. Her toilette is always *comme il faut*, and in the last mode of the month, for the family has an income which counts well on the continent; and her gowns, bonnets, and even light fancy jewelry, vary in the most systematic manner according to the orthodox law of the Parisian mode. She looks like a Follet fashion-plate done up into a charming little pastel study, as Philip aptly observed when he first saw her.

Her voice is in keeping with her appearance. She has been a pupil of Duprèz, and has one of those true Parisienne voices Scudo describes so graphically, as having "more sharpness than sonorousness, more vibration than force"; a true salon voice, and exquisitely cultivated. The freshness of youth and her frank, warm English heart make of this sharpness, or elevation of sound, and vibration an excellence rather than a defect; for the one is thrilling, and the other touching.

"She sings with a tear in her voice," Luigi says, and Philip last night compared her execution of the soliloquy in the last act of *La Traviata* to the misty light in an opal. Her voice is a little veiled, and the vibration in such heart-rending passages sounds as the hidden spark in an opal looks. Venitia compares her singing or execution of cadenzas to small diamond points, and quotes also Scudo's delicious description,—"little pearls falling on scarlet velvet."

But to my ears, her notes, while they are sparkling, are also round and liquid, not like diamond points or any hard gem, but as drops of dew, and they roll off in the air as we see glittering beads of water fall from the downy petals of a rich-hued flower. It is a pure soprano, very telling and bird-like in the upper division, and though trembling and delicate in the bridge-notes, there is a warm hue in them, which is not at all feverish, but gives just tenderness enough to create interest and almost love for the pretty singer herself, as well as admiration for the music.

Philip is completely infatuated with her, but he carries it off bravely, as if it were a mere fancy for a pretty girl, and compliments her openly, — compliments which are so bewitching from a man like Philip, for they come colored with all the rich hues of his genius. Last evening she was singing the Prayer in "*Assisa al piè d' un salice*," from Otello. Philip was leaning over the back of the lounge on which I was sitting, giving me the benefit of his short, enthusiastic ejaculations. I looked up in his keen, bright eye, as she ended the last cadenza on "*cenere a bagnar*," where the voice mounted finely to the upper B, resting there an instant, and making a half-ending in a very effective "Ah," then came rippling down, full of little sobs, to the throat-notes, giving the "*bagnar*" on the key-note with a most touching expression of sorrow. I whispered, —

> "'T is a sweet whirlwind (striving to get out)
> Heaves her soft bosom, wanders round about,
> And makes a pretty earthquake in her breast.'"

For one instant Philip looked at me as if he could have worshipped me, with that sublime generosity men show when you make them happy, and then electrified us all, and covered dear Florence's delicate brow with the happiest blushes by repeating to her, as a compliment, in his most impassioned and eloquent style, the whole beautiful description from Crashaw's "Music's Duel," in which is the passage I had quoted. His superb recitation of this lovely poem created the greatest enthusiasm in our little circle; as Janet said this morning, —

"Surely there can be nothing in this world so gratifying to a man, as a society-triumph such as Philip experienced then. It was free from the vulgar intoxication of public applause, and filled to the brim with that keen sense of pleasure caused by the sudden sensation one feels when conscious of carrying along on the brilliant magnetic current of one's own genius and eloquence hearts and minds equal to one's own."

A day or two since we had a fine dinner at Baiæ. We started early in the morning, for it is now the latter part of May, and the weather, though delightful, is very warm, especially at midday. Mrs. Folham, Janet, and Venitia went in the coach, for we cannot persuade Venitia to ride; she says the management of the reins and exercise of the arms unfit her for musical execution, making her fingers tremble and her touch uncertain.

We had a glorious day of course; lived over old Roman times, quoted Homer, Virgil, Livy, Tacitus, and the Holy Book, for this whole promontory is filled full to overflowing with sacred and profane memories, which rush along in swift currents together, making a wildering whirlpool at times. We have to leap back and forth in history with a mental agility that tests our skill finely.

It was a regular excursion, and every celebrated spot in that direction was visited; for although we have driven and ridden so often around the environs of Naples, we have never yet stopped at any of the remarkable or classical spots. The first place we visited was Virgil's Tomb, which stands near the entrance of the Grotto of Posilippo.

"I am indebted to Ottilie for my first idea of this place," said Philip, when we reached the brow of the hill in which it is built; "it was given me by a drawing of hers, which hung in my father's dressing-room when I was a boy."

"Clear away in those happy years long ago," I thought, as I sat down on the top of the ivy-covered columbarium, and remembered the little drawing. I recalled all the feelings of girlish pride I had on receiving Mr. Edelhertz's praise, and the long, pleasant talk we had at the time I gave it to him; he described to me in his precise, elegant English, as he examined my drawing, the situation and sweet surroundings of this delightful place, which he had visited in his youth. The past swept over me like a flood; and it seemed as if I was living two existences at once.

Philip and Florence rambled over the hill-top, talking gayly, and enjoying the delicious landscape, which the early morning sun made as fresh and bright as is her young beauty. Luigi and Venitia explored the inner part of the tomb, and I sat there listening to loved voices of the dead and gone, feeling very gray and ashen hued. I could hear Luigi's rich tones and Philip's clarion note gathering in around me; they were both loving, as I had been loved, giving to two women the same hopes which had been given to me. "But there let the likeness end," I said mournfully to myself, "for I sit here alone, on the brow of a tomb, with snow falling inward on the dead hopes of my heart."

Janet, who had been clambering about like a kid, came up to me, and leaned her hand on my shoulder in silence for a while, then she bent over and gathered a branch of Casimir Delavigne's laurel, saying with a merry laugh, —

"'Break from the sacred laurel the atoning bough.'"

The rest of the party joined us, and after a little talk on the numberless memories connected with the spot, from the time of Virgil to the present day, we descended the hill.

"Now, ladies," cried Philip, as he helped Florence mount her horse, "I have made myself guide-in-chief of this procession, therefore I shall announce when the enthusiasm must commence and when it must cease. The curtain now falls on Virgil's Tomb, and rises on the Grotto of Posilippo, sacred to the memory of Corinne and Petrarch, for when a lady is in the question she must be mentioned first even at the expense of a hundred years or so."

We trotted gayly through the dark grotto, which, although it was so early in the morning, resounded with the cries and shouts of the donkey-boys, and crowds of people, forever surging to and fro in this dark tunnel. When we reached Pozzuoli, we dismounted again in order to visit the numerous places of interest in this "Little Rome" of Cicero, — the Temples, the Baths, the Amphitheatre, and the Villa of the great Roman orator, in which he wrote the *De Fato* and the *Academicæ*. The portico, and its beautiful woods, which he called the Academy, and its lovely promenade along the shore, — the whole of this charming abode in which he said he "could be so happy if the importunate did not oblige him to desert it," — are all gone; only some ruined piles of stone, over which the sea washes, mark where the beautiful Villa Puteolana of Cicero stood.

Then we walked along the shore to the very spot where, nearly a hundred years after the orator was murdered, two unknown men landed, "after a perilous voyage from Cesarea, on their way to Rome," whither they were going to give to their Faith that which is its seed, — the Blood of Martyrs. These two men "tarried with the brethren" at Pozzuoli seven days, then travelled on to their great Life in Death.

Yes, at that very period while Nero and Poppea were sinning so madly, and the poor, frightened, lovely Julia Agrippina was fleeing to this Puteolan shore to escape the death she met so bravely, — in those wicked Roman days, described with such awful severity by Tacitus, when the old oracles were growing dumb, and "the gray old gods of Hellas" becoming palsied and dying out, — these two plain men of a despised and enslaved nation went journeying on wearily to Rome as prisoners of man, but glorious messengers of God, bearing strange news, "Great Pan was dead."

Venitia wished to go to the Cathedral to visit the tomb of Pergolesi. As we approached the church and saw its massive masonry and Corinthian columns, we remembered that when St. Paul and St. Luke "tarried to rest awhile with the brethren" in the town of Puteoli, this Christian church was then a Roman temple, dedicated to Augustus.

"Two thousand years nearly have swung around," said Janet, "and that little leaven has worked bravely."

After visiting the church, we went to the grand ruins of the Temple of Serapis, and looked up at the three mysterious pillars on which Nature has engraved her curious hieroglyphics, telling wondrous tales of age and change. We stepped carefully from stone to stone, and peered down wistfully into the fast-gathering waters which hide from the most searching gaze the once beautiful marble pavements of the temple.

Luigi explained to us as much as is known of the history of this marvellous ruin. The three columns which are standing were part of a *pro-naos*, or vestibule, of six columns and two pilasters, which supported a richly sculptured frieze ; fragments of the three other superb columns and the frieze lie scattered around. The three which are standing are each forty feet high, and formed of a single piece of cipollino marble. There was a court one hundred and forty feet long, and one hundred and twenty-two feet wide, surrounded by a portico of forty-eight columns; and in the centre of this court stood a circular temple, which had sixteen columns of African marble, that have been taken away and put in the theatre of the Caserta Palace.

Some suppose it was an Egyptian temple, but the learned disagree about it altogether. It is a grand, solemn mystery, as profound as the strange old faith said to have been celebrated in it. A semicircular niche is shown, where stood the Jupiter Serapis, which is now in the Musée Bourbonique. The many volcanic eruptions, and the various physical changes to which the whole of this portion of the Mysentine promontory has been subjected, at one time caused these ruins to be covered over and forgotten.

During the earthquakes of 1536 - 1538, in Don Pedro de Toledo's time, Monte Nuovo, a mountain about a mile from this temple, and four hundred and forty feet above the level of the sea, rose up in three days' time, formed by the accumulated ejections from the earth of red-hot pumice-stones. As the base of this mountain covers about a mile and a half of ground, the whole face of the country in its vicinity was naturally very much altered in making place at such short notice for the strange new-comer. The tradition tells of a village, royal villa, and other buildings being destroyed. At that time, this temple, which is spoken of by writers of the day as "the ruins recently uncovered," was again lost, and remained overgrown with trees and brushwood, forgotten for over two hundred years.

In 1750, when a palace which had been built for Don Pedro, over two hundred years before, was converted into barracks, the upper part of these fine columns was seen peeping above the ground. Charles III. — Don Carlos, that Bourbon hero — ordered the place to be uncovered. Then this fine temple, adorned with costly marbles, full of broken sculpture, was found. There were marble pavements and mosaic floors, and statues and vases; and also some curious hieroglyphics left by Nature, that silent, mysterious power, which told that this great temple must have known other changes than that of mere earth-burial; for high up on these grand columns, within a third of their summits, were distinct traces of ancient watermarks; also little holes, drilled deep in by a species of bivalve sea-shell called lithodornus; and above these busy little traces of ocean labor were marks of the restless, angry beating of sea-waves!

No wonder the antiquarians and geologists have been at a loss and not known how to find their place in a stone book whose weird leaves tell such contradictory stories.

I felt very solemn as I wandered through this mysterious old temple, stepping from slab to slab of stone, on the ruined fragments of superb sculpture, across the dull, sluggish sea-stream which is again slowly creeping through it. About thirty years after its last disentombing in 1780, the building was found to be slowly sinking again; and during the last half-century it has sunk two feet; probably in a few hundred years more it will be all gone and forgotten as before.

From this temple, or Serapeon, as it is also called, we went to the Amphitheatre, which was uncovered in 1838. It was here that Nero entertained Tiridates, King of Armenia, with a bull-fight, and surprised his royal visitor by leaping into the arena himself and killing two bulls with the same javelin. Foolish Nero! To use a *mot* of Jefferson, he must have had "a canine love of praise."

We left Pozzuoli and proceeded along one of the Roman roads bordered by tombs. Luigi directed our attention to the marks of the ancient chariot-wheels on the huge blocks of lava with which it is paved. This famous old Vesuvius is looked upon as a fearful destroyer, and so it is, of man and man's labor; but it creates more than it ruins, renders back more than it takes away; and one of its most marvellous creations is this fire-stone, called lava, which has been used for ages in the building of ramparts, great castles, and the paving of roads like these Appian and Flaminian routes, over which myriads of human beings have journeyed for centuries, and yet the huge blocks of stilled fire resist the wear and tear of time and use.

Yes, centuries and centuries ago this road was journeyed over by great Romans, who came to the Campania on warlike errands; or later, in more luxurious days, to visit their superb villas in this Parthenopian Paradise;—Scipio in his pride and then in his anger, Agrippina in her sorrow, Tiberius in his suffering, and the poor Aphrodite Julia in her fear.

Along its smooth course also rolled gay chariot-loads of pleasure-seeking people, coming to these luxurious Baths of Baiæ, to lakes covered with rose-leaves, that old Seneca talks of, where bathers floated in the perfumed waters by moonlight to the sound of ravishing music. Stately Roman matrons, with fair, cold brows of Pallas and Diana, but burning hearts of Venus and Psyche, rushed swiftly along in their mad pursuit of pleasure.

And along this road journeyed also those two travel-worn, unknown Israelites, towards the Capitol of the world, going there to plant an unpretending standard, which should wave through ages of desolation, war, luxury, learning, human craft and cunning, all unchanged,—the standard of the simple fishermen of Galilee,—to which king and kaiser bow.

It was an hour or two past midday when we reached Baiæ, and we were really hungry and tired, notwithstanding Janet's fine hamper of sandwiches and iced wine, which had been well used during the morning.

"I sent my Greek here yesterday," said Philip, "with Luigi's Andrea, and the report was anything but favorable as to accommodations; so that huge van which you see unpacking is for us."

We walked towards one of the ruins of the magnificent ancient Thermæ or Baths. It was the one called the Temple of Mercury; a superb circular hall with vaulted ceiling, and the blue heaven looking down through the ivy-crowned opening in the roof, shedding delicious rays and flecks of tenderness, as the sunlight broke through the delicate maiden-hair fern. Lycopodia and all sorts of bind-weeds, mingled with the fern and ivy, clambered around, set their little frail but firm-toothed roots into the stone, then fell pendant in soft, swaying branches, doing their best to hide and adorn this broken, irregular gap in the ceiling.

Directly beneath this opening was quite a little garden-wilderness, nourished by the rain and freshened by the sun which came daily streaming down upon it; mesem bryanthemums of vivid purple hue peeped out with their bright yellow eyes among the tangled mass of verdure.

Upon the ground were spread large carpet-mats, and there were camp-stools and small tables, and, best of all, nice cushioned hammocks. When we expressed our delight and amazement at the sight of all these comforts, Luigi and Philip, to whose gallant thoughtfulness we owed them, looked as happy as boys.

"Now rest yourselves," said Philip, "while Luigi and I consult with our men about that great business of the day, — dinner."

Such a merry dinner as we had on the little tables, where each one was served by one's self! And we had a pleasant lounge in the hammocks again, after the luxurious feast was over, — a feast which had all the elegance of a grand dinner, without any tiresome ceremony.

The gentlemen smoked, and walked in and about the ruins, and talked to us delightfully. Some girls came in with tambourines and danced the Tarantelle, which was as poor as stage finery looks by daylight.

"We are spoiled by the ballet," said Philip. "These peasant dances, like many fine national melodies, have the rich kernel taken from them when the clever theatrical or operatic artist appropriates them."

"Are you too tired for a little more sight-seeing?" asked Luigi, as we stood out on the roadside in the after part of the day.

Not at all. We were all as fresh as larks at sunrise, and quite ready to complete the well-planned excursion. We went to the birdless Lake of Avernus, the Mare Morto, the Elysian Fields, and the cave of the melancholy priestess of Apollo, — Deiphœbe, the Cumœan Sibyl.

The classical associations connected with the names of these famous old places gave rise to a delightful talk; and Philip's fine rhapsodies were as sparkling as the glowing beads on the golden Capri wine which we had been drinking.

The Piscina Mirabilis pleased me most of all that sunset sight-seeing. It can scarcely be called a ruin: it is as strong and firm as when the Romans used it as a reservoir for the waters of the Julian aqueduct centuries ago. We descended a flight of forty broad stone steps, then an inclined causeway, which led us to the bottom. There we found an apartment with a vaulted roof of grand masonry, supported by four lines of massive pillars, twelve in a row.

The whole hall or chamber was lighted by several circular openings in the roof, which, like the irregular ceiling-gap of the Temple of Mercury, were draped with all manner of lichens, ivy, and the soft maiden-hair fern, the loveliest of all the fascinating order of Felices. This clung about every part of the building, and, as the soft west wind of sunset came frolicking in through the ivy-crowned opening in the centre, it would ripple up the delicate, green, toothed leaves, like so many little waves on a streamlet. This fine old relic of the great Roman days is to be found on the summit of a hill between the Bay of Bauli and Mare Morto.

"Here, Ottilie," said Philip, as we came to some ruins on the Punta di Pennata, "this was the villa of that Roman matron who despised jewels, and considered two unruly boys of more value than precious stones. I remember, when you were a girl, you voted Cornelia, mother of the Gracchi, a woman of poor taste."

We laughed over the curious betrothal of this great and good daughter of Scipio Africanus. Tiberius Sempronius Gracchus, her husband, was originally an enemy of her father; but when the officers were taking L. C. Scipio to prison, and none of the tribunes interfered to protect him, Gracchus said that he did not seek to gain, by any act of his, the favor of the Scipios, but having seen Scipio Africanus leading the kings and generals of enemies to prison, he should never suffer his brother to be led to the same place. This generous and manly conduct had a curious effect on the Senators and Scipio, which effect is an evidence of the primitive, almost child-like state of feeling of the times, and shows also that their hatreds and enmities arose more from jealousy — as do those of children and immature minds — than from principle.

Some time after, the Senators were supping together

at the Capitol, and they unanimously requested Scipio Africanus to give his youngest daughter, Cornelia, to Tiberius Gracchus as wife; Scipio consented, and the contract was made in the presence of the whole assembly. On his return home he told his wife, Emilia, that he had arranged a marriage for her daughter. Madame Scipio did not like his taking such a step without consulting her in the disposal of their common child. In her resentment she said, "Why, even supposing you had given her to Tiberius Gracchus, her mother should not have been kept in ignorance of your intention."

Scipio showed a wisdom in managing this little domestic tempest which, unfortunately, he did not display when he had to deal with his countrymen; he waived aside all discussion, good-naturedly telling her she had named the very man, and that he was glad her opinion coincided with the Senators and his.

This young girl was the famous Cornelia, mother of the Gracchi. In her childless old age she bought this villa, and followed her father's example, dying in voluntary exile; but the Romans honored her memory by a statue, bearing the inscription, "To Cornelia, Mother of the Gracchi."

"This anger of the Scipio family," I remarked, "reminds me of feminine resentments, in which the injured one seeks a revenge which afflicts herself as much, if not more, than it hurts her opponent. Scipio's angry epitaph, depriving his countrymen of his bones, was so like a high-spirited, affectionate woman, who naïvely takes it for granted that her enemy will feel her reproaches as much as she should under similar circumstances; and the eager desire the Romans displayed to honor the family after death as much as they had wronged them in life, gives the whole affair the tone of a sorrowful family quarrel, which is fiercer and bitterer than other disputes, because of the pent-up love which feels itself scorned, and aching hearts stung almost to madness by fancied or real wrongs inflicted by the very beings held dearest and loved most fondly."

"I fancy," said Janet, "that these Scipios must have been like many other excellent and gifted persons, — too sensitive and difficult in disposition. An enthusiastic restlessness of mind and body enabled them to perform splendid and generous acts, but they exacted from plain, practical, commonplace mortals, with whom they had to live hourly, more capability of appreciation than they possessed; then, like all such exceptional persons, they suffered keenly, and, as they happened to be distinguished, they called on all posterity to sympathize with them, saying, 'Thus did I for my countrymen, and this was my reward!'"

"Nor was it vanity or self-conceit," observed Philip; "but, as Milman said of Tasso, that deeper pride which makes obligations painful, which cannot submit to injury or insult, which claims and maintains the position to which it thinks itself entitled, and expects that every one else shall render it the same reverence."

"And yet how deep-rooted was ambition in their hearts," said Luigi; "you remember Cornelia's famous reproach to her sons before they attained their sorrowful distinction, 'Am I to be forever known only as the daughter of Scipio?'"

"Here, ladies!" cried Philip, "is a tenderer spot, sacred to the memory of — I was going to say *sensiblerie*, but fear of Ottilie, who may call me cruel, makes me say *sentiment*."

We had reached the fine cliff-like promontory of Cape Misenus, the tomb of Æneas's trumpeter, and the spot made famous by the French Corinne. We were disappointed at finding her description of the promontory not correct in one point. Vesuvius cannot be seen from Cape Misenus. "The Gulf of Naples, the islands with which it is sown," — all this is exact; but neither Vesuvius nor "the country which extends from Naples as far as Gaeta,"* for hills intervene between the sight in the latter; and as to Vesuvius, the mountain sits too far back to be seen, and Punta di Posilippo extends like a screen in front of it.

After scolding a little about this harmless exaggeration of the gifted Frenchwoman, we took back our fault-finding, and agreed with Luigi, that the poet should not be trammelled by trifles; for,

> "as imagination bodies forth
> The forms of things unknown, the poet's pen
> Turns them to shapes, and gives to airy nothing
> A local habitation and a name."

Therefore, possessing such marvellous power, it was an easy matter for the Improvisatress to bring Vesuvius forward, when only a few miles of hill and distance hid it.

We talked of this wonderful woman, of her follies, some of which were the sweetest part of her nature, and of her wisdom, which, like most feminine wisdom, alas! was the most tiresome.

"'*Tout comprendre, serait tout pardonner*,' — If we understood everything, we would forgive everything," — I repeated musingly. "Mme. de Staël should be forgiven a great many of her parrot Schlegelisms, for the numberless loving truths, like this, which she was constantly uttering."

* Corinne, par Mme. de Staël, Livre XI. Chapitre IV.

"Then, her devotion," added Janet, "to that lovely creature, Mme. Récamier, was so wise and generous! 'If I could possibly envy one whom I love,' she wrote once to Mme. Récamier, 'I would give willingly all that I am to be you'; and it was not her friend's famous beauty which she thought most of, but 'those moral qualities which seemed to every one as remarkable as her charms.' "*

"The experience of poor Mme. de Staël's sorrowful and yet brilliant life," I said, "had doubtless taught her that which I once heard a great poet and good man say he had learned, — to value most those who were more remarkable for qualities of heart than head; and this can be applied particularly to women. As our heart-gifts surpass those of our head, so are we, in proportion, happier and better able to fulfil patiently our duty in life."

"You did not always think so, Ottilie," remarked Philip, in that provoking way which some men have of tossing up old worn-out opinions, like old slippers, after one.

" ''T is held that sorrow makes us wise,' " was my only reply to him.

As we walked along the shore, Janet and I talked of the capabilities of feminine minds and the quality of feminine studies.

"O, women read, they never study!" cried Philip, half jestingly.

"That is very true, Mr. Edelhertz, about the majority of women, at least," replied Janet, generously; for she has been, and is still, as capable and clever a student as any man. "Our reading, too," she continued, "is rarely

* Notes to Corinne.

for the purpose of acquiring exact knowledge, nor do we show that systematic holding-on to subjects which you men display; for even in your leisure reading you always keep your *spécialité* in view."

"Few women have *spécialités*," I said. "Reading, with us, is often a mere pursuit of food for our imaginations, which are ever rising hungry from the meagre meal that realities make of life's table; many times also it is, as I have heard Philip say cruelly, to soothe our ever-afflicted sensibilities."

"Then," asked Janet, "when clever women show that fierce book-hunger which they sometimes do, startling men with the quantity of books they are able to read, I suppose they are seizing on reading as a sort of mental or spiritual opium, to give them relief from thought and memory?"

"Exactly so," I answered; "and this reading very often excites the energies and rouses into action the creative powers. A lot of rubbish is gathered together by us, I admit; but in this rubbish are rough mineral stones, as it were, against whose iron of suggestion the flint of the feminine fancy strikes out a bright spark, which pleases even though it may not enlighten a great deal."

"Realities make life's table meagre, do they, Ottilie?" asked Philip, in a gentle, kind tone. "But you are right," he continued, without waiting for an answer. "You women endure realities because you are instinctively — nay, divinely — patient; but you have no love or even respect for them. There is one thing, however, which puzzles me in women, — your prejudices and preferences color all things; hence your judgments ought to be imperfect, and yet they are not. Why is this, Mrs. Dale? I ask you instead of Ottilie, because I know her of old;

she never gives reasons for her opinions: it is always 'because,' nothing else."

"It arises from a mysterious power we possess, Mr. Edelhertz," answered Janet, "which eludes all analysis, and which has no name, unless we call it instinct, as Ottilie does; but that is too poor a name, to my thinking, for these divine

'Impulsions, God-supplied,'

which are the best gifts of women, and worth all your reason."

"I call it instinct," I said, "because instinct has a swifter flight than logical reflection. It is, in fact, a sort of unconscious inspiration."

"Call it, rather, genuine conscience," observed Luigi, "which, according to Goethe, 'knows only feeling and no logic, and goes straightforward to its object, which it tries lovingly to comprehend, and, when comprehended, never lets go again.' This agrees best, I fancy, with your views of your sex."

"'*Prends le premier conseil d'une femme, et non le second,*' is a French proverb," remarked Philip: "'Take the first advice of a woman, and not the second.' Trench, in his Lessons in Proverbs, agrees with you, Ottilie, and old Montaigne too. The English Dean calls it moral intuition, and the wise old Frenchman *l'esprit primesautier*, the reckless, unthinking leap which gains all or none at the first bound."

"Instinct, conscience, or intuition, whatever it may be called," said Janet, "we women certainly show great cleverness and quickness through its aid, that is, when we act on the first warm impulse; for the French proverb is true, — few women have 'sober second thoughts.' We seem to be filled with those *perceptions aveugles* (blind perceptions), *pensées sourdes* (deaf thoughts), which Leibnitz speaks of, and compares beautifully to the thousand little noises produced by the shock of a wave on the sea-shore, and which compose, in their whole, the grand diapason of ocean melody."

"And this melody of the sea, too," I added, "is very like the workings of a woman's mind, — wild, sometimes wayward, confused, and vague, but having a mysterious meaning which attracts forcibly, and is filled with a never-wearying charm."

The two men looked in silence, and half unconsciously, on the two beautiful women whom they were loving, and I fancied they both agreed with us. A few short weeks ago, Philip would have turned into playful ridicule all this feminine *sensiblerie*, as he would have called it; but now Love, that divine messenger, who heals all differences between poor blind Adams and Eves, was brooding down over him, and filling his solitary, silent heart with sweet murmurs of hope and happiness.

At Baiæ we mounted our horses again for the last time, and Janet, Mrs. Folham, and Venetia returned to the barouche. We rode swiftly and silently on; the sweet moon shone down on us, and our horses' hoofs beat a martial measure on the hard lava-paved road; they kept as accurate time as if the dumb beasts, like their riders, had musical ears, and understood all the sweet subtleties of rhythm and accent.

The air was filled with the odor of orange-blossoms and the grape-flower; the glowing west had grown purple and wine-hued, while a ruddy glow flashed here and there most unaccountably over the heavens; but, as we doubled the point and came out on Posilippo, we discovered the cause of it, — Vesuvius was in flames!

"An eruption!" cried Philip; "at last, we shall see Vesuvius in its glory."

We had been hoping for this event during all our stay in Naples. There had been every sign of an eruption for months, and now, to our great joy, it had come; for, as it was unaccompanied by any destructive earthquakes, and seemed a peaceable display of the mountain's glorious powers, we felt no compunctions at rejoicing over it. Vesuvius looked grandly, as we rode briskly along the road facing it. Heavy columns of fiery vapor arose, touched on the edges by the moonlight, and streams of fire glided, snake-like, down the mountain-sides.

There was no terrifying darkness, no fearful explosions, none of the horrible attendants on preceding eruptions. The mountain seemed simply like a huge overflowing vase of fire; a beautiful and glorious spectacle, rather than a thing of terror and ruin; and so unlike the ordinary idea of Vesuvius in action, that we almost forgot its power to do harm. The flames and lava-streams did not pour from the summit, but from the sides. We afterwards learned that new craters have formed around it, and from these came streaming down the fiery rivers; there were two beautiful currents, which we could see, of the most exquisite fire-color, not sulphureous-hued, but mellow and almost rosy.

After the first expressions of gratification we said little, but looked on the beautiful mountain with indescribable, half-bewildered feelings, such as one has in a vivid dream; it seemed like some scene from a fairy tale of gnomes and mountain spirits, — some gorgeous, impossible vision of childhood, made real and possible.

Great phenomena of any kind are rarely seen under favorable circumstances; but surely our first sight of Vesuvius in flames could not have been more happily arranged.

SKY-ROCKETS.

AST evening, being Trinity Sunday and the Queen's birthday, the whole town was superbly illuminated. To form a complete idea of the extent to which town illuminations can be carried, and their frequency, it is necessary to visit Naples. I have never seen so many or such interesting ones as during the few months I have been here. Partial illuminations of some quarter of the town take place several times a week.

The decoration of buildings for illuminations is quite a lucrative business in Naples, they tell me. On the fête-day of a church, — that is, the day devoted to the saint whose name it bears, — its whole front is covered with hastily-erected scaffoldings, and several men can be seen running up and down ladders, from tower to roof, and roof to basement, suspending strings of small parti-colored glass cups, and arranging them skilfully, so as to form various symbolical figures when lighted; for each cup is half-filled with oil, on which floats a taper. Sometimes the houses and stores on the sides of the open square in front of the church are decorated in a like manner. At nightfall these lamps are lighted and the scaffoldings removed, with a celerity that seems hardly possible. The church façade then looks like a fairy scene, with its twinkling, sparkling, brilliant-hued letters and devices, and as they begin to pale and drop out, one by one, the attention of the crowd is attracted by the firing-off of petards and the sending up of remarkably fine fireworks. The pyrotechnical displays in Naples seem inexhaustible: there is one called the Girandola, which is remarkably beautiful; it is formed by a simultaneous discharge of numberless rockets, that fall back from a centre as they explode, looking like fiery petals of a gigantic lily-cup or bell.

After twilight this evening, while we were sitting on the terrace, looking at Vesuvius and watching the gradual brightening of the town, Luigi and Philip came in to propose a drive through the streets, to see the different illuminations and fireworks, and the equally fiery crowd. Janet, Venitia, Philip, and I went in the coach, Luigi on horseback.

We first drove to the Largo di Palazzo Reale, to see the illumination of the Royal Palace, and the grand sight presented by San Francesco di Paula, which is opposite. The magnificent dome of this fine church was outlined against the glowing sky by glittering gas-jets, whose tingling, tongue-like flames seemed like living things, as they mounted from the base of the dome to its apex, on which blazed a superb cross of fire.

After we have seen a moderate amount of wonders, we become very unreasonable; instead of being satisfied with our pleasure, we grow exacting, and ask not only for more, but for something greater.

To that dome and cross, whose graceful outlines trembled on the heavens and looked as if springing from the clouds themselves, and not belonging to anything on earth, we dared to suggest the addition of a new beauty.

"Instead of that simple cross-form," said our poet Philip, "it should have been like Constantine's visionary one, of which Eusebius tells us. Think how superb would have been the effect, to have seen palpitating in that gas-flame a cross, with the Greek characters, ΕΝ ΤΟΥΤΩ ΝΙΚΑ, 'Conquer through this.'"

"O," cried Janet, deprecatingly, "how can you trouble the beautiful thing by wishing for something beyond it? Surely, it is lovely enough to satisfy a poet's imaginings. Look at those porticos and that vestibule."

This church, San Francesco di Paula, has two semicircular porticos at right and left, supported by forty-four columns, and in front of the church itself is a vestibule with ten fine Ionic columns. These were all lighted by concealed gas-jets, and, as Janet spoke, a fresh head of gas was turned on, which glowed first at the base of the church and then mounted up to the summit, making these porticos look like enchanted aisles leading to some angelic cathedral.

"Do you remember," asked Philip, as we were noticing the resemblance of this church to the Pantheon, "what Stendhal said of it, when it was building, in 1816? Bianchi showed him the plan, and Stendhal wrote, 'Bianchi has adopted the circular form, which is a proof he appreciates the antique; but he has not remembered that the ancients proposed a very different end from ours in their temples. The religion of the Greeks was a festival, not a menace. The temple under the beautiful heavens was only a theatre of sacrifice, not immolation. Instead of kneeling, of prostrating one's self, and striking the breast, they executed in it sacred and beautiful dances. Shall our artists ever be able to read with their souls? Those of the present day seem unable to raise themselves to a comprehension that the ancients did nothing for mere ornament; the beautiful, with them, was only the natural growth of the useful.' But I do not see," continued Philip, "how Stendhal could have been long in Naples without discovering that this Catholic religion is a great deal like that of the old Greeks,—a festival of the gayest kind."

"The Neapolitans are neither Catholics nor Pagans," I remarked; "they are simply image-worshippers. But what higher religious form can be looked for in a populace so mobile, wayward, and, above all, joy-seeking? Of course, their religion must take the gay color of their pleasure-loving dispositions. Wait until these people, by some one of those great world-miracles, which take place every age or two, are changed into more thinking, intelligent beings, not needing visible signs like St. Thomas; then they can be St. Johns and St. Pauls."

"Yes," said Janet, "I do not think Protestants give enough weight, particularly in religion, to the needs of peculiar organizations, as well as influences of climate. Here in Naples the national appetite is for show, *éclat*, and bustle, not for quiet reason and calm thought. The people are quick at, and eager for, receiving impressions; but there must be new dies ready, as the burning lava of feeling and emotion is ever flowing. Their love of a sensation is a positive, passionate need, which, if not gratified, becomes as fierce as unsatisfied hunger. During this present visit of mine to Naples, while looking at the childlike throngs gazing at the spectacles in churches, or the throbbing, eager crowd in the streets, making up the religious processions, or kneeling devoutly as the sacred Host passes, I have repeatedly thought what fearful savages these people would be, without the help and control of this beautiful, tangible form of their faith. This grand old Catholic Church is very wise; it possesses the collected wisdom of experience, and knows best how to govern these people, who, as Ottilie says, are the St. Thomases of the Christian world, and must be treated as gently as he was. Even such unbelievers as Machiavelli and Voltaire admitted the wisdom of these gay theatrical devotions, and thought they prevented public misfortunes."

"What a true woman's use of an authority!" exclaimed Philip; "I am not surprised, however, at your employing such weapons, for your own religious views, as a Unitarian, are very free; but it is droll to hear Ottilie innocently wielding Voltairian infidel supports."

Janet seemed to feel that the conversation had gone a little too far, for she answered in a courteous, but rather cold and serious manner.

"You are disposed, Mr. Edelhertz, like many other formalists in religion, to regard persons holding what you call Unitarian views as unbelievers, if not heathen, because we do not subscribe to your Thirty-nine Articles, or your partial acceptances of old Catholic mysteries, such as the Trinity, and the like; and, indeed, it is not easy for us to comprehend each other, I fancy, for not only good breeding, but the dignified reticence of true pious feeling, confines the whole matter to a holier communion than differing mortals can hold with each other, to a commerce with their own consciences and God, in solitude."

"What is the subject of conversation?" asked Luigi, who, to my great relief, just then came riding up; he had left us a little while before to learn the cause of the shouting in the neighborhood of the Arsenal, and to see if it was practicable for our carriage to drive there.

"O, Mr. Luigi," answered Venitia, playfully, "they are talking like philosophers, who, you know, grow always unphilosophical whenever they enter into argument."

"No, no," interrupted Janet, with a sweet, good-natured smile, "we are not pretending to be philosophers even; we have simply been treading, as De Quincey finely says, 'that interspace between religion and philosophy which connects them both,' and which is neutral ground."

"But, like all neutral ground," said Venitia, slyly, "in warring seasons it is a dangerous one, for it can be converted into a *champ clos* on the slightest provocation, as I can testify."

A fresh shout from the distant crowd interrupted the talk effectually, and Luigi reported the cause of the noise. Some fine illuminations were being lighted up and superb fireworks preparing at the Arsenal. Before driving thither, we remained a few minutes looking at the picturesque scene which the street presented, and which within the past fifteen minutes had arrived at its full height of interest. Words can hardly describe it. The finely decorated stores on either side of the Toledo were in a blaze, but the most attractive sight was the centre of the street and the square.

Buying and selling, cooking and eating, were going on briskly. The perambulating orange-cars, and sherbet or ice-water temples, adorned with rude pictures of holy subjects, looking indeed very Byzantine and pre-Raphael, as Philip said, stood everywhere. These gay little booths on wheels were lighted up as fantastically as the houses; branches of the golden broom waved around them, nodding like feathery plumes; huge bouquets of what we call "hothouse flowers" glowed on their counters; and graceful, fragrant garlands were festooned tastefully around them.

On the sidewalks and corners of the square were literally hillocks of fruit, — for it is now the high harvest season; there were melting apricots, fresh, milky almonds, and huge, luscious Anana strawberries, looking as if carved out of pink coral. Old women sat by their braziers, over whose glowing coals they roasted sweet-smelling nuts, and brightened their fire by waving briskly, to and fro, reed fans; bellows, to be sure, would have been more effectual, but not half so picturesque; and it seems as if these people were just made for living pictures, to gladden the eye with fast-resolving forms and shapes, and keep throbbing for the artist, in this prosaic world, the warm pulse of Nature's beauty.

Little iron furnaces sparkled and blazed under huge boilers, and in these seething caldrons bubbled up mealy, bursting potatoes and yellow maccaroni; even fish-frying was going on; and almost every domestic and private occupation, as well as public, was there represented in a great square, in front of a royal palace, and at the foot of one of the gayest streets in Europe, while the screaming, roaring population poured down from the various stradas and vicos, — as the large and small streets are called, — and up and down the Toledo, like a hot lava flood, seeming as if it would demolish everything before it; a true Vesuvian current, with a human voice, which swayed and surged in almost bewildering confusion.

We turned at last and left the Largo di Palazzo Reale. Luigi directed the driver to draw the carriage up first on the Santa Lucia square, a position which gave us a fine view of the city in outline, and also of the bay and mountain. The gray phantom which always rises from

"Vesuvius' misty brim,
With outstretched hands,
O'erlooking the volcanic lands,"

was no longer visible. The whole summit of the volcano was enveloped in a rosy vapor, as with a mantle; and down the side towards Naples coursed two grand lava-streams, from which arose clouds as golden and ruddy as those preceding a mountain sunrise. Dante's

"Il tremolar della marina"

insensibly rose to the lips as we noticed the sparkling, trembling waters of the Crater Bay, that reflected the volcano's light, as the day-dawn was reflected from the mountains in Purgatory "on the ocean stream." Numberless little boats with winglike sails, or plashing oars, passed to and fro, from which arose snatches of song or the twang of a stringed instrument, just caught, and then lost in the thunderous roar of the passing multitude, who were divided, in their exultation and enjoyment, between God's and man's illumination.

After a few minutes given to this Santa-Lucia view, we drove around the Arsenal, to see the superb fireworks there. Even Vesuvius's grandeur could not pale them. Fountains and waterfalls of fire poured out their blazing flood; girandolas spread out their fiery lily-cups; and all the various pyrotechnic forms soared off on the volcanic air, as if their compounds rejoiced to be released from the bonds in which man had held them, and were dancing merry, exultant rounds, like so many Ariels, as they joined their brother-spirits of the mountain.

After looking until dazzled and deafened, we turned the horses' heads homewards. As we came around the Chiatamone, and across the Vittoria, to the stately palatial Chiaja, the Church of San Pasquale burst out upon us in a fine blaze of decorative light; a brilliant St. Catharine's wheel spun around, and little rosy crosses and stars and arrows of fire darted to and fro,

"Before you could say 'Come' and 'Go,'
And breathe twice and cry 'So, so';
Each one tripping on his toe,
Were all there with mop and mowe."

Luigi proposed we should go up into the drawing-room of his apartments, which are in the Palazzo, opposite the church, the side-windows of which look out on the San Pasquale square. We did so, and sat for some time enjoying this agreeable end of the brilliant spectacle. After a while Philip drew me away from the window, to show me Luigi's handsomely arranged bachelor apartments.

First, there are two pleasant ante-rooms, floored with deep-blue and white tiles, which made me feel as if I were walking on a great-grandmother's India dinner-set. These two rooms are furnished with tall, beautifully carved cabinets, and fine plaster copies of some of the master-pieces of sculpture in the Musée Bourbonique. From them we pass through richly draped doors into a handsome drawing-room which has two fronts, one on San Pasquale and one on the broad Chiaja. The furniture of this drawing-room is simple and elegant, like the man himself, in its perfect, quiet taste. Exquisite bronzes, whose subjects lead you, as through pleasant corridors, to memories of some of the finest galleries of Europe; two or three lovely bits of sculpture, each one telling its own classic birth in forms of divine beauty; some rare vases; a few fine copies of famous old paintings, and one or two undoubted originals; nothing ostentatious, nothing for display, but all governed by that exact taste which is so near akin to genius as to be almost identical with it.

To the west of the drawing-room is the library, whose windows also look down on the Chiaja and over on the beautiful Villa Reale, with the sea and purple Capri in the distance. This room is a place for sweet, calm thoughts, such as the owner must often have. He has had it decorated in the Pompeian style. The book-shelves run around the room, within a foot or two of the ceiling, separated at certain distances by airy columns; and the spaces between these columns, in which the books are placed, are hung with rich-hued tapestry, which falls from the finely-decorated frieze or cornice to the polished, inlaid floor. The light ornaments of the fretted ceiling, and the refined arabesque forms on the broad cornice and tapestry, give the room a graceful and cheerful appearance.

There is something peculiarly attractive in these Pompeian wall-decorations, especially under the bright skies of Italy, whose genial climate treats fresco and stucco decorations kindly. The forms, too, are so pleasing,—slender, straight lines, squares, right angles, and exact semicircles, adorned with exquisite garlands, graceful pendent baskets, and twining, climbing vines. These are all painted in bright, positive flat tints; but the extreme delicacy of the figures keeps the coloring from discord and tawdriness.

On top of the library cornice or frieze are beautiful vases, alternating with airy, winged figures; among these last I noticed the lovely Isis, and the floating figure of Fortune, just poised tiptoe on her globe, ready for a flight.

"Is not all this charming?" asked Philip, as he rolled a delightful easy-chair towards me, and placed under my feet a gorgeously embroidered Persian cushion; then commenced showing to me his favorites among the treasures of this pleasant retreat. Among other curiosities were some very fine pipes, one a gift from Philip, a superb chibouk, of black amber encrusted with diamonds.

But the books gave us both the greatest satisfaction. Luigi is the lucky owner of many curious and rare editions; he has an Aldine Odyssey, a Guntt Iliad, and an Elzevir Virgil with a margin of five inches, over which Philip's eyes looked notes of admiration of the largest size and greatest number.

"See this, Ottilie," he cried. "Here is an Elzevir New Testament, translated by the Port-Royalists, of which Jules Janin says so drolly, 'If you find this book in a good state, and have not money enough to buy it, go immediately to the pawnbroker, and pawn your watch or your gun, or anything that is yours, and buy this book; then sit down with satisfaction over it, feeling sure of having secured a good bargain.'"

He showed me some other Port Royalist books, and made me observe their covers. Great ascetics as were the Port-Royalists, they were very nice about their books. They had a binding made expressly for themselves, which is still known by the name of Jansenist binding.

While we were looking at the books, Janet, Venitia, and Luigi joined us. Luigi left Philip to do the honors of the library to Janet and me, and took Venitia to a book-stand on which were placed some fine illustrated folios on Architecture, Sculpture, and the various European galleries. They grew so interested over the prints, that they seemed hardly conscious of our presence; and yet I slyly noticed that they said little to each other,—they were too quietly happy to talk.

I leaned back in the easy-chair, half-listening to Janet's and Philip's intelligent talk over the books, but at the same time imagining I could read that sweeter, unspoken lore contained in the hearts of the two half-conscious lovers. I felt sure that a strange, sweet feeling was welling up in both.

Venitia seemed lapped in a soft, luxurious dream, doubtless caused by finding herself suddenly lifted into the very atmosphere of Luigi's daily, hourly life. It was a delicious mystery being unveiled to her. That subtle Frenchman who took women's hearts and clove them "deep down the middle," said very truly, "It is so sweet for women to know where and how those live who are dear to them."

To Luigi it was the simple but exquisite pleasure of having Venitia in his own home; it was a delicate sense of possession, as it were, which, though it could only last a brief season, still for that period it was real. This feeling showed itself in an expression which, though quiet, was exultant. As I looked at his fine face, lighted up with this happiness, I wished to whisper to Philip,

> "Open the temple gates unto my love,
> Open them wide, that she may enter in;
> And all the posts adorn as doth behove,
> And all the pillars deck with garlands trim."

Then I looked at Philip, and thought how different it was with him. He was talking earnestly with Janet, displaying all his fine powers of courteous argument, which he loves to do with her. He has a great respect for her almost masculine intellect, and an admiration for her lovely character and high-bred manners. Sometimes they have rather severe passes, arising from his forgetfulness for an instant of her superior abilities, and his treating her, as men always do women, when arguing with them, as a child or inferior, who must be tenderly borne with for its sweet ignorance' sake; but she soon brings him to a consciousness that he is measuring swords with an equal, and he likes her all the better for it.

I watched his animated countenance, full of life and

energy; and, I thought, he has no sweet dreams to preoccupy him, to make him gentle and at peace with all humanity; for love acts thus upon cultured, superior natures. Infatuated as Philip is with the young English girl, the feeling has not yet taken deep enough root to yield him the sweet fruit of joy and rest. There is some of the dull pain of sorrow left rankling in his heart, just enough to give him a little goading sting; for, upon bounding dispositions like his, which cannot be stilled by any power but that called death, sorrow acts as a sort of mental intoxication, producing a reckless, frolicsome state of feeling, which partially, but only for a brief moment, deadens the anguish of

> "That old wound ever aching."

De Quincey said he "made of grief a fiery chariot, for mounting above the causes of grief." Philip uses his as a bounding bark on a fast-running sea, under a head wind; or, as if mounted on Arcite's horse,

> "Who'd make his length a mile, if 't pleased his rider
> Put pride in him." *

And he does "put pride in" his, galloping bravely above his "causes of grief."

After a while, we were all brought to one common level, where love and divine philosophy were merged in the enjoyment of more material pleasures. A delightful fruit supper, with ices and wines, was brought in, and served on Sevres dishes, whose pink hue was as delicate as the Mediterranean conch-shell, and whose Etruscan forms were quite in keeping with the frescoes of the room. We drank each other's health in a parting glassful of the luscious Capri wine, which rested on the tongue and in

* Fletcher's Two Noble Kinsmen.

the throat with a fragrant, fruity taste; and as I held up the delicate-shaped, amber-colored Bohemian goblet to the light, I thought how like molten gold the two mellow hues united looked.

"Near midnight, on one side or the other it matters little which, does it, Ottilie?" said Philip, gayly, as he wrapped around me the pretty Arabian mantle he brought me from the East, whose rich goat's-hair fringe looks like the foam on cream, it is such a golden white.

We walked slowly along the broad Chiaja, for we had dismissed the coach on going into Luigi's. The clear, beautiful light of the young moon poured down a generous flood over the lava-paved streets, the high white palaces and thick foliage of the trees in the Villa Reale. The crowd had all left that courtly, stately part of the town; but every little while a chance petard could be heard, or a whiz of a sky-rocket, from the more densely-populated part of the city, and a distant murmur arose thence; but the whole affair looked like a public garden towards day-break, after a fête, very shabby and dilapidated. God's illumination, however, continued on, as fresh as at the beginning; the blazing lava streamed down the mountain's side unceasingly, and the glorious, fiery vapor rose up and curled superbly and slowly about the heavens, spreading itself everywhere, as if conscious of its inexhaustible powers.

Venitia, Janet, and Luigi walked together; Philip and I. We did not feel like talking, although Luigi tried to by snatches; but Philip remained silent, wrapped in his own meditations, yielding to the sweet influences of the night, and some graceful poetic thought, which, as a chaste young Muse, was wooing him on with pretty coquetry and tender waywardness.

MALEBOLGE.

A LARGE party of us yesterday ascended Vesuvius. We proposed going last Monday, but have been waiting for Luigi, who has been really ill since Trinity Sunday evening. Indeed, he is far from well now, and quite unlike himself in manner; so absent and preoccupied, that even he notices it, for he tries to recover his old self-possession, and in the attempt becomes unnatural and almost brusque. This afternoon when he joined us he seemed so ill at ease that I advised him to stay at home. But in a well-bred way, without any disagreeable words, he made me understand that he did not like my counsel, and appeared annoyed at the notice I took of him. I said no more, and felt relieved when I remembered that I was to go with the Rochesters, and not in our coach, where the constant sight of his altered countenance would cause me pain and anxiety.

I managed with all the adroitness I possess to have Philip go with Mrs. Folham and Florence. I found they expected to ask the handsome young Milnes, a nephew of Mrs. Folham, to serve as their attendant; but as he is one of the officers aboard the English royal navy ship which is anchored in the harbor, there was a little doubt about his obtaining a long enough leave of absence. Immediately I suggested to Philip that it would be much better for him to take charge of them, as, even supposing Milnes should be able to go, he was too young to have the entire care of both ladies: then, as I was to join the Rochesters in any arrangement, we could have two pleasant carriage loads, independent of the Minister's coaches.

I could hardly refrain from smiling while I was making this remark to Philip, he looked so intensely gratified at being able to arrange the party to please me, as he said; and he set about it with angelic alacrity, getting rid thereby of a grand attack of the blues, which have been tormenting him for some days.

Philip possesses all the sterling points and special developments which characterize the artist; and these make of him the most charming or the most disagreeable companion, the happiest or the most unhappy of men, just as his capricious humors direct. But it is good policy to make such persons happy, they are such delightful companions when they are in good spirits.

There are two grand high-roads, however, which women possess, if they only knew it, to the pleasant heights of every man's good humor and tenderness: — one, through the sweet path of his affections, which youth and beauty tread so naturally; the other, by making him feel comfortable in his surroundings. By the first, his heart is oftenest captivated; by the last practical, material one, — alas for sentiment! — the masculine citadel is held most securely.

Mais revenons a nos moutons in the shape of a burning mountain. Dr. L——, the famous encyclopedist, whom I met the other evening at Mr. Rochester's, told me that this eruption is one of the most remarkable eruptions that have taken place in the mountain during the seventeen hundred and seventy-eight years it has been known as an actual volcano.

I have never felt until now any desire to ascend Vesuvius; and during my visit at Naples I have often quoted the droll, original remark of Goethe's artist-friend, Tischbein: "Such a frightful and shapeless conglomeration of matter, which, moreover, is continually preying on itself, and proclaiming war against every idea of the beautiful, is utterly abominable."

Vesuvius is a marvellous sight, however, to look at from a distance, and adds a valuable feature to this peculiar landscape, — a landscape which is so widely different from any I have ever seen, — Elysium and Tartarus. Instead of calling the mountain a great altar, I feel much more like using the German artist's words, when I look at it, "This peak of Hell thus rearing itself in the middle of Paradise!"

But the present eruption gives the mountain a certain beauty; it has taken a voice, and shows forked, fiery tongues; therefore it is less terrible to me than when that fearful phantom-like cloud hung over its head, pressing down upon it the dread weight of silence, an appalling silence, like some indistinct approaching sorrows. For some time past the mountain has been showing symptoms of returning animation; the earth has been shaken, the springs of water dried up, and various other threatening signs of impending trouble and destruction have been given.

There is a curious volcanic group collected around this Crater Bay, as Strabo calls the lovely Bay of Naples; consisting of Ischia, Procida, the Solfatara, Monte Nuovo, and Vesuvius. In the centre of them lies the Aphrodite Naples on this

"Vesuvian bay's deep breast,"

which, like another Adonis, is forever fleeing from her. The subtle, dangerous volcanic fluid creeps beneath and around the city unheeded; and in some places, as in the Solfatara, the fiery vapor rises, like Hamlet's dead father, mysterious and ghostlike, out of the apparently solid ground. The ancients believed the whole of this country was subterraneously connected with the Sicilian volcanoes.

In speaking of Pindar's myth concerning Typhon, "upon whose shaggy breast the sea-girt shores beyond Cumæ and Sicily press," Strabo says: "Pindar throws more credibility into the myth, by making it conformable to the actual phenomena; for the whole strait from Cumæ to Sicily is subigneous, and below the sea has certain galleries, which form a communication between the volcanoes of the island and those of the mainland."

The only active crater among the Neapolitan group, during the last three hundred years, has been Vesuvius; but, like the others, it was at one time extinct, and only in legend, scarcely in memory, did its volcanic history remain.

Before the time of Titus there rested on its hot bosom, nearly to the top of its crater summit, peaceful, cultivated fields, such as can be seen to-day on Monte Nuova. Strabo, in his description of the Campania, speaks of Mount Vesuvius as being covered with beautiful fields, except on its summit, which he says looks as if it had been some time subjected to the action of fire, and that it might be inferred that the place was formerly in a burning state, with live craters.

Every lover of Plutarch will remember reading in the life of Marcus Crassus — the grandson of that solemn old Roman who was never known to laugh — the account of

Spartacus and his band, and their use of this Vesuvian crater. Its now "misty brim" was then made up of rough and slippery precipices, covered with wild vines, the stems and branches of which were of old enough growth to support the swaying, heavy bodies of those athletic Thracian shepherd gladiators, as they swung stealthily down to the sloping grass-covered bottom of the crater. And this feat of those "forty thousand huge barbarians" took place nearly a century before the birth of our blessed Lord.

In the present eruption, four new craters have formed along the sides of the mountain, some distance below the cone; and from these openings great streams of lava course down. Two are on the side towards Naples.

The eruptions heretofore have always proceeded from the summit; and it is feared that this new development may cause a great change in the form of Vesuvius, which would be a great pity, for no one would like to see this most prominent feature of the Bay of Naples altered in one jot or tittle. The eruption of 79 A. D.,—the one that destroyed Herculaneum and Pompeii,—made enough change in the form of this mountain, for it had then a great part of its grandeur of outline torn away.

Vesuvius must have loomed out finely before that eruption. All the semicircular mountain which lies around the north and east, called Monte Somma, was incorporated with it; and there are several points of view, especially at the Amphitheatre of Pompeii, from whence can be formed some idea how it might then have looked. It is easy to fancy the immense crater it formed; and the sight of the first gigantic fire lighted upon its summit, by unseen hands as it were, must have been glorious. Such an immense burning mountain!—a Titanic altar reared almost to the skies!—Jupiter Summus burning incense to the New Revelation!

During our drive yesterday, we talked over this past history of the volcano, each one contributing his or her little information to the conversation. We found the road thronged with persons of every rank and condition. Some frightened peasants, whose little homes lay alarmingly near the lava streams, were hurrying in to Naples with all their earthly goods on their backs or on their mules; other country persons, with some of the idle population of Naples, were following a grand religious procession, which was directly in front of our carriages, headed by the patron saint of Naples, San Januarius. The fine life-size silver bust — the same one we saw so superbly adorned with precious gems on the great festival day of the Liquefaction at Santa Chiara — was carried aloft by tall stalwart men, under a crimson canopy, whose gold cords and tassels swung and glittered finely in the sunlight. Around and behind us were equipages of princes, nobles, and commoners, mingled without difference together.

It proved a lucky chance for us that we were directly behind the procession, for a path was thus opened, which would otherwise have been entirely blocked up by the immense crowd, which swayed to and fro like waves under contrary winds, — a Neapolitan crowd too, that never budges but for a procession and a saint.

As we wound slowly up the mountain road, the view grew more glorious in beauty. The sun was setting; the surface of the bay sparkled brilliantly; the beautiful city rose gracefully up out of the swelling waters, and her Sorrentine and Mysentine promontories stretched out like graceful arms embracing the eager but fast-fleeing sea. The volcanic islands Capri, Ischia, and Procida were bathed in the golden purple of the sunlight; and, far off in the distance, spurs of the Apennines stretched along the dazzling west, whose summits glowed as with living fire; while level clouds were spread on the brilliant horizon, looking like heavenly floors for angels, such as can be seen in the works of the early painters.

The rose and the golden struggled together in the atmosphere. All the local colors of vegetation seemed to have disappeared. In some places the ruddy hue prevailed, making crimson the paler greens; while mingling with every shade was a sparkle like delicate golden dust. A landscape painter might have studied there curious effects produced by the light on the various tints of the scenery; but to have given the truthful tone, it would have been necessary for the artist to use gold itself for the highest lights, as did those old painters, Perugino and others, who sometimes gilded their distant trees, and the glorified threads of hair in their saints and singularly lovely Madonnas.

It was a glorious piece of harmony, like some of Beethoven's instrumentation or Chopin's mysterious melodic weavings. We were on a sufficiently high elevation to see the extent of Nature's marvellous power. The range of a magnificent orchestra of color was attained. There was the rich hue of the setting sun on one side, and the mellow light of Vesuvius on the other. Every variety of cloud was spread over the sky, from the level ones of the horizon to the dropping flaky bits near the zenith, that melted off and were "gathered up like young souls into heaven." The upper strata of clouds had a different tone from the lower, yet they all blended in perfect harmony, and seemed like many "golden aisles penetrating through angelic chapels to the Shekinah of the blue."

Even now as I write these words, striving to weave together, as in the sacred chord, the names of colors, in order to paint in language, as it were, my memory of this sunset, the whole rises up in that mysterious chamber of the mind called imagination, which is "tessellated with floating fancies of the blue shadow and burning gold," and

"With dreamful eyes,
My spirit lies,
Under the walls of Paradise."

But to feel the full meaning of these faint words, one must have seen such a sunset, on such a night, from the side of this famous old altar mountain, on the lovely shores of the Vesuvian Bay.

About nightfall we reached the Hermitage, where we supped; then proceeded with guides, torches, and our own servants up the mountain footpaths, in order to approach as near the lava streams and craters as was prudent. The stream of lava that is now coursing through the Atrio del Cavallo — the valley or gorge that lies between Monte Somma and Vesuvius — is the larger of the two which flow down the south side of the mountain. This stream is fed by an immense crater on the north-east. Of course this fiery spring was worth seeing; but we had to mount some eminence, from the top of which we could look over into the crater, and this was no easy task.

The only available heights were heaps or hillocks of old lava, standing on the edge of the crater, and through the bases of which the treacherous flood was beginning to creep. Notwithstanding this, we selected one which looked blacker and therefore safer than the others, and commenced the scramble up.

The surface of the lava hillock was almost as hot and steaming as a covering of wet ashes spread over a coal fire. At every step the lava gave way and crumbled under us, scorching our boots and crisping our gloves; for we had to clamber up on all fours, each one for himself or herself. At last, breathless and trembling, we reached the summit, which we found harder and cooler for our feet than the sides had been, and the view it commanded well repaid us for the labor.

We leaned over and looked down into the crater beneath, whose red-hot fluid came pouring out of the mountain's side like molten iron in a huge puddling furnace:

> "So fell the eternal fiery flood, wherewith
> The marl glowed underneath."

It was a veritable lake or gulf of fire, and vividly recalled Dante's fearful descriptions in the *Inferno* of the horrible gulfs in the Eighth Circle. While I was looking earnestly and in silence down into the crater, Janet, who was near by, asked me in a low voice if I felt like leaping over.

"I never stand on the brinks of precipices or great heights," I replied, "without recalling a constant dream possession or power I have, — flying. In my dreams, — and I never sleep without dreaming, — I do not seem to be walking, but always balancing in the air pleasantly, or soaring off gloriously, and so strong is the impression it leaves upon me, that sometimes in my waking moments I almost fancy I possess this impossible power."

"Well, my dear Ottilie, there is one thing certain, if you feel disposed to try your dream-wings in this place, it would not be many moments before you would know the great secret. All our mysterious life-problems, my friend, would be quickly resolved for you, and the 'distorted wills' that give so much trouble here on earth would soon be made wondrous straight after such a leap."

We were surrounded by a crowd, for we had found that little hillock swarming with human beings as venturous as ourselves; therefore we had to talk almost in a whisper. After a few half-playful, half-serious remarks, we concluded wisely not to leap over, but to stay and enjoy the gradual severing of life's hard knots, and the curious beautiful straightening of crooked human designs, which are sure to be made all in good time by God's own handiwork; for had not Janet, at least, seen these marvellous things down in her own past? This subject ended, I quoted, in halting lines, passages from Dante, of the place

> "within the depth of Hell
> Called Malebolge";

and as the flames of the fresh lava glided slowly up and around huge bits of stone or "glowing marl," — the oily character of the fluid showing itself everywhere, — we imagined the flaming feet of the poor wretches the Italian poet described as plunged headforemost into those fearful gulfs of fire.

The night was comparatively dark, for the moon had not yet risen. The whole mountain was alive with people, who were scattered over its sides. In every direction we could see the torchlights of different parties, but not the people themselves, and once in a while, in order to make a torch burn brighter, a guide would knock its end on the ground or against a stone, sending out myriads of sparks.

I looked up to the quiet star-lit sky, and then down the mountain-side on these thousands of torchlights. It seemed like a vast ocean lying beneath my feet, reflecting on its throbbing bosom the stars above, while around me rose up, in the place of ocean roar and rushing wave sweep, the hum of human voices and the muffled crackle of the lava flood.

We stayed on our perilous height as long as we dared. It was only when we saw through its fissures the red fire sparkle, felt the heat through our heavy-soled boots, and were assured by the timid Neapolitan guides that the mass was actually beginning to move, that we had power to break through the fascination which the glorious sight exercised over us.

The descent was as difficult, and to me more so, than the ascent. I looked with envy at Mrs. Rochester and Janet, who went bounding down lightly like little kids. My ankles trembled under me; and but for Mr. Rochester and his valet Domenico, I do not know how I should have accomplished the task. They lifted me from one slippery, sinking foothold to another too quickly to allow my feet to sink into the steaming crevices.

It was the work of only a few instants, but one of great excitement. After we had reached the ground we turned to look at the hillock, and could see the lava current sparkling through all its little openings. Before we left the mountain last night, that whole hillock was incorporated with the main stream and was one mass of flaming fluid.

After the bustle of descent was over, we seated ourselves on the banks of the Atrio del Cavallo, to rest our bruised, blistered limbs on the dry, scorched ferns, and also to enjoy the grand view laid out before us.

The forms into which the lava flood falls are beautiful. In its descent I watched its action, when it encountered heaps of earth, or stone, or mounds of old lava; the fire stream would seem to halt, as if accumulating its gathering forces, which were rushing army-like out of the crater above, and the fluid would creep around, under, and even through the obstructing mass, looking then like some Alpine cascades I have seen, where the intervening rock is formed of regular and horizontal strata, through which the water forces its way, spouting out in exquisite little jets; this would last a few moments, then the flood, receding for an instant, would come rolling over in one grand sheet of fire, with all the abandonment of a great cataract, then surge on in a quiet, flaming torrent.

Dante came again to our memories, as he does at every step in Southern Italy. Janet and I pictured, in the strange, weird forms of the lava flood, "the fell monster who taints all the world," Geryon, on whose serpent-back Virgil and Dante descended to the fearful Eighth Circle, and as the fire-fall poured on, we repeated with more intense interest than we had ever felt before, —

"Naught but the beast was possible to view:
He slowly, slowly wound in many a curve;
Though only from a wind, which upward blew
Against my face, his course I could observe.
Down on the right, I heard the whirlpool seethe,
Where splashing fell the horrible cascade;
And, straining forth my neck to gaze beneath,
At the dread plunge I grew still more afraid,
Such groans I heard, and saw such glare of fires,
Whereat I shrunk, all quivering with affright;
And marked his manner of descent, in spires,
Which until now the darkness kept from sight." *

Gradually we both stopped talking, and as we leaned

* Dr. Parsons's Dante, Canto 17.

back against the ferny bank, enjoying that singular luxury of a fatigue which arises from labor which has gratified the mind while it has wearied the body, we listened to the remarks of the others around us. They were talking of the appearance of the lava. Some compared it to melted gold (which not many of us had ever seen, I fancy); others quoted from Mrs. Jameson the word she applied to it, — "trickling"; to me it looked like molten iron, it poured on with the same oily, smooth sweep. Another peculiarity I noticed in this lava fire, — its slowness and stillness. It seemed like a furious torrent which was too far off for us to distinguish its rapidity or noise; and yet we were within a few feet of the fiery stream.

At last Mr. Rochester sounded the prudent signal of retreat, which I, for one, most unwillingly obeyed. With lingering steps, looking back all the while, we returned to the Hermitage of San Salvadore, where we re-entered our carriages and proceeded homewards.

Soon after we started, the moon rose on the opposite side of the mountain, — the Mediterranean side, — filling to the very "beaded brim" this chalice of beauty. The vapor rising from the mountain and lava streams was rosy, and the rocks and trees had a soft, delicate light thrown over them, like an early twilight. I have never seen the Vesuvius light accurately represented in any picture. Painters make it too fiery; on the contrary, there is in the light of burning lava a mellow, rich hue, which is soft and brilliant, with more carmine in its red than vermilion, and golden or rose-colored in its high light, not yellow or orange.

The whole scene was unearthly in its loveliness, and it exercised over my feelings the most beneficent influence. There seemed to be no past or future, no memory of sorrow. Life's hopes and cares and questionings were suspended, and for a brief season my spirit was lifted, as it were, into a higher range of being, where only the memories of the great and good things of this world existed, — into a region of eternal beauty, — for even the ruin and desolation of parts of the country through which we were passing were annihilated by the magical effects of that heavenly light.

> "And thou didst shine, thou rolling moon, upon
> All this, and cast a wide and tender light,
> Which softened down the hoar austerity
> Of rugged desolation, and filled up,
> As 't were anew, the gaps of centuries;
> Leaving that beautiful which still was so,
> And making that which was not, till the place
> Became religion, and the heart ran o'er
> With silent worship of the great and old, —
> The dead, but sceptred sovereigns, who still rule
> Our spirits from their urns."

A complete silence reigned in our carriage. Not until we rolled into Resina did we break the stillness; even then, we said but a few words, and, without apology, each one fell back into that "serene and blessed mood" which the beautiful night had created.

My pleasant dreamings were a little disturbed by entering the dark city, which was as still as if hushed by enchantment; and as the carriages rumbled over the stone flags of the Largo del Mercato, and the Largo del Palazzo Reale, where the gas seemed to burn with a weird and ghostly light, I shivered. It seemed like Nouronihar's and Vathek's descent into the fearful hall of Eblis by huge marble stairs, on each one of which "were planted two large torches." But suddenly we came out on the Santa Lucia, where the whole glorious sight of flaming mountain, rosy light, silvery moonbeams, and glittering waters burst on me again, and broke most pleasantly this transient illusion, which had been thrown over my excited imagination by the dimly-lighted, gloomy streets.

We swept around the Chiatamone into the stately, calm Chiaja, and on up to the Mergellina, where, at three o'clock of this lovely moonlight morning, we routed up our pretty, good-natured *portière*, feeling very willing, not only to rest our weary bodies, but repose our brains, which had been so stimulated by the sublime sight as to be overcharged with nervous fluid even to painfulness.

THREE DEAD CITIES.

 NOTICE, on looking over my journal, that I have not recorded one half of the wonderful things which I have been seeing and learning. On first arriving I gave conscientiously the history of everything which I saw; but this industrious spirit has left me. Churches, cities of the dead, ruins, all the marvellous spots which then stood out so boldly to be noticed, have fallen back under the haze of enjoyment which envelops everything in this lovely place, — one's self, one's actions, and one's associates.

Goethe said well of Naples: "You forget yourself and the world here, in going about with persons who think of nothing but of being happy." In Italy we soon grow acclimated in spirit as well as in body, and learn to prefer, as the Italian does, this life of sensation, ease, and pleasure to one of thought and mental labor.

Every cause of annoyance, too, appears to be with drawn from me; it is as if I stood on charmed ground. Even the dreaded letters do not arrive, and I have not felt for months that sharp heart-click which the sight of home writing causes me. Home! what bitter irony and sorrow there is sometimes in that little word. Yes, I seem protected, as by some sweet enchantment, from the power of the dread angel Ahrim, whose triple scourge of

Darkness, Misery, and Death I have so often felt. I "hide my life" in a luxurious, happy dream.

Philip also repeats Goethe: "Naples is a paradise; in it every one lives in a sort of self-forgetfulness. I scarcely know myself; I seem quite an altered being; and I say, 'Either I have always been mad or I am so now.'"

Lately I have been visiting various celebrated places in the neighborhood of Naples, making short excursions which have taken only a day for the jaunt. One of these pleasant journeys was to Amalfi. We went by rail to La Cava; there we took carriages and drove to Amalfi. This drive made a strong impression on me, for Nature showed itself so luxuriant and lovely in the foliage of the trees, the vast quantities of beautiful flowers, and the enchanting coloring of the mountains and sea; then the picturesque character of the villages scattered about added a great deal to the peculiar charm of the landscape.

The mountains were covered with chestnuts and oaks to their very summits, and were fronted by a secondary line of hills, on which rose up orange- and olive-trees; sometimes these hills were terraced, and bore various kinds of grain, whose different shades made them look like strips of brilliant-hued cloth or velvet rolled out on the hill summits. Garlands of the vine, laden with clusters of young grapes, hung in graceful festoons from the branches of the filbert, fig, and other fruit- and nut-trees. Then came a succession of cool-looking recesses in these luxuriant hills, little dells intersected by deep ravines, which were covered with rich foliage close down to the margin of a hurrying stream, or the garden edge of a peasant's home, clusters of picturesque houses, while here and there peeped out a *delizia*, or villa, as if to look us a welcome. Now all this scene must be colored with the entrancing atmospheric hue which is only to be found in Southern Italy, and the flashing sea introduced to give life to its loveliness.

It was quite late in the morning when our carriages approached Amalfi. There lay the beautiful gulf with the mountains rising up, shutting off the snow-white town from the interior; and as I noticed this, I remembered what I had read long ago in Mitford's Greece, that "Amalfi had always been subjected to the local disadvantages of being situated so as to be excluded from the neighboring country by a range of very difficult mountains." But its situation is fine for landscape beauty; there is a deep mountain gorge, a torrent dashing into the gulf, and the old dowager duchess of a city lies there mouldering on the coast.

Amalfi! I looked at the poor little ruined place while our donkeys clambered up and down the streets, which are forever mounting and descending, and it seemed hardly possible to me that this dilapidated collection of strange looking old houses could ever have been a great seaport, — the Athens of the Middle Ages, the rival of Venice!

It was once a successful republic which coined its own money; had extensive commerce; owned streets and quarters in far-off great cities, factories in Constantinople and Bagdad, and before the time of the Crusaders had a church and convent in Jerusalem for pilgrims: but it went to sleep many hundred years ago. Magnetica Amalfi! It gave to the world the mariner's compass, and during the Crusading wars the proud Amalfitan standard was emblazoned with the compass cross.

At last, man and the sea overpowered this bold, busy little republic. Bloody battles and fearful engulfings laid it low; and now nothing remains, not even ruins, of the once crowded quays and arsenals: for the plashing waters of the gulf ride as proudly over them as Amalfitan navies once did on the haughty and destroying breast of the glittering, treacherous sea.

I had not as much satisfaction as usual in the Almafi visit; the party was too large and gay, and Philip and Luigi were not with us. The whole affair was confused and bustling. We were a merry, noisy set, with more curiosity than reverence, and more quick-witted cleverness than information; but I will not be ungracious, for a great deal of care and indeed expense was generously given and incurred by the hospitable planners of the jaunt.

We first visited the Cathedral, a Saracenic building, with a joyful looking campanile, and gay-tiled cupolas and domes. St. Andrew the Apostle is buried in the crypt. Once this cathedral was a favorite resort for pilgrims; St. Francis of Assisium visited it, and many other holy persons; a wonderful miracle was here vouchsafed to the faithful in those believing days, but it is still and dead now!

Some members of our gay party hunted up two famous sarcophagi, one of which was found built into the wall of the church; and they traced with great interest in the fine bas-relief adorning it a classic legend, the Rape of Proserpine. Others gathered admiringly around the great bronze doors of the cathedral, which are over a thousand years old; they were made by some Byzantine artist, when Amalfi was still young and powerful; they have Latin inscriptions in silver letters, telling that one Panteleone di Maura erected them in honor of St. Andrew and for his own soul's salvation.

While the rest were loitering over some of the cathedral wonders, I stood alone on the top of the high broad stone steps, and gazed dreamily down into the square or piazza beneath; the elevation was so great that I seemed to be standing on the first platform of a mountain. I thought of those wonderful old Catholic days in 800 and 900 A. D., the first period of Amalfi's greatness. Then my memory swept on to 1200, 1300, and 1400, when the town was a place of holy pilgrimage for great saints and sovereigns. My busy fancy filled the spacious flight of stone steps and the broad piazza with stately processions, banners, incense, and all the superb adornments of grand religious ceremonies. Nothing for a little while interfered with my vision, which grew very vivid. The square was quite empty; a few idlers had collected there to look at the donkeys waiting for our party. The water of the piazza fountain spouted out from the stone statues grouped around it, and plashed refreshingly in the huge basins. Suddenly our whole party came out of the cathedral, eager for a new sight; the donkey-drivers gave shrill cries; some pretty girls of our company laughed merrily over the ragged trappings of the poor beasts, and my day-dream of the Middle Ages faded away in the bright noonday light.

" No voice, no lute, no pipe, no incense sweet
 From chain-swung censer teeming;
No shrine, no grove, no oracle, no heat
 Of pale-mouthed prophet dreaming."

First, the donkeys took us to the Convent of the Capuchins, at the west end of the coast opposite the town, to reach which we had to ascend the steepest of rocky paths. Even those of us who had never visited Italy before knew this place better than any other spot in or around Amalfi.

Years ago, when I was a girl, I sketched the beautiful cloisters of this convent as a drawing-lesson, and on their dwarf-coupled columns and lancet arches I had received my first impressions of Christian architectural symbolism; and after many long years, here I was standing, looking at the cloisters, the very stones!

I rubbed my eyes and wondered if it was not some fine dream; then in order to get rid of the people, who were talking busily, I left the cloisters and returned to a picturesque grotto at the head of the rock, near which we had alighted from our donkeys on first reaching the summit; there I stayed alone until the rest of the party were ready to descend.

I found some thoughtless young girls and youths in the grotto laughing, innocently though irreverently, at a rude representation of the Passion in wooden life-size figures. As I entered, they passed on and were soon out of sight. I knelt down on the stones outside of this wild place, and gazed off on the beautiful sea. Amalfi lay on the mountain slope to the left of me, and on the beach beneath were some Moorish looking persons, — fishermen, — and groups of children rolling over and playing with the sand, pebbles, and waves.

There was a wonderful loveliness in the sea, sky, and land, and, added to the beauty of nature, swift crowding memories of the great old past came flashing like lightning before me, hovering and vanishing just as I would try to dwell on some single one.

A boat put off from shore; its graceful undulating motion was like a satisfactory time-beat, or well-accented rhythm in a great symphony, after a passage of perplexed harmonies. A wandering stream of wind came from the west, sweeping like a pleasant wave over me, bringing an echo of the murmuring mountain woods, where it had been toying with

> "Meeting boughs and implicated leaves."

Presently I saw it catch the lateen sails of the bark; they expanded, and as the boat sailed off it looked like a huge nautilus floating just for beauty's sake. I wished to be in it, for it was speeding fast towards that famous colony of the Sybarites, now lying dead on the distant shore of the gulf, and whose mysterious ruins I am longing to see, — Pæstum.

The sea washed up with "hollow harmony" on the polished pebbles, which shone like gems in the sun, giving the beach a glorious brilliancy. It made me very happy to look at this wide expanse of rich-hued sky, the soft lines of the distant mountains faint and aerial as rosy melting clouds, the bold, beautiful Amalfi slope sweeping gracefully down to the beach, and the broad stretch of dazzling waters; to breathe the sweet fragrance of the foliage, and listen to the faint melody that surrounded me.

> "Delicious sounds! those little bright-eyed things
> That float about the air on azure wings."

To see and feel all this loveliness was such a pleasure, that for a while I forgot the perilous heights of pain I had had to scale in order to reach this point of my existence, I thought of nothing but the simple joy of living.

My pleasant solitude was soon disturbed by our noisy party assembling on the height behind me, ready to descend the hill. There is this advantage in large parties of well-bred society folk, — each one is taken up with his or her *impressions du voyage*, and so occupied with expressing them, that the doings of a silent recreant like myself pass unnoticed.

The brave little donkeys carried us pell-mell down the steep descent, urged by the laughs of the riders and cries of the drivers. It seemed very dangerous, and I have no doubt our high gale of frolicsome mirth made it perilous; but who ever takes heed of risk on a journey? There is a strange sense of security, which almost every one feels, and which is without reasonable foundation, I know; for, what merit or virtue lies in the responsibility of directors of either donkeys or rail-cars, after one's limbs are broken or life lost? But this sense is a lucky possession, and every traveller should cultivate it, in order to be free from all drawbacks of timid apprehensions.

We made a gay flight of it down that precipitous steep. Young girls, who rarely spoke in loud, natural voices in drawing-rooms, pealed out merry rings of the joyfulest laughter; the young men forgot their Sir Charles Coldstream indifference and society accent, and mingled their frank, manly ejaculations of frolic-fun with the shrill cries of the drivers: for there is something in nature's influence, if there is nothing in society; while the dear little serious donkeys trotted swiftly and safely from one rocky step to the other, seeming to pay no attention to us foolish human beings.

We did not dismount when we reached the town, but crossed the Cathedral square again, and went, in the opposite direction, to the Vallee di Molino, Valley of the Mills, where we were to dine *al fresco*. This short donkey-ride to the valley was one of the most remarkable features of the day, the road was so curious.

We first went through a dark passage, in which was a Moorish archway, with a shrine that had a flickering lamp and a vase of fresh flowers before the Greek-looking Madonna. The place grew more and more obscure, the air was filled with moisture, and we heard rushing, falling waters around us; but we could see nothing distinctly. The pretty, girlish laughs were stilled, and the young Coldstreams of our party grew courageous and protecting in their assurances of "no danger whatever."

This lasted but a few moments, when we came out into all the daylight to be found in narrow streets bordered by high houses. The little hoofs of the donkeys pattered up and down the rugged paths, which were like stone staircases. We were so close to the houses, that it seemed more like going through them than beside them. The inhabitants of the dwellings, some of whom were busy making the macaroni for which the town is now noted, left their work, and leaned listlessly out of the windows and over the terrace rails to look at our laughing cavalcade.

Arches and staircase-streets followed in succession, the donkeys trotting skilfully along; presently we came out on a mountain gorge, through which dashed a little glancing torrent. It was the Valle del Molino, Valley of the Paper Mills. High mountains rose up around us, and the foaming stream went leaping over the jagged, rocky bed, making beautiful cascades in its hurry; the shivering aspen-trees on the borders bent their branches down, as if to catch a sight of their trembling forms in the broken surface of the waters, and seemed to grow more quivering as the shattered reflection was cast up to them with the spray.

Along the sides of the gorge were ruins of the Middle Ages, which have since been used as paper mills, but are now deserted. The walls were covered with maiden-hair fern, and all the climbing bind-weeds and club-mosses peculiar to this luxuriant climate, whose soft, serrated leaves waved to and fro in the breeze. We went to the highest plateau of this lovely spot, where we found a low, picturesque wall, and some broken marble columns, which served for seats and tables. Here we dined or lunched. Champagne corks snapped; *pâtes de foie gras* and other delicious dishes were taken from the well-stocked hampers, and eaten with fine appetite,—indeed, with a hunger that is rarely given to such luxurious food; peals of laughter rung out; snatches of opera melodies and barcarolles were trilled; pretty words of society compliment talked: it was a true Boccaccio fête, and, as I looked at the white walls overrun with verdure, and the branches of orange- and myrtle-trees leaning against the building, I recalled that poet's admiration of Amalfi. Some day our own little family party must go to Valle di Molino; the four lovers will be very happy there.

The drive home did not seem a repetition of the morning's pleasure; it was like something new. I noticed more carefully the beautiful route. All the way from Amalfi to Vietri the road lies along the coast and winds around the bend of land which forms the western shore of the Gulf of Salerno, doubling and redoubling as it follows the irregularites of outline.

The superb scenery looked even more attractive in the late afternoon glow than it had in the morning light, and I understood better its geographical position. I traced with my eye the high mountainous country of the Sorrentine promontory, which lies on the west side of the Gulf, the Apennine offsets; and then, turning, gazed down the eastern shore, which stretches out to Pæstum's coast, far off in the almost invisible distance.

Close at hand new points of scenery opened on us, and we noticed fresh beauties. The golden, poetic fruit and snowy bridal blossoms of the orange and lemon scattered perfume around us. Every little while we saw groups of olive-trees, standing midway up a hill, their dull leaves turned gently back by the western breeze, which was dying away; and as their gray masses rested against the dark foliage of the chestnuts and oaks above and around them, they looked like soft

> "Clouds suspended in an emerald sky."

Undine waterfalls tumbled down the numberless ravines, and sung their sunset song, as they danced gayly on to the Gulf. That beautiful Gulf! Not a zephyr ruffled its surface, and it was

> "Filled with the face of heaven, which, from afar,
> Comes down upon the waters."

Amethystine blue lay near the shore, while farther out it looked like broad plains of malachite and gold. There was not a cloud in the heavens, and all the various colors seemed indeed to be

> "Melted into one vast Iris of the west,
> Where the day joins the past eternity."

After we left the coast-road and turned in towards La Cava, our attention was attracted by the numberless wild-flowers which were spread in lavish profusion over the banks, on either side of the road. We stopped the carriages, and gathered huge bunches of cowslips, daisies, musky wood-violets, and blood-red anemones. At La Cava we again took the rail-cars, as we had in the morning, and crossed this little point of land, which forms the left side of the Bay of Naples, — the same Sorrentine promontory over whose western shore, on the Salerno Gulf side, we had just been travelling. When we reached Pompeii, we found our carriages waiting for us, as we had ordered they should in the morning. We could have gone all the way to Naples by rail, but we wished to enjoy the evening drive on this lovely Mediterranean shore, of which we never grow weary.

We visited Herculaneum and Pompeii a few days ago, and I brought back only a few pleasant memories. As I walked through the confined streets, and looked at the little houses of Pompeii, it was difficult for me to realize that living people had ever inhabited them. The place seemed less like a real town than a collection of models, made to show in miniature the way the ancients lived.

There are in my memory two separate and distinct images of these exhumed places. One, the more agreeable of the two, was gained by looking at the curious and interesting things taken from these towns, which are collected together in the Musée Bourbonique; the other, and totally different one, was produced by the visit I paid to the towns themselves. The first fills me with wonder and admiration; the last with disagreeable disappointment: moreover, I can never connect the two.

It is incomprehensible to me how a people who displayed such perfect artistic taste in all the appointments of domestic life should have put up with such contracted accommodations. The mere door-latches, bolts, handles, locks, and keys were of bronze, and richly worked, showing that the Pompeiians possessed a microscopic eye for ornamental detail, but no refined need for home space and personal comfort. Shop weights, braziers for boiling water, portable stoves, made also of bronze, graceful in form, of exquisite workmanship, small and elegant enough to set on a table as ornaments, were used daily by these people, who had not even comfortable sleeping apartments, whose home rooms were mere side-closets, and whose largest dining and reception-halls were only twenty feet square.

Rich decorations, however, were lavished on these little rooms. The floors were covered with costly mosaics; the ceilings and walls with frescoes; while columns, hung with rich tapestry, bordered the inner courts, in the centre of which were always little gardens and fountains.

The men lived abroad in the superb public buildings, the temples, forum, and luxurious baths; as for the women, life was not equally shared with them, nor arranged for their comfort, as in these pleasant days; for in this good nineteenth century, though there may be instances of old heathen injustice and selfish disregard of women's real rights, they are rare and individual ones, — exceptions, really, to the general spirit, which is disposed to be honest, and give us a fairer portion in life than has ever before been granted.

The solemn, dark labyrinthine passages of Herculaneum were more attractive to me than the baby-house appearance of Pompeii; there was at least the mystery of darkness hanging over them. Luigi told me that one of these galleries in Herculaneum led to the villa in which were found the beautiful sitting statue of Agrippina mourning Germanicus, the divine Plato head, the dreamy Scipio, and the troubled, perplexed Seneca.

Whose villa was this? What an abode of luxury, refinement, and pleasure was darkened in one single night, — a night, too, that was to last for centuries.

Notwithstanding the little disappointment which is first experienced on seeing these diminutive houses, it is impossible to stand in the streets of these buried towns without feeling deep emotions, and such, too, as no other place in the world can create.

The busy waves of life were surging as roughly and rolling on as swiftly in those buried towns as in our crowded cities of to-day. Human beings were gathered together, each one of whom had his or her own secret history. Hopes, fears, and ambitions choked the life current, and caused the same faintness with apprehension, the same exaltation with fast-fading success, which we suffer. Existence was glorious to some; others carried hopelessly aching hearts, or secret sins, hidden, like the man's viper hand in the legend, in the discreet folds of life's mantle, which devoured noiselessly to the heart-core. Vigorous life, feeble health, each were alike suddenly suspended; and here beneath these ruins they have mouldered and mingled, with lava and dust, for nearly two thousand years.

The situation of the Tragic Theatre at Pompeii pleased us very much. The building was above the general level of the city; it stood on the southern slope of a hill, was semicircular, and every part was lined with Parian marble. The seats faced the Mediterranean; and as the Theatre was open to the air, the audience commanded two luxuries at once: while enjoying the play, they could lean back and gaze over the beautiful free sea.

We imagined them listening to the words of womanly sympathy, chanted by the tender Sea Nymphs to Prometheus Bound, as they sat there looking out on the fast-speeding waters of the Crater Bay, while old Typhon's resentful roar made a murmuring accompaniment to the sad words of the poor chained Titan, —

> "for grief walks the earth
> And sits down at the foot of each by turns."

And if they felt terror-stricken when they heard the mountain's sullen moans, while watching the sparkling waves dashing myriads of gems on high, and hearing the

> "multitudinous laughter
> Of the ocean billows,"

they could find the answer to their fears in the response of the rock-chained enemy of Zeus to Oceanus, —

> "*Chorus.* — How didst thou medicine the plague fear of Death?
> *Prometheus.* — I set blind Hopes to inhabit in their houses.
> *Chorus.* — By that gift thou didst help thy mortals well."

The Pompeiian visit, though pleasant, wanted the *élan* of our usual family excursions. In the first place, Luigi, who is not well yet, was spiritless and sad; even Venitia seemed in a "sweet trouble." Then Florence Folham met some young English naval officers among the ruins, one of whom was her cousin, young Milnes, a handsome youth, and very devoted to her; of course they joined our party, and were quite in Philip's way, as can readily be understood; this put him out of humor, and made him silent and moody to the rest of us. Thus Janet and I had all the classical talk to ourselves, — and not much either, — for in the presence of strangers it sounds a little pedantic to indulge freely in conversation on the subjects suggested by these places.

We are not as united as we have been, it seems to me. There is some little tangle in our golden chain; but it will soon unknot. I fancy our two lovers are discovering that they are not mere admirers of these pretty young girls. The affair for both of them is in a troubled state, like some perplexed music which works itself out, through strange resolutions into perfect peace and security.

So must it ever be in this life. The fullest joy is often born out of the throes of a great sorrow. He said well who wrote, "Without a basis of the dreadful, there is no perfect rapture." Life's jewel must be set in jet to display its fullest radiance; and even these innocent lovers must have their tender trouble to make the bliss all the more perfect.

The closing of the day at Pompeii, however, was satisfactory. The young officers had to leave early, in order to join their ship before nightfall; thus we were left to ourselves for a little while. Luigi and I went to the Amphitheatre to look at the sunset, which was peculiarly glowing and gorgeous. While we sat there, we talked, not of these "mummied cities," but of musical coloring in Nature. This was suggested to us by the exquisite shades which the enchanting atmosphere was throwing over the landscape. The rest of the party were loitering idly near us, and joined us just as I was saying, —

"Flowers and leaves of trees are forever modulating; they are true living harmonies; they strike one key of melody in their youth, then modulate and resolve through series and series of tones, in every phase of their short existence, but always breathe their last in the minor; it may be a grand, full, high-sounding chord, like the red, orange, and purple of autumn foliage, still it is the solemn minor of death."

"That is all very pretty, but fanciful, Ottilie," said Philip, laughing, as he took a seat beside me. "That theory of classing musical tones and harmonies in colors is impossible; every sensible musician will say so; and for this reason, my friend: color has not, like music, a gamut of harmony, nor certain tones which serve as data, from which shades and combinations can be formed by divisions of tones into semitones, then woven into subtle expressive forms. The Tone tongue is vague enough, heaven knows, but not so vague as Color."

"You are right," I answered, "in saying musical tones and harmonies should not be literally classed in colors; nor did I mean that. Each form of art-beauty has its separate and distinct individuality; but one form can very properly suggest to the observing and imaginative spectator or hearer other art manifestations. It is difficult to express in words clear descriptions of either music or color, without borrowing technical terms from one for the other; for music and painting are nearer akin than poetry or any word form. Indeed, I never look at the works of great colorists, without thinking what fine musicians they would have made."

"That gifted man Alfred Tonnellé," said Luigi, "made a beautiful observation, which is *apropos* to your remarks: 'If the lips of the young man of Urbino could have opened to music, they would have sung the melodies of the young man of Salzburg.'"

"Charmingly true. Mozart was indeed the Raphael of music!" I exclaimed.

In all the short arguments which Philip playfully provokes, Luigi if possible helps me, partly for the reason that we think alike on most subjects, but chiefly because he sees, what is really the truth, I am not a fair match for Philip; so on this occasion he came as usual to my rescue.

"You are right also, Ottilie, about the fitness of drawing comparisons between color and music; and, as you say, using the technical terms of one in describing the other often helps two cultured artists to understand each other. Thus, for example, when Euler said the strength and intensity of a color depended on the vibrations of light, he compared the sun to an immense clock, whose movements, transmitted by ether, acted on the optic nerve in the same manner as the vibrations of the air act upon the nerve of the ear in producing sound.

"Yes," I said, "it is in these vibrations of light that the great melodic secret of color lies, just as in the vibrations of sound skilfully arranged agreeable harmonies exist."

"Exactly so. The science of color consists in producing equal vibrations, and the great skill of the colorist is shown in making tones which are wide apart harmonize together and produce an equal vibration on the eye: but the variable fashion in which ether vibrates makes it difficult of command; the colorist has not the same degree of power over it that the harmonist has over sound. This very variability of vibration, however, enables us to regard in Nature the marvellous and complicated assemblages of colors without confusion and fatigue. Nature is always perfect in color as in design."

Janet added her information to this pleasant sunset talk, and told us of the gamut of harmony which M. Chevreul, the director of the Gobelin and Beauvais manufactories, has given to color. He produces ten chromatic circles from the three primitive colors; these ten circles make thirty series; each tint has its gamut of twenty-four tones; thus over fourteen thousand tones are produced, all of which are said to be needed for the "chromatic arsenal" of the Gobelin and Beauvais works. We talked afterwards of the wonderful variety of colors which the skill of chemists is now producing.

"But the cleverness of chemists," said Philip, "is destroying the power of the eye for delicate effects of color, just as the so-called improvements in brass instruments is destroying the ear for subtle effects in orchestration. The purple shadows accompanying chemical reds, blues, and greens are totally deficient in transparency, and are quite unlike those suggested by the clear cochineal red, the carnation of Adrinople, the soft China indigo, or the tender azure of *lapis lazuli* and cobalt. Shadows no longer resemble nature, nor do they fulfil the meaning of their name, for they have become opaque and unvarying."

With something of a woman's obstinacy I added, as we arose to leave the ruins, "These modern chemical colors have been justly styled, 'false harmonies in the place of resolving discords.'"

And thus ended our day at Pompeii.

A MUSICAL EVENING.

AST night the Folhams and Rochesters called to see us, on their way home from a fine dinner-party. Luigi also came in, and we had a charming evening without ruffle or tangle. Philip and Florence sang together, which they do very cleverly, and their voices harmonize nicely. I had been riding with Philip in the afternoon, and had the excuse of fatigue for my silence; so without much interference from loquacious Mrs. Folham, I rested on one of the window lounges, listened to the music, looked at the happy young people, and felt so comfortable that I found myself wondering if there was any real trouble in the world.

> "What pang
> Is permanent with man? From the highest
> As from the vilest thing of every day,
> He learns to wean himself. *For the strong hours*
> *Conquer him.*"

But the sweet and happy hours are conquering me. Last evening a powerful charm was worked on every one, however, by that subtle and delicate interpreter of hidden emotions and inexpressible thoughts, — music. Some one has said finely, "Music's form, composed of vibrations of the air, lives in space and gives form and shape to the impalpable." Indeed, the most impressive, direct, and irresistible language for the ideal is the Tone tongue; it is a much more powerful expression of feeling than any other art form.

I watched its effect with great interest last night. Our lovers are just at the most difficult point of their intercourse; their love is unacknowledged, even half unknown to themselves. It is without speech, words have not given it tangible form, therefore music is a pleasant relief to their full hearts; it produces the happiest harmony of feeling. Last evening Venitia and Luigi stood near each other in tender, gentle silence, and during some passages in the singing I observed their eyes meeting without startle in long, quiet looks.

The merry conversational intercourse between Philip and Florence formed a pleasing contrast. He complimented her gayly on the success of her toilette, making her blush bewitchingly; and she tinkled out her pretty foam-bell laugh, which always reminds me of dancing waters rippling over pebbles. These blondes are truly "the stars of the earth."

She was dressed in exquisite taste; the texture of her robe was as delicate as gossamer; its flounces and light ornaments were in perfect keeping, and she moved gracefully about in a half gliding step. I fancy a Parisian modiste would have thought her an exact representation of an Aphrodite rising from the foam of the sea.

Her beautiful hair seemed more radiant than usual; it was turned off from the blue-veined temples, and rolled back in that style called "*L'Impératrice*," which suits so well a blonde like Florence. The hue of the roots of the hair and the skin is so nearly the same as scarcely to show the line of separation, and both seem to have gold-dust mingled in their precious compound. The rich mass rose in ripples all over her head as if lifted by little waves of wind, and made me think of Chaucer's Queen of Love, —

> "It shone as gold, so fine,
> Dishevel, crisp."

Florence sings the *Sonnambula* music better than any other, — that is, for my taste. It may be because her fresh young beauty seems so well suited to the charming pastoral story of this opera, — "this true Bucolic of the country of Virgil and Theocritus," as Scudo calls it. It is indeed a delicious creation, full of the freshness and perfume of spring; its sadness is only a short shower at sunset, refreshing the young, springing herbage which was a little bent down by the rays of an over ardent noonday sun; then, after the little shadow of trouble is over, the air is filled with resonance, and the young rising moon of love is greeted with the delicate notes of Arcadian reeds, piping sweetly and tenderly a ravishing epithalamium.

She sang last evening the aria in the first act, "*Come per me sereno*," in the most winning manner; and in the ensuing allegro, "*Sovra il seno la man mi posa*," her high notes were thrilling, and filled with that mysterious, invisible fluid which escapes from a fast throbbing soul. I think I liked her execution of this passage better than the finale, "*Ah non giunge*," although she did throw into that an *éclat*, a bounding girlish joy, which was delicious.

Philip sang with her the duos following the arias, and his ruby-hued voice mingled with hers delightfully. They gave us almost the illusion of the opera; for added to their very clever singing was an unconscious display of deep emotion, which was equal to the finest acting. The two lovers were evidently speeding off just as fast as the swift locomotive of a mutual infatuation could carry them.

During the little dialogue in "*Prendi l'annel ti dono,*" Janet glanced at me once or twice, and she had to check a merry quivering of her expressive lips, and drop her eyelids quickly to hide the frolicsome dancing of the eyes. Florence's reply to "*Sposi or noi siamo*" was very naive. She had yielded up her whole being unconsciously to the new element which music and love combined had created, and on its tender pulsating waves her spirit floated happily. Her violet-hued eyes were full of sweet meditation when she sang, *sotto voce*, "*Sposi*"*;* then she struck the E flat, and the sound was fruity. Although it is a head-note, the sudden gush of deep feeling made it "full-throated" like the nightingale's tone. A soft swell followed, the voice floated down on the A with the most ravishing little turns soft and silvery, and "*Tenera parola*" lay on the air like little swaying flower petals.

Philip, I knew, was thrilled by it; for his reply, "*Cára, cara nel senti posi questa gentil viola,*" was so full of emotion it almost choked him. Florence's response was sung as if she were unconsciously uttering aloud the sweet echo his "*gentil viola*" had left in her love-touched soul, "*Pura innocenta fiora,*" — it was inimitable!

Luigi stood near Venitia; his long dark eyes were half closed, and rested on her; he seemed lost in a sweet dream. Dear Mrs. Folham, delightfully innocent of Italian, sat bolt upright, looking on the whole affair in the most practical English mamma manner; but Janet and I were "the chiels amang 'em takin' notes."

When it was over, the young people gathered around the piano, and tried to cover their real feelings by earnest talk about nothing. Wenzel, a music teacher, who plays accompaniments for them, preluded softly; the rippling arpeggio passages he played were not meant to attract attention; the discreet Italian only wished to fill up a gap. Janet stood a few moments by the piano, then went to Mrs. Folham, who was talking with Mr. and Mrs. Rochester. After saying a few words to them, she came to the lounge where I was lying in a true hypnotic state.

"This music makes me think of a passage I read in Scudo to-day," she said, leaning over me. "'It is not high art producing a grand dramatic emotion; it is a delicate pleasure, a sensuality of the ear tempered by a light moral feeling, which sweetly penetrates the heart, *per aures pectus irrigatur,* as a Latin poet has said so happily.'"

I could not reply to her; to be spoken to by any one gave me a keen sensation, which was almost like pain. After a glorious flight on "music's mighty wings," it is impossible to return to ordinary mortal means of communication; the soul has been soaring off in its own ether, and comes back as *folâtre* and rebellious as an Ariel; the poor body seems like a prison, and it beats the bars of the cage mercilessly. The body, too, becomes impregnatic, as it were, with some of the same emotion, and a vertigo and irritability result which few know how to control; so I only smiled back an answering assent, and leaning my head on the cushions closed my eyes. Janet sat near me in silence; she rested her little hands on my head, and kindly smoothed down the hair bands; her soft magnetic touch was very soothing, and gave me great comfort.

Venitia finished the evening by playing that Polonaise of Weber in E major, which Liszt calls dithyrambic; in it life, warmth, and passion glitter on the wave crests without disturbing the grand ebb and flow of the majestic ocean of deep feeling. I listened, still in my *raptus* state, and whispered to the beat of the measure, —

"Thou art the wine whose drunkenness is all
We can desire, O Love! and happy souls,
Ere from thy vine the leaves of autumn fall,

"Catch thee, and feed from their o'erflowing bowls
Thousands who thirst for thy ambrosial dew;
Thou art the radiance which here ocean rolls

"Investest it; and when the heavens are blue
Thou fillest them; and when the earth is fair,
The shadow of thy moving wings imbue

"Its deserts and its mountains, till they wear
Beauty like some bright robe; — thou ever soarest
Among the towers of men, and as soft air

"In spring, which moves the unawakened forest,
Clothing with leaves its branches bare and bleak,
Thou floatest among men ; and aye implorest

"That which from thee they should implore; *the weak*
Alone kneel to thee, offering up the hearts
The strong have broken, — yet where shall any seek
A garment whom thou clothest not?"

MRS. ROCHESTER'S BALL.

T is a glorious night, — or morning, as it is after two o'clock. I have been out on the terrace; I cannot sleep; my heart is too full of tender inquietude about a strangely-lagging happiness I would fain hurry on, if I knew how, for those who are very dear to me. Every one else is asleep; stillness reigns in this vast palazzo, and even the great city is quiet. The season is just on the verge of June; the moon is at the full, and its sharp, clear light lies on the "straight-up tufa rock" behind the terrace, pointing out

"Where lichens mock
The marks on a moth, and small ferns fit
Their teeth to the polished block."

A "love-lorn nightingale," hidden in the dark foliage of the orange-trees which are in that garden on the terraced hill, pours out a perfect flood of song. What a delicious note! It is as if the rich odor of the starry fruit-blossom had become a voice. At first, the bird trilled a little faintly, then the notes fell into a heavy gurgle, and she stopped, as if frightened at her own voice, recalling to me Chaucer's

"New abashéd nightingale,
That stinteth first when she beginneth sing";

but now she utters a peal of glad music, and "showers a rain of melody," without stint or limit,

> "Like a poet hidden
> In the light of thought,
> Singing hymns unbidden
> Till the world is wrought
> To sympathy with hopes and fears it heeded not."

But why is the nightingale called "love-lorn"? That song is full of joy and rapture. I know Shakespeare says,

> "The nightingale's complaining notes,"

and the ancient poets gave the same description. Sophocles calls the bird "lamenting Itys," and likens her to Electra. Homer, too, in the Odyssey, compares Penelope's restlessness to the nightingale; but, while listening to that gush of gay melody, — there, it bursts out afresh! — I cannot agree with these great authorities, but rather side with jovial Chaucer, who, in his Flower and Leaf, calls the nightingale's song "a merry note."

Beyond the broad Mergellina the sea sparkles like cloven gems, and off in the distance Vesuvius glows. It is indeed a glorious night; and this loveliness of nature and my tender thoughts make "civil wars within my brain," as Sir Philip Sidney says. Like him, I have

> "Smooth pillows, sweetest bed,
> A chamber deaf to noise and blind to light,
> A rosy garland, and a weary head."

For if the garland on my head this evening was of rich lace, instead of rosy flowers, it was none the less a festal one. Mrs. Rochester gave a ball to-night, and it was a very brilliant affair; "a success," as Mrs. Folham reiterated, "yes, my dear, a positive success."

Our two beauties looked well. I love the detail of

dress, and have a true feminine weakness for all those delicious nothings which go towards the making up of a beautiful woman into a charming Watteau or gorgeous Titian picture; and Florence and Venitia were to-night the living counterparts of those two masters' creations. Florence's toilette was one of those indescribable but veritable inspirations of the French *modiste;* and its delicate pink hue, with puffings and flounces of airy tulle, and all the accessories of rose-buds and light ornaments, suited well her dainty little person.

Venitia's fine, large form needs something more exact in costume than the pretty blonde does; her dress to-night was a rich, heavy silk; its color was that lovely Venetian green; and the haze of soft, costly lace which fell over it made it look like sea-foam. The drapery of the robe was fastened on her superb shoulders, and over the breast, with large onyxes, set around with fine-sized pearls; the head-dress and armlets were adorned with the same gems. There are nine of these finely-sculptured stones, which Janet has owned for years, unset, — Paul's gift. A few weeks ago we were admiring them, and Luigi suggested the setting of them as a costume decoration, very well suited for Venitia's style in full dress. Janet took to the idea, and had them arranged by a jeweller, under his supervision. They were only completed a few days since, and to-night Venitia wore them all.

A sleeping Medusa forms the girdle-clasp. A Psyche gathers the drapery across the bosom, while an Iris and Hebe fasten the shoulder-bands. The armlets are formed of a broad, fine network of gold, clasped with Egyptian Bacchantes. The head-dress is composed of fillets of gold network, something in the style of the Sappho bands;

three or four of these are plaited in a caul, in which the rich braids of Venitia's hair are gathered, and this rests on the back of her finely-shaped head; another band, set with large, oblong pearls, is clasped, at each ear, to the caul by small, exquisitely-cut butterflies; this band passes across the front of the head, rising in a diadem shape, after the fashion of that on the brow of the Ludovisian Juno, and in the centre of this diadem of gold and pearls is placed the largest and finest onyx of the collection; its subject is a sleeping Psyche, with a butterfly hovering over the temple and another nestling into the breast,—sad emblem of the double awakening love causes in brain and heart.

Janet and I served as foils to these two pretty girls. We were in the orthodox costumes of our age. She wore a queen's-gray *moiré*, and I a Parma violet silk, both gowns shaded becomingly with rich black lace, accompanied with a discreet sprinkling of diamonds. When we all met in our drawing-room to drink tea together, before going to the ball, Philip and Luigi talked of coloring and artistic grouping.

"But the fine effect of this beautiful dressing," I said, "will be ruined by the bad taste one is apt to meet with at an evening party. Just think of the discords that will be made by some horrid chemical-blue gown passing near Venitia's delicate sea-foam, or Pompadour pink clashing against Florence's rose-bud hue."

"Like a public picture-gallery," replied Philip; "but Luini and I will appoint ourselves hanging committee, and give you all the best lights."

Soon after we arrived, Venitia was taken to the music-room by Mr. Rochester, to play for him and a small circle of friends a lovely Ghazel, to which he has lately taken a great fancy. Luigi, of course, followed her, attending on Janet and Mrs. Folham. At the other end of the fine suite of apartments was a large, brilliantly-lighted ball-room; a band of music was playing there, and, as Florence and I stood talking to Philip in the centre drawing-room, we could see the resolving forms the dancers made in a Lancer quadrille.

A group of young men came out of the ball-room, and looked about as if searching for some one. They were the English midshipmen we had met at Pompeii, and it was Florence for whom they were looking. They saw her almost immediately, and, coming up, shook hands cordially with us all, even with stately Philip, whose coldness did not affect these brave, happy young fellows in the least. Just then, that beautiful Galop from the *Vêpres Siciliennes* poured like a rich topaz-hued current on the air, and swiftly-gliding and whirling couples flashed before the broad, open doorway.

"Florence, the Galop!" cried her handsome young cousin, hurriedly. "Come, you have missed one already, for I have been waiting nearly an hour for you."

"Miss Folham, Miss Folham!" exclaimed the others, eagerly, all talking together, "do not forget I am on your tablets for the first Lancers after"——"And I for the second"——"And I for the next Galop"——"And I——."

She turned to us, hesitatingly, and, with an attractive thoughtfulness not very common in a young, admired girl at a ball, surrounded by gay officer-partners, said, "Neither of you dance, I believe; and yet—" She stopped, as if not knowing what to say, while young Milnes tapped his foot, impatiently, and Philip looked haughty and indifferent. I replied, with a laugh, "And yet you do. I am sure, my dear, it is very natural you should; so hurry off with Mr. Milnes, who is quite out of patience with us all. We shall follow you, for I shall like to look at you very much."

Philip and I walked slowly into the ball-room; he was very sullen, said not a word, and I rather enjoyed his annoyance. He needs a little contradiction once in a while; and, moreover, I fear he will never see his way clear with Florence, unless some younger rival shows it to him. Florence looked very lovely, as she floated by in the dance; her light form rested gracefully on young Milnes's firm hand, and, as he is a skilful waltzer, he bore her along swiftly and beautifully; more than one person stopped to admire the two handsome cousins.

"I never liked to dance," I remarked; "and yet it is a pretty sight, especially when the dancers are such graceful young creatures as Florence and that fine-looking lad, Milnes. Is she not charming?"

Philip did not deign to reply to my question, but said, in a low, angry voice: "Few sensible women, Ottilie, express such contradictory and inconsistent opinions as you indulge in constantly. Often I have heard you say you thought society dancing absurd, and all kinds of waltzing, without exception, unladylike, and worse, — immodest."

Of course I made no more remarks. After a few moments' silence he asked: "How long do you intend staying in this noisy ball-room? I wish you had not taken the office of chaperone on you. All dancing young ladies should hunt up their mammas, and not bore mere acquaintances in this way."

"Florence a mere acquaintance!" I thought, with a repressed smile. Poor Esau! I am sure he was willing at that moment to barter his glorious birthright of genius for a mess of the sweet savory pottage of gay youth. No wonder he was cross, for

> " 'T is a bitter thing
> To see our lady above all need of us;
> Yet so we look ere we will love."

"I do not see that it is necessary for me to chaperone Miss Folham here," I replied, "although I am quite willing to do so on our riding parties; her mother will soon hunt her up. Suppose we go into the music-room and listen to Venitia."

On going there, we found that Venitia had only just commenced. Some gentleman was at the piano when she came, and he had finished but a little while before we entered. She was playing the Ghazel, which is a curious little creation. The composer of it has made his music-poem correspond to the rule of the mental word-lyric; there is in it one positive, well-expressed thought, reiterated in various keys; the modulations are close and intricate; the accentuation strongly marked and skilful. Venitia executed it not only with the dexterity it required, but threw into it that delicacy and poetry of feeling which the composer had left to the *executante* to supply.

Of course it was received with great applause, and many earnest requests were made for "something more." Venitia remained at the piano, as if she intended complying with these requests. While she was listening to the pleasing compliments of Mr. Rochester and some other persons, I saw her eyes fall under a glance from Luigi. This look of his acted like a magnetic touch on her imagination; straightway sprang up within her that subtle emotion which the true artist feels at the moment of creation, and which spreads throughout the thoughts, enabling them to transform themselves into vivid, graphic pictures, adorned with rich coloring, so warm and glowing that they enchain not only the senses, but the mind and will.

Her fingers commenced slowly threading together some full chords, stringing them in groups, which reminded me of brilliant-hued gems, well contrasted. While she did so, her eyes wandered slowly over the room, with that calm expression of magnetic subtleness which they now possess at times; she seemed to be weighing and measuring her little audience. The compliments she had just received had been those of taste and discernment, of the very nature to encourage an *executante;* there was not one breath of petty jealousy near her, but a great deal of high, artistic culture and good breeding.

I felt sure she meant to improvise, and I was right. It is only lately that she has ventured on doing this in society; Luigi's encouragement, as well as capable, friendly criticism, have been of much help to her. Few who were present this evening knew what she intended doing; thus she was spared the embarrassment of an announced improvisation. The conversation ceased, and every one listened. Luigi caught her resolve with the instinct of a lover. He stationed himself near the end of the grand piano, with folded arms, and brow a little bent, as if listening with the critical but appreciative ear of an artist.

Venitia shows in her improvisings the promptness she has in her character. She has a great deal of decision and common sense, — two qualities particularly needed, and often found lacking in the artist; these enable her to make a rapid choice of the thousand and one suggestions which crowd in with perplexing confusion on the instant of conception. Her subjects too are always simple, —

like herself, open and candid, — sweet succeeding harmonies, and resolutions whose tangles are intricate, but not thorny; she manages them also with a freedom that is remarkable in one so young; she has good breadth of handling, as a painter would say, — a quality that partly arises from her close, rigid practice of many years which makes mechanical difficulties of little moment, and also the strict scholarly culture she has received, which removes from her all the embarrassment of raw, newly acquired information.

But on this occasion, I noticed much variation from her usual style, — the girl's genius is developing under the influence of love. After the resolving chords of the short interlude were over, and the spirited melodic thought well defined, the beautiful image was suddenly disturbed, as a swift wind ruffles a streamlet's mirror; weird chords, so combined as to sound like questions, fell in syncopation, leaving the response mute in the measure; little bits of the *motivo* mingled in producing a curious effect, and some vague but soft and pleasing passages flitted about, reminding me of the pearly-gray shadows which creep out of dingles and wood hollows.

Venitia uses the chromatic gamut in her *rêveries* as a skilful singer employs it, pointing it with a trill; she also controls the pedals with nice art, thus giving her melodic phrases the necessary sweep, — horizon, as it would be called in painting. This clever pedalling enables her to produce as fine contrasts in Tone distance as her melodic chord groupings give of Tone coloring. After a powerful assertion of the Tone thought, she often follows it with a passage *con sourdine*, as a violin player would say. This dexterous combining of the soft and loud pedals does not change the timbre of the sounds, but throws over them a haze, — an atmosphere of space and distance. This obtained she advances the retreating sounds by adroitly removing the *sourdine* effect of the soft pedal, then her vigorous trill, which is like the shrill throat-beatings of a lark, comes pouring down, bringing out the foreground firmly and clearly. Her improvising this evening possessed all these characteristics, and she carried us along with her so forcibly that we forgot to criticise.

Her admirable self-possession adds very much to the effect of everything she does. Her execution is never flurried; her hands always retain their position. A French gentleman said to-night they reminded him of Mme. Pleyel's hands; "*Si bien posées, — elles ne grimacent jamais*," was his remark ("so well placed, — they never make grimaces or affected movements"). No matter what may be the difficulties she encounters, the general position is never lost. This good command of her hands is like a firm seat in the saddle, and it makes her execution clear and flowing, every note coming out with satisfactory roundness. The divisions of time, too, are accurately marked, which produce that delicate shading and undisturbed rhythm so necessary to true musical expression. Her manner in everything is a little measured, like the time in a fugue, and this precision shows itself in her music, but the frankness of her nature allows the warm breath of love which is now affecting her, to flow over her creations, bestowing on them a freshness and vitality which is like the expression given to a great fugue by a passionate and poetical *executante*.

Through all the mysterious windings of her improvising this evening, not one of us felt for an instant a shadow of anxiety; our faith in her power and ability was not only unshaken, but it received a deeper hold;

as I have said, we forgot to criticise, and followed her lead obediently. The description I have given is long, but her improvising was short, and yet so complete, so full of suggestive thought and deep feeling, as to feed and occupy the minds of her listeners, without wearying them.

Presently the dark commingling harmonies grew clearer; the sorrowful questionings ceased, as if the cause of doubt had been forgotten; no dissonances were heard; the resolutions mounted joyfully; the broken bits of the *motivo* blended cunningly together, ruling with rejoicing triumph as it were over the whole; and the improvising closed with one of her best executed chromatic gamuts, on which sparkled here and there beautiful trills, as bright, Philip said, as small diamonds, but they reminded me of pulsing auroras.

The sensation which was produced by this display of poetical power in the person of so young and beautiful a woman was very great; and it might be injurious, but for the sweet balancing power of love. I am sure Venitia cared little for the compliments paid by the crowd of notabilities who thronged around her. Luigi's few words of praise, and the superb look of exaltation which sat upon his fine brow, gave her all the satisfaction she desired. He seemed to forget his late reserve, and during the rest of the evening was lifted up on this mighty wave of love-music as on a throne. He took possession of Venitia without hesitation as if she belonged to him, and she looked like a happy young queen who would fain put diadem and kingdom down, and be a humble handmaiden to her beloved.

But my old friend Philip was not so happily affected by the music; indeed, he was very wretched I could see.

He stood in a corner silent and moody, and I looked about for something to divert him.

"There is the great encyclopedist going into the library," I said.

"What, L——!" cried Philip, arousing himself. "He is the very person I wish to see. I was not at home when he called this morning. Let us go to him; if it will not be a bore to you, I should like to have a little talk with him."

I was only too happy to find my bait successful. We went into the library, and Philip buried his chagrin in the pleasing excitement of a conversation with Dr. L—— and two or three other agreeable men; but I could see that he had not overcome his discomfort, and his annoyance served as a sharp sting to his conversation, giving it pungency and point.

I began to wonder in that way we women have of blending our sentiments and intellects together, — driving four in hand as it were, — listening to cultivated manly conversation, and all the while weaving our own little web of romance and sweet folly; — I began to wonder, I say, how this affair of Florence and Philip was going to develop, and all this I worked at while listening admiringly and understandingly to a masterly description Philip was giving me of a subject which is deeply interesting the learned encyclopedist.

"You see, the thing is simply this, Ottilie," and he explained to me with some little help from Dr. L—— and the other gentlemen, the plan of that famous tunnel under the Straits of Dover, which the first Napoleon conceived, and the third Emperor dreams of completing.

"The bare idea is an epic!" exclaimed Philip.

After Dr. L—— had pointed out to me the plan of the

tunnel on a beautiful little map or chart he had with him, Philip threw off, in his bold, impassioned style, a description of the descent of the cars from the high land, glowing with sunlight, to darkness far below the bed of the ocean; the roar and whirl of the steam-engines, united to the dull din of the sea waves dashing imperiously against that cuirass of rocks which shall separate the wild waste of waters above from this world below; and then the sweeping grand ascent upward of the cars in the middle of the Straits, to that Pharos of nations standing out in the sea on the coast of the Bank of Warne.

"Imagine," he said, "this subterranean road; a locomotive comes rushing along, vomiting flame and fiery vapor; it ascends a vast well-like tower, and finds itself on an island in the wide ocean. This island-port of Warne, as Lemoine says, will be the most complete representation of cosmopolitanism and fusion of people ever dreamed of, even by that great half-unknown French Franklin, Abbé de St. Pierre. Ships from every nation, with the produce and people from all parts of the globe, will assemble at this vast bureau of universal correspondence and intercourse; at midnight, as vessels come sailing by on the open sea, the great ocean light-house will beam on them, and its immense quays, lighted up by huge reflectors, shall point out one neutral spot of land, ruling over two seas, a star of hope and faith to peaceful nations."

All this he sketched out with a graphic force and energy which set my blood to tingling. While he was making one of his finest points, I saw his eye sparkle, lip quiver, and I fancied I noticed a slight waver in the voice, as if some sharp, sudden emotion had stung him: at the same time I felt a soft hand creep around my waist. I turned, and there was pretty Florence, looking almost penitent and entreating.

Philip never noticed her, never stopped the shadow of an instant, but poured on his fine eloquence as if unconscious of the sweet flattery her coming displayed; and yet I knew that the haughty creature was feeling it in every bounding pulse of his body. I drew the darling girl quietly down beside me, making room for her on the large sofa, held her soft little hand with its pretty pink finger tips tenderly in mine; and while Philip's lava current of description poured on, I thought how lovely and refreshing youth is.

The dear child sat looking up with rapt, half-conscious admiration of the brilliant man. She, who had been a few moments before the little queen of the ball-room, had thrown aside her rank and station and admirers, drawn by the subtle, strange, but sweet magnetism of love to his side. How dreamy and happy I felt as I looked at the two. I wished to say to him, Strange Philip!

> "Look at the woman here with the new soul,
> Like my own Psyche's; fresh upon her lips
> Alit, the visionary butterfly,
> Waiting thy word to enter and make bright,
> Or flutter off and leave all blank as first.
> This body had no soul before, but slept:
> Now it will wake, feel, live — or die again!
> Shall to produce form out of unshaped stuff
> Be art, — and further to evoke a soul
> From form be nothing? — This new soul is thine!" *

* Browning's "Pippa Passes."

CONSEQUENCES OF THE BALL.

WAS up so late last night, that when my maid came at the usual hour this morning I dismissed her, and slept until ten o'clock. After I had breakfasted, I learned that both Janet and Venitia had gone driving. Feeling as if I needed some pleasant occupation out doors, I sent for a carriage, intending to drive to the Church of L' Incoronata. I wished to be alone in the gallery of that old building, and dream my waking visions beside those ceiling frescos of Giotto, which are so suggestive to me of pleasing memories both in history and art; for if, as old Montaigne says, "*les historiens sont ma droicte balle,*" the early artists are also "*le vray gibier de mon estude.*"

> "At any rate, I love the season
> Of Art's spring-birth so dim and dewy."

While looking at Giotto's pictures, after studying those of the Byzantine school, I understand well what F. Schlegel meant when he wrote, "Where clear intelligence is combined with an instinctive power over the mechanism of a work, the glowing apparition called Art, which we venerate and welcome as a stranger visitant descending from loftier regions, springs at once into existence."

Giotto! With that name what rich associations are

connected. The friend of Dante, Petrarch, and Boccaccio. The popular artist of one of the most brilliant and luxurious courts ever known, where beauty and genius, and, alas! sin and sorrow also, dwelt. From this painter's pencil has come to us, in the ceiling frescos of L' Incoronata, the face of that lovely, hapless queen, Joanna. In this portrait she looks pleasure-loving and *insouciante;* her long, almond-shaped eyes ask only tenderness and ease; her full lips, soft cheeks, and beautiful head, which bears the crown with sweet dignity, all express love and joy more than pride and ambition.

The haughty beauties standing behind her in this fresco picture of her marriage — her cousins, Boccaccio's Fiammetta, and the Countess Durazzo — have enough of these dangerous passions in their faces; but the countenance of this calm, happy-looking woman is free from all harsh emotions.

> "E tu madre d' amor, col tuo giocondo
> E lieto aspetto."

Pretty creature! She and her gay, pleasure-loving cousins had great poets for lovers; world-poems to fetch down their names to us; and Giotto, "the lord of painting's field," to give us their delicious forms; but alas! they had history, also, to stand grimly by, and point with red, dripping finger to their poison bowls and headsman's block and axe!

> "merely born to bloom and drop,
> Here on earth they bore their fruitage, mirth and folly were the crop;
> What of soul was left, I wonder, when the kissing had to stop?
>
> 'Dust and ashes'! so you creak it, and I want the heart to scold.
> Dear dead women, with such hair, too, — what 's become of all the gold
> Used to hang and brush their bosoms? I feel chilly and grown old." *

* Browning's "Toccata of Galuppi."

When the servant brought me word the carriage was ready, I stepped out of my window on the terrace, and found Philip there reading.

"I thought I smelled your cigar. Why did you not announce yourself?"

"I have been waiting patiently for you ever since Mrs. Dale went out," he said. "You are going out also. May I accompany you?"

"Certainly, if you wish to."

"Where are you going?"

"I intended driving to L' Incoronata; but as you doubt the verity of my beloved Giotto frescos, you would be bored. Therefore we may go somewhere else, and I can visit the old ceiling another time."

"Of course," he said, in a gentle tone; "you allow me to be bored, and you yield to instead of controlling me, and making me more amiable. Dear Ottilie, you are an angel!"

"Not quite, Philip. But say, where shall we go?"

"To L' Incoronata, my friend; and I will promise not to utter one slighting word against the objects of your sweet faith. Where is San Lorenzo? I wish to visit it some time, for it is the church in which Boccaccio first met his Fiammetta."

Love is making Philip heavenly, I thought. I let him lift me into the carriage, arrange the cushions and foot-stool, and do everything for my comfort he could, while I directed the coachman to drive to the Largo de San Lorenzo. While we were driving there he said: "Ottilie, you and I should have been lovers. You understand me so well. I wonder if any other woman could now be as patient and forbearing with me as you are?"

"If you loved her, Philip, she would not have the

need; and as to understanding you, the knowledge I have a wife should not wish, — indeed, would be better without."

"Why, fair Portia?"

"Because a wife does not need to understand her husband as I do you. Sweet love and faith are her best gifts."

"And have you not love for and faith in me?"

"Yes, both; but, with them, a deeper knowledge of you, which places us abreast. I am not the sort of wife you should have."

"What sort of wife should I have, Ottilie?"

"Some one to love you trustingly, confidingly, adoringly, with a young, fresh, happy heart; just as I could and ought to have loved your father, Philip."

Philip remained silent, but he held my hand in his kindly, and once in a while grasped it with a firmer clasp. We reached the Franciscan church of San Lorenzo. As we looked up at the great marble doorway, which is one of the last remains of its original Gothic glory, and then stood under the vast stone arch, which spans the interior with stern beauty, we helped each other's memory in running back over the famous history of this great old church.

Every stone we stepped on had a legend or commemorated a great name. The very ground on which the church stands is classic. Here was the Forum, the Augustinian Basilica, and near it a temple of Castor and Pollux, in old Roman days.

The church was built by Charles of Anjou, that warlike, adventuring brother of St. Louis, to commemorate his victory over the "flaxen-haired Manfred," at Benevento (1266). Robert the Good and Wise, his grandson, finished it. Good and Wise! How sad those titles make us feel; for when this good and wise king died, all those virtues seemed to be buried with him.

"Heavens!" wrote Petrarch to Cardinal Colonna, after his arrival in Naples, when sent there on an embassy to the new government succeeding good old King Robert's death, — "Heavens! what a change has the death of one man produced in this place. No one would know it now. Religion, justice, and truth are banished. I think I am at Memphis, Babylon, or Mecca."

On entering the church, our first footsteps fell upon the tombstone of Giambattista della Porta, that friend of all hasty, eager, nineteenth-century students, who have so much to learn; for Time's book has grown very ponderous, and life has not one day more added to its length, nor is its strength any greater.

"Blessings on the memory of the old Italian!" I said, as we stooped to read his name chiselled in the stone, and the date of his death, 1515. "From his plan came all these great digests of knowledge, called encyclopædias, which has formed a true community system for the mind, more successful than those which political dreamers have attempted for governments."

Then Philip hunted up the tomb of Tasso's enthusiastic friend and biographer, the young Neapolitan nobleman Manso. After that we groped back in the old Chapter-house, where we admired a remarkable window, and the vaulted halls, now in ruins, which retain the original Gothic form of the church. As it was very dusty and close there, we returned to the front and sat down in one of the polygonal chapels, near the tribune or choir, where we talked over the Petrarch and Boccaccio history of the building. It was in the monastery of this church Petrarch resided during the period of his embassy from Rome to the court of the ill-wedded sovereigns, Queen Joanna I. and her cousin-husband King Andrew.

"Do you remember, Philip, the account Petrarch gives of the great storm which took place while he was here, 25th November, 1343?" I asked. "Just fancy this church at midnight, with the raging tempest outside and the poet Petrarch prostrate before that pulpit; the friars and prior of the convent holding crucifixes aloft, chanting litanies and prayers and burning incense, while the great body of this church was filled with the shrieking people. Then the lightning flashing in at the Gothic windows, and peals of thunder shaking the building 'from turret to foundation-stone.' And as day dawned, the holy service of the mass commencing; 'but though the priests chanted *Kyrie eleison, Christe eleison*, the rest of us,' says Petrarch, devoutly, 'did not dare lift our eyes to heaven, but remained prostrate on the ground.'"

"The closing of that famous letter," said Philip, "has the best part of the story, and shows the courage of the poet as well as his piety. After mass was over, and day had fairly dawned, he writes: 'Despair inspired us with courage. We mounted our horses and arrived at the port. What a scene was there!' They found the shore strewn with shipwrecked bodies, and a thousand Neapolitan horsemen assisting in the burial of the poor mangled bodies. 'I caught from them a spirit of resolution,' writes the poet, naively, 'and was less afraid of death from the consideration that we should all perish together.'"

"O yes, Philip, and when the sea sapped the foundations of the ground on which they stood, and they rushed to a higher point of land, what a touching scene they saw! The young Queen Joanna, with naked feet and dishevelled hair, — those beautiful feet and that amber flood of hair, Philip! — attended by a number of her ladies, rushing to the Church of the Virgin, crying out for mercy and help, — that very Church of L' Incoronata we are going to presently, which is not far from the port, you know. Poor young queen! Very blessed instead of fearful would death have seemed to her then, could she have only known her dreadful future. Why do not mortals accept death willingly when it first comes? Averted by prayers, it always takes a more frightful form in the end, which end must come some time. Better would it have been for her to have been swept out of existence by the fury of the elements, than to live as she did through years of black, bitter shame, and then have her sweet loveliness mangled by man's rage and brutality."

"The Fiammetta must have been in that group of beautiful, frightened women," said Philip. "Let us leave that sorrowful memory, and recall the gay Easter-eve a few years before this terrific storm took place, when Boccaccio saw for the first time, in this very church, — probably by this very column, — who can deny it? — the Princess Maria, whom he made known to fame by the name of Fiammetta, forming thus a quartette of beautiful women in the poetic diadem of Italy, — Beatrice, Laura, Fiammetta, and Leonora."

"Yes, Philip, but we shall put the gay, naughty Fiammetta in the back part of the diadem. Beatrice shall be the centre gem, with the cold, chaste Laura and the suffering Leonora on either side of her. Fiammetta must be content to shine alone, and in the background; she is not worthy of being placed in any closer companionship with these pure, good women, though a great poet did immortalize her."

Philip shrugged his shoulders saucily, and said, as we left the chapel and church, "Commend me to a woman's charitable judgment of her sex."

We drove to the Strada Medina, in which is the Church of the Virgin, of which Petrarch speaks, — L' Incoronata, — near the street or Vica delle Corregge (Corteregia). It is a small, unpretending building. On entering it there is a descent of several steps, which De Reumont says is in consequence of the elevation of the ground which has taken place since the sixteenth century. The exterior is unsightly; and the crowding in of more recent buildings makes the place more difficult to find. I remember I spent two or three mornings hunting L' Incoronata, when I first came to Naples, never thinking it could be this insignificant-looking chapel.

We stopped, before entering, to look at the sculptures over one of the portals, — the arms of the Neapolitan princes of the house of Anjou. On the right is the red cross of Jerusalem, on the left the golden *fleur de lis* of France, with the border of difference, and near these arms are little angels holding up a crown of thorns. Poor Joanna! It was indeed a crown of thorns thy wise and good grandfather placed on that golden head which he loved so fondly.

The famous frescos are in the choir of this church, which choir was formerly the Capella Regis, or Royal Chapel, of King Robert's Palace of Justice. In this chapel Joanna was married, when a girl, by her grandfather, to her cousin, Andrew of Hungary, who proved to be not only a bad husband, but a wicked sovereign. He was poisoned some time after his accession to the throne; the queen was accused of being privy to the act, just as Mary of Scotland was charged with a similar crime two centuries after, and for the same reason, — an ambitious cousin coveted her crown.

In 1352 Joanna married another cousin, Louis of Tarento, and built this church, L' Incoronata, in commemoration of her second marriage, and also in honor of the sacred crown of thorns of our blessed Lord. She incorporated in her new building the little Capella Regis, making it the choir; for on its vaulted ceiling were the fresco gems Giotto had painted for her grandfather, and they were a desirable possession for the new church.

This little bit of history is very precious to me, for it settles the doubts against the authenticity of these beautiful frescos; which doubts were founded on the anachronism that Giotto was dead fifteen years before L' Incoronata was built. To be sure; but this little Royal Chapel of the Palace of Justice, the scene of Joanna's first marriage, was decorated by this great painter when she was a girl, many years before its annexation to her new church. Her grandfather was alive and on the throne when Giotto painted the frescos on the Capella Regis. When L' Incoronata was built King Robert and his painter friend were both dead, and had been many long, sad years, and the girl-bride had grown to be a woman, was a queen, had been an unhappy wife, a widow, and was dreaming of new happiness in a second marriage.

The authority for this opinion is Chevalier Stanislas D' Aloë, the distinguished Secretary of the Musée; he has written a fine and exhaustive work on the subject, which sets at rest all doubts.*

The vaulted ceiling of the chapel, or choir, is divided into eight compartments, on which are these great old

* *Les Peintures de Giotto dans l'Eglise de L'Incoronata, à Naples.* Berlin, 1843.

frescos; seven represent the seven Sacraments of the Church; the eighth contains the Triumph of Religion, an allegorical picture, in which King Robert and his son Charles the Illustrious (Joanna's father) appear carrying royal banners sown with *fleur de lis.* In the Sacrament of Baptism the portraits of Petrarch and Laura are supposed to be; and in the Sacrament of Marriage (the one containing Joanna's portrait), Dante is pointed out. To see these frescos to advantage, it is necessary to go into the gallery of the choir; to reach this a narrow, dirty staircase and then a steep, unsafe ladder have to be clambered up; but they are worth that or any trouble to me.

On reaching this gallery of the choir, we sat and gazed up at these strange and beautiful old creations. We traced out the fabled portraits of Petrarch and Laura; then looked at the golden, gay wedding, — that sorrowful, ill-starred marriage of Joanna to her cousin Andrew, commemorated by Giotto so gloriously; and we hunted out in it a stern, hook-nosed, long-visaged face for Dante.

"That face, Philip," I said, "whether it be Dante or not, is harsh enough looking to be one of those wretched beings, in the existence of whom Italy believes yet, — the *jetatori*, — they who have power through their eyes to cast an evil fate over those they look upon. That man is the *jetatore* of the picture. His priestly mantle and cowl hang meekly enough, but that stern face sees farther into futurity than the rest; and while all are gazing at the ceremony and the soft, voluptuous beauty of the girl-bride, and the gay, imperious princesses behind her, — some tenderly, some rejoicingly, — he averts his look, as if loath to cast his *jetatura* there. He need not fear his own sad power, for Fate has been beforehand with him, and already cast her evil destiny in the forms of unbridled licentiousness, strong will, and freely indulged passions. What a sermon that Dante face preaches, however!"

"I had rather hunt up the brilliant Fiammetta," replied Philip, laughing, "than let those sorrowful events 'cast their shadows before.' On the whole, I think King Andrew quite ugly and silly enough to be put an end to in any way. That fat, leering priest beside him, looking like such a sycophant, is doubtless the wretch Petrarch hated so bitterly, of whom he wrote with droll pedantry, 'In vice and cruelty he was a Dionysius, an Agathocles, or a Phalaris.' But help me with your woman-wit, Ottilie. Which one of those imperious-looking princesses is Fiammetta?"

"She who is standing to the right, directly back of Joanna; you can only see her face and head. The pretty chin is raised, the full nostril dilated, and her superb brow a little bent, as if looking at some one in the distance. She surely spies her lover, Boccaccio, in that gay crowd of knights and ladies."

"The outline of her face is beautiful," said Philip.

"Yes, but it is not a face or a style of beauty I like. It is sensual, haughty, and reckless."

"She should have been queen," remarked Philip, "in the place of that luxurious creature. Joanna should have had more firmness and less heart, if she intended to be wicked."

"No, Philip; if she was wicked, as you say, I like the way history gives it best. Had either of those two imperious women stood in her place, the story would have been revolting. The sweet, womanly touches of tender weakness, which we see in the sad history of poor Joanna's regal sorrow and shame, give a soft haze to the crimson flood of sin and grief that flowed around the beautiful motherless girl as impetuously as love and pleasure coursed through her veins. But look at that violin-player, Philip! how tenderly he rests his cheek on his instrument! He seems to have forgotten the gay crowd, the royal pageant, the courtly dance, everything, to listen to the sweet tone he is drawing from his instrument: surely it is the voice of his ideal speaking to him. Look, he has just caught it! Poor fellow, when you were alive, you lost it the next instant; but Giotto seized you and it, and put you both there forever."

It was a pleasant hour we spent in that old choir gallery; at last we rose to go.

"It is not yet three o'clock," said Philip, looking at his watch; "have you not another church to show me, Ottilie?"

"Yes; Monte Oliveto."

And there we went. This church is a perfect gallery of monumental sculpture, as well as of exquisite inlaid work of precious marbles. While we were admiring the high altar, with its gay flowers and strange birds formed of malachite, lapis-lazuli, verd-antique, and mother-of-pearl, skilfully blended, some clergymen entered, and an afternoon service commenced. We withdrew into the beautiful Piccolomini chapel, at the lower end of the building, to the left of the entrance. This little chapel is the crowning jewel of the church. Over its altar is a famous "marble picture, in relief," of the Presepio, or Nativity, by the Florentine Antonio Rossellino. Vasari gives a glowing description of this work. There is a great deal of tender life in this sculptured picture; as Vasari says, the little band of angels hovering in the air over the Holy Infant, their lips parted, chanting the Gloria in Excelsis, seem almost to breathe. The Virgin Mother looks like a young, innocent girl; she has a round, immature forehead, with soft hollows on the temples, which give the brow an infantile expression, and childlike features; innocence, calmness, and simplicity characterize the whole creation.

But the finest thing in the chapel is the tomb of the Duchess of Amalfi, to the left of the altar when standing in front of it. This tomb is by Rossellino also, and an exact copy of one he made for the Cardinal of Portugal, in the Church of San Miniato, near Florence. When the Duke of Amalfi buried in this chapel his young, lovely princess-bride, and with her his ambitions and hopes, he ordered Rossellino to erect over her a counterpart of the Florentine tomb. She was the daughter of a king. Her father was the unfortunate Ferdinand of Aragon, whose ancestors' ashes rest in the velvet-covered chests in the sacristy of San Domenico Maggiore, and who was so sorrowfully betrayed by the Great Captain, Gonsalvo de Cordova, to that other Ferdinand of Aragon, Charles the Fifth's grandfather and Isabella of Castile's husband.

Duke Amalfi had also good lineage to boast of. He was a Piccolomini, and nephew to a great Pope. His uncle was the celebrated Eńeas Sylvius Piccolomini, Pope Pius II., the learned secretary of the Council of Basil, and one of the finest scholars that ever wore the triple crown, but who died of disappointment and mortification, because, when he summoned all the princes of Christendom to go fight the heathen, he found only a few pious old men ready to embark with him.

Five years before this last crusade, projected against "Paynim dog," the beautiful young Duchess of Amalfi lay down to sleep under this superb sarcophagus, surrounded by worldly prosperity. Death must have sounded an unwelcome summons to her, and yet it was a friendly, tender withdrawal from approaching sorrow; a few years after, her royal father was wandering about, a deposed king, seeking a home and a grave in an enemy's land.

The fine tomb raised to her memory by her husband occupies the whole of one side of the chapel. There is a large marble chest, of beautiful form and workmanship; above this is a stone couch, and at each end a young child holds back the head and foot drapery, showing the sculptured marble form of the Duchess, who lies in the dreamless sleep of death; floating above her are two angels, and in the centre of the panel behind her is a medallion, containing a Madonna and an infant Christ. A finely-sculptured arch rises above the whole composition, and from this arch falls a marble curtain, which is drawn and looped back on either side, knotted up in light, graceful folds.

After we entered the chapel, we sat still for some time on a high marble seat, which runs along the wall opposite the tomb. There was some fine music being played for the service at the high altar, and heavy, rolling pedal-notes from the great double diapasons of the organ were filling the air with glorious sounds.

I looked at the lovely marble effigy of the Duchess, and framed fanciful notions about the invisible music-current, which like a subtle, permeating fluid was making its way into recesses and around columns, in a manner very different from light; it came pouring down from that great organ, like the rays of light from the bull's-eye of a lantern, travelling forwards and sideways, upwards and downwards, spreading as it proceeded; yet, from being more reflexible than light, it was able to make its way around solid interpositions such as columns and walls, instead of lying against them as light does, and casting heavy shadows.

Sweet philosophy of sound! So should we wind around our pillars and columns of grief. But we stand under the glorious arch of Divine Wisdom; we are as little children; we cannot take in its perfect proportions nor see its sublime intention; we can only sit down and mourn sadly in its shadow.

The music filled the little chapel with its rich golden and purple tones; chords and harmonies seemed to blend like curious broiderings on a fine tapestry. The full, sonorous sound of the open diapason formed a solid groundwork. The music was slow, the harmony dispersed, and many suspensions occurred in the progress of the piece. Once in a while the stopped diapason was added, giving body to the pure sounds of the open pipes; then the dulcinea was drawn, adding a haze or atmosphere.

Philip, who had been wrapt in meditation, suddenly started, and, leaning towards me, said in a low voice: "Ottilie, there is a fine passage in De Quincey's Suspiria which tells just the effect this music has had upon me: 'This harmony has displayed before me, as in a piece of arras-work, the whole of my past life; not as if recalled by an act of memory, but as if present and incarnated in the music; no longer painful to dwell upon, but the detail of its incidents removed or blended in some hazy abstraction, and its passions exalted, spiritualized, and sublimed.'"

He fell into a still deeper meditation, and gazed with glowing eyes at the richly sculptured tomb raised by a husband's love over his young wife's dead beauty; presently he turned to me, and said to me in a hoarse whisper: "That Duke of Amalfi loved his wife, Ottilie, did he not? Tell me, what does the legend say? Did he ever love another? Or had he enough cold firmness to go through life without the warmth of a living love beside him? Tell me."

"I do not know, Philip. But he could have loved another and not wronged her; do you not think so?"

Philip looked at me keenly, and I returned his look with steadiness. I understood the meaning of his strange talk, but I could not venture on such a sacred subject unbidden. It was but an instant I had to wait, however, and then it came,—the whole full tide of confidence. He loves Florence Folham with all the force and strength of his matured nature, of his "old sorrow put to new uses."

"Yes, Ottilie," he said, with deep feeling, "I, who had given up all hope of ever loving again, and should have condemned myself for even thinking of such a possibility, am out in that old whirlpool of doubt and fear and hope."

"And why not, Philip? It is very right and natural."

"You do not condemn me, then? You do not call it perfidy to the past?"

I knew what he meant: he was thinking of Ellen; but we could not either of us speak of her, and yet we were both true to her dear memory. I remained silent a few moments; then taking his hand I said,

"'Because we love instead of sorrowing,
When life is shriven,
And death's full joy is given
Of those who sit and love us up in heaven,
Say not we "loved them once"!'"

The organ ceased; after the benediction the high-altar service ended, and we left the chapel. We drove along in silence for a while, I thinking much of Philip and Florence. The love for her is beautiful, and comes most graciously in season. His affection for Ellen was different: it began in his boyhood; there was no doubt, or fear, or sweet, wild delirium about it,—a quiet, sweet blossom of the spring-time of his life, which, if death had not intervened, would have ripened into golden fruit. Just before we reached home, he turned half playfully to me and said with a laugh, which was intended to hide his real feeling, "She may not love me after all, Ottilie, for I have not asked her; and upon my soul when I think of doing so, I wonder at my presumption in supposing such a blessed possibility."

"How can you doubt it, Philip? Why, her love is as plain to be seen as yours; clear as the sun at noonday. She reminds me of Coleridge's Genevieve. Go tell her some tender love-tale; she would forget and fling herself into your arms as naively as the poet's pretty maiden did."

He shook his head doubtingly, and began to look very solemn. As he lifted me from the carriage, when we reached our own court-yard, I whispered to him gayly, "Have courage, and, like Móntrose,

"'put it to the touch,
And win or lose it all.'"

He did straightway. This evening he came to me triumphant. When he told the dear girl of his love and asked her to be his wife, she rose from her seat, stood frankly before him, rested her two little hands in his, and when he put his arms around her, she buried her glowing face on his shoulder and wept like a little child.

BEGINNING OF THE END.

I HAVE been neglecting my journal for quite two weeks; and now I have so much on my heart, that, woman-like, I wish to begin at the end, and tell that which is troubling me most, instead of that which makes me happy. But, soberly and in order.

Philip is married! Yes, married and off. A few days after his pleasant and gratifying acceptance by the Folhams, — who showed a very frank satisfaction at having their daughter so "nicely established," as Mrs. Folham said, — he received news of the death of an uncle in Germany, his father's eldest brother.

The death of this uncle brings a great deal of business on Philip. He has to go immediately to his father's old home in Saxony, to attend to the family affairs; thence to America, to settle up the business interest which his uncle and father had for many years together there, and which has been hanging half unravelled since the death of Philip's father, owing to the age and ill-health of this uncle. All the heirs look to Philip to settle matters; and he feels himself responsible, as his father's representative, to have the business arranged promptly and advantageously for all parties. But to do this might require a year's absence; and to be separated from Florence such an age seemed to him an impossibility; yet go he must.

"Why separate at all?" asked the practical, straightforward Janet. "Why not marry at once? You are no stranger to the Folhams, so far as name and position are concerned; nor are they,—to me at least. And as for *qu'en dira-t-on*, why need any of you care?"

Common sense carried the day, especially as common sense and inclination went hand in hand. Mrs. Folham, to do her justice, demurred a little, very properly; but the approval of such persons as the American Ambassador and his wife, and Mrs. Dale, also Philip's distinguished position, had great weight with her, and overcame her "natural scruples," as she called them. Such scruples, arising from that sort of delicacy which is the growth of society, not nature, generally seem satisfied with a mere announcement of their existence; and as they are convenient mythical feelings, perfectly innocent, on which society's proprieties can be hung, they surely may be treated respectfully, as, half the time, they only ask to be acknowledged, not yielded to.

Florence behaved beautifully. The good, sweet girl, without any boldness or forwardness, said frankly and trustingly, "I should rather be married at once, if Philip wishes it, than wait for his return."

So the affair was settled; and yesterday morning,—as midday is called, in such matters,—they were married in full and proper state. I cannot stop to give all the details, which at any other time would be so agreeable for me to dwell on,—the costly gifts, the ravishing toilet of the bride, the touching, impressive ceremony;—no, I must hurry on to that other romance, which has been blending its scarlet and purple threads in with this lovely golden one, making up the sacred life-chord of joy and sorrow. At the breakfast yesterday Luigi and I stood beside each other.

"Now Edelhertz is off your hands, Ottilie," he said, with an attempt at playfulness, "you can have a little time for me; shall you not?"

I have been neglecting Luigi lately; but, to tell the truth, I have thought he showed a disposition to avoid me. He has seemed for several weeks indisposed for any companionship except that which we could have when all together. He has excused himself from our rides, preferring to drive with Janet and Venitia. Our little family circle has thus divided off during the daily pursuits of pleasant occupation; uniting, however, always in the evenings over the music, or in conversation with visitors on the terrace.

But I have willingly yielded him up to Venitia, hoping that his love for her, which has seemed to have an unaccountable tangle in it, might announce itself in some way. I could not see how I was able to help him in the matter; and his seeking Venitia's and Janet's society instead of mine appeared the most natural path to the conclusion, which I had convinced myself, from outward appearances, must come sooner or later.

And it has come; but Heaven knows in a form and shape I little anticipated! Eager and hasty as I was, a few pages before, to begin at the end, my pen falters as I approach it. O, to shut up Life's book once in a while, and not open it again until all the sad pages are passed over!

I was very gay yesterday, as I always am when under the high-pressure of memory. Philip's marriage could not be a true merry-making to me. It struck on the hundred portals of the past; and there came thronging out around me the invisible presences of the lost and gone, holding to my lips the weird goblet filled with that rare wine of Cyprus, whose draught

"Stirs the Hades of the heart,"

and gives an intoxication to the laugh and looks and manner, more subtle and brain-wildering than any grape-juice of this earth's vintage can cause. So I laughed sharply, and wore my gay face-mask bravely; but Janet, who knows me so well, came silently and tenderly to me every little while, resting her hands on me with sweet looks of sympathy and love. Luigi, too, who looked very pale and haggard, kept close by me, and gazed wistfully at the scarlet hue which the secret dripping of the old heart-wound sent glowingly up into my cheeks. After we had seen Philip and Florence off in the steamer, and had returned home, I was standing in the late twilight on the terrace with Luigi alone. He said, "I wish to have a long ride with you, Ottilie. Can you give me to-morrow?"

"Certainly. I shall need some pleasure of that sort badly. You know I believe in appeasing the tumult of the heart by rapid movements of the body, my friend; so it is very kind of you to think of it. But you are not going! Stay and drink tea with us."

"No, do not urge me. I cannot. I shall be here early in the morning. Say seven o'clock, that we may go to Lago d' Agnano before it grows warm. We shall be gone all day, remember; and—" he hesitated, then added hurriedly, "Ottilie, I wish to have you all to myself to-morrow; so, let us be entirely alone."

At seven o'clock this morning, therefore, before Janet or Venitia were awake, we were trotting out of the court-yard gate, on to the broad, lava-paved Mergellina. The morning was glorious, and we cantered nearly the whole route, for both of us felt an indescribable embarrassment. We soon arrived at our old haunt of Lago d' Agnano, and rode around it, and through the neighboring paths, until we felt tired of the saddle and wished to breakfast.

We found the lovely lake as still and delightful as it had been in early spring, when we used to go there in the commencement of our pleasant friendship. The woody hills which surround it closed in more shadily than then, and the soft, grassy banks we found not yet touched with the heat, which is growing so oppressive in Naples as to make us talk of the necessity of seeking some Capri or Sorrento retreat for the midsummer months.

We rode up to the *trattoria*, where we dismounted, left our horses, and ordered refreshments for the day. The beautiful Roman woman Delaïta, who keeps this Lake inn, gave us a friendly greeting. She helped me off my horse, and took me from the saddle in her strong, beautiful arms as if I had been no heavier than one of her own "iron-jointed, supple-sinewed," dusky babies who rolled jollily about on the ground, almost under the horses' heels.

Luigi and I had a pleasant chat with her; then as we walked slowly off from the *trattoria* to go into the woods, we talked of her beauty as if we had not observed it a hundred times before. We stopped a little way from the house, and noticed her fine points as she moved gravely around, with the slow, dignified step of a Roman matron of antiquity.

Delaïta indeed seemed more beautiful than usual this morning, giving us a good excuse for growing enthusiastic over her. She stood sideways for a while, affording us a chance of observing the simple but powerful outline of her person, the fine poise of her head and neck, and the richness and quantity of her glossy black hair. The form of the necks and shoulders of these Roman women is bewitching. Some one has said that the graceful lines formed by the movements of their heads and throats recall those of swans and doves; and it is so.

We admired the gay yellow and green of her dress, the rich knot of hair fastened at the back of her head by a long gilt bodkin, and the bewitching little curls that strayed rebelliously out of the pin-fastening and clung as caressingly around the broad, firm base of the head as that brown boy of hers who clambered up at her feet.

We noticed her self-possession and tranquillity with the restless children, the screaming donkey-boys, and the passing travellers, the calmness with which she responded to the thousand and one demands made on her by babies, boys, and people, and her still dark eyes gazing on everything quietly. Those eyes of Delaïta have a rich, full look, such as may be seen in those of some fine cow, or beautiful dog, or horse; and when we see this look in them we say, "How human!" Yet, again, when we see it in human beings, the animal look, free from coarseness, just in its simple, true nature, is always suggested to us.

This subject thoroughly discussed and the pleasant little savory breakfast Delaïta had sent us — of fruit and curds, delicious bread, and really good black coffee — finished, we took a leisurely stroll among the hills. We walked along in a silence which was only broken by some vague, half-understood, indeed only half-uttered, remarks on the beauty of the landscape. We had chosen the side of the lake to the west of the *trattoria*, on a beautiful slope, where, under the shade of the trees, we could loiter or ramble at will.

Each was full of an unexplained anxiety. I knew Luigi had asked me to take this ride purposely to give himself a chance of relieving his mind of some annoyance. To request me to be his intercessor with Venitia seemed absurd; the girl's frank acceptance of his attentions, and innocent, unconscious admiration of him, his superiority in her eyes over all other persons, surely must have made him certain of her love already.

No, there must be some other obstacle than doubt as to her feelings I was certain. His restlessness and unhappiness at times, his fits of "frolic grief" after these sombre moments had passed, all proved to me that there was some impediment to a disclosure of his love; an imaginary one I felt sure, heightened by the exaggerated apprehensions of a young man in love; such as comparative poverty, or the fear of inflicting on his beloved the troubles and privations of exile, which to him, an Italian of high rank, brought up without a profession or positive means of support, might seem terrific. But although I thought whatever obstacles the young man's delicacy had conjured up could be readily dispersed by the plain light of a friendly talk, there was a silent anguish about him which made me feel — I did not know why — uneasy.

A shady, solitary part of the woods attracted us, and I sat down on a rustic seat under some trees, while Luigi walked leisurely up and down, trying evidently to appear occupied with the enchanting scene around him. How I pitied him, and yet I could not help him. For is not Venitia almost like a young sister to me? Therefore I could not urge him to an avowal of what should be voluntary. He turned suddenly and looked at me. I suppose my face must have expressed very strongly my perplexed feelings of sympathy and anxiety.

He came to me as if intending to speak, then sat down on the ground near me in silence. Luigi is never melodramatic ; his Saxon blood tempers the Italian fire, — indeed, the southern current seems to make him languid under intense excitement, where a northerner might show something like emotion. He has always about him a refreshing repose of feeling as well as physical quiet, which is so very attractive in a person who possesses as he does capability of passion and energy. It is this self-control which gives him an unconscious air of superiority, and has made me feel from the beginning, he could do nothing ignoble. He gathered some delicious violets that grew within a hand's grasp of him, put them in my lap, and then looked earnestly up in my face.

"We plighted brother-and-sister faith, Luigi, soon after we met," I said, half playfully; "let me claim a sister's privilege in entreating you to tell me if I can help you in any difficulty you may have."

I could not endure silently the appealing look of this usually self-sufficing man any longer.

"I do not wish to intrude on your confidence, my friend," I continued; "but intrusion or not, however it may be, I do wish to relieve your mind, if possible, of this unspoken trouble which is making you so very miserable."

"Ottilie," he said abruptly, "after all, I think the expansive confidence of some natures, like yours for example, is far better, nay, wiser and safer, than the prudent reserve of mine. Now, of your whole life I know, and also of Mrs. Dale, and —" he stopped as if he had touched a nerve, then he continued: "But how little you know of mine. Fear of intrusion keeps me silent; then the reserve which is taught us early in life, here in Europe, — where concealment of one's personal matters is regarded, if not exactly a virtue, certainly a mark of refinement, — acts upon me. But" — here he sprang to his feet, and stood erect before me — "no matter what may have been the reason for my yielding insanely to a wildering temptation, you, you, Ottilie, will surely do me justice, — you never will accuse me of meaning anything dishonorable by this reserve."

"Never, Luigi," I answered promptly. "I would trust you, my friend, as I should Janet or Philip, and I have felt so from the first."

I held out my hand to him, for he was looking intensely sad; he took it, and as he sat down on the bank again he pressed it to his lips with the graceful courtesy of an Italian.

"But, Ottilie," he said in a low voice, the anguish of which I shall never forget, "this reserve is now becoming dishonorable."

He trembled with emotion, and remained silent, as if not daring to trust his voice, and I felt a hot tear fall on my hand. I was perplexed and distressed. I rested my other hand on his head as if he were a boy whose young heart had been wounded bitterly by some injury or insult; but I could not say anything, except a tender, soothing reiteration of his soft Italian name, "Luigi, Luigi."

Then followed a sad story, which put us both in a woful tangle. An obstacle to his love for Venitia! I should think there was. And this obstacle is nothing more or less than a wife.

He had married very early in life one to whom he had

been betrothed by his parents in infancy; it was a *mariage de convenance,* so common, as we all know, in Europe. Soon after, he discovered that his wife was no companion for his heart, head, or life. She was wealthy and high-born like himself, but ignorant, — and worse, — vain and impure. When Luigi made himself obnoxious to the government and had to leave Milan she gladly returned to her mother's house, where, under the protecting shelter of her roof, she could lead, as a married woman, the life she best liked, — a life of veiled impurity, shrouded by all decent attentions to the outward proprieties of social life. They luckily never had children, and their separation, so agreeable to both, had continued for years, indeed would last for life.

"Indeed," said Luigi, "I was beginning to forget I had ever been married. My immediate kindred having all died, my associations lying far, far away from the social circle in which my wife moves, and this for so many years, I have had nothing to recall to me that which was for a short time the misery of my existence. I do not suppose any friend or acquaintance I have in Paris, Rome, or Naples, except his Eminence, know of my former real position or marriage; the name I bear is an obsolete one of my family, quite forgotten. I have always known that my wife and her relatives would be only too happy if they never heard of me again, and I — I embraced willingly the life of freedom which a humbler and unknown station afforded me.

"When I met you and your friends, I entered frankly and without scruple into the pleasant, friendly commerce which an acquaintanceship with you offered me. Had you belonged to the ordinary class of women, having a daughter or sister to marry off, I should have avoided you; but we met as intelligent, thinking, active-minded people; we had no thought of marrying or giving in marriage. For a while I imagined our happy intercourse might last forever. Some nights, after leaving you, I have sat in my library and lived over, in fancy, a future spent with you as your brother, travelling, studying, living real life with you. But now," and the young man looked hopelessly up at me, — "now, my dear, dear friend, it is at an end, — all this future; for I love Venitia. Love! my God, I adore her!"

There was no reason for condemning the young man. My straightforward woman's wit saw that. There had been no perfidy meant. Had he intended to be dishonorable, he would never have disclosed his real situation, but gratified his love by marrying Venitia. We had been completely in his power.

This young man had met with us, liked us, visited us. We were three women, as he said, who had no thought of hunting up husbands, and were quite as ready to enjoy a frank, honorable friendship with a good, intelligent man as with a pleasant, honest woman.

Thus I rapidly reasoned on the subject; consequently, there was no mute reproach in my manner, but a freely expressed sympathy. Venitia has drawn a prize of passionate true love in her life-lottery; the prize simply cannot be made available. I think I felt all the time more sorrow for Luigi than for her. He will be so hopelessly lonely in the future. Self-sufficing as men are, their loneliness is more withering and desolate than ours.

We spent the whole day wandering about on the banks of that beautiful lake, talking of Luigi's past life. During all this long conversation, I gathered that which I have been able to put into immediate information, for he was loath to condemn his wife when he first told me his story.

Sunset came, beautiful, golden, gorgeous. It had been a glorious day; but we had not enjoyed as much as we usually do this lovely place, — the overarching trees, the soft, half-sleeping winds, the buoyant clouds, and the deep pulsating blue of the sky. But the fever and torment of acknowledgment was over; a generous, just sympathy had been given; and now, as evening approached, we both felt calmer. Before leaving the lake, we sat down again to enjoy as much as possible the beautiful close of the day.

All the tumult of life seemed to me to be suspended. The wind rose up as if it had been reposing on the broad bosom of mother earth, and commenced toying with the branches and leaves of the trees on the other side of the lake; then it came frolicking over the water, breaking it into a million of sparkling ripples, while the tops of the trees on our side bent down to meet its passionate grasp. I grew reconciled with life and its shortcomings. A superb balance appeared to be established before me, as I thought of the "mighty and equal antagonisms" of grief, which are rolling up forever like waves, making broader and deeper our capabilities of feeling for each other's sorrows.

But Luigi, though calmer, seemed more sad than he had in the morning. Then, something remained to do; now, it was done, and the certainty of his fate stood sternly before him. There was a quiet melancholy on his face, which was very sorrowful to see. We returned home as silently and rapidly as we came, and parted in the court-yard with yearning looks for a hope and a help which neither of us dare give to the other.

A NOCTURNE.

LL day Venitia has been so constantly with us, I have had no chance to talk to Janet alone. However, after tea this evening she went into the *salon* to the piano, and Janet and I remained out on the terrace.

Where a deep feeling or an urgent necessity imposes explanation, the words come naturally if we will only let them. I never trouble myself about preparing what I shall say or do in an emergency; the power that permits the difficulty will supply means of supporting or extricating us, if we only trust firmly; and so it was in this case.

I told Janet, as soon as we were left alone, all that had passed between Luigi and myself yesterday; and the just, generous-hearted woman received the sorrowful information as I knew she would. I felt instinctively, without his telling me, that Luigi dreaded Janet's first hearing of his position. He could not comprehend her as I did, of course.

There is in Janet's character a clearness of mental sight, a strength I love to call manly, and a nobility of feeling, which, with a little more demonstration, a little more show of tenderness, would make the life-harmony sound exact to unskilled ears. She is so just in her judgments, and so charitable and indulgent withal, that she has taught me many a lesson of true love; and yet our ordinary friends would much sooner come to me, in a questionable difficulty, than to her.

But I am more expansive, more demonstrative, although not naturally so free from prejudice or so capable of generous judgment as she. She is cold in manner, and so strict in judging of her own actions, as to leave the impression she would also be of others; and this debars many from seeking and receiving her truly valuable counsel and sympathy.

She has a way of knitting her fine broad brow and pressing the forefinger against the firmly compressed lips, on approaching a subject, which somehow, I don't know why, arouses antagonism, and makes those who do not know her shrink from baring their wounds; while probably all the time she is interrogating or giving herself a rigid self-rebuking, not judging unjustly her opponent or companion.

The broad brow grew terribly tangled, and, as she leaned on the railing of the terrace, listening to my low, rapid, earnest words, her finger pressed like a wedge of iron on the lips, which seemed to rebel in an eager pout against restraint. I fancy Luigi would have shrunk in pain had he seen her then, fearing the cold, worldly judgment of a selfish woman, who intended obstinately to see nothing but the falseness of his position towards us, in the inevitable trouble it would bring to her. But I knew her better. I had not one instant of doubt as to how she would receive it; only I could not help thinking of all this. She spoke not a word, but sat for some time in deep thought. At last she turned towards me and said, in a voice of deep emotion, which she tried, in her usual way, to veil with a little laugh, —

"What mad people we have all been, to be sure! Poor Venitia, Cleopatra-like, she has melted a priceless pearl in the cruel acid of an impossible love."

I made no answer; I had nothing to say.

"Come, Ottilie," she continued, "you must not sit so silent, so dreamy. I do not often want word-comfort, you know, but I do now. Can you not tell me some of your satisfying philosophy about art's needing trials, and artists requiring the heat of disappointment to ripen them?"

This forced lightness could not last; she came towards me with a curious look of mingled appeal and distress, and as she rested her forehead on my neck, this self-sufficing woman said, in the most tender and touching tone of voice: "Am I not almost the girl's mother? Tell me, Ottilie, what am I to do when she hears this solemn hour of renunciation striking?"

I knew it was not counsel my strong friend wanted; it was words only,—words which might give her something on which to hold as human, in this first wildering moment of a kind of trouble she, so experienced in all such lore, had never encountered. And I had so little to say of that, which I thought would be most fitting. Indeed, to the clear, crystal tone of that heart-note, what mortal words would not sound dull? But she was out on the waves of a wild ocean, and, as I said, any human voice of tenderness and sympathy was something to hold to, to help her to think and grow firm. So I did as we always do in such cases,—I talked platitudes.

"Dear Janet," I said, "I think a love which is prevented by oppositions of some kind from becoming tangible, from taking positive form and shape, is to a highly intellectual creature the most perfect incarnation of love. Love that reaches its consummation in this state of being is apt not to survive its own peculiar season; but love which is altogether pure and holy, such as this of Venitia and Luigi, which angels might witness and feel, and which is free from all mortal soil, is immortal; and if those to whom is given this divine grace remain true to the gift, they will already have in their possession a sweet, mysterious blossom, which has come trembling down into their hearts from a purer sphere, in whose celestial soil they shall find the roots of that delightful tree which bears fruit and flower, and no thorn."

We sat in silence on the balcony; the undemonstrative Janet leaned her head on my shoulder, and allowed my hands and lips to rest caressingly on her soft cheek. Venitia was alone in the drawing-room, improvising, as she loves to do at this twilight hour. She enveloped us in her harmonies. A broad, grand musical thought lay superbly sketched out before us in the moonlight. Then she wove around and out from it a curious musical web of involved modulations, and as De Quincey, in his enchanting description of the Palimpsest, says of the pursuit of the various lost handwritings, she "hunted back the chords through all their doubles, and as the chorus of the Athenian stage unwove through the antistrophe every step that had been mystically woven by the strophe," so she chased back in a chorus-like chain all these tangled suspensions and modulations until she reached the glorious starting-point, and her original *motivo* rang out supreme.

"Talk to me, Ottilie," whispered Janet; "your words comfort me. But do not tell me you have no belief in the perfect, purple fulness of wedded love; for, my friend, I have seen and known it, even though for so short a season, still it was a reality and must also be immortal.

The appointed and peculiar season of Paul's love and mine will be eternity."

Venitia's vague, questioning improvisings wound around us like graceful, weird arabesques.

"The love of husband and wife," I said, "when the holy sacrament of Love is partaken by both, the sacred chrism anointing both brows, and the Real Presence in their hearts, is rare and almost too great a happiness for mere mortals."

Step by step Venitia's modulations mounted to dizzy heights, reminding me of poor Piranesi's aerial dream flights of stairs, forever ascending, forever overhanging perilous abysses, and he forever standing on their highest rounds.

"But," I continued, and my words, said to the measure and beat of that wondrous music, — unwritten language of the newly-awakened Psyche in the girl's passionate soul, — sounded more effective than these poor written ones, — "but, Janet, beautiful as such love is,

'With darkness and the death-hour rounding it,'

there is much more attraction to me in an unavowed or unaccomplished love, — one which is set to that divinest key of life, the minor key of renunciation, and which gives rise to the most wildering soul-harmonies.

"Love, struggle, suffer, — then comes the true harvest of the soul; and such a love and such a fate has tragic beauty and sublimity, far exceeding those which are called happy loves, for there is shown an exercise of power, the overcoming of some great contending force, all telling an exultant tale of a moral combat and a moral victory."

Venitia commenced weaving in skilfully with her own

thoughts chords which were leading to the solemn portals of Beethoven's *Marche Funèbre* (Funeral March on the death of a hero, Op. 26). The grand drapery of purple and gold seemed to envelope us, and give even a tinge to the moonlighted air, which was heavy with the odor of orange-blossoms; and the fair starry flowers turned up to the cool night as if asking also for tenderness.

"Such loves," I said, drawing my friend closer to me, —"such loves, Janet, have carved great statues, painted glorious pictures, and written grand poems. Vittoria Colonna put life into stone; and she, with the two Beatrices, — one with the myriads of Madonnas surrounding her, like the palpitating *fond* of angel's heads in her Sanzio's pictures, and the other with the 'Divina Commedia' encircling her heavenly brow as with a halo, — shall tell age after age how Angelo, Raphael, and Dante loved."

The solemn chords of this sublime March tramped with majestic step on the air, and we listened in silence to Venitia's touching execution of this creation, which tells of death, not in its sorrow, or its despair, but in all its pomp and glory.

WANLUCK.

OW prompt Janet is. This morning while I was at breakfast she came into my room to show me a note she had just written Luigi. It was this: —

"DEAR LUIGI, — We know all. We must part, my friend. Do not let us drive you from Naples, however; for we shall make our arrangements to leave immediately. Before we go, of course you will come to see us. Venitia wishes to say good by, and I a God-speed to you.

"Keep up heart, my poor friend. How many of us live over the separation caused by death, and are able to do our duty; and so must you in this trial. I cannot ever write or speak half I feel, especially when my heart is fullest; so do not think my note cold. You have no warmer, more sympathizing friend than

"JANET DALE."

The note was sent to his apartments, and I was certain he would reply to it immediately in person; so I dressed quickly and went out. I thought it wisest to be absent during their interview. I knew Venitia and Janet could manage their trouble best alone.

We do not need our friends in the first moment of sorrow. When all is over, and the new grief and old way of life meet, — ragged, rough, obstinate selvages, that must be fitted and adapted together patiently, — then those who love us can help us.

I spent the morning at the Church L' Incoronata, studying the Giotto frescos; for if we leave Naples so soon, these are among the things I shall wish to keep freshest in my memory. In the afternoon I stopped at the nice cake-shop in the Strada Chiaja, near the Toledo, and took dinner. That over, I lounged in at Detken's awhile, looked over their new books, and selected some fine large photographs, which they have just received, of the surrounding places. One, of our glorious, mysterious Temple of Serapis, took my fancy, — it was so finely executed. We must have it, and indeed all the others, to take with us as pleasant mementos.

Leave Naples! It makes me very sad to think of doing so. I am not half or quarter through. There are the old palaces with their pictures, and Pæstum unvisited; and — O, so many places! But some time in the future I may return. However that may be, I shall not separate myself from Janet in her sorrow. Italy is full of delightful abodes for persons who have our tastes and pursuits, so one place is as agreeable as another. At all events, I must try, in my little way, to make a new resting-place pleasant to them.

Near sundown I drove into the court-yard, and found Luigi's carriage there. As I entered the anteroom of the *salon,* I was witness to a touching little scene. Near the door were Luigi and Venitia. Neither of them saw me, for I was hidden by the muslin curtains and drapery which hang over the archway between the two rooms. She stood facing me, calm, pale, and still. He had hold of her hand, and was just bidding adieu. His back was towards me, and I could not see his face.

"Grant me one favor, Venitia," he said.

"Certainly," answered the girl, frankly.

"Let me kiss that pure, clear forehead of yours, which will always rest in my memory as the brow of an angel."

Without hesitation she leaned forward to him and received the kiss. Then resting her strong, beautiful hands on the young man's shoulders, she looked earnestly in his face for a moment, drew him close to her, put her arms tenderly around him, and, with a faint little sob, kissed him on his lips.

"Now go," she said in a broken voice, "and may God help us both!"

She left the room without looking at him again, and he tottered by me, never noticing my presence, blind and deaf with his great sorrow; for the parting was as hopeless as death to both.

Luckily the Rochesters came in this evening, and several other visitors. I say "luckily," because it broke up the *gêne* of our trouble. Venitia was excused from receiving them on the plea of a headache,—that convenient, available indisposition for a woman. Janet and I talked to them all the evening composedly, and I even sang a few ballads; but we both felt as if acting in a dream.

Before parting for the night, Janet and I had a little talk on the terrace. She told me that Luigi came immediately on receiving her note this morning. He leaves to-night for Paris. We shall go to the Baths of Lucca for the summer, and decide there where we shall spend the coming winter.

Janet says he spent the whole day with them, talking tranquilly, and was more self-possessed even than she had dared to hope. She bade him good by a little while before he left, in order that he and Venitia might be together alone. I did not tell her what I had seen. Some day I shall give her this journal to read; then she will know what was too sacred to be put in spoken words, even to her.

When I came to my bedroom, I found on my table a short note from Luigi, bidding me good by, enclosing his banker's address in Paris, reminding me affectionately of our brother-and-sister troth-plight, asking me to write to him, and signing himself my "brother Luigi."

God bless and help him in his sorrowful future, which will be very lonely. Now, if I were a man, I could go and be a brother to him, and make life much more easy and bearable. And if life in this social world was as pure as it should be, I, a woman, could be his true sister-companion. But there is no use in trying to alter the prejudices of the world by fretting at or acting contrary to them. It is much wiser to adapt ourselves as patiently as possible to these judgments and rules, unjust and petty as they may seem to us; for, on the whole, they are right, and we find them safest in the end.

It is now full time for letters from America. Even supposing the missing mail should be lost, which I fancy is so, a second one is due, and from it I must hear the worst or the best. I look for these letters anxiously; in the centre, as I am, of all this joy and sorrow of those I love, I cannot forget my own causes of inquietude. Happiness is, after all, comparative. For instance, I, who have so little in a worldly or social point of view to make me happy, and not at all likely ever to possess any more, should feel something akin to happiness if I could see the time when the arrival of home-letters would cease to be a cause of anguish to me.

O for a draught of Lethe! O that the separation

between us and the living dead might be as silent and impassable as the grave! The powerlessness of the dead to wrong the living is a merciful limitation. But man governs this life, God the other; and knowing this, why do we not, the little time we live here, submit more patiently to a power which we know is a fleeting usurpation? The old Greek gave wise counsel: —

> "Do not spurn against the pricks,
> Seeing that he who reigns, reigns by cruelty,
> And not by right."

Good old John Newton said that he worked at the crosses and difficulties of this life until his knuckles were sore; then he gave up and left them all for the Lord, and straightway they were righted and removed. How I wish I could rest mine fully in his all-powerful hands! But this capability of yielding up one's anxieties is a grace in itself, for which we must also wait patiently. So many of us, when shouldering weighty burdens of grief, feel like poor Constance, —

> "That faith would live again by death of need;
> O, then, tread down my need, and faith mounts up;
> Keep my need up, and faith is trodden down."

. . . . .

Venitia has been very ill. To my surprise, she gave up immediately after the separation from Luigi. I should have fancied, from my previous knowledge of her, that she could have borne, almost stoically, any amount of grief; but this subtle power of love has changed her whole nature. She is out of danger now, and as soon as she is able to travel we shall leave here.

. . . . .

My American mail has come, and with it a wilderness of woe.

. . . . .

A sudden shock of grief takes away the moral strength, and leaves scars behind that open and ache with every breath. Such sorrows as these are the real diseases that make both body and mind aged, even more than those fierce physical attacks which leave the body broken and infirm.

. . . . .

The cold-hearted calumny, the pitiless persecution, the cruel laugh and sneer, the torrent of bitterness poured into a heart which God has already bruised, is a woful human work. And when is the anguish ever to end? For, alas! there are some natures who, while they tread down a falsehood and walk boldly, proudly, yes, even highly and holily over it, apparently unharmed by the adder, feel a fang which strikes in at their hearts, and leaves a mortal misery gnawing there forever.

O for a vigorous, well-educated will that is able, like Janet's, to mount to the level of any summit of emergency, and bear unflinchingly the fierce storms of trial. Very beautiful is her character; its material was firm enough in the beginning to bear the sharpest instruments of sorrow, and the master hand of discipline has sculptured it into a lovely shape. Then her will, instead of being warped and weakened under the fierce heat of trial, has grown into crystalline firmness.

Such beings remind me of what I have read about the formation of mighty mountains; some fiery process compressed together their atoms, and the sharp cuttings of Heaven's storms chiselled out their fair outlines; thus purified and formed, they lift up their lofty peaks in serene, majestic silence, piercing the great empyrean.

But there are volcanic hills as well as granite heights, alas! and as I look over on Vesuvius weeping its fiery rain, bathing its sides with a hot, angry flood, I cannot help murmuring, —

> "Great Architect of all!
> When Thou didst build the fire-devoted hill,
> Thou gav'st it but the semblance of a life!
> Say, was it merciful to frame man's heart —
> Sò finely fibred — on the selfsame plan?"

. . . .

Several days have passed in consulting, arriving at conclusions, and making arrangements. The mind becomes fearfully bewildered when a wave of sudden sorrow first breaks over it; but if one waits patiently, this wretched indecision passes away, and the confusion takes manageable form and shape.

I have resolved to return to America and face full front this shameful grief. I have written to Philip that I shall meet him there; I shall need his presence and protection. Nor shall I be left alone in the mean while. Dear Janet and Venitia instantly decided on accompanying me, — kind friends! And Janet makes light of their generosity.

"Why, you know," she says, cheerily, "it will be of infinite service to Venitia, such a total and complete change for her in every way will be obtained by it."

Venitia, too, takes great interest in the proposed journey. It seems to give her a fresh impulse. When the news of my trouble came, it was the first thing that aroused her and brought back her natural self. The resenting of my wrongs by indignant words of sympathy appeared to be a relief for her, — a vent for her own unuttered suffering.

We have had in view many ways of returning. As Philip cannot be in America until autumn, I do not care to arrive there before he does, nor do I wish to remain in Europe; therefore we have plenty of time before us, and Janet proposes we should return by a sailing vessel. We have often longed for the chance or opportunity of taking a slow, leisurely voyage on the ocean; and as Venitia is still feeble from her severe illness, it will be better for her.

Janet thinks that the monotony and stillness of such a voyage will be beneficial mentally to us, as well as physically; quiet down the fever and fret, cause the fierce vibration of feeling to fall back into a steady pulsation, give me courage for the coming struggle, and Venitia strength to accept with woman's endurance the new life.

So we have concluded to take the sea-voyage. Mr. Rochester and our banker have kindly undertaken to charter for us a nice, safe fruit-ship on a return voyage. They have in view a pretty little clipper, now at Constantinople, but which will be in Palermo in a fortnight.

And now it is not a mere partial farewell to Naples I am taking, with the prospect of a fair journeying to some other delightful place, but probably an eternal farewell to Europe, — a sight of the Promised Land from Mount Pisgah and then a mournful turning back into the old Wilderness. A mysterious, wayward destiny controls some lives.

LEAVING NAPLES.

UR last night in Naples. Dolce Napoli! We sail to-morrow afternoon in the steamer which runs between this city and Palermo. There we shall join our little clipper, which boasts the fanciful name of "Zephyr." It was originally a war-steamer, built with great care for Santa Anna of Mexico; but the news of his downfall came just as the little naval toy was completed, then it was altered into a sailing vessel, and put on the Mediterranean and Levant fruit service.

Every arrangement has been made for our comfort. Janet, whose easy means enable her to indulge in extravagant luxuries when she wishes, — and this she loves to do for the pleasure of others, — has had a good cabinet piano fitted into the cabin. She has also had strong water-proof cases made, and had them lashed to the quarter-deck; in these have been placed a small, well-selected collection of books. The preparing for this voyage has given her infinite satisfaction, and she has not forgotten even such pleasant and palatable luxuries as wines, fruits, and the like. She came to me yesterday holding up triumphantly a peculiar looking tin box; it had a curious arrangement for the lid, which I did not comprehend.

"It is a water-proof case, and can be closed hermetically," said Venitia, examining it. "What is it for?"

Janet enjoyed our surprise a little while, then going to my desk, took this journal, clasped it, and laid it in the box.

"For Ottilie's journal!" exclaimed Venitia.

"Yes, she is the only member of our family who keeps one; and if any accident should happen to us during the voyage, I should not like to have the book lost. We shall not be sunk at sea any the sooner for making preparations for such an event," said Janet, coolly.

So nightly I am to shut up this precious volume in the box.

To-day I heard from Luigi. He wrote to me immediately on receiving my letter which informed him of our intended return to America. He begs of me to keep him always advised of our movements, and to do as he shall, — write at stated times unfailingly and trustingly, even though we may sometimes miss hearing from each other. He makes no allusion to his late trouble, mentions Janet and Venitia naturally, sends his remembrances to them; altogether the letter is just such a one as he might have written two months ago, before he and Venitia had gathered the sad fruit of knowledge, which has driven them from their paradise.

I knew that from his writing thus, he wished his letter to be seen by them, so I handed it to Janet. She gave the letter to Venitia without any remark. When it was returned to me I found pencilled on the margin, in Venitia's handwriting, "Dear Ottilie, remember me affectionately always to Luigi whenever you write to him."

Jean Paul somewhere speaks of "concluding a great past with a little present"; such has been our farewell night in Naples. We have had a crowded, talkative evening; all our friends calling to say good by. We shall miss many of them a great deal, for our social surroundings here have been very agreeable. The Rochesters, who have been our most pleasant acquaintances, we hope to meet again in America, and keep up unbroken the intercourse which has ripened an acquaintanceship into a very deep feeling of regard.

But we shall miss most of all our beautiful surroundings, — this lovely home, — for home it has been, — a home that has seen the birth and growth of pure, deep love, a strong temptation resisted, the brave facing of bitter sorrow, and the triumph of honor and true feeling.

Beautiful, golden, glorious Naples! with thy rich sunlight, pure moonbeams, pulsating blue sky, and atmosphere filled with delicious life-drops and exquisite odors. Often in the future, while far off in my American home, my heart shall stretch out tender, yearning memories to this enchanting place.

Angelini the sculptor, who also called to bid us good by to-night, said to me, in his soft, melodious Italian voice, "Ah, in Naples one needs so little. The simple act of living, the breath Nature gives us here, is a priceless luxury in itself. Here sight and sense are fed most gloriously by the good God."

They have all left, and I have come to my room to be alone with my fast-rushing thoughts. Janet and I have been walking up and down the terrace silently together, looking over at Vesuvius, whose lava streams still flow, though sluggishly. The beautiful lichen-hung hill above the terrace is buried in sombre shadows, although the sky is glowing with stars, — the hundred-eyed Argus watching for the lost Io, — for the moon is gone. It is near midnight, and this living whirlpool, this noisy, shrieking Naples, is comparatively quiet; around us all is still, but from the more densely inhabited part of the town arises a hum and beat like the roar of a distant ocean or the fevered throb of a factory.

Venitia is in the drawing-room, "holding commune sad and sweet" with her lovely Erard, from which she is to be parted forever. Now her hands sweep voluptuously over the ivory rocks, like the grand swell of some shining wave holding aloft on its dashing crest a divine sea-nymph. That most delicious of all nocturnes, Chopin's "Murmurs of the Seine," floats on the air, — a true music mist and spray. The plaint and descending gamut in the *motivo*, sparkle just as I have seen the shafts of moonlight, when standing out on the terrace in the Villa Reale, fling themselves passionately down on the innocent bosom of the sea, and break into golden spears and arrows of light, while the waters washed up against the stone foundations of the terrace, as if in sweet pain and sorrow.

Venitia is in a true playing mood to-night. Now she is improvising. She seizes the music-grapes, and, Bacchus-like, crushes out the purple and golden flood of music-wine. Her fingers seem dripping with the rare, priceless juice; and as they rise and fall on the keys the rich, invisible liquid sounds gather around me like a delicious flood of many waters, and bathe my suffering senses in the sweet intoxication of

"Desires and Adoration,
Winged Persuasions, and veiled Destinies,
Splendors and Glooms, and glimmering Incarnations
Of hopes and fears, and twilight fantasies,
And Sorrow with her family of sighs,
And Pleasure blind with tears, led by the gleam
Of her own dying smile instead of eyes."

O, this potent rhetoric of music that stealeth away all weapons of pain and steepeth the whole being in a wave of exquisite rapture, soothing the sting of "wounds that will never heal, and silencing the pangs that tempt the spirit to rebel"!

But, alas! just as this gloomy pageantry of "Winged Persuasions" had quieted all unrest with their Lotus draught, there comes creeping on the ear a despairing interrogatory, — solemn, dumb, questioning chords, followed with wildering, maddening doubt, — pure Wanhope! And with these sorrowful chords the music ceases. Poor Venitia!

And now to bed and to sleep, but not to partake of sleep's sweet refreshment; for it spreads no banquet for the heavily laden, but sits down a solemn veiled ghost beside the sepulchre of our buried hopes, like Buonarotti's spectre, watching over the dead Duke Lorenzo.

> "In our hearts
> There is a vigil, and these eyes but close
> To look within."

"CONCA D' ORO."

E arrived quite early at Palermo yesterday morning. On approaching the town we were charmed with its loveliness. Putting Vesuvius out of the question, it is as beautiful as Naples in its ravishing surroundings. It rests on the bosom of a sloping plain, which plain is called, on account of its luxuriance and fine situation, Conca d' Oro, — Shell of Gold.

First, the city spreads graciously out; back of it are rich forests of orange and lemon trees, and here and there the curious nut-tree with tufted top; — these form a rich framework; then around and above this foliage arise sloping mountains, ascending in terraces four thousand feet high, whose bold edges lie clear against the soft blue of the heavens.

This lovely island was the home of ancient mythology, the throne of the gods of Hellas. Jupiter reigned on Etna, and held chained under its fiery feet the giant Enceladus. On its plains of Enna, Proserpine was roaming, when Pluto carried her off to his dread abode. The whole land was Ceres' kingdom. In its forests, Diana and Minerva rambled in their girlhood. Here Vulcan forged his thunderbolts, — hence the name of the island Vulcania Tellus; and here also the terrible Cyclops lived. The story of Acis and Galatea, the myth of Polyphemus, with old Homer's songs, all bubbled up in our memories, as we fell stormily into port under the raging, shrieking sound of our steamer.

> "Arethusa arose
> From her couch of snows
> In the Acroceraunian mountains,"

I chanted half to myself and half to Janet as we stood in the end of the boat looking with eager eyes on this island, which spoke like a huge, many-leaved illuminated book to us.

"You are thinking of that delicious story and poem of Alpheus's pursuit of Arethusa, which the poet Read has painted with as much inspiration and beauty as Shelley's verse tells it," said Janet; "but the memory roused in me is a more strange, mysterious one. The shrieking noise of this steamer, the various things around me which tell of man's strength, remind me of that weird myth of Polyphemus. Do you remember, or did you never hear, the old Norwegian version of this Polyphemus myth?"

I nodded my head affirmatively, and she continued: —

"The child, through adroitness, not strength, you know, deprived the Trold, — the northern Polyphemus, — of his eye, and thus not only took from him a divine power, but held him in subjection. He made the Trold give him gold and silver, and also two bows, the arrows of which were unfailing in their aim and flight.

"So it is with man the pygmy. He has cunningly seized on the eye of Nature, and is wresting from her all her secrets. She gives him the treasures of the earth, the steel bows of lightning, and that unknown power called magnetism, on whose viewless current fly with unerring aim the swift arrows of intercourse. Then the relation between Man and Nature, how like to the legend also.

"After the Trold granted the child's requests, he and his brothers retired sternly and quietly into darkness, leaving the boy in ignorance of their greatest secret,— who and what they were! All he knew was, that they represented a vast, mysterious, giant power, which could be governed only through adroitness and skill.

"So Nature acts with man. He may wrest marvellous gifts and secrets from her, but after a sullen and unwilling bestowal of them, the great Cause of all these wonders recedes into the darkness of silence and mystery."

Just then the current of passengers ebbed back against us; there was a dragging of luggage, and a bustle which interrupted our pleasant talk. The steamer struck the wharf, and people sprang eagerly ashore and aboard; among those who came on the boat were the courteous American Consul, Mr. B., and our captain, who were in search of us.

We went with them directly to our vessel, and were much pleased with it. This beautiful little sea toy, which is to be our home for so long a time, the gentlemen tell us is a safe, swift sailer. The appointments of the clipper are very satisfactory; there are three nice state-rooms, small, but prettily finished, as indeed the whole vessel is, with mahogany; then there are berths back of the cabin for our two maids. The piano fills up most of the space to be sure, but we do not intend using the cabin as a dining-room. We shall take our meals on the quarter-deck, where a low awning can be stretched to protect us from sun and rain.

After establishing ourselves aboard, seeing that all the

trunks, boxes, provisions, etc. were arranged properly, and dining comfortably, we accepted the kind invitation of the Consul to drive through Palermo, and drink tea with his family.

"You have arrived just at the luckiest time," he said. "To-night is the vigil of our great *fête* of Santa Rosalie."

The first thing we did was to drive out the Palermo Toledo, to see a colossal statue of the saint, which we found in a huge pavilion, mounted on a car or chariot, that is to be drawn by over fifty oxen. It was a curious compound of stucco ornaments, gay flags, plaster statues of various saints and flying cherubs, with our old Neapolitan friends, the little colored glass cups and tapers, arranged in all manner of forms, so that when the whole structure shall be illuminated, which is to be every evening of the *fête*, it will produce a superb effect.

The *fête* continues five days, and we wished we could stay to see the whole of it, but the captain was anxious to sail with the first fair wind; the illuminating of the cathedral dome with twenty thousand lights was in itself a sufficiently strong temptation to us, but such experienced travellers as ourselves know we cannot see everything that is attractive.

On our drive through the town we found them decorating the houses and stores with the inevitable glass cups; strings of them were suspended in every direction, forming stars, crosses, monograms of "Mary" and "Our Lord," and every other religious device and shape that could be thought of. We were glad to see one more illumination before we left Italy.

First, we drove out on the fine old promenade of Palermo, the Marina, or Cours de Bourbon, which used to be the fashionable drive. It commences at the Porte

Felice, — the entrance to the Toledo, where the statue and car stand, — and extends along the bay shore to a public garden called the Flora, with its beautiful Villa Julia, which was built nearly a century ago in honor of a viceroy's wife, Julia Guevara Colonna. The Marina is also adorned with fine statues by various Italian sculptors and costly buildings, but its most striking adornments yesterday were the large transparencies and preparations for the evening's illumination and to-day's procession.

After leaving the Marina we returned to the Toledo and drove out its full mile length. This Toledo, when it reaches the centre of the city, is crossed at right angles by the Strada Nuova, another grand avenue or city artery like the Toledo. The square or place where the two streets intersect each other is an octagon called the Villena, beautifully decorated with fountains, statues, and fine buildings. These two great streets of Palermo divide the city into four equal quarters, the Loggia, the Kalsa, the Albergaria, and Siricaldi. Very Moorish sounding are these names; the old name of the Toledo, too, was Al Kassar. Indeed, I noticed on driving through the town the Saracenic and Moresco style of its architecture. Some of the houses have high, large, iron balconies to the second floor, like those in Spanish towns, recalling to me what Philip had said of Palermo, "that it should be the city of iced sherbets, serenades, and silken ladders." The convents have grated fronts to their balconies. The whole appearance of the city is pleasure-loving and luxurious. Palms and cacti on the surrounding hills and by the roadside Moorish buildings, Saracenic names, — we felt as if transported by some enchantment suddenly into the Oriental atmosphere of an Arabian tale.

We did not visit any churches or interiors of public

buildings, as we had only enough time to drive through the town to its most prominent points; for, beside supping with the Consul, we wished to see the Marina illumination, and our captain looked for a favorable wind at midnight. When we passed the Cathedral Santa Rosalie, the sight of it deepened the Moorish impression which the other buildings had already made on us. It is half Norman, half Moresco in its architecture; for in Saracenic days it was a mosque.

It dates back to the twelfth century; but the delicious climate of this fabled home of the gods has not blackened or injured the stone. The indentations of the festoons and other carvings which run around its margins and domes lay against the sky clear, fresh, and golden-hued, adorned with the gift of eternal youth. We were told that the interior would disappoint us; but we knew it contained some tombs we should have liked to have had time to look at.

The tomb of Roger — the great Roger, who was father to Tasso's Tancred — is there; also his daughter's, that "mighty Constance" whom Dante's "gentle Beatrice" unwillingly condemns; and her son's, the gallant Frederick II., "the third and last great Suabian blast," as Dante sings; these three famous old tombs still stand in that Cathedral, though the world has swung around with many fierce plunges during the long six hundred years' sleep of their famous occupants (Roger II., 1154; Constance, 1198; Frederick, 1250). Janet caught my eye as the carriage rolled slowly by the handsome old building, and heard me saying to myself,

> "This is the luminary
> Of mighty Constance, who from that loud blast
> Which blew the second over Suabia's realm,
> That power produced, which was the third and last."

"Yes," she said, "it is a pity we cannot see her tomb. I, too, should like to stand beside the resting-place of that woman, who 'held affection to the veil,' even after she was wife and mother; and, to uphold her son's rights, 'did what she would gladly have left undone,' as 'gentle Beatrice' says."

"I always thought Beatrice made a delicate 'distinction without a difference' on that point," I replied. "Divine judgment did not agree with her also, for the great Nun-Empress had a pleasant place allotted her in Paradise: Piccarda's glowing description proves this. She describes her as

> 'This other splendid shape which thou behold'st
> At my right side, burning with all the light
> Of this our orb.'"

It was useless to lament over the pleasant talk we might have had beside that "single slab of precious porphyry, and the superb canopy of six columns of white marble," which are said to mark the resting-place of this wedded nun, who at fifty years of age left her convent, where she had lived from early youth, to become an empress, and mother to one of the greatest monarchs history has chronicled.

"At an age when a woman has few hopes left of obtaining a brilliant establishment," Janet drolly remarked, as we lost sight of the church, "this cloistered Princess became the bride of the handsome young son of the mighty Barbarossa, and mother of that imperial warrior, philosopher, and graceful troubadour-poet, Frederick II. During the reign of this great son of Constance, Palermo was one of the most polished cities of Europe; and it was in her father's reign, King Roger II., that the first Italian verses were written."

We drove out to the extremity of the Strada Nuova (also Macqueda and Favorita, as this other great street has been called at different periods; for, like the Spaniards who built it, it carries a legion of names). There we found what Europeans call "an English garden"; a sort of park, with fine walks shaded with trees and shrubbery, and pleasant drives. This place is now the popular promenade of Palermo; that capricious authority, Fashion, bids "everybody" to come here, instead of going to the old and much more lovely resort on the Bay, the Marina, with its superb sea-view, fine Flora garden, and pretty Villa Julia.

We left the carriage and walked through some of the paths. The whole fashionable world was there. It was at the hour of sunset; and the rich dark foliage of the orange and lemon trees, the livelier greens of the other shrubs and trees, the sweet odors, golden sunbeams breaking in between the branches, and gay world around, made us also forget the Marina and its deserted loveliness.

The fashionables were in every variety of modish costume,—gay walking, dinner, and even light gossamer evening dress, as can be seen in all Spanish and Italian summer-evening promenades; and they displayed also every style of equipage that could be thought of. A dashy little affair flew by us several times; it was something like an English drag, painted in gay colors, and "picked out" in gilt, looking like a royal state-coach; it had four horses, two abreast, and two jockey-like postilions; the livery and mountings were brilliant, and it did not appear so gaudy as one might suppose, under the glowing sky and fine Vanity Fair surroundings. We were told that the young gentleman who was in it, its master, was the Duke of Monte Leone, whose mother is a woman of immense fortune and curious reputation. We remembered, then, having seen this Duchess and suite on board the steamer which brought us to Palermo, and observing that she was a bold, handsome-looking woman.

The whole scene was Parisian, a bit of Bois de Boulogne. It was strange to be thus suddenly jostled against modern artificial life, after driving through those old Saracenic streets, our memories filled with Middle-Age legend and poem, and those old legends too seeming new, alongside of the myths we had recalled when first landing on this "happy island of the gods, these eternally classic heights of the ancient world."

After leaving this gay throng, we drove to the Palazzo in which the Consul lives. Its court-yard, stairways, corridors, and rooms made me think of old Moorish tales. We supped with the Consul and his family, and then re-entered the carriage, which was waiting in the court-yard, and drove through the streets, blazing with illuminations, to the crowded Marina.

We drew up in front of a large marble building, designed by King Ferdinand II. as a shelter for an orchestra,—a costly, unsuitable place; for the columns and architectural construction cause the greater part of the music to be lost, or to fall upon the ear with muffled sounds; but on this evening I rather liked the effect.

Our barouche was on the outside of a throng of fine equipages, and very near the sea. The Marina was superbly lighted. Near our carriages were some large transparencies, which made the place look like a grand picture gallery. They represented, in glowing colors, various incidents in the life of the famous Sicilian Saint whose *fête* was being so superbly celebrated.

This Princess Rosalie was the niece of the Empress Constance. When she was a young girl, she was so saddened with man's doings that she left palace, court, and knightly lover, and went clambering up, all alone, the rugged, thorny sides of Monte Pellegrini,

"To liberty and not to banishment."

There on this lonely mountain the pious maiden lived out her innocent existence, far removed from the storms which the fierce Barbarossa and haughty Hildebrand, the struggling races and faiths, were making together out in the world. But she was safer in those dripping mountain caverns, with the thorny cactus fortifications and in far-off, forgotten loneliness, than if, like her brilliant aunt, she had chosen one of the gay new convents in the royal city of her grandfather, Roger.

In this abode, rude and harsh for one so tenderly reared, she lived and died in sweet ignorance, I will dare vow, of all the vivid stories her "exalted mount" could read to me; her saintly thoughts were never disturbed by the gorgeously illuminated myths, which would dance before my eyes, from every island point, as brilliant as some of the rare, gay-colored leaves in one of her own curiously painted Missals or Hour Books.

Blessed ignorance, and thrice-blessed faith! The gentle maiden soon slept a quiet sleep; "in the flower of her youth and beauty she died,"—so the legend says; and her long slumber was undisturbed by the clashing of arms, the swaying to and fro of the Christian and Paynim world; for five stormy centuries she rested there quite, quite forgotten.

Then a fearful pestilence raged in the island; and holy men were directed, in sacred visions, to go to a lonely cavern on that grand old headland for relief. They went in solemn procession, holding the Cross aloft, with banners swaying to and fro, and clouds of incense arising; priests and peasants clambered up the rugged, zig-zag paths, to whose rocky sides the moss scarcely clings, and in a dark, dripping cavern, near one of its highest points, they found the remains of the fair maiden. They gathered together these sacred relics with pious reverence, and carried them to the suffering world. Wherever the procession moved, sickness ceased; and the grateful Sicilians made the saintly girl their Lady Patroness. For over two hundred years her memory has been lovingly preserved.

The bleak, bare cavern in which she wept tears of anguish for that poor father whose name has come down to us laden with the sorrowful title of "Bad," and where she sighed out in solemn solitude her last gentle breath, has been adorned with all the costly decorations the loving Catholic faith so tenderly hangs around its beloved sanctuaries. A monastery and a church spring finely out from the side of the mountain-height, and cathedrals and churches are raised to her memory in every Sicilian town.

I thought pleasantly of all this old history and legend while I sat leaning back in one corner of the barouche, looking out on the dim outline of the coast towards Cape Zaffarina, which stretched off its picturesque indentations of bays, isthmuses, and headlands, with the starry heavens above and sparkling waters beneath.

The dull plash of the waves against the shore mingled curiously with the heavy, muffled sound of the Overture to Sicilian Vespers. The undulating rhythm of the opening movement in the Overture, and the clarinet solo, sounded like the mysterious beat of muffled oars in bright waters, and the violoncello passage was as dark and sombre as these very waves of the Palermo bay are said to look even at the brightest noonday, for the shores and mountains hem them in so jealously that they keep every ray of sun-glitter off from their pure crests. We did not talk, — not a word was spoken, — each one sat still, enjoying the pleasant sights and sounds.

Midnight struck, and we drove along the Marina to the vessel, which we found ready to sail. We bade our kind, gay entertainers good-by, and after the little rocking, dancing boat had carried us to the ship's side, and we had clambered up the ladder, we settled ourselves in the hammocks, which are slung on the quarter-deck, and there watched in silence the starting of the vessel. The beautiful outlines of Monte Pellegrini lay sharply cut against the clear sky, which was crowded with thickly studded stars, while Palermo, with its many lights growing a little dim, looked like some half-extinguished meteor dying out on the bosom of the valley.

On leaving the harbor, we sailed towards Cape Zaffarina, at the eastern arm of the bay. This movement gave us a fine view of Santa Rosalie's home, Monte Pellegrini: it is one of the boldest mountain headlands in Southern Europe, and said to resemble Gibraltar, being nearly as high.

The scene produced a delightful effect upon me. I listened to the plash of the black water against the vessel's side, breathed the novel and peculiar odor of the sea, noticed the graceful outlines of the mountains, the bright, starry heavens, whose fire-points seemed to throb and scintillate like pulses and sparks, while quick-changing memories pursued each other with shadowy haste through my mind. The surging of the vessel rocked all sights, sounds, and thoughts into a curious compound, from which arose a succession of strange, grotesque forms, created by that mysterious "chemistry of sleep called dreams" and the opium-like power of the sea.

Solemn processions seemed to wind up the mountain-paths, contending armies thronged the coast, and gay pageantries filled the ocean. The various epochs of the past presented themselves before me, and these shores gave up their dead in a brilliant, curious phantasmagoria.

There was the magnificence of Tyre and Sidon blending with mediæval splendors; the fierce conflicts of Punic wars, raging beside crusading knights, when

> "Christian swords with Persian blood were dyed."

Romans, Northmen, Saracens, and Christians all mingling in one wild, hot contest; while floating over the whole changing vision, as a brilliant sun-lighted mist, was the faint memory of strange myths glowing with the far-off light of ancient poesy, — fleeing nymphs and pursuing gods, quick-leaping fountains holding aloft exquisite forms of beauty, cresting waves bearing divine shapes, —

> "The feast of Neptune, and the cereal games,
> With images and crowns and empty cars;
> The dancing Salii, on the shield of Mars,
> Smiting with fury, and a deeper dread
> Scattered on all sides by the hideous jars
> Of Corybantian cymbals, while the head
> Of Cybelé was seen sublimely turreted." *

* Wordsworth.

IBERIAN COASTS.

ULY 13. — On land I rarely date my journal; here on the sea I must hold fast to dates; having no busy world around to do it for me, I shall forget how time passes in this "cycle of Cathay." Yesterday we did nothing but lie in the hammocks on the quarter-deck; for although we do not suffer from actual sea-sickness, we feel a delightful, indolent languor and an unwillingness to commence any regular occupation.

Janet laughingly reminds us of Novalis's saying, "Rest is peculiar to the spirit. Life is a disease of the spirit, a working incited by passion." From this she concludes that we are in a more healthy spiritual state while feeling this enchanting indolence. I must confess my usual restlessness is quieted, and a sweet peace, which must come from mental health, fills my whole being.

Sicily is still in sight, with its bold, beautiful coast. Last night we passed three islands, Ustica, Alicuri, and Felicuri. The blue of the sea is of the deepest hue, but the sky is clear light blue, and yet the most perfect harmony exists; there is not a shadow of a discord between the two shades. Nature is unerring; and he said well who told us that "Art is a prudent steward that lives on managing Nature's riches."

The haze and atmosphere over the mountainous coast of Sicily are very soft, and the heavens are filled with light floating clouds, that dissolve into the blue as the white crests of the waves do into the sea. The sharp cutting which the prow of our swift little ship makes through the waters dresses up the waves with glorious white crests.

15th.—We are all doing very well. We have commenced our regular employments. As we have no sight-seeing or land-journeying to keep us occupied together, we separate immediately after breakfast, each to her own pursuit. Venitia goes to her music, the theory of which she is examining very closely. Janet studies languages; and two hours daily I join her in French, German, and Italian. After that, I lie in the hammock and read, or dream waking-visions while listening to Venitia's earnest study of modulations and intricate tone-webs woven from curiously blended chords; sometimes I talk and walk the deck with Janet or read aloud to her.

16th.—We are having glorious sunsets, beautiful moonlight, and glassy seas. There is very little wind, and the sails flap lazily to and fro in this July calm. Ah, how charming is this life! Not luxurious like that Neapolitan existence of two baths, five repasts, and three sleeps in the twenty-four hours, but possessing its own peculiar pleasure. Out on the broad sea we are cut off from all provocations to anxiety, and, such as we are, enjoy this calm episode to the very full. On land, humanity and humanity's cares, hopes, ambitions, likings and dislikings, press in upon us, and disturb our tranquillity; here all is divinely still.

At sunset this evening the scene was what might be truly called "fairy-like." The whole horizon opposite the sun reminded me of Shelley's "dissolved opal." The sky had the delicate pink hue of a conch-shell, then it melted itself into a soft blue, wedding itself to the ocean without a line of separation, while over the mysterious union of sea and sky flitted fitfully faint but exquisite shades of color; here a blue, there a rose, and then a green, while the soft west-wind hovered over the waters, rippling them prettily together.

On the other side of the heavens hung the "infantine Moon, with her attendant star." As the twilight darkened and the moonbeams shone down, we leaned over the guards and watched the fiery line made by the sharp cleaving of our quick little vessel through the brilliant phosphorescent waves; small diamond-like sparkles danced and trembled over the waters. While noticing this phosphorescing of the sea, Janet's classical memories were quickened, and she rhapsodized playfully, with "divine frivolity," about the Nereid Mera, who, according to Hesiod, was the one to whom these mysterious ocean beams belonged.

These medusidans give the sapphire-hued sea a metallic lustre in the daytime; at night, sweeping by in huge shoals, they look like smothered flames; and when the vessel strikes them, they emit sharp electric sparks.

In the morning the waves are adorned with dozens of baby nautili sailing gayly along like fairy fleets, with their tiny sails erect. Venitia caught one on the handle of my riding-whip to-day. I fastened it to this page of my journal, but it was like a delicate flower-petal from poor Kilmeny's fairy-garden; it faded and crumbled away in our mortal atmosphere; and yet I wished to preserve the pretty thing, for the deep blue base and transparent lilac and pink sail were bewitching.

The veriest trifles on shipboard possess interest. We are like children in watching them, and find not only quiet as children do, but food for thought and fancy in our observations. This morning the captain and his men amused themselves by catching turtles. The lowering of the boats, the going to and fro of the men up and down the vessel-side, the rowing off, the silent, stealthy approach to the poor, silly, sleeping things, and the shouts made over their capture, gave rise to more entertainment for us than one might fancy.

Then we leaned over the side of the vessel and watched the playing of a rope in the water while a boat was lowered and drawn up. As it caught the sun's rays, it looked as if made of molten gold; and the most fantastic lines and traceries were formed, every change brilliantly beautiful, offering studies of divine shapes for arabesque ornaments.

To-day has been very calm. At times we did not seem to stir. The whole image of the vessel, sails, cordage, and masts, lay reflected on the truly glass-like bosom of the sea with startling clearness, like the ancient mariner's

"Painted ship upon a painted ocean."

I try to grow learned over the various sails, and to distinguish them by their different names, but in vain; that which is apparently so easy to these uneducated sailors is *grimoire* to me. Our ship carries a great number; yesterday I counted thirty-three at one time, spreading out their white wings and making the little vessel skim over the waters as swiftly and lightly as a true zephyr. But a good deal of skill, and of watchfulness too, is needed in using them, for an unlucky squall of wind might make us pay dearly for our top-heavy finery, by giving us an unexpected capsize.

21*st.* — There is a brisk wind, and the pretty little clipper cuts sharply through the waves. We are now passing Fromantera, one of the Balearic Islands. A little while ago, we were close to Majorca; its sharp cut coast lay clear against the purply blue sky, with beautiful leafy indentations running along its edges, formed by the aloes and palms.

I leaned on the chain of the quarter-deck watching the island as long as I could see it, and recalled Chopin's sufferings. I thought of the desolate winter he spent there, the intense loneliness and sadness he felt, when the cry of the hungry eagle, the wail of the north-wind, and the sight of the desolate yews covered with snow, united to the heart-weariness of the woman he loved, wrung from his soul those divine cries of music sorrow.

Venitia evidently had the same memories awakened, for she also gazed intently at the island.

I looked at her and observed how much her face has altered in the past month. The arch of her brow is, as I have said, a shadow too prominent, and formerly the expression was hard; now it is stern and reflective. There is also a sombre and mysterious look in her eyes, which is like distant thunder and far-off lightning, making me think of the flashing of a storm through the painted windows of a chapel.

The same smile has settled on her face which rests forever on Janet's, and which first attracted me to her. This smile has a pitiful meaning, is sadder looking than tears, and both mouth and eyes rebel; it can be seen on the face of every proud, self-contained person in a season of fearful uncertainty, or after some great loss has been experienced.

To-day Venitia's deep prophetic eyes had an expression that was too intense for one so young; and the blue-veined eyelid drooped with a tender weight over them, as if heavy with unshed tears. The thin, flexible nostrils dilated with the passionate memories that were agitating her. Her beautiful mouth had lost the bewitching child-like pout of the under lip, the short Greek cut of the upper one grew thinner, and both became like two trembling crimson lines, under the influence of the quick quiverings of emotion excited by the sight of these Majorcan rocks.

After the island was quite out of sight, she went down to the piano and played, as if improvising them, those great Majorcan preludes of this master, which make "a single instrument speak the language of the infinite, and where in ten lines of music are enclosed poems of the highest emotions, and dramas of unequalled energy." *

23d. — The coast of Spain is still in sight. The graceful outlines of its mountains and hills are beautifully traced out against the sky in the morning sunlight. We have just passed Cape di Gata, and the captain has pointed out where Almeria should be. Now we are sailing in front of a beautiful plain, to which slope down laughing hills, bathed in a "leafy tide of greenery," rippling in the shadowy wind; and equally charming ones wrapped in a soft green misty haze, make a lovely background.

Farther along toward the southwest, high mountains can be seen, topped with dazzling snow. Soon we shall be coasting in front of old Granada, so rich in Moorish

* George Sand, *Mémoires de ma Vie.*

legend. We are going very fast,—ten miles an hour. If we continue making this good time, we shall be at Gibraltar before this hour to-morrow.

Night, Velez Malaga.—The fine sail of to-day from Cape Gata to this point has been charming. The mountainous coast was enveloped during midday with a soft, peach-colored haze; the hills rose up, one above another, amphitheatre like; and the distant ones were topped and dashed along their sides with glittering white snow.

This Iberian peninsula has a garden-like coast; vines cluster around precipices, and here and there little chapels peep out from the rich groves of orange, lemon, myrtle, and cypress trees that wind around, or sweep across the mountain sides in graceful ascending terraces. We have coasted quite close to shore; moreover, we have fine spy-glasses, which give us a full view of the distant part of the country.

24*th.*—Becalmed off Velez Malaga. The sails hang as if wearied with their swift run of yesterday. Now one flaps lasily as a teasing little breeze steals over and under it. The vessel sways dreamily to and fro on the water, giving a true opium feeling to the brain. The sun has a white hot beam, and its rays pour down like a molten silver stream, bathing sea and sky, and even the whole landscape, in its dazzling atmosphere.

THE GADITANIAN GATES.

ULY 27. — Last night we remained awake until after midnight, watching the vessel as it passed around the Gibraltar Rock, and entered the Gulf of this Calpe of the ancients. We had a very rough sea yesterday, with strong head winds; but this ship lies the closest to the wind that is possible, and the captain, by dint of tacking and patient going to and fro, managed to arrive here notwithstanding the difficulties.

The sun went down behind the purple hills of Spain slowly and languidly, enveloped in rich golden and yellow clouds. About ten o'clock the moon arose full and clear, and poured down upon the waters a flood-like stream of silver light. As we approached the Rock, the sight was superb; the moon shone upon the gray old height, the light-house on the point burned brilliantly, and over on the African coast the revolving light of Ceuta by turns flashed out sharply, then died away.

We could not help thinking of the effect produced on ancient voyagers by the sight of these high headlands which terminate the two continents, standing like pillars of boundary to their own world, or grand gates of entrance to a new one. The Iberian Calpe and Libyan Abilyx are no longer such imposing places. Men are too busily employed in rearing invisible Babel towers of lightning and magnetism to be awed now by such tangible forms as Pillars of Hercules or Gaditanian Gates.

This morning we went ashore to visit Gibraltar town. After landing, we took an open carriage, and spent an hour or two in driving around the Rock beyond Europa point and the light-house, to the Mediterranean beach. We passed the Governor-General's gardens, and saw his Excellency sitting in the balcony of his summer villa, reading very comfortably behind a bamboo shade, which was propped out as a blind. During the drive we observed some exceedingly pretty cottage homes, snug and English looking, evidently officers' residences; one was a charming place buried in shrubbery, and over its partially hidden front clambered vines with luxuriant clusters of white and purple flowers.

The fig-trees on the roadside were in full fruit; the aspens trembled in the west wind, showing their white-lined leaves, reminding me of the silver poplar. There were several other shade-trees, the names of which I did not know. One was particularly beautiful; it waved long golden-hued, feathery blossoms in the air, which looked something like the acacia flowers at a distance. The roads were bordered with blood-red wall-flowers, scarlet geranium, and brilliant cacti, just as at Naples; indeed, many things reminded me of our sweet Italian home, especially the houses clambering up and clinging to the rocks and the terraces, or hanging gardens to the residences, filled with beautiful flowers and shrubbery.

After our drive we walked through the town; did some "shopping," as women do everywhere, and hunted up a piano-tuner. The streets are very clean,—a strong evidence of that "well-regulated family," England having the control. The population is of the most curiously mixed character. We saw Barbary Jews with black skull-caps, flowing robes, and red scarfs knotted around them for girdles; Moors in white turbans, full drawers, and yellow slippers; Spaniards with their peculiar padded brimmed hats, braided jackets, and velvet breeches, tinsel trimmed on the seams, slashed at the knees, and hanging full of tags; Spanish women with rebosas, high combs, dark skins, white teeth, sparkling eyes, short petticoats, trim feet and ankles; and among them all, fresh, hearty-looking English men and women went striding about as perfectly unconcerned and at home as if walking on the banks of the Thames.

The stores gave us infinite pleasure. There were Persian leather cushions, covered with curious embroidery; Gibraltar black lace, recalling the Havana blonde; and a variety of rare ornaments. The bracelets were wildering: strings of strange golden coins, looking as if they had been gathered from a Haidee's brow; amber beads curiously carved, each one holding a god and a charm; different kinds of small, rich-colored seeds, strung with gold in pretty forms. The fans, too, were of course beautiful, and had a cunning, coquettish air, as if they almost knew how to carry on a flirtation by themselves.

We shall stay here a day or two, to have the piano tuned thoroughly, ramble about the place, and get a little change off shipboard. We have concluded to sleep aboard the vessel, as we shall find ourselves cooler by doing so; for the town is now intensely hot, suffering from a long drought. But if the town were never so cool, our ship-home is preferable; for it gives us a perfect rest and freedom in the evening, which we find very refreshing after the day's ramble; then the rowing back and forth in the boat is agreeable.

What could be more pleasant than the *laissez aller* of our ship-life? This evening, for example, is a fair specimen picture. Janet is lounging in her hammock; Venitia in hers; I am writing by the carcel lamp, the base of which is clamped to the table-top of the little bookcases; but its works are skilfully arranged in a swinging globe, so as to adapt them to the swaying of the vessel. It is near midnight, and sea and land are still.

All the evening we could hear plainly the music from the public grounds of the town. At sunset, the Rock gun was discharged, and then we watched the gradual lighting-up of the town and the vivid sparkle of the lamps. The different light-houses shone out brightly; and the green, blue, and red lamps of the steamers in the harbor made them seem, in the twilight and night, like some huge, panting animals with fierce, staring eyes.

Above the hills, over on the African shore, glowed a fierce red light of some inland fire, — bushwood burning, or something like that. After the sun went down and the night darkened, this fire reminded us of Vesuvius: tongues of flame darted up, and, as they crept around the edges of the mountain, they resembled a little the lava-light, only the smoke was more dense and black than lava-smoke, and the forked, sharp forms of the flames told they came from blazing wood.

Gibraltar is a free port, and thus offers great facilities, and indeed temptations, for smugglers. About sunset, a little boat rowed up to us and lay under our stern. It had in it about a half-dozen Spaniards, with some parcels and packages. They were a merry, white-teethed, brown-skinned set of rogues, looking as picturesque in their Spanish costume as a set of operatic heroes.

Janet amused herself by "airing" her Spanish on them.

When she asked their business, they replied candidly that they were smugglers, and told her with amusing frankness that they were only lying around our ship under pretence of business with us; at nightfall they should row off to Spain and smuggle in their contraband goods.

While Janet was talking to them, Venitia was swaying indolently to and fro in the hammock, singing in an undertone a little Spanish melody she had picked up among some music at a music-store to-day. One of the smugglers overhearing her, drew out a guitar, and began singing it gayly to sparkling, rattling words. She left the hammock and came to the guards to listen to him. When the men saw her beautiful face, and large, languid, well-shaped form, which looked very lovely in the soft, white mull robe, and purply, golden atmosphere that surrounded everything, they grew enthusiastic, and burst out into a chorus which had a glorious fulness. They also sang us an Ave Maria, that reminded me of Gordigiano, and they accompanied it with a pretty plash of the oar, which had an enchanting effect.

28*th.* — Our poor, poor smugglers! They were seized and shot last night. They hung around our vessel until just before moon-rising at midnight, singing, talking, and making themselves very agreeable, poor fellows! They were perfectly proper and respectful in their deportment. Venitia's beauty evidently delighted them: she sat nearly all the evening, leaning over the guards, talking in her captivating, indolent way, which is as unconscious as bewitching. The men looked at her as if she was some beautiful saint. She took their guitar and sang Neapolitan boat-songs and Venetian barcarolles in her soft, low voice and clear articulation, which are peculiarly adapted to ballads, making them sound like sweet talking.

About half past eleven they asked us the hour, seemed startled, said they were very late, bade us good night hurriedly, and rowed off in great haste.

We watched the moon rising, which was superb; it came slowly up over the centre fortification, and the high, firm chiselling of the Rock was set off finely by its clear light. While we were looking at this lovely sight, and expressing a little fear about our smuggler friends having overstayed their time, we heard a distant report of firearms, that came booming across the waters. We did not associate the sound with them, but fancied it was a signal from a vessel in the distance; and I remember, just as the shot came echoing around the hills, Janet answered our fears about their safety in her ready, healthy tone, that will not admit trouble of any kind in advance: "O, do not feel uneasy about them; they rowed back to Gibraltar; they did not attempt their perilous trade to-night."

But this morning the captain brought us the sad news. We feel very mournful about it. They were so merry and full of life, poor fellows! And now all is over with them for this world!

30*th.*—Last night, our captain looked for a suitable wind to make the passage of the Straits, and we sat up until after midnight, not wishing to lose the fine sight of leaving the harbor; but it proved a hopeless affair, and we went to our state-rooms. At four o'clock this morning we were awakened by the noise on deck. We hurried up, and found all the ship's crew and captain making preparations to beat through the Straits against the head-winds and contrary currents.

All day the good little vessel has labored industriously against wind and waves. It was very exciting; for the ship had to tack to and fro, first approaching the coast of Africa, then the Spanish shore, so close at times that we could distinguish the fields covered with grain, the various trees, and even people and houses. Africa showed some curiously shaped hills, bluffs, and rugged peaks. The Spanish hills were rolling, and tufted as if covered with purplish-green velvet. Some one has said prettily of this passage through the Straits, that Europe and Africa look at themselves in the same Mediterranean mirror, and seem to struggle for the palm of beauty.

A schooner from Valencia to Boston was trying also to make the passage through. Several times, when tacking, we crossed each other's paths; once we were alarmingly near. Every one on both vessels expected a collision, and the fierce thrill that passed through us was like a magnetic current. The danger over, we drew a long breath; it was almost a luxurious feeling: the excitement had been so keen, so sudden, as to be free from pain,—Saladin's scymitar cutting the velvet without ravel.

It has been a glorious day. The little slender ship, as she tacked about, careened first on one side, then on the other. The waves danced madly; and they were as fiercely obstinate in their opposition to our purpose as if they had been living things. The wind was fresh, and we inhaled fine draughts of the invigorating breeze. There was no reading or writing, or indeed much talking, done, for the motion of the ship was too great; and the noise and dash of the opposing waves, united to the beating of the wind, sounded like roaring thunder. This motion of the vessel we all compared to the sensation felt on a fast-galloping horse,—the bounding, free feeling which fills the rider with enthusiasm, making, as that fine line says,

"All the queen in one's nature put on her crown."

After all the toil, at nightfall the vessel had made but four miles in the whole day's sailing; so the captain wisely determined to give up the present attempt, and in one short half-hour we were back at Gibraltar, in front of this old Rock, which towered up, gray and grim, against the mellow sky.

As we neared the point, the Rock gun fired, an eagle swept grandly around the cliff, and soared off into mid-air. Janet and I quoted impulsively, and in one breath almost, as if we had been thinking with one mind,

> "Thou winged and cloud-cleaving minister,
> Whose happy flight is highest into heaven."

Since our return, we have each withdrawn into ourselves, as it were. I am filling up journal; Janet is lying in her hammock, gazing silently up at the starry sky and the Rock, which looks as unflinching as she sometimes does. Once in a while she stretches out her hand and rests it tenderly on my shoulder, for she never likes me to be far off from her; I turn to give back the caress, and see her dear, true eyes looking at me with an expression full of firm, unchanging, mother, sister, and friend love.

Venitia is in the cabin, improvising. Most mysterious is this power to me, this capability of expressing passing thoughts and feelings by quick-succeeding and blending harmonies. I have spoken before of Venitia's remarkable possession of this gift; but since her separation from Luigi her improvisations have taken a deeper tone; they are very often now what the Germans call subjective, and are a true tone-language; not a fiction of art, but a lovely, mystical, cipher-tongue, telling her heart and soul history.

She never names them, never writes them off, never talks of them, and only plays them when she is alone.

Sometimes they are so masterly, I cannot resist calling out to her; but though I veil my admiration or interpretation of her musical thoughts under technicalities, my remarks check her on the instant, and she breaks off into vague chords, simple pursuits of harmonies and dry reasonings.

But if, like to-night, they are objective and descriptive, then my comprehensions and remarks stimulate her, and make her develop her musical thoughts more brilliantly. Now, as the music rises up from the cabin, I notice its spirituality; image after image is summoned, and yet only a gentle hovering over each, for the fancy roused by the scene of to-day is so rich in such descriptive wealth as to silence thought. Curious inharmonious dissonances are wedded so skilfully as to make perfect concord; indeed, the chords proceed rapidly, without reflection; they fall instantaneously from each hand, dissimilar as possible, and yet their union is divinely complete. This is not the result of mere "grammar rules." The study and knowledge of theory may, does, help the improvising artist; but the power or gift which Venitia possesses to so high a degree arises from some subtle, spiritual influence, which is exercised over the mind, and the best name to give it is inspiration.

It resembles the divine harmony of nature, where each sound in itself, like these chords, if taken separately, may be unmusical; such as the hot, grating chirrup of the grasshopper, so fretful and petulant; the crackling of dried leaves; the rustle and tumult of the winds among the branches of the trees; the regular rise and fall of an oar, the drip of the water from its blade, with the complaining creak of the thole-pin; and sweeping along, upon the surrounding air, from the distance, a hum and throb like a sad minor undertone, telling the sorrowful tale of human labor, toil, and pain. But Nature never errs; these sounds are all blended harmoniously, and lull to rest, with vague, delicious fancies, the happy dreamer, who, resting under the trees by the shore of "sweet running waters, with a soft south-wind blowing over them," listens with gentle rapture to the divine symphonique whole.

And the improvising artist, to produce a similar effect, must possess that power which has been happily called "prophetic action of the mind," which bestows this marvellous and inexplicable ability to seize on the instant, without taking time for reflection, upon the best out of a throng of fast-crowding fancies, and create, from this little pallet of twenty-four gamuts, things of beauty.

TEMPTING FATE.

ULY 31. — We are again trying to beat out. The captain proposed we should have the vessel towed through by a steamer, but we refused simultaneously: it shocked all our poetical fancies.

"Just like an omnibus to cross the Desert," cried Venitia, half indignant.

Even the practical Janet said, "O no, that would never answer"; and then, as we walked the deck together, she quoted Humboldt about these "Pillars of Hercules at the west margin of the earth, on the road to Elysium and the Hesperides, beyond which were first seen the primeval waters of the circling Oceanus, in which the source of all rivers was then sought."

"And here was the fabled margin of the earth," she continued. "Now, according to these wise men of old, we should be sailing towards, not from, Elysium. We are striving to enter these 'primeval waters of the circling Oceanus,' and probably, my dear," she added, putting her arm tenderly around my waist, "we are approaching a true elysium, not the sorrow you dread so much. Your troubles at this very moment may be graciously righting themselves, — some happy influences working, like sweet Ellie's Knight, to

'Make straight distorted wills.

When we reach home, darling friend, we may all find peace and pleasure instead of trouble and trial."

"Home!" I replied, sadly; "it has been some time, Janet, since I have regarded that word as representing a reality for me. My home, henceforth, will only be a country, — a wide space, a land, not a fireside with sweet possessions."

We paced the deck silently for some time with quick, elastic tread, as if our wills intended to control the feelings through the physical motions, and Janet's only answer was a firmer grasp around my waist.

Evening, off Al-Kazar Point. — The sun has just set beautifully, but now a dull, heavy cloud hangs around the horizon, like a curtain partly drawn up. Cape Trafalgar stretches out in the distance golden and glorious as a "heavenly hill," and Cape Espartel, the northwest point of Africa, also catches a gleam of the radiant light.

Behind us lies Gibraltar, just faintly seen, for a misty cloud hangs over it; but the last rays of sunlight give us a sight of its stone walls and houses clambering up against the rugged old Rock. Opposite to us is a beautiful bit of landscape; Al-Kazar Point, a rugged, sharp, gray bluff runs out into the sea, forming a bay; behind it are several hills, each covered with a different shade of green, and the atmosphere which hangs over them is deliciously soft. One catches the sunlight, which throws a silvery sheen over its verdure; another has a clear, open hue, like Shakespeare's "lush and lusty grass, with an eye of green in it"; and beyond there is yet another, wrapped in a semi-opaque greenish haze. Meadows stretch out, and there are clumps of trees, which tell of sweet shady woods that must now, at this hour of nightfall, be full of all manner of solemn sounds, and where

> "the silent air
> Lays her soft ear close to the green earth."

To-day the Spanish coast presented a curious sight; trees stood in closer and more regular groups than nature arranges them; then there were rows forming belts or boundary lines around large tracts of land, which land was yellow as if covered with grain stubble, and some looked like pasture which had been cropped off by cattle.

The western horizon is glorious just at this instant. Cape Trafalgar and its surrounding hills are covered with a dissolving green haze, which has "an eye of fire in it" like the opal. Tarifa light-house gleams out fitfully on the Spanish shore, and the opposing currents of the Straits beat noisily through. We have been talking of those early voyages of the ancients, their earnest attempts to advance beyond the Mediterranean shores; of the old tale of the Argonauts, which is enveloped as thickly in poetical myths as these beautiful mountains are with the glowing haze.

No wonder those early voyagers clothed their adventures with legends, for when they reached these pillar-like mountains and saw such a dark unknown expanse of waters stretching out beyond, they must have felt startled and awed; then the aerial perspective of time gathered gradually around their expeditions, and naturally gave them poetic, mystic forms. Like us, these early adventurers must have had fitful, capricious winds, and listened with terror to this thundering roar of the contending currents in these Straits, forbidding them to advance — as they seem to do us — towards Elysium.

How curious these water currents are to the unlearned, such as I am. I traced to-day upon the globe the course of that mysterious Gulf Stream, which sweeps river-like across the ocean, flowing past the opposing and circling waves as if they were simple earth-banks; retaining, it is said, forever unchanged its own high temperature through all its intercourse with other waters.

The captain, who is an intelligent man in his business, told me that the ocean current propelled by this gulf current, which flows from the Azores towards the Straits of Gibraltar and the Canary Isles, drives round the waters of the Atlantic Ocean in a continual circular course of three thousand eight hundred miles!

The night thickens, the wind changes, and the sea is treacherous. The captain and men look anxious, but we three women, who carry such heavy loads chained fast to our hearts, — one a grave, the other a hopeless love, and the third a living death, — are not appalled by the presence of mere physical danger; indeed, presenting itself in this sublime form, it possesses a strange attraction, to me at least.

"I should feel loath to risk the lives of these men," said Janet just now, "but there are boats enough to save them, and despite all the fine stories told of disinterestedness and generous self-sacrifice at such fearful times, I know, in such an event, these sailors would take good care of themselves, no matter what became of us and our poor maids. But we shall get through safely"; and she added in an undertone, as if to herself, turning away from me, "I fancy death is too great a blessing to come to us just yet."

A perfect fleet of vessels set out with us this morning, — over two hundred; it was a fine sight to see them stretch out their huge wings against the morning sky, looking like so many gigantic birds. Some of them have sailed steadily on like us, contending bravely with wind and current, but most of them have fallen back. We have concluded to stay in our hammocks all night on deck, to see the termination of this attempt.

Midnight. — We have drifted back in spite of all our trouble to Gibraltar again, just outside the grim old Rock! Janet, who is swaying to and fro in her hammock, quoted gayly just now, —

"'Ever striving to pass onwards, Phœnicians, Greeks, Arabs, Catalans, Majorcans, Frenchmen from Dieppe and La Rochelle, Genoese, Venetians, Portuguese, and Spaniards, in turns attempted to advance across this ocean, this dark and misty sea, — *mare tenebrosum,* — until proceeding from station to station as it were, they finally came to the New Continent,' — and so shall we, notwithstanding all this contradiction."

We have been talking of the fabled Continent of Atlantis.

"It must have been here," said Janet, "just in front of these Gibraltar Straits, that it lay. I have heard famous hydrographers speculate beautifully on the mysterious tradition. Homer and Hesiod mention it; and Plato, in his Timæus and Critias, designates this very spot. He says in the Timæus, 'There was in front of the Straits which you call Columns of Hercules an island greater than Libya and Asia.'

"On this great island reigned famous kings, and brave warriors lived. In one fatal night and day there came a fearful earthquake and heavy flood, when this wondrous island with its mighty men disappeared. Ever since, the solemn, voiceless ocean has swept over its face, obliterating its great cities, fertile countries, innumerable animals, and all its marvellous beauty of landscape, — vast plains and high mountains, which in extent and beauty surpassed all we possess.

"I have heard very learned men say that they did not regard this legend as a poetic fiction or allegory; that the configuration of the ocean just here accords strangely with the ancient tradition, and that the accidental elevations which occur on the bosom of the Atlantic, which have made hydrographers despair, can thus be cleared up, for the Archipelagos of the Azores, Madeira, the Canaries, and Cape Verd, can be regarded as the high table-lands and mountain-summits of this lost continent."

We are still working out, notwithstanding our rebuff. It is now two o'clock in the morning, and the whole vessel is alive. The good, energetic captain and his brave men seem to have caught our adventurous spirit; a pride has taken possession of them, and they have determined to make this passage unaided. I do not believe they would now consent to employ a steamer, even if we should urge it.

Sunday Morning, August 1.—Safely through the Straits at last, and fairly out on the broad ocean. At four o'clock this morning we had worked out to Tarifa again. The rising of the sun was very, very curious; coming up above the horizon without any dazzling rays, round and red as a full moon, it seemed to sway to and fro like a ball of liquid flame.

At ten o'clock we were once more in front of Capes Trafalgar and Espartel; when we were lunching at two o'clock, we had reached the open sea. We have just enough wind against us to make fine work with the waves. Venitia and Janet seem fatigued and sleepy. They are lying in their hammocks, enjoying the swift sweep of the graceful little ship, the mad dash of the waves as they come rolling by, carrying proudly their white-crested crowns, and the far-off dome of the sky.

A fine salt-bath has refreshed us after our days' and nights' watch, but we all feel too weary even to talk, and I think I shall find it pleasant to doze, awaken and enjoy with dreamy pleasure this "fine fluent motion," as Janet called it just now.

"Ottilie, stop writing, and come to your hammock. Do you remember De Quincey's speaking somewhere of 'the fine fluent motion of a mail-coach'? The expression is very descriptive; and the dash and sweep of this clipper over the fast-rushing waves may readily return to the memory some time when we are rolling along a superb road in a swift-going, well-balanced coach."

MARE TENEBROSUM.

UGUST 9. — The sea is very rough, and the ship rolls tremendously. If I did not know how to write in any position I should not be able to manage my pen. The waves dash up feathery spray, which catches the sunbeams, making rainbows play and dance over every crested billow.

The grand ocean swallows all our little chagrins and complaints. Its superb symphony sweeps up and on, drowning all human moans and griefs, and the sorrows of humanity seem as the veriest trifles in the presence of its sublime terrors and divine beauty.

Humboldt says, whoever builds his own world within himself must be excited by the view of the free, open sea, the majestic picture of boundlessness it presents; but he speaks of "a shade of melancholy longing" mingling with the enjoyment. And this is so. Not that we are sad outwardly, — indeed, the captain says we are "a cheery set of passengers"; I know, too, that we are happier here than we should be on shore, or probably ever shall be again, — but there is at bottom an intense melancholy, and it is soothed by finding itself in perfect unison with the ocean diapason.

The simple-minded captain doubtless thinks us a gay, happy trio; he knows of no other merriment than that proceeding from animal spirits. Ours, which results from mental excitement, deceives him, as it does nine out of ten in the world, who take it for real mirth and true humor, and do not see that it is simply a pleasant garment with which we clothe ourselves to hide even from our own eyes the unseemly rags and rents made by sorrow.

15*th.* — Our sunsets continue to be glorious. The clouds this evening formed veritable landscapes, in which there were mountains of silver, and lakes, rivers, and waterfalls of gold. Then followed a brilliant, sparkling night, when the starry vault of the heavens rested the edges of its superb dome on the profound ocean base.

We enjoy very much the various changes of the ocean and sky. In the heavens the pale green modulates by ascending full harmonies into brilliant carmine and gold, just as some glorious music; then in the finest weather, when the sky is clear and a steady blue, the sea will vacillate and waver from one shade to another, — from dark indigo to deep green, and sometimes a dull, solemn gray.

22*d.* — We are having fine weather, fair winds, and smooth seas. These "primeval waters of the circling Oceanus," after battling against us, have generously extended their huge arms and laid us on the broad, palpitating bosom of the sea. Not a storm, or anything that could throw the faintest shadow of danger over us, has occurred. Just three weeks to-day since we left Gibraltar.

The ocean is enchantingly beautiful this morning. A fine fresh north wind is blowing, and the sea is with us. We ride gracefully over the waters, and the waves rise and fall with gracious dignity and beauty. Now a slight breath trembles above the sea, breaking it into delicate ripples, which spread along in silvery radiance under the sun sheen; but soon a fresh swell or white-crested wave comes sweeping along, and the surface is again calm and smooth. As I lean against the bulwarks, looking at these changes, all manner of pretty poetical conceits are suggested to me.

Venitia's comparison which she made just now, when observing with me this ripple and wave break, pleases me. She says it is like some music, in which the melody goes trembling along with a half-trilling sound, then comes a grand chord, or brilliant modulation, or noisy resolution, which dissolves and annihilates the whole pretty trilling *motivo*. Janet says we remind her of good old Jeremy Taylor in our disposition for making comparisons, therefore I shall not write mine.

Venitia has gone down to the music. We are in good luck about this piano. At Gibraltar we discovered that one of the crew, a Sicilian, who had admired Venitia's music very much, knew something about tuning. She made the piano-tuner at Gibraltar give him some counsel, and go over the instrument several times; now he keeps her piano in capital order, examining it every morning. She provided fresh strings in hermetic cases before leaving Naples; and no one could imagine, from its pure and beautiful sounds, that the instrument was in so trying an atmosphere as the ocean. The chords and harmonies blend most mysteriously, too, with the ocean's roar: no matter what key Venitia opens in, the wave tone-pitch seems always to adapt itself, and we never have enjoyed music so much.

Venitia has just been playing her favorite Sonate of Beethoven, — the one in D (Re). (Opus 31, No. 2.) The glasses of the cabin skylight are raised, and I am resting against the casement, listening.

"A charming and accomplished friend of mine," said Janet, as Venitia concluded it, "used to compare this Sonate to trackless paths in a wild primeval forest."

"Yes," murmured Venitia, in a low tone, as if to herself, "but a forest of one's own passions, in which one follows the trackless paths of bewildering, hopeless desires."

Dear girl! this love-sorrow has ripened rapidly her heart-fruit. I once said she was as brilliant as a diamond, and almost as hard; now she is as tender as an "awakened Psyche." She turned over the leaves of her Beethoven volume, and said, looking up at me, "Listen to the Adagio of this Third Sonate, dedicated to Haydn."

She played it over several times, then added: "This Adagio contains the very essence of unbelief, it is so rebellious. A little light beams out toward the close, reminding me of the last scene of Manfred with the Abbot, for a reconciliation with lost faiths and hopes is almost reached; but this F double sharp destroys the promise, and the C which follows confirms the sad truth. I tell you, Ottilie, there is in this Adagio the positive expression of a confirmed, almost maddening despair; it does not even contain so much hope as Manfred's last words, —

'Old man! 't is not so difficult to die.'"

I did not answer her, and she continued playing; but I thought of the marvellous and weird power contained in this vague, beautiful Tone-tongue, the suggestions it makes to us of life experiences; as Spohr said, "It is the sole expression of some complicated feelings and struggles in the human breast." Janet was lying in her hammock, reading, and did not hear Venitia's remark; but the music had its effect on her, for she looked towards me and said, "While I was listening to that Adagio, Ottilie, a tender and touching remark of Mrs. Jameson came to my memory, — 'In this life there is always something to be done or suffered, when there is no longer anything to be desired or attained.' "

25th. — We are still on the beautiful wide ocean, and it is very calm and tranquil, so unlike the sullen repulse it gave us when we entered its inhospitable gates. We shall be very sorry when this voyage is ended. It is quite late in the evening. Janet is pacing the quarter-deck, and only the man at the wheel and the first mate are on watch. A little while ago, Venitia and I were walking the main-deck together, talking of the pleasant voyage we had had thus far, and she exclaimed: "O, to go on always thus! To live forever, Ottilie, in this way, would it not be Elysium?"

"Like the Phantom Vessel," I replied.

We were near the cabin door; she left me and went down to the piano, and soon rose up on our ears the strange harmonies of that curious composition, Wagner's "Flying Dutchman."

FUGUE IN E MINOR.

UGUST 28. — I do not write very regularly now in my journal, my life is so vague and dreamy. I read a little, talk a little, but most of all lie in my hammock and listen to Venitia's music; or give up my whole being to the delicious influence of the sea, when I forget all "the before and after," and am so still and happy in this state of simply existing without the torture of thought or memory, that I feel

> "Like an unbodied joy, whose race is just begun."

We are six hundred miles from America yet, and to-night will make it seven weeks since we left Palermo. We are sailing at a fine speed, — ten miles an hour. There is a superb sky, brilliant sun, fine fresh wind, and sublime ocean. The rolling, dashing waves ring out grand harmonies in full, open diapason, and the white-crested billows dance madly on in a wild, gay leap, and throw aloft their snowy foam as if they felt the same glorious exultation their sweep and dash create in me.

I have been sitting in the forward part of the vessel alone. I clambered up to the very end of the ship, that I might be able to watch the various changes of the waves. The prow cut through the waters sharply, throwing myriads of sparkling gems up and around. Whole clusters of wave-diamonds would be flung out on the sea, and mingle so quickly with it as to produce the effect of being caught back by invisible hands. The waves dashed along madly, smoking like ice; and, as the sun arose towards the zenith, and the short perpendicular spar under the bowsprit end, called the martingale, dipped into the rising waves, numberless segments of rainbows flitted over the racing waters. I thought of the Harpy Podargy in the Iliad, the white-footed nymph who slid before the tempests and made the crests of the waves foam as she tore them up while passing over them.

A troop of porpoises came rolling along, — a mournful sight to superstitious sailors, for they betoken a storm; but our voyage has a fair white star on its front, and its end shall be peace. Some dolphins bounded over the martingale-chains, and little flying-fish, about a hand in length, flitted in and out of the sea, as white as the wave-crests on which they sported.

31*st.* — A bright and sunny day, with a gentle wind. The sea seems full of floating amethysts and emeralds, the mollusca are so plentiful; at night, huge floats of them pass near us, glittering like lightning half hidden by clouds. Beautiful nautili sail by the ship, nearly as large as my hand. Janet had a boat lowered to catch some, and we have dried them very successfully; their sails look like large flower-leaves, — lilac rayed with black and tipped with a rich rose-pink, thin as gauze and frail-looking as a convolvulus-petal.

Midnight. — My journal seems very fragmentary to me, and yet Janet likes it. She has been reading it the past few days, and said yesterday, on returning the volume to me: "Why, Ottilie, it reads like a story. Suppose you give it a name, write a preface, and publish it. I wonder if persons would take it for a fiction, and not 'an ower-true tale'? Alas! if there was not so much heart-aching truth in your journal, my friend, it would not be amiss to publish it."

Then we talked playfully about working it up into book form, and speculated on its title. This led us to thinking of the difficulty some great authors have had in finding suitable names for their literary offspring. We recalled the story of Ariosto, who, after seeking a long while in his brain for a title to his famous poem, arose one midnight, awakened his retainers, and had the great bell of the fortress, of which he was governor, rung in grand rejoicing. His poem was named!

The stately, grave poet must have felt very proud while he listened to the loud pealings of his castle bell, as it rung out in the dark night over the Apennine solitudes, telling Nature that a great poem had been born from the invisible world of romance into the visible one of language.

To-day I have amused myself by giving headings to the various divisions of my journal, hunting up a title, and writing a preface, all of which work Janet has superintended with an approving pleasure almost as grave as Ariosto's. "Some day," she said, "Venitia, poor child! will also enjoy reading this book. You must give it to me, my friend, when we reach America. There this volume shall end, and a new journal, and a new life indeed, begin for us all."

The new life has commenced for Venitia. But, alas! this new existence, the mysterious emotional life from which spring Art's most luscious fruits of tone and word-poesy, is, like all mortal things, born of pain, Novalis's "disease of the spirit," or that human-like gem, the pearl, created by a wound! And yet it is happiness and gladness, not pain and sorrow, that make the blessed birds break out into song.

This strange emotion, love, too, in what different forms it presents itself: to Philip it has always been a joy and a blessing, while to others it is a tragedy; and to Venitia, what is it to be? It must be her inspiration, the key-note of a higher life. Now she suffers and struggles, but the pure pearl of peace must come; for both she and Luigi are loyal and true in their natures, not fitful and wavering, like some poor feeble hearts. The perfect faith which will be established between them shall sustain her yet; though she may never see him again, this one thing will not fade away from her mind, — the memory of his firm, quiet repose of heart. It will be to her

> "An ever-fixed mark,
> That looks on tempests and is never shaken."

But I would fain have her a word-poet instead of a tone Sappho. Music, alas! is only "known through gradations of joy and sorrow," listened to and uttered with an emotion that is sharp as pain; and leaves behind it a regret. The *ivresse* of the *executante*, too, is as exhausting as the intoxication of the earthly grape; and the wildering sounds so full of beauty, which are poured forth "from the voice and the instrument," are restless waves of the great heart-ocean, speeding along under the fierce storm of sorrow, and breaking against the sharp reefs and desolate shores of longing and memory.

I remember saying once that Venitia could not play fugues, and also that one must be far out on the deep waters of trial to comprehend fully the real meaning of a great fugue. Now she has attained this sorrowful comprehension. To-night she played the fine Handel fugue in E minor, and I listened with surprise to her different rendering of it: it throbbed with a life-pulse. After she had finished it, she said: "I am so glad that at last I really love fugues. I used to play them as a duty; but now they are a pleasure, and they sound like solemn, inspired poems to my ears. This fugue of Handel, I never tire of reading it. Bach's fugues are more severe, but this is full of melodic sublimity. Listen to these three warning notes in this passage."

And she played over the three following measures, which are the fourth, fifth, and sixth ones of the fugue:—

"These three notes," she continued, "must be *martelé*, that is, struck persistently, in order to usher in fitly the melodic ripple which follows. One hand teaches the other the strange story in many keys; it comes and goes; it sways and surges like a river widening in its course. You used to compare it to the roll of mid-ocean, Ottilie, and now I feel the truth of your comparison. Yes, it leads to a wide, boundless ocean of thought; but through all its changes you still hear these three mysterious warning notes.

'Weird sisters hand in hand,
Posters of the sea and land,
Thus do go about, about.'

Sometimes they carry me, indeed, to Hecate's Cave, and I hear the solemn, thrice-reiterated 'Show!'

'Show his eyes and grieve his heart,
Come like shadows, so depart.'"

"Venitia, a dear friend once said to me, with all the eloquence of sadness, that 'Belief plays at hide-and-seek with disappointment in life, like the first voice in a fugue.'"

"That is beautiful!" she exclaimed, and she repeated it over. "And so true! But, Ottilie, it is very long before we see the truth. We believe and hope so blindly, then comes the solemn resolution of the minor chord, and that is the end of the believing life."

"The end?" repeated Janet, stepping up quietly behind us and putting her hands on our shoulders. "The end? O no, my friends; not the end while life lasts. We women never lose hope; we always 'attend' the coming of our vision in some form, as the Jews forever expect the Messiah."

"Attend a delusion," I replied, with some little bitterness.

"So be it," answered Janet, calmly; "but let us respect this 'delusion,' as you call it, — I call it the ideal, and so do you, Ottilie, in your better moods. Come; both of you must walk with me on the quarter-deck; the moon is glorious, and the waves are trembling like a young Endymion, —

'A symbol of immensity,
A firmament reflected in a sea,
An element filling the space between
An unknown —'

and mysterious spirit of beauty, which your marvellous

Tone-tongue describes better than the word-poems do. Let us go breathe and feel it, for its influences will be healthful for us all."

We walked, with Janet between us, up and down the quarter-deck till near midnight, and her good, wise words at last brought a calm, trustful feeling into our hearts. We talked indirectly of the past, present, and future, and Venitia and I were at first not a little stiff-necked.

"Janet," said Venitia, with an attempt at playfulness, "when I was a child you should have given me elementary thinking-lessons."

"It takes the whole experience of life to give us the power of thought, Venitia. We are only learning to think here. First we feel, then we suffer, then we *know;* and with this beginning of knowledge comes the dawning of true thought, — then for hereafter the wisdom."

"But after all, Janet," I said, "how few of us really wish this knowledge; it is almost always forced on us. We enjoy the delicious sense of feeling, and are even willing to take the suffering which follows if it will only come blind and deaf, and not leave with us the fearful responsibility gained from experience, whose painful fruit is thought and knowledge."

"Ah, but it is like Ruskin's hawthorn, my dear Ottilie, which must grow with the spirit of the triangle in it. When we have a stern necessity put upon us, — whether of duty, performance, or self-abnegation, — awful as it may be, we grow stronger and better for facing and accepting it. We may transgress, — we may reach forth longingly to some other more delightful end which we see sweeping swiftly and temptingly by us, — we may even feel other needs pressing in on us and demanding food; it is all useless, — the 'triangular necessity' is on us, and towards that form must be our souls' growth, if we have any power of growth in us."

"A soul-growth is it, my dear?" I replied, obstinately; "I can tell you that one of the severest purgatories which can be inflicted on a proud spirit is the acceptance of this 'triangular necessity,' as you call it. You are right, however; my own experience has proved it, for I have often seen myself doing quietly, and sometimes even with a strange sense of willingness, the very things I had fought furiously against in the beginning; but I have never yielded without a keen sense of mortification."

They laughed, and Janet said she fancied, if the truth were known, this confession I had just made had been one of these purgatories to me. Gradually we shifted our talk to other and gayer subjects, and before parting for the night had some very merry laughs. They are both asleep now, and I am sitting on the quarter-deck alone. It is nearly three o'clock in the morning. The weather has changed and grown chilly. Dark clouds hang around the horizon, and a fitful, angry wind is beginning to agitate the sea.

The man on watch shivers, walks up and down the deck, and looks inquiringly around on the sky. He has gone down now to the captain, and I hear them talking earnestly in low voices. The captain is preparing to come up on deck. I will close my book, and look out hopefully toward the west as I go once more to sleep upon the treacherous sea.

Cambridge: Stereotyped and Printed by Welch, Bigelow, & Co.